THE
GAUNTLET
AND THE
BROKEN
CHAIN

IAN GREEN is a writer from Northern
Scotland with a PhD in epigenetics. His
fiction has been widely broadcast and
performed, including winning the BBC
Radio 4 Opening Lines competition and
winning the Futurebook Future Fiction
Prize. His short fiction has been published
by *Londnr*, Almond Press, *OpenPen*,
Meanjin, Transportation Press, The
Pigeonhole, No Alibi Press,
Minor Lits, and more.

@ianthegreen
www.ianthegreen.com

THE GAUNTLET
AND THE
BROKEN CHAIN

IAN GREEN

An Ad Astra Book

First published in the United Kingdom in 2023 by Head of Zeus
This paperback edition first published in 2024 by Head of Zeus,
part of Bloomsbury Publishing Plc

9 7 5 3 1 2 4 6 8

A catalogue record for this book is available from the British Library.

ISBN (PB): 9781800244184
ISBN (E): 9781800244092

Printed and bound in Great Britain by
CPI Group (UK) Ltd, Croydon CR0 4YY

Head of Zeus Ltd
5–8 Hardwick Street
London EC1R 4RG

WWW.HEADOFZEUS.COM

For Benjamin Dragon & for Abigail

There are worlds beyond our own –
I hope you find them all

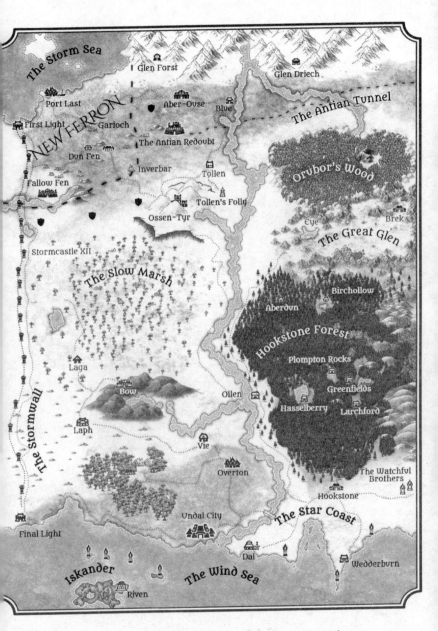

Map of the Undal Protectorate after Ferron invasion,
year 312 from Ferron's Fall (1123 Isken) – **Private
collection**, Knight-Commander Salem Starbeck

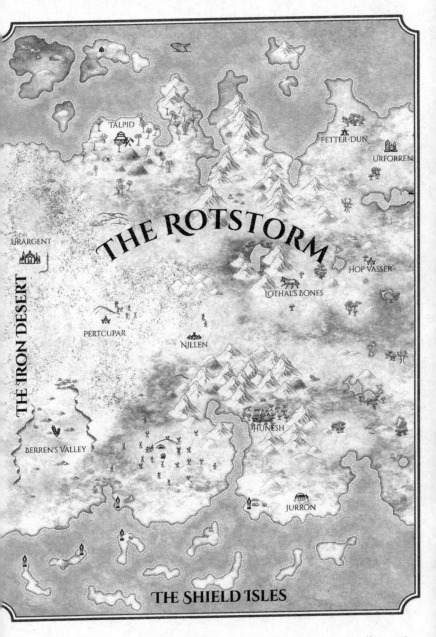

Map of the Rotstorm and Ferron ruin, year 307 from Ferron's Fall (1118 Isken) – **Stormcastle XII archive**, Commander Benazir Arfallow

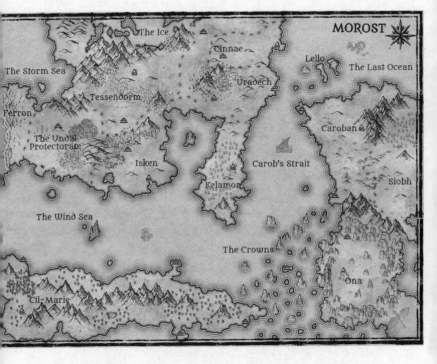

Reckoning of the lands of Morost, year 312 from Ferron's Fall
(1123 Isken) – **Castrum library**, Commissar-Mage Inigo

ᛈ ᚷ ᛏ ᚠ

THE STORY OF THE ROTSTORM

Across the ruins of Ferron the rotstorm ever rages – a nightmare of arcane lightning and acid mists where the spectre of the god-bear Anshuka hunts children, twisting them into monstrous beasts. The crow-man Varratim, corrupted by the rotstorm, found a cache of lost technology deep in the ruins of Ferron – orbs of light that can fly through the sky and shoot fire and force. With these orbs Varratim kidnapped children sensitive to the magic of the world, the skein, to empower an ancient dagger that could kill a god – a dagger he stole from Deathless Tullen One-Eye, the most powerful mage ever to live. Tullen was sentenced by Anshuka to wander the earth forever and watch the ruin of his people and has spent three centuries seeking to escape his chains.

Varratim tried to kill the god-bear Anshuka to free his people, but he was stopped – Floré had left the violence of the rotstorm behind, but when Varratim's orbs stole her daughter, Marta, and killed her husband, Janos, she hunted him down. Floré saved her daughter and her god, but the skein-mage Tomas took the ancient dagger for his own devices.

With Varratim dead and their scheme for absolution failed, from the nightmarish depths of the rotstorm demons and goblins and rust-folk have struck forth and claimed as their sanctuary

*the Northern Marches of the Undal Protectorate. To help her
people and Marta, who was sickening from the skein-magic
inherited from her father, Floré sought out the besieged island
of Iskander. She aimed to find the whitestaffs, mages sworn to
support the Undal Protectorate who had abandoned their posts
when Varratim's orbs first flew. Instead she found betrayal and
a horrifying revelation – the whitestaffs had taken the mage
Janos from his deathbed and were using him as a font of power,
hoping to realise new extremes of magic. Meanwhile, Varratim's
successor, the brutal war-leader Ceann Brude led the Ferron on
a devastating campaign of terror across the protectorate.*

*Floré and her comrades managed to save Janos, but the folly
of Tomas came to fruit – Tullen One-Eye manipulated him into
breaking the chains of magic binding him. With his power and
his dagger returned, Tullen faced down Janos at last, and the
deathless mage was victorious. With the power he harvested
from Janos's magic, he resurrected the god-wolf Lothal, who
once led the armies of Ferron to blood and glory.*

*Through the Undal Protectorate the land is gripped in a Claw
Winter, a frozen mirror of the punishment of the rotstorm laid
down to the west. Abandoned on the island of Iskander, Floré
and her comrades must find their way back to the protectorate.
Marta is hidden somewhere in the north, dying from the skein-
magic she cannot control.*

*After centuries of bondage, the immortal mage Tullen One-
Eye has been unchained and the great god-wolf Lothal hunts
again. And deep in Orubor's wood, the god-bear Anshuka stirs
from her slumber. The last time these Judges warred, an empire
fell.*

*If she is to save her daughter and free her people, Floré
will have to defeat the great wolf and kill the man they call
Deathless. But how can she kill the unkillable man? And is
steel alone enough to take down the gods?*

PROLOGUE

THE WAR AND THE WOLF

Ceann Brude watched the village of Garioch burn, spirals of black smoke and dancing flame filling her eyes as thatch and timber caught and blazed. The snow was piled thick in drifts and clumps, but her soldiers had oil and patience and the flames danced out from barns and houses and sheds and sties. Somewhere, a child cried. Somewhere, a horse screamed its death throes. Wooden beams cracked like bones, wet and sudden and bright. Through the streets of the village, gangs of goblins ran amok, small grey bodies clad in rags and armed with rust and malice, black eyes flashing and ragged teeth glinting as they sought any who would resist. Their rust-folk minders chased and corralled them with rough words and quick blows to correct their courses, to pull them off those who surrendered before the villagers were torn apart. She could hear the goblins chittering and screeching, some individual words climbing up beyond the crackle of flame. Brude leaned back against the stone at the top of the shaman tower, hiding from the snow flurries in the lee of the old dark stone.

The tower was perhaps forty feet tall, a simple tight spiral of wooden stairs walled in stone. It stood proud over the village, looming over the stark stone of the temple building underneath. Her hunched back had scraped at the beams of the stairs above as she climbed, but at the peak it was only her and the bronze-coated shaman bells marked with the runes of the Judges: XYFꞱ, *feather, claw, flower, and eye.* Nessilitor the Lover, Anshuka the Mother, Berren the Fair, and Lothal the Just. Anshuka's bell was double the size of the others, and Brude turned to it and watched the reflection of the flames below dancing on the beaten bronze. She shivered and remembered a bear of red mist stalking the rotstorm, hunting her when she was only a child. Changing her. *Never again,* she thought. *I will take the children from the storm.*

'A shame,' Amon said, emerging from the darkness of the stairwell and smiling up at her. His scar-pocked face was all crags, his smile pulling at one half of his face as he leaned to the edge of the tower top to look down at the flames. Brude sniffed and drew further back into shadow, felt her shoulders hunch lower as she tried reflexively to appear more human – less crow-man, *demon*, elongated and broken by dark magic. It made no difference. Still she towered over him, and she was as aware as ever of the pains in her joints and bones and sinew and blood.

'Why a shame?' Brude asked, her voice smoke-rough, and Amon shrugged and moved closer to her, sheltering from the wind and snow. His proximity made her hands flex, a nervous reaction, her overlong fingers curling back until her fingertips touched the hem of her shirt. Through snow and cloud she thought the sun must be setting – she could barely make out his eyes in the darkness, just two black spaces rimmed in shadow. *He is tired,* she thought. *We are all tired.*

'This is good land,' he said, pulling his cloak tighter. 'Rust-folk could farm here, could live here. But examples must be made. I do not question your decision.'

Brude's eye twitched and she loomed over him and stretched to her full height, a head taller than any man, gaunt and bent, arms and legs oddly jointed and aching in the cold even more than normal. She rubbed around her eye, tracing the symbol tattooed around her eye socket: Ø, the Ferron symbol for salt.

'Examples must be made,' she said, and Amon reached up and laid his hand on her shoulder and smiled at her placatingly, his face still cast in shadow.

'They are ready below,' he said, 'if you are.'

They descended the tight spiral of stairs, Brude following Amon, her hand reaching down and almost touching the back of his cloak. She held herself back. Emerging into the courtyard below, they stopped at the well and Amon drew up the bucket from deep below, and in turn they drank the cool crisp water of the Northern Marches, untainted by the peat and acid of the rotstorm or the acrid tang of rotvine sap.

'I'll not get tired of that water,' Amon said, and Brude wiped her mouth and grinned at him.

'You'll not have to, my friend,' she said. The water was cold beyond cold, a cold that flooded her throat and spread through her chest and then seemed to dissipate only when her whole body had shivered. Even the aches in her bones seemed to ease, for a moment. It tasted so clean – this wasn't the fetid water of the rotstorm. She had spent her life drinking water tainted with rotvine sap, water red with whatever hell leached from the sky down into the peat. Water in the rotstorm was a pain to endure, a necessity to survive. You would strain it and boil it and filter it over and over but the taste was always there. *Don't we deserve clean water, clear skies?* Brude let the bucket fall to the snowy ground.

Amon led on, his old, oiled cloak of worked leather over his new uniform. The uniform was a simple thing. A thick sash of red from shoulder to hip – they could afford no more, could spare nobody to work loom or dye or needle. Together Brude and Amon walked through slush and snow to the village green and when she saw her rust-folk – spear-wielding, wild and worn – each had the red sash. Some of them wore new strips of cloth, sashes clearly taken from what clothing or fabric they had found in Garioch. It brought a smile to her face. *An army needs a uniform,* her adviser Jehanne had said, *no matter how simple. It is cohesion. It is discipline. Those who wear your colour will answer to your word, or they will be other.*

Brude could not fault the Cil-Marie soldier's teachings. Her rust-folk, men and women scarred by the rotstorm and its acid mists and brutal flora and fauna, hair braided, weapons stolen and broken and worn, looked like an army – not a rabble.

The rust-folk surrounded the few remaining inhabitants of Garioch. Most had fled spans before, fled when rumour of war and a Claw Winter on its heels sent them to the south – *to safety.* Brude smiled at that thought – she had struck at Undal City itself, had left it ablaze and in turmoil. *Let them feel the fear we have lived with all our lives.* Brude's adviser stood at the edge of the village green in the shadow of a wall, hood raised and cloak drawn close against the cold and the eyes of those watching. A few goblins ran to the square and the captives, with their broken blades of stone and jagged iron, but were shooed away quick enough by Brude's soldiers. The grey-skinned monsters were sent to search the unburnt houses and barns for supplies.

'There must be an example,' Brude said again loudly and, in the centre of the green, standing in packed snow and slush, the people of Garioch looked up at her. Brude was a head taller even than the tallest of them: a grizzled heavily built man who stood straight in his grey Stormguard tabard – the only tabard amongst the cowering villagers. He wore no cloak and bled freely from a wound in his head, and stood a step forward of the others, placing himself between them and her. There were perhaps twenty Undal there, a mix of old and young, even their poorest clad better than her rust-folk. Well-fed but with hard lines to their faces. The wounded soldier had blood caked in his beard, grey in his hair and a set to his jaw. He was not afraid of her.

Brude focused her gaze on the man in the tabard as she spoke.

'The Northern Marches belong to Ferron. You were warned, but now the snow has come and with it your last chance at survival.'

Behind her the shaman temple burned, the tower above it wreathed in guttering flame. Through the flurries of snow the last light of sun fell behind the horizon far to the west. What had been a faint light behind the clouds was gone, and all that remained was the red of flame.

'Garioch has suffered before,' the man said, and he spat at her feet. 'A rotsurge passed the town three decades back. We rebuilt. Before that, raids in the Antian wars. We rebuilt. Before that, half the town dead to the corvus plague. We rebuilt. Three centuries back, this was all slaves minding sheep for Ferron masters. They died, we rebuilt. We will always rebuild, crow-man, no matter what fires you set or chains you forge.'

One of Brude's soldiers stepped in and slammed the butt of her spear into the man's stomach, and Brude watched his hand twitch to intercept it, watched the man decide to take the blow. *A soldier.* He went to one knee but then slowly stood and Brude could see the corded muscle of his shoulder as he tensed.

'You want to kill me,' she said, 'but you cannot. You are City Watch? These people are your responsibility. Why would you not flee when we told you? You were told. You were warned.'

One of the others went to step forward and speak, a young man with thinning hair and a broken nose, blood dried around his mouth in thick rivulets that shone black in the firelight. The City Watch soldier held a hand back and the young man deferred, returned to the old woman he had been standing next to, placing an arm around her shoulders for support. Brude looked at the wrinkles on the old woman's face – *wrinkles of age*. She felt a burn in her gut, that familiar cleansing anger – an anger that always reassured her of her course. *How many of my people get to grow so old?* Not many, she knew. Most rust-folk died in the rotstorm long before they tasted old age, died of pestilence or wound or acid cloud, arcane lightning, the twisted flora and fauna of the rotstorm all hungry for flesh.

'Some too old to flee,' the soldier said. 'Some stubborn. Some foolish. I stayed to watch over them, if I could.'

Out in the bogs and hills beyond the edge of town, a wolf howled and Brude grimaced. *I must trust in my reeve*. Brude was *ceann*, war-leader of the rust folk – but the reeve was the one the people turned to, the one who made the true decisions that would determine their fate.

'You thought to protect them,' she continued, banishing the thought of the reeve and his plans from her mind. 'You thought the Stormguard would drive us back, as it ever has, and the great bear Anshuka would watch over you in her sleep, even as her nightmare brings snow and storm and ruin across the land. Penance for your sins, is that right? This is what you Undal believe, what your shamans preach?'

The man just stared at her, so Brude flexed her fingers and reached into the storm within herself. In a moment she could sense the tempest within her and around her, the chaos of connection and disconnection and pattern and influence. Each person was a tangle within that storm, an impossibly complex layering of chance and connection and chaos. Turning her gaze down to the soldier before her she could see him inside and out, from marrow to skin, see the pulse of nerves firing and the intricate dance of thought inside his skull, unfathomable in its complexity. *I must trust the reeve.* Brude closed her eyes and threw back her head and howled, a long howl – *a wolf's howl.* She pushed her power into it, the tempest of pattern – she gave her howl power, the way she had been told.

From the darkness beyond the fires of Garioch, her howl was returned, once, twice, a dozen times over, each howl a different note responding in chorus. The wolves of the Northern Marches, lingering in the darkness at the edge of town. The howls died down, and Brude dropped her senses deeper into the storm below and pushed outward. *Is he here?* The reeve had promised her that her howl would be enough, but the deathless mage had said so many impossible things to the reeve and the reeve had told Brude only what he deemed necessary.

Silence, except for snowfall and the crackle of burning thatch, the whimpers of the old and the weak in front of her, the breath of her soldiers. With her senses so heightened through the storm of the skein she could hear the friction of rough hands on spear shafts, could feel each snowflake that landed on the shoulders of her cloak. Then, at the northern edge of town, a presence…

Lothal the Just entered the village of Garioch silently, and all turned to look, and all were humbled. Their eyes were drawn not by noise, nor by flash of arcane light. The god-wolf exuded a presence that drew focus – like the edge of a cliff, or the depths of a well, shadowed and unknowable. With his shoulders hunched as he stepped forward with loping strides, the wolf was a full forty foot in height, rivalled in sight only by the tower of the shaman temple. Black fur glistening with snow, small drifts of it cascading from his back with every step, the wolf stepped forward and sniffed, stared down at the rust-folk and the Undal below. Through and below the black of his fur, streaks of glowing silver flowed in curving arcs. His eyes were pits of darkness, drinking all light. The wolf stared down at them from the edge of town and panted, hot breath blowing out in huffs of cloud past a tongue wet with slaver, past teeth long as swords made of thick black ivory. Garioch was silent, save the sobs of the villagers, but even those were quiet, muffled sounds – as if the Undal believed that silence could save them.

Brude looked at Lothal for one moment through the storm of her connection to the skein and had to back away, return her sight to the physical world. *Too much!* If a single leaf was an intricacy enough in the storm to draw her eye for hours with its infinite complexity, Lothal was a forest – complexity upon complexity, for every pattern a pattern below in a recursive chain of detail that never stopped. She could only take him in at the top level – to look any further was madness. The wolf was something beyond nature, beyond the world of little spirits and mortal creatures. There was a fey oddness to it. *It does not fit.* Brude had been raised in the rotstorm, where all ecology and nature were subject to the wrath of a god, where all that was natural was twisted into a dark reflection, but here in the Northern Marches where the trees grew deep roots and the deer roamed the hills she could see the oddness of the Judge. *It is too much for this place.* Brude dropped her gaze to the snow and held her breath.

'The mage told true,' Amon whispered beside her, and she felt his hand slip into hers – she was too startled to even quake at that.

The wolf will aid you, the reeve had said to her, *but the one-eyed mage has other work.*

'No,' she heard a voice say, a meek voice audible only in the tense silence Lothal had brought. It was one of the old women in the crowd. The others stood still around her, or had fallen to their knees at the sight of the great wolf. None cried or wailed but she could see the tears on their faces. They did not stay silent through bravery, but through awe. All save the old woman, face lined and mouth dour.

'The wolf is dead,' she said, her voice finding strength, her gaze locked on Lothal. 'The wolf has been dead three hundred years. This is a trick. The Mother will protect us!'

Lothal stepped forward onto the village green and snuffed at the snow and dirt, one heavy paw the size of a horse crushing a fence as it came down, and the old woman fell silent. Brude watched, her eyes flitting from the wolf to the woman to the City Watch soldier, whose jaw hung slack as he stared at the slowly advancing god.

'There must be an example!' Brude called out, though her voice shook. She could pretend bravado, could will herself strong, but her voice betrayed the fear in her heart. Lothal the Just was a dead god reborn, a legend come to life, a creature beyond the bounds of any power she knew. *He will aid you,* the reeve had told her. But she had no way to make her intentions known to the Judge, no way to order such a creature to her whims. She could only hope it understood her, and knew her as an ally.

Brude pushed her hood back and felt the cold dance over her neck and the sides of her head where the hair was shaved close. A strand of red hair slipped over her eye and she pushed it back and blew out a breath. She turned her back on Lothal, and felt her spine itch under the weight of the god wolf's gaze. 'I am Ceann Brude,' she called out, 'war-leader of Ferron. I killed the Salt-Man, the skein-wreck Janos. I burned the shaman temple of Undal City. I broke the northern Stormwall and put Port Last to the torch.'

Brude let herself draw straighter as she listed her accomplishments, and with a thought she pulled upon the storm within her and drew its power, *her* power, and rose from the ground to hover three feet higher. Amon's hand dropped from hers and then her hands were wreathed in red flame, raised at her sides. She looked back at Lothal and lost a moment staring into those eyes, unreadable. *An example,* she thought, willing him to understand. The wolf scratched one paw at the dirt, leaving plough furrows in the street with talons each as thick as a man. He closed and opened his mouth, muzzle twitching as something like a snarl crossed his face, a face the size of a barn door. Brude forced herself not to flinch as the wolf stepped forward and lowered its head and *sniffed* at her.

'Look now upon Lothal reborn,' she said, and the gaze of the wolf was on Brude but the prisoners were looking only at him. 'Know now that the Northern Marches are forever lost to you. You may leave this place by the Aber-Ouse road, and you will not be harried. There is a Stormguard fort new built halfway to Aber-Ouse at the border of the Marches – they will find you on the road. If you survive the snows tell the Stormguard that the Northern Marches belong to Ferron. Tell the Stormguard that no Undal shall enter here and live. Tell them that Lothal is with us. Remember this example.'

With a look to Lothal, Brude pointed a flaming hand at the muscled City Watch soldier, and as one, the rust-folk retreated until only the Undal villagers of Garioch were left in the dirty snow of the village green. By the light of their burning homes the villagers huddled together as the wolf stepped forward, and Brude willed herself to float back, away, her boots a yard from the frozen earth below. The City Watch soldier stepped fast from the crowd as Lothal approached, seeing that the wolf's eyes were locked on him alone.

'Travel fast by the Aber-Ouse road,' he called to his villagers, his eyes locked on Lothal. 'Leave none behind for the wolves. Trust in each other!'

Lothal stepped forward and with a whip-fast motion sent

him sprawling to the snow, paw pressed on the man's chest, covering his tangled limbs. Brude lowered to the ground and licked her lips and her seeking hand gripped Amon's tight. She had seen the bones of the old Judge Lothal, Lothal the Just, Lothal the god-wolf. She had gazed up at ribs thick as the mast of a ship forged from black rock, a skull the size of a barn half-buried in the peated mire of the rotstorm. *This Lothal is not even yet full grown.* She did not know if it was the same wolf, reborn, or some new iteration of an old pattern. She knew the bones remained, deep in the storm. *A new pup, with the same name,* she thought, but the idea of referring to the beast looming over them all as a pup made her stomach clench.

Down came the wolf's head until it was held over the squirming City Watch guard, who fell still under the gaze of the beast. Brude stared at him as his face slackened for a moment with fear and then set stern with resolve.

'Suffer no tyrant!' he yelled. 'Forge no chain! Lead in—'

With a press of the paw Lothal cracked his ribs and spine and then drew back his paw and his head came down and snatched the soldier up, no air left in his lungs to scream. Lothal held him a moment aloft in his mouth and then with a single clench of its jaws bit him in two, legs falling back to the snow in a spray of blood. With cracking bites the wolf broke his bones, chewed and swallowed him, and then snuffled at the snow and picked up the still-twitching legs in its mouth. Without a backward glance Lothal padded away, black fur streaked in silver fading into nothing as it moved past the village and the pyres that were once houses and out into the dark wilds beyond. Sound seemed to return to the village, and Brude could taste ash in the air. She felt her muscles relax a mote as the wolf left – its presence was so powerful that it was like standing by a river in spate, or gazing into a blazing fire. She had been taut, ready to die. It was too much.

The Undal were not screaming, were too stunned to scream. The rust-folk were touching hand to chest and murmuring to themselves. Next to Brude, Amon did the same, and she felt her lips twitch as his hand pulled from hers.

'Honour to the wolf,' Amon whispered, and Brude let go of the storm. She leaned away from him, back in on herself, her shoulders hunching down and her bones aching. Her joints felt like they were tearing, but it was the same feeling she had endured every moment for fifteen long years. Brude closed her hand but Amon's hand was not in it anymore, only air. His hand was clutched to his chest, his eyes locked on the darkness where Lothal had stood. *It cannot be.*

'Get them out of the village and on their way,' she said, swallowing and grimacing. *It cannot be.* She looked down at the spray of blood that arced across the dark snow. 'Cloaks and food and water for the journey – more than they ever gave us.'

She turned before waiting for Amon to acknowledge her order and stalked away from the village green to the wall of the blacksmith's where her adviser waited in shadow, her face hidden by the hood of a fine cloak lined with fur.

'Your mage told true,' Jehanne said, and with a hand clad in delicate leather gloves she slapped the wall of the blacksmith's, shaking her head in astonishment. She swept back her hood and then twitched open her cloak, and Brude could see the thin smile on her face and the beautiful black leather armour embossed and embroidered with symbols and curved script, the hammer wrought in black metal and incised with twisted patterns of silver and gold that hung on her belt. *She is beautiful,* Brude thought, looking at the olive skin and amber eyes and thick black hair cascading down to her shoulders. Brude did not envy her face – Brude had a face as human as any other, and her pale skin and flaming hair would be the envy of many were it not for the horrors wrought to her body – that wrung out and stretched body whose marrow ached with dark magic. Brude envied the woman her body – the body of someone untouched by the ghost-bear. A human, not a demon – *not a crow-man*.

'This changes the situation,' Jehanne said, and the woman adjusted the scarf of patterned weave she always wore around her neck. Commandant Jehanne of Cil-Marie, always watching, always ready to advise. Amon had fetched her back from distant Cil-Marie and she had brought ships and tactics, a brutal focus. Brude stared Jehanne up and down and chewed at the inside of her cheek.

'Our deal remains, of course,' Jehanne said with a tight smile, 'but if Tullen One-Eye and the wolf Lothal are both returned then Cil-Marie may be able to offer more than just advice and a few ships.'

Brude nodded and gestured towards the blacksmith's forge, where two rust-folk stood guard with spear and hatchet. From within, the pale yellow of torchlight spilled through the gaps in shuttered windows. Together they went to the door and as they went to enter, across the village green, the shaman tower finally collapsed as the flames in the temple below ate at its foundation. The crash of stone and wood and tile was quieted by the snow all around, a snow that made all noise feel muted and distant. Of the bronze shaman bells Brude could see no sign. Even with the snow, as the final stones fell Brude could hear wolves howling in the forest – dozens of wolves, and then above and below them the reverberating deep howl of the god-wolf Lothal, a howl like thunder. She could feel it in her bones. She could feel it in her heart.

'Come, then,' Brude said, 'let us talk of the war and the wolf.'

ACT 1

THE BALANCED BLADE

'Dawn and cold, Father slept, Father dreamt.
Wake I said, wake I said; still he lay.
Father wake, wake I said – never; no.'

#6, *Sea Collection*, Yggrid the Bloodless

1

STEEL FOR THE CHILDREN

'As ever, with troubled times the mood shifts and the people seek someone to blame. Thirty years since our elders tried to wrest Aber-Ouse from the Stormguard – a foolish quest. The witches read the signs, the elders bayed for blood and conquest as if this was the age of shining blade and broken stone. It is not. We are a people diminished. Twenty years since the amnesty, I have lived in exile for my crimes, living amongst the tall folk. Spy, they have called me. Dog. I have been beaten and chased. My bakery has burned down twice. I hold no office amongst our people. I claim no great mind. But I have watched them long.' – **Letter to the Hidden Council of the Undal Redoubt,** Bellentoe Firstclaw

Between black cloud and black water the orb of light cut through the sky. Skimming low over choppy waves or dancing upward to gain a better vantage, on and on it flew, a pale white brilliance shining outward from the smooth stone of its hull. *Marta,* Floré thought. It was all she could think, all she could bear to focus on. Within the orb, strapped into a seat with her face pressed close to the thin crystal view strip that bisected the flying craft, Floré gripped her knuckles and felt the ache and twinge of pain up her right arm. It was the same old ache that always came with her nerves, where a spark of lightning had charred her nerve and sinew. *Marta,* she thought, and twisting Janos's wedding band on her finger she closed her eyes and felt the weight of her daughter on her chest, the warmth of her, the scent of her hair and the slow blink of her eyes as she first woke in the morning, the burst of her smile.

Floré knew Marta was alive. She was far north, north and north and north again, if the whitestaffs could be believed with their rituals and their claims, but she did not need them to tell her that Marta was alive. *I feel it.* Inside her heart was fire and ice, light and dark. Marta and Janos. Her love for her daughter and her fury at the one who had taken Janos from her. As they flew, she allowed herself to focus on the flame in her core, the part of her that knew Marta was alive. Behind her in the orb there was the noise of the others, but she did not let it in. Instead she thought of Marta, and allowed herself to hope that Protector's Keep would hold answers.

At last on the horizon – dark on dark, a change in the texture of night. *Land.* Cutting east, the orb raced along the coast of the Undal Protectorate faster than any ship or horse or bird. The sight of land, of *home*, was enough to raise even Floré's spirits. She didn't know this patch of coast, but the geography was familiar. The little rocks, the leaning trees, the fields bordered in stone or hedgerow. On they flew and she tried to think of what she would say to Marta – the girl had been so angry when she left her in the keep, left her to seek a cure for Marta's sickness from the whitestaffs. *I failed in that,* Floré thought, *as I've failed in so much. What kind of mother am I, to leave her in that place alone?*

Next to her Yselda came forward and said something, but

Floré did not listen to her. She stared out at the ground far below, willing the miles to pass.

As they flew, the Claw Winter made itself known – flurries of ice and flakes of snow pressing at the thin crystal view strip that bisected the orb, obscuring their view of the ground below. Road and field and village all blurring to the same white and grey and variations of shadow. After an hour the flurry was past, and from blackness, a hellish throbbing light grew as the orb neared its destination. Floré's eye twitched and she shook her head, reaching for her belt, and felt the weight of Marta on her chest turn to a millstone. *It was never going to be easy.*

Ahead, a rotsurge rained hell down on Undal City. A momentous cloud of roiling purple and black and red hung low over the towers of Protector's Keep and the dome of the mage's castrum, and within and from the cloud unceasing lightning pulsed, thick bolts of white and gold and red and purple bursting down in unpredictable rhythm. The lightning lit the cityscape below – the shaman tower of the high temple was charred and half broken, but Protector's Keep stood stalwart, a fortress of worked stone and ramparts, torches and braziers lit against the rain and titanic cloud. The rest of the city was darkness.

The orb grew still for a long moment as their pilot – Ruemar – hesitated, but Floré waved at Benazir who leaned low and gave the Tullioch child direction, and then they were swooping low along the coast. A hundred yards from the entrance to the east harbour, the ancient stone lighthouse False Friend glowed steady through the storm. The light spilling from the crystal at its peak was a soft yellow, nothing compared to the brilliance of the flying orb, and the rain around False Friend danced in spirals as gales from the Wind Sea clashed with gusts from the unnatural storm above.

Floré tried to keep her panic in check. *I must find Marta,* she thought, for the thousandth time that day. It was a burning mantra that was seared across her mind, a purpose to keep going. *I must save her,* she thought, eye twitching. *I* will *save her.* She knew the torches at the keep meant there was still hope, but she felt herself embracing the cold in her heart, the anger. A rotsurge meant goblins, rottrolls, trollspawn, creeping vine and burning rain. *I cannot fail her now. I cannot be weak.*

Protector's Keep faced down onto a huge square, and even as the Tullioch Ruemar slowed the orb and began to manoeuvre downward to land, the interior was flooded with light and the orb juddered and fell from the sky.

'Lightning!' someone yelled, but Floré focused on blinking the blaze from her eyes. The impact of the orb with the ground slammed her into the strange harness that held her in place, and she felt the sickening tear of old wounds reopening. Beyond the crystal strip the white light of the orb flickered and Floré was left in darkness, her face pressed close to the strip and the stone above and below. The black stone was the same seamless stone as the overseers' fort that made up Protector's Keep's lowest level and the tower holding aloft False Friend's light – Ferron stone, *mage* stone not crafted in three centuries since the old empire fell. The stone of slave roads and overseers' forts.

Behind her and around her the silent orb had filled with yells and groans as the passengers being transported were flung into a brutal heap. A glance showed her Cuss and Yselda and Benazir and Tomas all extricating themselves slowly, pulling themselves up, and then she heard the clattering between the heavy thrum and resonance of thunder. Arrows.

From the ramparts the arrows sought the orb, clattering harmlessly from the stone and down into the slush and ice of the square. Floré could see just enough through the crystal to glimpse movement on the ramparts, and she could hear the faintest edges of yells as, through wind and thunder, orders were cried, ballistae and heavy crossbows were wound and brought to bear. A spear clattered to the flagstones not halfway to its target.

'The ramp,' she said, and Ruemar nodded weakly next to her. There was a flicker of light within the orb as the intricate metal controls in front of the Tullioch glowed in response to the girl's touch.

As the ramp of the orb began to lower and Floré squared herself, a bolt of black and red lightning twisted down into the square from the tempest and rent the stone.

'Floré, wait!' she heard Benazir call, but all she could think about was Marta. *North and north again.* She would not find her daughter tonight. The ramp lowered slowly, and she saw where the lightning had struck. The torn flagstones smouldered and, after a few breaths from the crater, arms reached up and goblins began to pull themselves free from the ground, naked and steaming, earless grey-skinned beasts, slavering and howling. They screamed as they clawed at the dirt where the wet-lightning had planted them, seeds of the storm budding and exploding into violence in heartbeats. Their black eyes turned as the ramp from the fallen orb crashed with a jolt onto the stone below. Floré bit her lip and tasted blood, and embraced her anger.

She descended the ramp at a run. It was a sixty-yard sprint to the goblins, but seeing her approach they ran to meet her. The rain felt good on her skin, good after so many hours crammed in the orb. Floré wore her red Stormguard commando tabard over a shirt of leather, but wore no other armour save her gauntlets – dark grey iron, utilitarian and heavy. In one hand she spun her sword as she ran, feeling the weight of it, and from its pommel her sword-knot fluttered in the wind, red with a stripe of white. Lightning flashed above and a thunder rolled that masked the howl she gave as she descended upon the goblins.

Children, she thought, gnashing her teeth as she cut the first rushing goblin clean in two. The runes on the black blade of her sword began to glow as they tasted blood and the blade burst into white flame, and then she was striking again and again, both hands on her hilt driving the blade down with a brutal ferocity. The goblins were unarmed, nothing but rough grey skin to try and fend off her blade's edge, huge eyes of ceaseless black reflecting the flame of her blade as she chopped and thrust. This was not the finesse of some Kelamor duel or the clash of warriors testing their strength. It was butchery, but Floré was a Stormguard commando. She could butcher with the best of them.

Children, she thought again, and she was screaming as she hacked through another, and another. They were so small, so weak, but she had seen them chew the faces from commandos in the storm. She had seen a dozen swarm a man and drag him down, tear him until there was nothing left to tear, rip and bite until there was no fight left. Floré had seen those frail arms draw stolen knives across the throats of the weak after a rotsurge brought them to a village. One dived and grabbed at her leg and Floré drove her sword down, feeling it jar in her hand as it passed through flesh and sinew and bone and caught on the stone below. She let out a gasp.

There were three more, and they began to circle her.

'*Kill you,*' one said in Old Ferron, and as it leapt Floré quickstepped back and backhanded it with the pommel of her sword. The other two were on her, gnawing mouths full of jagged teeth searching for flesh to bite, and she rammed her sword down into the chest of the dazed goblin she had just hit and dropped the blade. With a hand for each goblin clambering over her back she reached and gripped.

Children! she thought, throwing them from her and back into the rubble of flagstones where the wet-lightning had hit. Where the rotsurge had dropped its seed. One of them reached for the rune-sword she had left still flaming in the other goblin, and then it fell back to the dirt and slush as an arrow sprouted from its chest.

Yselda stepped to Floré's side, shortbow already nocked and drawn with another arrow. Her long tresses of dark hair had been brutally chopped back, and the last few spans stuck on the island of Riven had hardened something in the girl's face. Floré did not look at her for more than a moment, her gaze locking back on the final goblin as it scrabbled in the pit where the wet-lightning had struck, trying to claw down into the dirt, frantic.

'Children,' Floré heard herself say, and then the gates were opening at the base of the keep and figures in the red and blue and grey and green of the Stormguard were emerging. Yselda fired an arrow through the final goblin's back, her face expressionless, and Floré stood in the rain and looked at the corpses as above her the rotsurge roiled. *Every goblin, every rottroll, every wyrm a child.* It was the brutal truth of the rotstorm she had learned – that the divine punishment of Anshuka did not spawn monsters in the unceasing storm over Ferron's ruin, but rather *made* them from the children it found within.

How can I fight for her?

Cuss was there, pressing her sword back into her armoured hands. Sweet Cuss from Hasselberry, now looming at her side, brown curls plastered to his forehead as the rain pounded down on them. Floré could feel herself swaying, but could feel no injury. She felt sick, and a heat in her skull was pressing at the backs of her eyes even as her heart was ice.

'We clear, sir?' he yelled, and she blinked and glanced about the square. *Go to work, Floré. Marta needs you.* There was no movement save the Stormguard at the keep. No noise save for the rain and the thunder above, around, echoing down the alleyways. Another bolt of the black and red coruscating wet-lightning blasted down, coming to ground a few streets east. It left an imprint across her eyes that she blinked away. *East*, she thought, and remembered walking these streets with Janos, with Marta holding a stuffed bear years before. *The Star Market.*

'Get them in,' she said to Cuss, and with a slow exhalation tried to will herself still. It felt good to have her blade in her hand after six spans on the island, sixty days stuck and stewing. Sixty days of visiting Janos's grave and honing her anger to a razor edge. *Every goblin, every rottroll, every wyrm a child,* she thought, and felt the lightning scar on her arm burn, heard thunder above. Around her Undal City was in ruins, half the buildings burned or abandoned and the remainder shuttered and ragged.

Every goblin, every rottroll, every wyrm a child.

So be it. What were her choices? She could not let them destroy the protectorate. She could not let them hurt Marta. She would do what must be done, until she found another path.

Behind her she heard the yelling, heard Benazir's voice call clear to the Stormguard pouring out from the keep.

'Bolt-Commander Arfallow!' she was yelling, identifying herself. 'Get these whitestaffs to the infirmary! Get me to Starbeck!'

From the orb of light down the ramp to the slush and filth of the city came their cargo – the last of the whitestaffs, the two dozen who had survived their own civil war and schemes and Floré's end to it. They were led by Deranus, the old man's white hair and beard now unkempt after six spans of winter on Riven, living on rationed food. The beating Yselda had given him had left its mark – his nose was crooked and bent, and his right cheek sunken where the bone had given way. Hustled along by the mage Tomas and Sergeant Buchan and their remaining soldiers, the final travellers debarked – the shaman Jule of Hasselberry, gaunt and pale, stalked down the ramp. He spared her a glare as he crossed the square, a sword point at his back and his hands bound in rope. Next to him, the sailor they had found washed up on the harbour after the rust-folk's failed assault, his olive skin and amber eyes a mirror of Floré's.

She did not know what it meant, that a sailor with the look and manner of Cil-Marie had washed up with the ruins of the rust-folk's flotilla. Floré was descended at least in part from Cil-Marie, her ancestors amongst the slaves sold cheap from one empire to another. Many across Undal were. Cil-Marie was south across the Wind Sea, past the wild reefs of the Tullioch. They traded slaves but the Undal had no truck with that or with them. An alliance between Cil-Marie and the rust-folk could be devastating. Floré stared at them both and then heard a scream from the east where the wet-lightning had struck the Star Market.

Seeds of the rotstorm, hatching. She believed in her heart that the goblins and monsters who sprang from the lightning were children, cursed by Anshuka to become monsters, transported through the rotsurge by arcane machinations. She did not know if they were new creatures, monsters true, of if some remnant of what they were was still there. Floré heard the scream, a human scream. She left the orb and its cargo of whitestaffs, left her friends, left her soldiers. *Save who you can,* she told herself, and the fury inside her crooned for blood and death and vengeance.

With a clenched jaw she went hunting.

~

Floré ran the three streets to the Star Market, feeling the pounding of her boots on snow-slick flagstones and rutted roads, feeling the pulse of her heart and the acrid taste of adrenaline on her tongue. She didn't think about children, about Judges and ghosts and the violence she had wrought. She thought about the scream and the black-red lightning – *someone needs help*. She could not allow herself to think about her Marta, could not allow herself to think of answers that would only lead to more questions. *And even if I find her,* she thought, with a twist in her gut, *she is still sick. I've solved nothing.* She blinked and focused on the cobbles slick with snow and muck, focused on the weight of the sword in her hand. *Help who you can.*

Skidding out of the last alley she saw the source of the screaming – a house at the edge of the abandoned market square. The market was long and thin, and normally full of stalls whatever the hour – perhaps closed for the night, but there, nonetheless. Now Floré could see only a few broken shells of stalls, cracked wood covered in snow. The snow was a foot thick across the square itself, worn down to ice and slush at the peripheries and pitted with the rain from the rotsurge, but that rain had frozen in a slick sheen crust over the powder beneath. Charred in the centre of the square was a blackened wound in the snow where the wet-lightning had struck, and from it a chaos of tracks all heading towards the nearest house – a townhouse with a peaked roof where screams still came from the upper floors. *A woman,* she thought. *And at least one child.*

The rain from the rotsurge above was mixed with flurrying snow and it deadened the noise across the city, but Floré could still hear the screams between distant growls of thunder, and she could see the cause of them. At the doors to the townhouse four goblins were chittering as two larger creatures kicked at the heavy wood of the door – *trollspawn*. They were perhaps six foot tall apiece, well muscled, skin the same rough pebbled grey as the goblins – rough and grey like sharks. One had an overlong right arm ending in a club fist the size of a war hammer, and the other was thinner but its head was huge, its jaw splitting back to reveal a mouth of teeth like knives and two twisting tongues of red that lashed around each other.

Floré spun her sword and flexed her off-hand in the dark steel of her gauntlets. *Halas's gauntlets.* She had taken them from the dead commando Halas on Riven, stripped the padded red leather gloves from the ornate gauntlets Starbeck had given her and sewn them into the utilitarian steel. True commando gauntlets, no ornamentation or design – just function. She had barely exchanged a dozen words with the dead woman, but she had been a commando, like Floré. She could trust the steel.

Floré whistled long and loud and kicked over a broken wagon wheel that was half buried in a snowdrift. The goblins turned, and so did the trollspawn, black orb eyes settling on her as they huffed steam in the cold night air. The rain and snow were coming down in sheets and swirls, and she was already soaked through. It slicked the skin of the goblins and trollspawn, and she could see their own breath rising in clouds as they turned to her, lean and slavering. A true rottroll could reach fifteen feet in height, could rip a horse in half. The two trollspawn were closer to human in size, but Floré knew they were freakishly fast and just as violent.

Children.

The thought came to her as she stared at them and they at her. Eight goblins, two trollspawn. *Ten children.* Floré felt the sick heat in her arteries, the rage in her chest. *Monsters. Children.* Two competing voices in her head. *Anshuka, what have you done?* The screams of the civilians inside the house. The children inside the house...

'Surrender!' she said, and said it again in old Ferron. '*Opphore!*' *Was that right?* She remembered Janos reading her a poem in Ferron, remembered a crow-man screaming Ferron curses as she cut him down in the storm, stabbing over and over with a silver blade to stop the preternatural healing power of the demon, both of them sticky with his black blood as it sprayed up with every blow.

'*Please!*' she said, but they were already crossing the snow, and with a shiver she passed the sword to her left hand and drew a silvered dagger from her belt. It was a standard-issue Stormguard Hawk knife, weighted for throwing, the blade coated in silver to burn any demon or rottroll or goblin like hot acid. They were coming for her, and a tiny spark in the back of her mind was glad of it. At least they had made the decision for her. It was not a slaughter, but a fight.

At thirty foot she threw the dagger, but the goblin she aimed it at ducked easily. *Bollocks.* Reaching to her boot she pulled out Captain Tyr's old knife, Tyr from Hasselberry who liked his pints and his chissick stones and a quiet life. Its blade was silvered, but the weighting and design were different – a Hawk knife was murder, a thin blade built to pierce, handle and grip designed not to slip even when slick with blood and the handle cored with lead to add momentum to any throw. Tyr's knife was an old lancer dagger, simple, wide-bladed. Floré measured the heft of it and when the beasts were twenty feet away she feinted with the blade, locking eyes with one goblin, and instead hurled it into the nearest trollspawn – the one with the overlong arm and the club fist. It squealed, a wet piercing cry that cut through the snow and rain, its charge stuttering to a stop as it writhed to pull the silver free from its gut with clumsy hands.

Fifteen feet. Floré slipped her sword back into her right hand and braced for the melee. *Kill the trollspawn. Goblins after.* All of them were unarmed, sent naked through the lightning by whatever arcane force the rotsurge unleashed – but Floré was barely armoured and her wounds from the past season were still fresh. In the freezing air she could feel the heat of her blood around rune cuts on her leg and face, the rapier wound in her shoulder, the dozens of welts and tears and slashes that had been sewn with catgut and meditated over by whitestaffs as they waited sixty days in Riven for a ship, for any hope.

Floré went to meet them, feet skidding on the ice and snow. Her sword was still burning softly from the goblins she had killed in front of Protector's Keep, the blade red-hot and wreathed in flickers of white flame. She could feel her gauntlets heating through the thick leather of her gloves to her skin below. There were no other lights in the square, only the faint glow of candlelight behind barred doors, the distant braziers of the high ramparts of Protector's Keep shedding no light or hope here.

Floré ran with her sword in a high guard over her head and as she reached the trollspawn she brought it down with all her might. The trollspawn reached a lazy arm up to block it, but the blade chopped clean through the arm and buried deep in its head, that head split in twain by a jaw full of knife-teeth now split again vertically. The goblins were on her, claw and tooth, but her blade was stuck in the thick skull of the trollspawn, spewing flame as it fed on the blood within. Floré let it drop and she crunched her fist down onto the nearest goblin's skull, and again, and again.

One was on her back biting at her but she threw back an elbow and then grabbed it and flung it to the snow and stamped, and then she was on her knees in snow and blood and charnel, goblins clawing at her, squeezing the life from one even as another tore at her arm. *Children!* They were screaming, and their chittering voices shouted words half remembered – *kill rip tear blood*. With a yell Floré forced herself to her feet and threw the last two goblins off. She stood on the dead trollspawn's chest and yanked at her sword, a spray of charcoal-black blood leaving a smoking trail across the snow.

'*Opphore!*' she yelled, and still they came at her. She lashed out and another fell, gouts of blood spraying across the snow.

'*Stop!*' she screamed, but they wouldn't stop. They kept coming, and she cut them down with brutal hacking blows, another, another. Around her the square was a mire of blood and ice and snow, black and green blood, red blood. *My blood?* She realised she was standing still, and there were no more attackers. Looking at the bodies all around her she dropped her sword to the snow and fell to her knees and retched, a torrent of bile spilling down into the mess below. *Children.* The screams kept coming from the house. Always, a child needed saving from someone.

Who will save them from me?

A roar pulled her gaze upward. The trollspawn with the club fist was back on its feet, its guts spilling black blood onto snow, and it was running for her. Floré pawed in the snow for her sword desperately, but then the trollspawn staggered as an arrow and another sank into its chest, and she turned and saw Yselda nock another and draw, even as Cuss ran in. Yselda stood tall in her Stormguard commando tabard of red, the gold trim and lightning bolt across the chest catching the glare of the lightning dancing above. Her face was pale and set, no emotion showing, what was left of her fringe plastered to her face by the driving rain and snow.

Thunder rolled and Yselda loosed her third arrow, and the trollspawn flinched away to dodge it but that left him open to Cuss's attack. Cuss was near as tall as the trollspawn even at its six foot, wide-shouldered and heavy, as he loped in. From under his cloak he drew the long axe he'd spent the last six spans with, an axe liberated from a dusty library in the Riven citadel. Its three-foot haft swung back and with an explosion of movement Cuss swung it around and up, a look of utter fury on his face as the blade buried deep under the ribs of the trollspawn. It staggered back and he let the weapon go, stepping backward and slipping in the snow. The trollspawn reeled and roared, and above, lightning flashed again, purple dancing light blasting down to a rooftop at the edge of the square and exploding chunks of masonry and tile. The thunder and the blast filled Floré, the noise overwhelming every sense, but then in the snow she felt the handle of her sword and beneath a layer of snow the flame on the blade caught and burned, and as the trollspawn swung at Cuss again and again she ran for it.

Yselda's arrow took the creature in the throat before Floré made it three steps. She stopped and lowered the sword as the beast tried to paw at the axe in its side, the arrow at its throat. Cuss stepped in and grabbed his axe handle, wrenching the weapon free with a fountain of black blood, and the trollspawn fell still.

From a side street, six lancers in blue were running.

'That house!' Yselda yelled, pointing to the door half broken in, and four of them ran to check it as the others stalked the dead goblins and trollspawn.

'Many thanks,' one said, but Floré did not make eye contact with him. Cuss came to her as Yselda talked to the lancers.

'Commander,' he said, reaching a hand to steady her, 'are you okay? We need to get to the keep. We need to find Marta!' The rage that had covered his face as he fought the trollspawn was gone and he was Cuss again, sweet Cuss, earnest and simple.

Floré let herself sink against his steadying arm for a moment.

Cuss and Yselda. Her soldiers. Her children. She couldn't put words to the fear she had for what she would find at Protector's Keep, but Cuss didn't need her to say anything. Wiping his gore-slick gauntlets on his cloak, he pulled one off and put a hand on her shoulder.

'She'll be all right,' he said. Floré looked back at the carnage of the Star Market, the blood and bone and death.

'I don't want her to see me like this,' she said, and looked away before he could see the tears in her eyes. Cuss didn't say anything. He always knew when to be silent. Instead he pulled a rough cotton handkerchief from his pocket and pushed it into her hand, gestured at her face. Yselda was standing over the fallen rottroll, gazing around wide-eyed at the square. They stood in the rain and Floré looked up and closed her eyes, letting the cold rain pour over her. Cuss pulled his hood up over his tight brown curls and stood wringing the neck of his axe, looking across the square at the snow and carnage, looking up at the roiling sky above, the turmoil of the rotsurge.

'Just a bit of blood, Boss,' he said in the end when Yselda eventually joined them. 'It'll come clean.'

The lightning danced in the clouds above, slower and slower, and the wind began to drop. Floré turned her eyes back to Protector's Keep and allowed herself hope. Hope for news of Marta. The whitestaffs had done their rite of seeking for her, every day for six spans – with a drop of Floré's blood they had sensed her daughter, *alive* – north, far far north. *Far past Undal City. Where are you, girl?* She had found no cure for the skein-sickness. Marta reached for the pattern, and it took from her. Janos had told her before he had died that he could fix it. *That a skein-wreck could fix it.*

Floré wiped at the blood on her face and rolled her shoulders and, together with Yselda and Cuss, she walked from the Star Market as the rotsurge began to calm over them. The rain turned to snow and Floré heard the screaming from the Star Market calming, becoming distant sobs, and then nothing at all.

2

Forge No Chain

'Mistress Tree, Master Soil, Master Wall, and Mistress Water. In every city of the protectorate there stands a statue to Mistress Water, robed and hooded at her insistence – her face and form hidden to show she could be any of us. "Every change in history began as a thought and a hope," she said, and through her connection to the skein she went to the great mother Anshuka. How did she pass the guardian Orubor? No tales tell. How did she wake the mother? No tales tell. We only know from the teachings she left us that she asked, and was answered.' – **History of the Revolution,** Campbell Torbén of Aber-Ouse

When they made it into Protector's Keep through the thronging lancers and City Watch at the lower gates, a brown-clad steward was waiting for her.

'Your presence is requested in the grand chamber, Bolt-Commander,' the steward said, and Floré looked them up and down. Her old steward had tried to kill Starbeck. *Are any reformists left fool enough to keep rebelling even now?* Floré knew that for decades the most recent band of reformists had

34

sought changes in the structure of the protectorate – less power to the Stormguard, a separation of the military from the core of government.

When Fallow Fen was taken their support had dwindled, and Starbeck's triumphant recapture of the city and the destruction of Urforren had bought him years of good favour with the people. *But now it is a Claw Winter, and all hell is breaking loose.* Floré nodded to the steward and with Cuss and Yselda at her shoulders they rose through the keep, from the black stone passages wrought by the Ferron up to the tall rooms of limestone the Undal had built above. Over the three centuries since Ferron fell, the keep had been abandoned, becoming a fort, a palace, a council hall. Now it was a fortress. Everywhere, there were Stormguard tabards below hungry faces. Braziers burned down each corridor, and there was a hustle of civilians towards the infirmary. Orders being yelled. Floré itched to focus on it, to get stuck in with the response – anything other than think about Janos dying in her arms, Marta racked with fever…

Focus. Even in normal times a rotsurge would be a disaster in a city like Undal – goblin and rottroll and trollspawn escaping to hide and hunt through alley and sewer. Stormblight as well – the rotvine and pepper-thorn and bite-kelp, creeping plant life – and black fungus that turned food to rot, which made weak lungs hack blood for a season. Floré glanced out of a window at the snow, still falling thick, the Claw Winter upon them when they should still be harvesting. *Perhaps the cold will kill the stormblight, this time.* The rotsurge was the enemy's worst weapon. How could you fight a storm? The commandos tried to stop them at their source, capturing the strange rotbud crystals that grew deep in the storm, but if the crow-men found them first they could funnel power into them and send a vortex of chaos the breadth of Undal.

Floré focused on memories of the rotstorm and the tactics of containing a rotsurge as they walked ever upward in the keep. The alternative was Marta and Janos, and if she thought too long on Marta she felt her heart would burn to ash. If she thought about Janos, about *Tullen One-Eye*... Floré's jaw clenched as she walked, and her focus was gone. *Deathless Tullen One-Eye*. Once more she thought of how to kill the unkillable man.

They arrived after many minutes of stairs and long hallways. The grand council chamber was high in the keep, a dome built for the mighty of the land to discuss and debate and decree. Floré had been there only once before, when Knight-Commander Starbeck and the council had begged Janos to stay. Janos had refused – had refused even non-military application of his power. Refused to touch it ever again, after what happened at Urforren, a city turned to a mile of burning salt. *And I told him to do it.*

As they waited at the heavy doors for their presence to be announced, Floré slipped her blood-wet gauntlets from her hands and onto the hook of her belt and let her hand linger on the hilt of her sword, her fingers stroking the sword knot tied there. Red silk with a core of white, damp to the touch even now after three hundred years. It was a strip cut from the robe of Mistress Water herself, the first whitestaff. Mistress Water who raised the slave rebellion against Ferron – who began the first revolutionary council. Mistress Water who spent her life in the hell of a Ferron salt mine, and forever after wore her eternally damp robes to keep her scarred and ruined skin as soothed as she could. *Mistress Water who wrought violence for peace.*

Even after all these years, Floré was unsure if she had made the right decision at Urforren. *What would Mistress Water have done?* Urforren had been a garrison of monsters, rottrolls, goblins, crow-men. Rust-folk who raided the protectorate and killed without mercy. It had been a garrison, but also a city, and Floré bit her cheek as she remembered the cold knowledge in her heart – that the chimneys and thatch of Urforren housed more than just monsters. She shook her head and stared at the stone of the floor. Next to her, Yselda shifted her feet and kept smoothing her tabard and Cuss was sniffing, all of them dripping water onto the dry floors of the upper keep.

Two stewards opened the doors to the chambers and Floré kept her head high as she entered past City Guard armed with shortsword and cudgel. Inside, the long council table was covered in a sprawling map of the Undal Protectorate, from the rotstorm in the east to Brek and the Cimber hills in the west, the Storm Sea and Wind Sea cosseting it from north and south. Starbeck was leaning over the far side table, and next to him Commissar-Mage Inigo of the Castrum. Starbeck was lean as ever, an axe of a face with grey stubble and close-cropped hair, his face lined. Inigo was a complete contrast, expansive, his wild beard lustrous and brown, eyes darting at her.

Tomas and Benazir were opposite along with the Antian Voltos, all speaking at once. Tomas no longer needed the goggles he had worn to hide his skein-scarred eyes, and he turned to look at her as she entered and gave a tight smile. His beard had grown out as they waited for rescue on Riven, a thick lustrous black that only broke for the burn scars up his right jawline and cheek and forehead. He gave her a nod and turned back to the maps, and Benazir smiled to see her. Benazir's hair was cropped short, her face still crossed with scars from the wyrm she had killed at the Stormwall, but her flesh less sallow than it had been when last they were in the city – six spans on the whitestaffs' provisions, even on rations, had her back to strength.

Voltos the Antian looked at her and smiled as well. He was

just over four feet tall, covered from head to toe in black fur edged with grey, his high ears mobile and expressive. He was dressed in silk robes sewn through with ceramic plating, a decorative obsidian knife at his belt and spectacles on his nose. The Antian were somewhere between a mole and a dog to Floré's eyes, astute tacticians and fearsome warriors. Despite their short stature their hands were subtle and their muscle strong, as the Stormguard had found thirty years before when they had fought for control of the mountain city of Aber-Ouse. She nodded to him and behind her – and Cuss and Yselda – the door pulled shut.

Along with those at the map table, three prisoners knelt with their hands bound at the edge of the room, a City Watch guard standing over each. The gaunt shaman Jule, who had stolen Janos's corpse, stared at her unblinking. The Whitestaff Master Deranus, who had killed half his order and wrecked a dozen ships seeking to harness the power of the comatose skein-wreck. He was old and broken, his posture stooped. His eyes did not leave the floor. The final prisoner was the sailor who they had found washed up after Janos destroyed the rust-folk fleet, the sole survivor. *A fleet they should not have been able to field,* Floré thought. Floré had previously noted that he had the look of Cil-Marie about him – but Cil-Marie were secretive, barely trading outside of their island nation that was across all the Wind Sea and the wild reefs of the Tullioch. The implications of a Cil-Marie fleet transporting rust-folk, goblins and rottrolls and all, made her grimace at the sight of him.

'Floré,' Starbeck said, and she winced at his informality. *When has he ever called me Floré?*

'Sir.'

She locked eyes with him, and couldn't bring herself to ask the question. She felt her arm twitch and made herself look up as she clenched her fists, up at the ornate dome of stone above them with its high arched windows. Four braziers warmed the centre of the room but they were scarce keeping back the cold, and she could still feel cold fingers of snowmelt seeping through her clothing.

Starbeck blew out a breath and raised a hand for calm and silence as Benazir and Tomas and Voltos and the Castrum Commissar-Mage Inigo all spoke at once. They quieted at his simple gesture.

'The first rotsurge was six spans back,' he said, voice as careful and clipped as ever. 'Three ships assaulted from the sea, but they were a distraction. Six wyrms came over the walls, which could have ruined us. We lost nearly the whole Undal commando garrison trying to repeat Commander Arfallow's trick with the rune-blade, and killed two of the beasts. But they were a *distraction*. I got Marta out and north, with Nintur of the lancers and twenty of his best men – a mage as well. But it was all a distraction.'

Starbeck circled the table and drew up a long stick, and began to prod at the map. His eyes were lined and reddened, his jaw clenching and unclenching in any gap between words.

'When they retreated, they took their four wyrms but they left us many gifts. Rotbuds. Normally one in a year would be a disaster. We have seen one a span, for six spans. Every ten days as sure as the tides. They are hidden through the city, and once a span, an orb appears, and the next day, a rotbud surges. The storm gathers, the wet-lightning falls. Monsters crawl from the ground, brought by the storm. Our people die.'

With a swish his stick came to rest on the Northern Marches.

'So far they do not expand outward. The ships debarked west of here and the rust-folk headed straight north, through the Slow Marsh. They burned as they went but did not stop for any town outside their straight path. They are back in the

Northern Marches now. And while we fight rotsurges, they have fortified. A ditch from Fallow Fen to Inverbar, then north to the Storm Sea. They have spent six spans digging in, and we have spent six spans fighting fire after fire in the lands we still hold. The rotsurges. The Claw Winter. The refugees from the north. Trade ships are still not making it through from the east. The Orubor are still refusing us access to Anshuka or the orbs you captured in summer. Reformists have been rallying those without hope and blaming all of this on *us*.'

Standing straight, Starbeck adjusted his tabard and turned to them all.

'In this our darkest hour, the hope I sent out has come back to me. What is the news? An orb of light brings you, but leaves within moments. I hear already murmurs of whitestaffs in the infirmary – the muttering reached my guards before you had begun climbing the stairs.'

Floré let out a breath and went to the table and drew out a chair and sat, laying her blood-coated gauntlets and sheathed sword on the table. *Hope is for fools.* Benazir came and stood at her shoulder and scratched at the scars on her cheek with her remaining hand. She gestured with the hook she now wore on the stump of the other wrist.

'Short version, then the full debrief sir?' Benazir asked, and Floré poured a cup of wine from a carafe on the table and drank it without looking.

'Aye, Bolt-Commander.'

The rest of them drew chairs, and Floré stared at the map. *North with Nintur of the lancers and a mage and twenty men. Alive.* She looked at the regions north of the city – Undal City sat on the south coast. There was the whole country, from Hookstone forest to the mountain city of Aber-Ouse, the great glen of Brek… hundreds of miles and thousands of places to hide. *Or be lost.*

'I'll save the heroism for the full report. In sum, our mission was threefold. Retrieve the whitestaffs; learn how to kill Tullen One-Eye; learn a cure for Marta. Beyond that, the god-killing dagger of the demon Varratim is in play, lost by the Orubor after his defeat in the summer.'

Benazir went to the whitestaff Master Deranus and used her hook to pull up his chin until he was forced to meet the gaze of Starbeck and Inigo.

'Deranus here deposed Master Vilni, and killed all who objected. He did this because the shaman Jule, under guidance from his church, stole the body of Janos. Our Salt-Man. Our skein-wreck. With the body of a skein-wreck and the communal magic of the whitestaffs, Deranus devised a way to access the power and pattern of Janos – who was *alive*. With this power, he killed Vilni. He killed over half of the other whitestaffs, who had been recalled to co-ordinate their response to the orbs of lights. He captured an orb of light, presumably sent to raid the citadel of Riven, and used it to kill any who would tell of their betrayal as he worked at harnessing Janos's power more fully, to whatever end. I'm sure his final plan was something grandiose. Some ships you sent to Riven were lost to the rust-folk's wyrms and rottrolls, to be sure. But most you sent were destroyed by a man who had promised to serve the protectorate, to give him time to consolidate his own power.'

Benazir paused and let Deranus off her hook, a thin trickle of blood welling up into his beard.

'I can explain,' he started to say, but Starbeck silenced him with a raised hand.

'She just did. You will talk more, tonight, to one of my men,' he said, 'and in the morning you will hang. The shaman too.'

Deranus slumped his head and, after a gesture, the City Watch guard behind him dragged him from the room.

Jule struggled to his feet.

'I have only done as I was asked by the Shramana,' he said, voice quick. He had eyes only for Starbeck. 'You must understand, Knight-Commander. The skein-wreck was refusing to aid the protectorate. His power came from Anshuka. What right did he have? What pride, to think he knew better than the church, better than the whitestaffs – better than the council? You must understand!'

Starbeck waved a hand curtly and the guard behind Jule brought his cudgel down on the back of the shaman. He slumped to the floor. The guard dragged him away, and Floré did not watch. Instead she turned and looked up at the high windows set in the Grand Council dome, looked at the darkness beyond, strained to listen to the sound of snow blowing hard against the glass. Next to her Cuss adjusted his axe against the map table and began wiping at a patch of black blood he had left on the table edge, the end of his sleeve pulled tight in his hand. Floré smiled. *Sweet Cuss.*

'The shaman in your village, the whitestaffs in our halls,' Starbeck said softly. 'How quickly our brothers and sisters forget their oaths when power is at hand. I have not looked to the Shramana and their church in too long.'

Starbeck fell silent, and next to Floré Tomas stared hard at the map. *Hope is for fools,* Floré thought, looking at Starbeck. She could see Starbeck did not let himself hope that Janos was alive. Did not let himself hope at all. Benazir rubbed her jaw with her hook and then seemed to deflate.

'This is troubling indeed,' Commissar-mage Inigo said. 'If what you say is true and Deranus learned to… *tap* the power of a skein-wreck, we must beware the consequences, and beware this power in the hands of our enemies. For now, it means the whitestaffs are greatly reduced. What else did you find, Bolt-Commander?'

'More than half were already dead,' Benazir said. 'We took

back who we could in the orb, and sent them to the infirmary. Others we left behind, and they should have supplies enough to get through until a ship reaches them. The important thing… Janos was alive, sir. He fought with us, against a fleet of rust-folk, wyrms, all of it, burned a whole fleet to nothing. But the one-eyed mage was there.'

Benazir returned to the map table and spread her arms wide to encompass Tomas and Floré and Cuss and Yselda.

'Tullen One-Eye has his knife. He has done something to the black luck stones, some skein-magic that has set him free from Anshuka's chains. He has his knife, he can *fly*, and he killed Janos and left us all to die. We are only here because a Tullioch who was left behind in that business in the Blue Wolf Mountains stole the last orb there and came for her father, who we picked up on the voyage south. They agreed to take us back here, and return now to their folk to speak of what might come next. Luck and chance, chance and luck. He killed… Tullen killed Janos, sir. He has a knife that can kill gods, and magic enough to turn this city to ash in a minute if it crosses his mind. Like Urforren.'

Silence, except for the wind at the windows, the press of snow on glass, the movement of feet in the corridor outside.

'Lothal has been sighted,' Starbeck said at last, and pressed the heels of his hands into his eyes for a long moment. 'The last two spans. Near Ossen-Tyr, near one of the new forts by the borders of the Northern Marches, we had the lancers pull up. Garioch. In Hookstone forest. A wolf forty foot at the shoulder, eyes of deepest black. From the forest, even here we have heard him howl.'

Floré pictured ribs thick as tree trunks and black as pitch, ribs rising from peat next to a skull the size of a barn, teeth long as spears. She had seen Lothal's bones, deep in the rotstorm where Anshuka defeated him three centuries past. She had knelt in the flower meadow beneath Anshuka's sleeping form, the sleeping god covered in rock and dirt and grass and with trees looming over her. In the cold of the grand chamber Floré shivered and pictured Urforren burning, a burning column of salt a mile high for an instant, leaving an ever burning wound in the earth. *Does it still burn, now he is dead?* The works of a skein-user fell apart when they died – would Urforren still burn now that Janos was dead? *Would killing Anshuka stop the rotstorm?*

Months before, she had beaten the demon Varratim to death as he tried to do just that. Varratim who had snatched children in the night, Varratim who had mutilated livestock and spread fear and hate as he moved towards his final goal. Now in the depths of the unnatural Claw Winter, enemies at all sides, Floré stared at the cup in her hand. It was simple clay, but etched with a bear motif. *What would have happened if I had let him kill Anshuka?*

Commissar-Mage Inigo scratched at his beard.

'How do we kill an invincible mage and a god?' he said at last, and Floré sniffed and met Benazir's eye. Benazir nodded. Floré pulled her gauntlets from the table and clipped them to her belt and then rubbed her eyes.

'This sailor washed up after,' she said, gesturing to the final prisoner. 'Cil-Marie, we think. So we have perhaps another front to think of. I said I'd not imprison him, so I suppose you question him and then kill or free him, as you choose. From what I can tell, Cil-Marie have been supplying ships to the rust-folk.'

Starbeck nodded, and turned to her, locked his pale cold eyes to hers.

'What is the plan you two are hatching?' he said, and Floré nodded to herself and pictured Marta. *Hope.*

'Kill a god, kill an invincible mage, cure Marta,' she said.

'I've got a plan. Well. In fact, *Cuss* had the plan, but I think it's the right one.'

All of them turned to Cuss and Floré managed a tight smile. He had a mouthful of bread, the rest of the small loaf clutched in one hand. *All we've done is fight monsters and march up a hundred stairs, and the lad found a loaf.* He grimaced and swallowed.

'Well, sir, well,' he said, and Floré nodded to him to continue. 'Well, the first thing we need is an Orubor.'

~

Hours later, Benazir almost felt warm.

'We left thirty sailors and a score of whitestaffs and a handful of commandos behind,' Benazir said, 'but you managed to keep the cat?'

Tomas held up the kitten Jozenai and scratched under her chin.

'I'm not hearing a question,' he said, and Benazir huffed. They were up in a suite of rooms in the commanders' corridor, she and he and Voltos, with most of a bottle of wine now gone along with a few bowls of soup and hard bread.

'Did you want me to leave her on a frozen island full of mad whitestaffs? Poor wee beast has suffered enough madness. Floré didn't want to join us?' Tomas asked, and Voltos rubbed at his whiskers. Tomas rubbed Jozenai's whiskers and held her up facing the Antian. 'Do Antian like cats?'

'She hoped to find Marta,' Voltos said, his voice precise as he worked his mouth around the Isken trade tongue. 'Even though she knew from the whitestaffs that she would not find her here. Antian do not like cats, or dislike cats, Tomas. It is pointless to like or dislike cats – cats simply *are*.'

Tomas nodded as if this was wise and set Jozenai down on the floor; watched her wander off. She had been such a little thing when he found her, but a few spans and she was already bigger, plump and long-legged. He turned back to the table and withdrew his wand of starmetal from the holster in his sleeve, pointing it delicately at the candle. Its tip was a ruby, worked and faceted and inscribed in arcane geometries. *Just a little.*

The wick sputtered into flame, and Tomas smiled and sheathed the wand.

'I didn't even touch the skein for that,' he said, and Benazir and Voltos exchanged glances.

'If you didn't touch the skein,' Voltos said slowly, 'then that tool presents perhaps the greatest leap forward in technology in history.' Tomas shrugged and ate a little more bread until Benazir held out her hand.

'The castrum have had these since summer,' she said, 'and I've heard nothing about them not needing the skein.'

Tomas passed her the wand and saw her focus, and with a gentle hand he directed the end of the wand away from his face and out into the room. Benazir furrowed her brow.

'The castrum have been busy,' he said, 'and rumour of a weapon that might make them obsolete is certainly enough to drive a little secrecy, don't you think?'

A thin stream of flame sputtered from the end of the wand and Benazir dropped it to the table.

'Berren's black blood, that was bloody magic!'

Tomas laughed at that; a laugh as good as any he could remember having.

'Bolt-Commander, you are now a mighty mage!'

The air stank of flame and Voltos sniffed and gingerly reached for the wand, inspecting it all over. Benazir drained her glass of wine and refilled it with the end of the bottle.

'Every hell there is… that is a strange feeling, Tomas.'

Voltos was gazing into the gem, holding the candle close to better read the runes inside.

'Old Ferron runes?' he asked, and Tomas nodded.

'Aye, but could be whatever. The trick to rune tattoos or scars or whatever is the pattern of it calling to a memory of a pattern far more complex. I suppose the question here is, where is that more complex pattern stored? I don't think it's the runes themselves; I think it's their distribution.'

'The industrial applications...' Voltos said, voice quiet. 'How many skein-users are there in Undal, Tomas?'

Tomas frowned. *Skein-users?* From the doorway Jozenai mewled and disappeared around the corner and then returned dragging a piece of cloth she had found. Benazir got up and rummaged until she found another bottle of wine, and she poured them all a healthy glass. It was an orange wine from Cil-Marie. Tomas took a sip and grimaced. *Sour.*

'For a country that only exports wine and slaves, you'd think they'd have the decency to at least export *good* wine,' he said, and Benazir and Voltos didn't even pretend to be listening. Both were staring at the wand.

'Can you make more?' Benazir asked, and Tomas shrugged.

'Do you understand what it would mean,' Voltos said, 'to have this power in the hands of an artisan? Tomas, I ask again how many?'

Skein-users. Tomas frowned and pictured Janos, Janos the Salt-Man flying in the air over Riven Citadel throwing fire and force.

'Not many,' he said, and took another sip. 'There are whitestaffs, say a couple per large market town, a dozen in a city – in total there were no more than a hundred and fifty, and now at least half those are dead. Skein-mages, perhaps two hundred competent in the country, perhaps another hundred in training at any given time. It's not an easy thing.'

Voltos was nodding, and then he drained his glass of orange wine and held the wand out into the bare heart of the chamber and squinted. A burst of flame spewed out, white fringed with red, and then Voltos was cackling as Benazir flapped a cloth at the smouldering wooden shutters.

'Judges' sake!' she said, snatching the wand from him and handing it back to Tomas. 'If you've a point, make it, but no more bloody fire!'

'My point is,' he said, 'if Tomas could make ten of these and string them in a row, what might that do? If he could make fifty and line a forge with them, how would that compare to the heat from bellows and coal? What might the metallurgists be able to make with higher temperatures, the chemists, the alchemists? My *point* is that this is a tool that can perhaps only be constructed by one who understands the skein. But it can be *used* by any peasant. You do not see the threat? You did not touch the skein to use it, but it still costs the user, oh yes. I feel the exertion.'

Benazir scooped up Jozenai from the floor – the kitten had dragged her cloth close. With her hook hand she gestured at the fireplace, which was dying slowly. Tomas went and threw another split log onto the fire and took his seat.

'What would you do with it?' Benazir said, and Voltos shook his head.

'I would slip it in my pocket and never have to look for a match again,' he said, and Benazir laughed, but Tomas squinted at Voltos. *He isn't as drunk as we are.* He sheathed the wand at his wrist.

'It still costs,' he said. 'It costs less than it would a mage, to be sure, but there is still a price. Your blacksmith would be winnowed and dead in an hour. Your ten-wand bundle would leave a man gasping as if he'd run from here to the Stormwall. There is always a cost, Voltos.'

The Antian tilted his head.

'There are those who place less of a price on the energy

in a body than you would dare think. How many desperate folks would sell their strength? How many slaves would be given no choice? This is old magic, Tomas. Remember who made it. Ferron were not kind to their slaves, and many disappeared and were lost, so many. How many do you think were powering the wands beneath the empress's bathhouse to heat her water, at the end? What machinations might we find if we could brave the storm?'

Tomas pocketed the wand and dropped some bread for Jozenai, and together they drank the wine and did not speak about the other things that might change the world – the orbs of light. The wolf in the wood. The one-eyed mage. They drank the wine and when the others were talking, Tomas stared into the fireplace and pictured the symbols Janos had drawn in the air over the harbour of Riven – a series of symbols that had burned as bright as the sun, that had burned a fleet from the water and left nothing but ash. *The burning sun.* Next to it his wand was nothing. A toy. *Next to Janos or Tullen One-Eye, I am a child.*

'I am worried about the reformists,' Voltos said, and Tomas could see the Antian's eyes flitting between himself and Benazir, always gauging reactions. Tomas did not give him the benefit of a reaction, and instead waited for Voltos to continue. Benazir tapped on the wood of the table with her little metal claw, and he did give that a smile. *Finally her outside matches the inside,* he thought. *Scarred and sharp.*

'My sources say there have been meetings, across the city,' Voltos continued. 'Agitators for elections. For a change in leadership. For negotiation with the rust-folk. There was a riot at the forest gate, cobblestones thrown. None dead, yet – none that we know of. But they are organised, and they are angry, and the whole place is close to breaking.'

Benazir took a slug of wine and wiped her mouth with her sleeve.

'Bugger the reformists. Not our problem – let Starbeck keep them in line. The only question we need to be thinking about is: will our plan actually work?'

Voltos laughed again and poured himself another glass. Tomas pictured the one-eyed mage, the dagger at his belt. *Where is it from?* From the wand he had learned so much, but the dagger had sent him half-mad. *Only half-mad,* he thought with a grimace. He felt his true self again, after so long. *It was your true self that took the dagger from the Orubor and caused this mess,* he thought, and the memory of it was an ache in his heart. He had killed the Orubor, had broken treaty and tradition. He had been obeying no orders other than his own desire for power. *Power to what end?* Benazir and Floré had not told Starbeck or Commissar Inigo that it was *Tomas* who took the dagger from the Orubor, and not Tullen. *That it is my fault.*

The skein-wreck Janos had cured the sickness in Tomas's eyes without a second of hesitation. Tomas stared at the fire and wondered how they all seemed to know the right thing to do – when rules should be broken and when they should be obeyed, who to save and who to sacrifice. He had seen Tullen One-Eye, seen a man who had every scrap of power that could be gained, a man who had conquered nations and murdered gods.

Tomas stared at the little kitten and he stroked his beard. He had seen Tullen, who had that power, and he had seen Janos, who did not want it. *Which of them would you rather be?* Janos had used his power and it had broken him, sent him running to the forest to hide. Tullen had broken half the world. Tomas shifted in his chair. *Could he wield that kind of power without breaking, without being broken? Could anyone?*

'Will it work, Tomas?' Benazir asked again, and he found himself nodding slowly.

'Suffer no tyrant; forge no chain; lead in servitude,' he said at last, and toasted them both with a forced smile. 'The plan could work. Orubor, demons, an invincible mage, ancient magic technology, and on top of that it's snowing. What could go wrong?'

3

THE STONE PRINCE

*'Dearest, it is as you said. He has gone. He has taken the orbs and he has taken the wands, has taken our twenty best mages. Only in you and I would he trust the realm in his absence. Ferron has left us with the Judges and your power to follow his dream. The old man built this haven from his will and his magic – know that I have his will, and know that you have a magic even greater than his. Together, darling, we can rule. With the Judges at our call we can make Ferron the greatest nation ever to exist in this world. Let my father have the stars – we will have earth and water and tree and berry. You must come now.' – **Private letter,** Empress Seraphina of the Gilded Spire*

In the shadow of the Watchful Brothers, Ashbringer crouched behind a pile of crates and tried to calm the panic in her heart, tried to ease the tightness in her chest. The Watchful Brothers were two looming statues of black Ferron stone, the same unmarred black as the slave roads that connected their outposts across old Undal, the same seamless black as the walls of their overseers' forts. The Watchful Brothers – one a knight grim-faced, one laden with a bounty of scrolls and coin and fruit extending a hand of friendship. South of the Cimber hills they marked the old edge of the Ferron Empire three hundred years past – and now the edge of the Undal Protectorate.

In the shadow of the hundred-foot statues, the market sprang up each day, the fastidious traders of Isken travelling the mile from Flous-Tar with their bureaucracy and orderly stalls, itemised receipts scribbled, each vendor with a pad of ink and an intricate stamp from their guild. Opposite them the disorder of the Undal, the chaos of commerce unfettered tramping from Wedderburn and the little villages that grew up overlooking the border valley. Neither country claimed the valley floor – an area for trade. A few hundred yards in each direction of the market a line of stones marked the point where the Stormguard or the Isken Guild of Order would behead or hang thieves, respectively.

Ashbringer huddled below her heavy cloak on the Undal side of the shallow valley and pulled her gloves tighter. As she glanced at the patrolling Stormguard City Watch overlooking the path down to the main market, she gripped the hilt of the broken sword tucked in her belt. The hilt was the antler of a little god, shed in a season many years before her own birth. Of the blade there remained only a jagged inch of silvered steel. The weapon had been intricately forged and folded and patterned by the rune-smiths of Elm with a single purpose – *kill Tullen One-Eye.* Ashbringer gripped the crate next to her until her hand hurt, gripped it to keep the world from spinning again. She could picture him, Tullen One-Eye smiling as her sword broke on his magic, as he cut her from the world and left her to drift. *Failure.* Her bow was lost, her belt knife gone somewhere in the fight on the mountaintop high over the Riven monastery. *Breathe,* she said to herself, and tried to sing the hunting song Highmother Ash had taught her as a girl. The melody would not come – only words disjointed.

'Run, run, towards the light; run towards the mother,' she said quietly, but there was no tune, and crouched behind the crates in the frozen mud Ashbringer shivered and tried not to weep. The brutality of the Claw Winter was all around – after the attack on Undal City, the fishing villages and market towns of the eastern Star Coast were flooded with those seeking refuge. Ashbringer pulled her stolen cloak close, and wrapped her scarf tighter to better hide the blue of her skin. With the ravaging cold winds and the nightly flurries of snow and the attacks in the Northern Marches, the Undal were on edge – Ashbringer was sure the sight of an Orubor would lead to disaster. Blue-skinned with serrated teeth, eyes unmarred golden orbs, skin scarred in rune and pattern, she knew she was *other* to those here. *Not even Tullioch or Antian,* she thought, *not some strange neighbour.* Orubor were wraiths who never left their impenetrable woods – mind-readers and cannibals and murderers.

And now I have become a thief, she thought, almost giddy with the madness of it all, and the hunger in her stomach. She had no coin for food, no bow to hunt, even if any game was left in the fields and woods. Tullen had taken her from the skein and locked her off from the connections of the world. *Deaf to the chorus of all things.* Rather he had plucked her eyes or ripped her tongue by its root. Clutching her cloak tight Ashbringer walked to the central market, head bowed. The Undal stalls were few, the last desperate traders seeking coin as if coin could save them from the cold.

She carefully avoided the end of the market where the Isken were processing those who wished to leave the protectorate. She could hear yelling from there. She had roamed into Isken from the deep woods of the Cimber hills, had seen a few of their towns when ranging and hunting sign of the Deathless mage in years past. Patrols ran the borderlands, and would imprison and deport any who tried to enter without the proper papers. They loved paperwork. Ashbringer pretended to inspect a pile of coiled rope, to better glance at those queueing for asylum. *No asylum,* she thought, *only chains for warmth.*

The Claw Winter would not affect Isken so harshly, and it was a rich country. For those without a guild sponsor or a pouch of coin, entry could be had on terms of service. Indentured labour for a guild, and after a set time or cost, freedom to work and live in Isken was granted.

'Bloody fools,' the man beside her said, and the smooth familiarity of his voice made her gut wrench. *Tullen One-Eye.* She had not sensed his arrival. He was tall and dark-skinned with the thick locks of his hair pulled tight behind his head, and the mage had trimmed his usual long beard and was eating a carrot as he stood next to her, so casual. *I'll rip out his throat with my teeth and...* and then Ashbringer was focusing on the grain of the wood of the crate beneath her hand, the knots and whirling pattern of growing wood now dead. She felt a wave of nausea spread over her from head to toe as she even contemplated violence against Tullen, a wave of confusion and pain in her mind. Her mind saved itself by turning to input and pattern, so dull as it was without the skein to drop into.

Tullen One-Eye had cut her from the skein, and placed on her a limitation – she could not harm him, or act to bring him harm. Her mind could not even conceive of hurting him, try as she might. On the rooftop of Riven citadel, she had watched silent and still as he duelled the skein-wreck Janos to the death. She had allowed herself to be carried away in Tullen's flight, limp and wretched. The will was within her, but as soon as she formed thought against his strictures her mind would flit; her hand would falter.

'Fight, fight, fire so bright; fight for root and tree,' she heard herself say. *The hunting song.* Tullen ignored her words and took another bite of his carrot, glancing around the market. Aside from those waiting to be processed into Isken, the Undal traders were surly and the Isken traders surrounded by more caravan guards than during Ashbringer's previous visits. Garlands of flowers and bushels of hops, vegetables and trinkets piled equally high. Mirrors from Kelamor, fine linen from Uradech, black pepper and books from Cinnae. Undal was cut off by the rotstorm to the west and the Tullioch wild reefs to the south and the bleak black water of the Storm Sea to the north. Its only neighbours were Isken and Tessendorm, and three centuries of border wars with the latter meant Isken held the keys to the wider world.

The Undal had wool and bricks of peat, rough Brek whisky, barrels of pickled eels, what little grain or root or bog cotton that could be called excess, books with rougher bindings and poorer type than those of the strait kingdoms. The skins and meat of the crocodiles and lizards that slunk through the Slow Marsh in the west. Ashbringer brought herself to her feet and lowered her head against the biting wind.

'Why are they fools?' she asked, and Tullen threw his carrot stalk to the ground and turned to her, smiling.

'They think they can earn their freedom, but the Isken know their trade. They hold no slaves, but you work until your debt is paid or find yourself in a debtor's gaol. But each day they add a little cost – your food, your shelter, the clothes on your back. Rental for the tools you must use to complete the work. Breakages, medicine. All of it combines so that perhaps you can leave but it will be more than the season or year they tell you – and by that point, you are likely well under the thumb of whatever guild you are indebted to. Clever, really – we used chain and force to make you work the fields and mines, but the Isken use the market. Progress, eh? Charge your slaves for bed and board!'

Ashbringer reached her hand for the hilt of her sword and drew it fast to her own neck, but as the stub of blade moved close to her skin she felt herself relaxing and staring at a cloud, a lone cloud scudding across the sky. Then the hilt was back in her belt and Tullen was three caravans away, inspecting a stall of weaponry, his long fingers careful as they ran across the hilt of a rapier in the ornate style of Kelamor. Ashbringer followed and waited a few steps back for him to buy the sword, and then she followed as he bought a brooch the vendor claimed as Cinnae that looked like a star of battered tin.

What does he want from me? Why won't he let me die? He had taken her with him from Riven as a companion, but then left her in Undal, abandoned as he flew off to destinations unknown. He would return, and then depart. She did not know where he went. He could find her anywhere, it seemed. *There is no hiding from the Deathless one.*

Finally Tullen left the market, heading back into Undal, and the guards did not stop him, did not question him. Mute and hooded she followed, her legs leaden and her mind clouded. For three hundred years her line had been tasked with bringing him to justice. In her mind she saw Highmother Ash's face, free of rune scars but lined with time and the burden of responsibility – *you must ask him, will he change his course? Will he submit to judgement?*

After they passed the Undal Stormguard, Tullen turned south and together they climbed a low hill crowned in a rough circle of standing stones, each four foot high. Of what were once perhaps thirty stones, half were gone, and many fallen. Ashbringer shivered as Tullen sat in the snow, and without looking at her he waved his hand and the air around her was warm, as if the summer sun was stirring it from a meadow.

She sank to the snow a few feet from Tullen and watched as he opened his pack, set out kettle and pot, and lit a fire with a blink of his eye. *Obeisance to the Highmothers,* she thought. The warmth he had given her was so good, so calming, so *wanted.* She felt sick in her heart at how weak she had become without her magic. *Is that all I was? My magic?*

'I am bound to ask you,' she said, voice thick with pain, 'will you change your course? Will you submit to Anshuka's judgement?'

Tullen poured water from a skin into his kettle and placed it in the fire, and then took his pipe from inside his cloak. The pipe glowed with no match or taper. Ashbringer knew he was using the skein, using it as easily as any who had ever lived. *More easily than I ever did.* She could not think of the skein, could not think of how severed she was from the world. If she did she would be lost. *Obeisance to the forest.*

'Why did you take me to Undal only to leave me? What do you seek now that you are back?'

Tullen did not answer until the kettle billowed steam, long minutes of silence. From a small box he pinched tea into two battered tin cups, and when he had poured both and handed her one he finally met her eye.

'I had tea on this hill over four hundred years ago,' he said, and smiled at her, though his eyes did not change. 'Empress Seraphina, her Tullioch guard resplendent in gold and copper, and I. We met the old princes of what are now Isken and Tessendorm and Kelamor – noble families from the east come to pay homage and make peace, that we might stop our expansion here.'

Ashbringer drank the bitter tea, and stared from the circle of standing stones down into the valley below where the Watchful Brothers stood.

'You have done many things in your long life, Tullen

One-Eye. Was this a good thing, or a bad thing? Will you submit to her judgement?'

Tullen stared at her and then down at the Watchful Brothers.

'They tried to kill us that day,' he said at last, and with a sniff put his cup down into the snow and took another pull on his pipe, the smoke snatched away by the wind in a heartbeat. 'I forget his name – some prince of somewhere, son of someone, heir to something. Lord of so on. He had good boots but too much jewellery. Gaudy, and poor metalcraft in the housing of the gems. In truth there was only one prince there that day – all the rest were skein-mages, the best skein-mages and wizards and sorcerers and witches and necromancers of two dozen houses, enemies and rivals bound in an alliance with a single goal. Kill me, and thus force the empress to withdraw.'

Obeisance to the mountain, Ashbringer thought, and sipped at the tea. The mountain was Anshuka, the great Judge and god of her people. A mountain that was a bear that was a mountain. *The will of the world manifest,* Highmother Ash had told her.

'A sad thing that they failed,' Ashbringer said, and drained the last of her tea. 'Many a life would have been brighter.'

She flinched as Tullen laughed, and with a spring he was standing and pacing the remnants of the stone circle.

'Seraphina was *here*,' he said, 'and I was *here*, and old Pelomar the Tullioch was at her shoulders. What do you think happened next? Two dozen skein-mages all coming for blood, and me sat here, a bottle of wine in me. The stones were all in place then, and they had lifted a canopy of red silk over us – Seraphina hated the sun. It was summer. Can you picture it, Ashbringer? What do you think happened next?'

She closed her eyes and pictured the scene, two dozen mages dressed as nobles climbing the hill from the valley below. Two dozen people with mothers and fathers and siblings and perhaps children of their own. Two dozen people connected to the world and its history.

'You killed them all,' she said. 'One-Eye. Red Hand. Deathless. I think you killed them all and made slaves of their kin. Woe, I name you. Death. Perhaps you killed their gods as well.'

Tullen drew her up roughly by the arm and Ashbringer did not resist. A lifetime of reflex and training to *fight*, to tear every vessel and snap every bone... she found her eyes tracking a sparrow flitting through the sparse hedges that clung tight to the side of the hill. *You should be east or south, little one.*

'Will you submit to her judgement?' she heard herself say, but Tullen wasn't listening as he dragged her along.

'I let the crier start his work with their false names and false titles, but in each mage's mind I placed a message. *I mean you no harm.* "Before we start," said I aloud, "let us begin with a show of good faith." With just these hands I pointed to the valley below and I drew up the Watchful Brothers. A hundred foot each, seamless black stone, unending and unchangeable. Skein-magic beyond what any of them could begin to conceive of. I drank a glass of wine as I did it, and as the dust settled I took Seraphina's hand and I said to them these are the Watchful Brothers – one looks east, for trade and friendship. An exchange of power and knowledge. The brother Boon. The other also looks east, an eye sharp for threats, a reminder of the power that protects this realm. The brother Bane.'

Ashbringer stared at the sparrow, and then tried to connect to the skein. She closed her eyes and dropped into that tangle of light and colour that connected all things – what they were, what they might be, inside and out, the connection of all things to all others through an endless series of nameless forces and links. *Connection.* She could see herself, the complexity of her own essence and physicality, but where it should reach outward there was a veil of shadow and her sight lost the trail of any connection moving beyond herself. Still the connections were there, but she could see them only as though through flame or smoke. *Blurred and unreadable.*

Ashbringer dropped the skein and realised Tullen's hand was on her shoulder.

'Not too long now, my friend,' he said, 'and I will free you. I have only put a leash on you – our mother bear cut me off almost entirely for three centuries. I could scarce warm a cup of tea, and could not think my own thoughts. I need you to understand, before the end.'

'Run, run, towards the light; run towards the mother,' she said, tonelessly. 'Fight, fight, fire so bright; fight for root and tree.'

Tullen shook his head at her. 'You will sing again, one day perhaps. Now – what do you think happened when I raised those statues? Do you think the mage prince and his cohort bowed at the empress's feet?'

Ashbringer stared down at the valley, the hundreds of Undal in a ramshackle queue at its northern end trading freedom and fear for safety and bondage.

'You killed only one,' she said, and clicked her teeth together.

'I said to them, "I am not your enemy." But treachery must be punished. With a wave of my hand I turned the mage prince to stone. His defences and preparations did not slow me a moment. I had the Tullioch Pelomar break him with the hammer they used to peg down our canopy, and to each mage I gave a piece. A hand, an arm, so on, to take back to their masters. You understand? I made an example. "Think on this," I said, "when your rulers turn to folly." If you wander the halls of many a palace east of here, even now, in a chest someplace secret will be a piece of that stone prince. A reminder of the power of Ferron. To protect your lands is noble, but to defy nature itself is foolishness.'

Standing in the circle of ruined stone, Tullen raised a hand and the Watchful Brothers who had stood three hundred years both cracked, jagged fissures across their cores, and the upper halves of each slid and then fell with a crash that shook the valley. The screaming began, traders and refugees and guards all fleeing from the spumes of earth and snow that the falling statues sent flying up into the sky. At the feet of the statues there had been market stalls and figures sheltering from the wind, and they were lost in the avalanche of stone. Ashbringer saw the sparrow fly up, and then east. She looked at the dagger at Tullen's belt, the thick handle of twisted bone with a pommel of green gemstone and a blade of obsidian.

'Is that what you are, Deathless? You are nature? You are the storm, the shaking earth, the burning mountain. *Nature.* Will you submit to judgement, Deathless?' she asked again, and Tullen kicked a stone. The stone bounced off into the snow atop the hill, disappearing beneath the deeper white.

'*Will you submit to judgement?*' he said, and she saw a flit of anger cross his face. 'Judgement from a bear, assassin? Or judgement from you, the night guard? One can only be judged by a peer, and I have none. At least, none on this continent.'

'You lost once before,' she said. 'When you faced her, you lost your wolf and your dagger. Your empire. Your empress. Is that why you walk with me at the border, and watch refugees in the dirt? Or do they remind you of yourself – afraid, and without a home?'

Tullen spat and broke eye contact, stared down at the valley below.

'The sailor fears the hurricane, no matter how skilled he is.'

Ashbringer bowed her head and felt the familiar taste of her own despair, the blackness growing in the back of her mind. *He could kill the mother,* she thought, *and all the trees, and all the little beasts. All the Undal, and their songs and their dancing.* She pictured the little gods she had met as she travelled the world. *What would the world look like, with Tullen's reordering?* Ashbringer had known no empire. Tessendorm and Isken were Undal, but with different rules. She had never dared enter the rotstorm when Tullen's trail had led there in the past. The Highmothers had warned her to stay clear – the demons and monsters within were already living under Anshuka's wrath. When he entered the rotstorm, she would retreat to Orubor's wood to pray to Anshuka, to commune with the Highmothers, to confer with the bladesmiths and singers.

'What is it you are going to do, Deathless?'

Tullen walked across the snow to his kettle and settled down with his back against the stone. With a pinch of tea from his box and a top-up of hot water, he made himself comfortable. The spasm of rage that had crossed his face was gone and he was smirking, implacable. Cupping both hands around his tea he met her questing eyes and held her gaze.

'I'm going to make an example.'

4

WOOD, WATER, WOOL, AND WINE

'*Many of our kin are dead since the orbs first flew. Since the summer heat it has been a swift collapse into this Claw Winter. Their bear god curses us all with unnatural cold even as they praise her for the storm she brings down on Ferron. Their shamans preach piety, as if these spirits care for individual action. Their leaders are people of the blade – their answer is, as it will always be, the blade. There was panic, and in the panic the other was sought. Within their own ranks religious practitioners of Baal, or the gods of the strait kingdoms, were viewed with distrust. Those few Antian who have sought a life on the surface were soon to follow. Do not mistake me. Many hands and voices were raised in our defence, but fear is potent. Children stolen and livestock mutilated. Threats from before their meagre histories. The Undal have killed Antian this year – how many, I do not know. This is not the state – this is the people.*' – **Letter to the Hidden Council of the Undal Redoubt**, Bellentoe Firstclaw

'She is with the Antian,' Starbeck told her, and Floré cleaned

64

her sword blade and began trying to get the goblin blood from inside the scabbard with a scrap of cloth and a wire from her belt pouch. 'I sent her with Nintur – my best lancer captain. They have made for the redoubt. She will be safe there. The Antian witches may even have medicine we do not, or some idea how to stop her from reaching the skein. Our treaties are strong, and she will be safe in the redoubt from orb or storm.'

Floré sagged in her seat but kept cleaning the blade. She pictured Marta, the same red-brown skin as her father, the same curls of hair and amber eyes as her mother. Angry and sensitive. Kind. Sick. Burning with fever, screaming in the night. Floré felt a wave of relief wash over her. The redoubt. It was as safe as anywhere could be from the Claw Winter, and the rust-folk had no war with the Antian. She rubbed the oilcloth along her blade and tried to be strong, tried to hold the composure in her face as underneath she wanted to weep. Floré knew Marta was safe, knew the Antian redoubt was a clever choice with the city besieged and winter upon them. *But it is so far,* she thought. *She is so far from me.* The sadness threatened to drown her, as it had every night on Riven when she was alone in the darkness, no Janos, no Marta. Only cold blankets and silence.

'Thank you, Knight-Commander,' she said at last.

'Floré,' he said, and she stopped cleaning her blade but did not meet his eye. They were in his private chambers – a simple hearth and a simple table, a thick rug of undyed wool spilling over the floor. There was a bookcase piled with treatises on war and politics, thick bindings, and piles of reports covered a table pushed against the wall. Floré had scanned the spines of the books and found the blue, the red, the green – *Janos's poetry collections.* She had already squared most of her gear away when the steward came for her, requesting her presence in Starbeck's rooms. Floré rubbed at her scalp and met his gaze.

'Sir?'

'The boy's plan is a good one, your element of it more so. I wanted to talk. One of the mages came to me – Artus. Benazir told me when we debriefed, as well. Your theory.'

'Sir.' Floré loved the word sir. It could convey every emotion under the sun. *Sir, you had me slaughtering children in monster form for half my life, sir. Sir, I'm not sure you were wrong. Sir, our god is perhaps the worst monster of them all.* Starbeck was too old a hand to fall into it. He sat in silence and waited for her.

'The theory that some wraith of Anshuka hunts the rotstorm,' she said slowly, watching his eyes. 'That it finds children, and when it does, it twists them. Turns them into crow-men. Goblins. Rottrolls. Trollspawn. Wyrms. That leaving rust-folk in that storm was not a punishment, a hard life in a hard place. That it was not defending our border. That they fled for good reason, and turning them back was murder.'

Starbeck's eyes did not change, sharp eyes, cold and pale. Floré put down the sword, took a drink of water and flexed her fingers, and twisted her wedding band around on her finger, and Janos's silver ring below it.

'Did you know, sir?' she asked, and he did not answer. Together they sat and listened to the hearth crackle, the press of wind against the glass outside, the distant commotion as the castle carried on its life – civilians to be made safe, injured to treat, patrols to organise, and reports to be written and read. Blades to be sharpened and arrows to be fletched. Floré looked into the fire.

'Did you know, sir?'

Starbeck tapped the pommel of Floré's sword – what was once *his* sword.

'Anshuka's rune etched on the pommel of a Ferron blade,' he said. 'When I found it, I thought that strange – but I was a young man, and I did not heed my lessons. The Ferron worshipped the four Judges equally – Anshuka the bear; Berren most fair; Lothal the Just; Nessilitor the Lover. Think on it – they did not live with the idea of a distant protector as we do, a slumbering god in a hidden wood, tangible only in the rotstorm, the Claw Winter. The Judges walked their realm, or flew above it. As real as you or I.'

Starbeck looked into the fire and drew his hand back from the sword.

'I knew, Floré,' he said. 'Reports going back three hundred years. Rust-folk begging for mercy. At some point, we used to drag them back and send them into the storm, instead of killing them. For a decade after the corvus epidemic, quietly a few bands were allowed in to work the Slow Marsh – not that any would admit to that heritage now. At one point there was the chance of passage, a ship from the southern edge of the storm, once a season, from Final Light to the port south of Flous-Tar in Isken – indentured servitude and, perhaps, freedom. It has been to varying degrees legend, joke, and reality over the last three centuries. Our policy has changed, but the Stormguard and the council have been resolute in Knight-Commander Jozenai's legacy – *draw a line and burn a ditch*. It is divine retribution, Floré. It is the will of Anshuka. Who are we to change that?'

Floré drank her water and bit her lip until she tasted pennies, until the pain was sharp enough to drive through the sadness, the disappointment. Starbeck had been a father to her as much as her own had, a distant figure, always there, always sure. *How can it make no difference to him?* She felt the well of anger, the burning coals in her heart flaring. *How could he send us to do this, for so long!*

'I spent the last six spans stuck on Riven with the traitor whitestaffs,' she said, 'and I asked them all. I found their expert on Judges; I found their texts. You know what they told me? Anshuka is a god, the way the old man of Loch Hassel is a god. Just bigger. You know what a bogle is, Knight-Commander? The current theory on Riven is that they are the manifestation of thought and emotion, our thought and emotion manipulating the skein. The Judges were bogle, and old Ferron took them and had a whole nation of wizards or whatever, servants, *citizens*, and they focused on those four and fed them thought and emotion, tried to give them ownership. A wolf that thought only of justice. An owl that thought about love. *Whatever.*'

Floré sighed and sheathed her sword and began packing away her cleaning kit.

'Mistress Water was a skein-wreck, and she convinced Anshuka to fight Lothal, who was goaded by another skein-wreck. Anshuka won, and then what? Fell asleep. Mistress Water died in her sleep not ten years after, if the history is right. The rotstorm is the nightmare of a god, sir, but it is *our god*. She does what we want her to, twisted through whatever insanity her mind must be. The only divine judgement is the one we've chosen. Hells, the Claw Winter is probably our own dream of the punishment we deserve for treating the Ferron so badly.'

Starbeck shook his head. 'It is all immaterial,' he said, and Floré cut him off.

'No. No! It's not. If we could stop the rotstorm tomorrow, would you? If you could stop the wraith of Anshuka twisting the rust-folk to monsters tomorrow, would you? I stopped Varratim from killing the mother, but if I hadn't... would the storm be ended? Why would the rust-folk attack us if they had their own lands, their own chance at peace?'

Starbeck stared at her. 'I don't think it is for me to decide how our god metes out her punishment. You have been talking to academics, and they have filled you with theories. What do you *know*, Commander?'

Commander. Floré deflated. She felt so helpless, and as ever, Starbeck offered certainty – but for once she was not sure she wanted his certainty. She wanted him to question, as she questioned. How could they worship a god that did what Anshuka did? *How can the Stormguard send children back into the rotstorm, when all that awaits them is death?* Floré had spent her years on the wall patrols as well as ranging into the storm itself – she had turned back many rust-folk, often at the end of a sword. It had been so easy. *I have so much blood on my hands.*

She sat in silence for a long moment and pictured Marta, dancing with her in the safe stone kitchen in Hasselberry as they sang together and fed each other slices of sweet apples. She always pictured Marta when she thought about all the horrors she had wrought. *I don't deserve her,* she thought. *I don't deserve her, and she deserves better than me – but I will protect her, no matter what.*

'I know we have to stop Tullen One-Eye,' she said, and she let the cold anger in her core take over. *Be the weapon you always have been,* she told herself. *Be the weapon you have to be.* 'This plan should do that. He can't be allowed to live – he could kill us all on a whim. I know that we need to stop the wolf, and for that Anshuka is our only option. I know the mission, sir. Regardless of the rotstorm, regardless of what we have done, I know the mission right now is to protect our people.'

Starbeck nodded, and they both looked up as the door opened. It was the two City Watch guards on duty, two pale tall men who could have been brothers. Both were ashen-faced, and each had their cudgel drawn.

'What is it?' Starbeck said. Floré saw the twitch in the right-hand man's shoulder, the subtle change in stance of a man ready to attack. She saw the grimace on the face of the left-hand man. In a heartbeat her sword was drawn, and she stepped between Starbeck and the two men, each of them a head taller than her, each of them in heavy boots and chain mail where she wore only a simple tunic and trousers and thick woollen socks. The right-hand man shook his head.

'Knight-Commander,' he said, the heavy wood of his cudgel twitching nervously in his hand, 'this madness has gone on too long. In the name of the Reformist Council, you are under arrest.'

~

Cuss tried to get it all to fit in his pack but it wouldn't go. Waterskin, mess tin, four days' rations, flint, sword cloth and oil, Hawk knife, belt knife, whetstone, fifty feet of rope... *why do I have so much rope?* He emptied his pack again and started again, and Yselda laughed at him.

'We aren't going to the moon,' she said, and he just shrugged.

'You know where we're ending up then, this time? Last time I thought we were going for a span to Riven and ended up six spans in the snow. Time before that I thought I was going to check Yulder's farm, and ended up eating grass under Anshuka's nose with about a thousand goblins.'

She laughed at that, and came and helped him, piling up all he could wear the next day to one side and filling his mess tin with all the little items he had been trying to ram around the edges. On the top she even folded an extra blanket. Her own pack was finished and done and neatly set aside, her gear for the next day stowed. They were in one of the commando barracks, but most of the commandos were gone. The room was freezing, but Yselda had found the two bunks nearest a hearth and the fire was slowly starting to do its work.

'You killed a trollspawn,' he said at last, and she sniffed and looked out of the high window – nothing but darkness and a creeping web of snow climbing from the bottom of the pane, climbing higher every minute.

'*We* killed a trollspawn,' she said, and punched him on the shoulder. 'Sorry for taking the piss out of the axe the last few spans. It was a good choice.'

Cuss grinned at her. 'Right? I feel like it's a bit more my speed. I'm not going to be doing fancy parries, but I can barrel through anyone's nice guard if I swing hard enough.'

They sat and watched the fire until it started to die, and Yselda threw another log on.

'You still want to do this?' she asked. 'Be a commando, fight monsters?'

Cuss smiled at her and scratched his hair.

'I suppose. You know how it was with Ma and… and Jana. And Petro, of course. I think… I think I was doing it because I was mad, you know? But the last six spans have let me think a little more.'

'You aren't still mad?' Yselda asked, and she shivered and huddled closer to the fire.

What am I trying to say, Petro? Cuss was always the one waiting to speak, or saying the wrong thing. Petron was the one who knew how to say what he meant. Cuss sighed at the memory of his little brother. He still could barely think of his ma and little Jana. She was barely walking, just a little thing, so perfect. Whenever he thought about Jana it made the anger come back, the sadness. He could think of Petron though – Petron wouldn't have wanted him to be sad.

'Petro always knew what to say. I'm not good at this stuff, Yselda. You know that. I was mad, I'll always be mad. But Sergeant Buchan helped me with the axe, you know? And he told me: don't let anger make your choices. You can be angry, but you get to decide what to do next.'

'So you *are* mad?'

Cuss threw a pair of socks at her head. 'I'm mad but that's not why I'm here. The commander, *you*. You're my family. Commander needs help, Marta needs help, so I'm going to help. If helping means fighting, I'll fight. And if someone else needs help, someone like Ma or Petron, or little Jana, I'll help them too. Would I rather learn how to make boats and spend my day sitting by Loch Hassel eating fried fish? Absolutely. And maybe I'll get to. But that isn't the world we are in. There are monsters and bad people, and someone needs to stand between them and people who can't protect themselves. Every one of them I kill is one less that could do what they did to me. Does that make sense? I'm not fighting *them*. I'm protecting us. I don't know if that makes sense.'

Yselda was quiet at that, and Cuss was happy with that. He didn't like talking, didn't like talking about *feelings* especially. But it was good to have it all out there. He reached for his axe and felt the cold steel of the head of it, pictured the trollspawn. *Whatever Floré and Benazir say,* he thought, *even if that was a child, it was a monster by the time I got to it.* He looked into the fire a long time before he realised Yselda was crying.

'Oh,' he said. *Stupid.* 'Hey...'

He went to her and pulled her close and she cried into his shoulder. *What did I say?* Cuss didn't know what to do about this. He'd gone to her but not thought about the angle he was sitting and now she was crying on his shoulder as he kind of half sat, half squatted, and his left leg was beginning to shake at the weird angle he was holding it.

'Hey,' he said again. *Why do I keep saying hey?*

'I don't know if I can do it,' she said eventually, and Cuss just waited. From a lifetime of saying stupid things, he had learned that sometimes not speaking was the better option. Yselda wiped her nose and then snuffled a laugh. 'It's ridiculous, isn't it? I was only in the cadets to give Esme and Shand a break from me, to learn how to shoot a bow better. Something to do other than chores. And now here we are. I don't want to be a soldier, Cuss. I never have.'

They sat in silence for a long moment watching the logs burn, and Cuss realised she was looking at him, waiting for him to say or do something. He smiled, too broadly, and then settled on his most thoughtful face. Cuss gave her shoulder a squeeze and then took the opportunity to reposition his leg so it had more support.

'What do you want, then?' he asked, and she gave him a hug.

'You aren't going to try and convince me to stay in the commandos,' she asked, 'to stop the rust-folk and stay with you and the commander, are you, Cuss?'

He frowned. 'Why would I do that, if it's not what you want?'

Yselda wiped her eyes and smiled at him, and he felt like he had missed some point but couldn't tell what it was.

'I'll figure it out,' she said. 'Don't worry. Like you said, we need to get Marta. After that, I'll figure it out.'

The door to the dormitory was flung in and Benazir was there in nothing but a shirt, fussing with the straps of her hook-hand. Cuss blinked at her and then looked down at her bare legs and then she was running up the dormitory towards them.

'Reformists!' she yelled. 'Get your shit! We need to be gone – this isn't our mission.'

As she came closer Cuss realised there was a spray of blood over her shirt, and her left hand was soaked and dripping red.

'Sir?' he said. 'Are you hurt? Do you need… trousers?'

Yselda paused from where she was grabbing her pack, and in unison she and Benazir stared at him for a long moment. Cuss kept his gaze locked on the dormitory door and prayed for a reformist with a sword to walk in. He felt the heat rising in his cheeks but he kept his gaze steady.

'It's... cold outside,' he said at last.

Benazir pulled the last cinch tight on her hook and flexed her elbow, sending the bright sharp point cutting through the air.

'That it is, lad,' she said. 'Now let's get me some trousers and get us the hell out of here.'

~

Floré's socks were soaked in blood, and the rune-blade clutched in her bare hand shone bright with flame. A step behind her, Starbeck had one of the shortswords of the City Guard who had tried to arrest him. They had left the two men dead in Starbeck's quarters, fast enough to hear the first screams echoing through the keep.

'You should get Highmother Ash from the Orubor embassy and be gone,' he said, and Floré led them around another turn in the keep – a split junction, and all of the torches and braziers extinguished. Floré flexed her toes and felt the hot slick of blood between them, blood coagulating and sticking the wet wool of her socks to skin. *I liked these socks.*

'Floré!' Starbeck said, and then together they pressed tight to the wall as three arrows shot through the darkness. *Piss on that.* Floré pulled Starbeck back around the corner of the junction.

'Three archers at least,' she said. 'We need to get you out of here. Who can you trust?'

'Everyone I can trust is either dead or doing something more important than waiting here,' he said. 'This is the skeleton crew, meant to keep the city alive long enough for the peace talks in Ossen-Tyr to *fix* this.'

An arrow slammed into the stone of the corridor wall three

foot closer to the junction and snapped in two, the broken pieces tumbling to their feet. *This sword is a bloody lighthouse.* Floré sheathed the still-flaming blade, and the fire died as soon as her hand left the hilt. The only other thing on her was her whetstone and wire and rag, her sword-cleaning kit folded in a patch of leather and tucked in her belt.

Another arrow, this one flying low, and a murmur of voices from that same left corridor.

'Peace talks?' she asked and pulled Starbeck further back again. Her left arm was aching – one of the tall guards in Starbeck's chambers had managed to land a cudgel blow to her shoulder before she severed his spine with her blade. With the sword extinguished the only light was from distant braziers outside filtering through narrow windows packed with snow. It was almost pitch black, and she could feel Starbeck next to her, still and poised. *I must remember that he is a wolf. A wolf in a trap.*

'We cannot fight this war and the Claw Winter,' he said. 'They sent an envoy a span ago. A gift of wood, water, wool, and wine. Good oak from the Northern Marches. Clean water from the Northern Marches. Thick fleece from the Northern Marches. Sweet wine from the cold vineyards, of the *Northern Marches*.'

Floré heard a whistle low and short at the far end of the corridor and held a hand to Starbeck's chest, listening to the blackness. *Wood, water, wool, and wine. Like a fairy tale.* She could hear the slow step of feet down the left hall, and tried to build a map in her mind. *The left hall to the commanders' corridor. To Benazir and Tomas. The right hallway to the old motte where the Orubor embassy is.*

'On behalf of the Council of Reformation,' a voice called, 'you are under arrest pending trial. The Stormguard will relinquish all power over the Undal Protectorate, and a council of merchants, thinkers, and citizens will reign until this crisis has passed.'

Floré held her hand over the hilt of the sword an inch from the wrapped leather.

'Last guy said it was the Reformist Council,' she called, her off-hand cupped to her mouth to throw off the source of her voice. 'Are you telling me there are two councils? Or that you can't get yourself straight?'

There was a muffled argument, and the steps grew closer. *Ten paces?* The corridor had nothing useful in it, no suits of ornate armour like a Tessendorm banquet chamber, no axes hanging below slain beasts like an old Undal chief's mead hall. Just bare stone and doused braziers. *Doused braziers...*

Floré moved them both back ten steps until she reached a lamp sconce and began feeling at the niche carved behind it in the stone of the wall. *Yes.*

'Reformist or Reformation,' the voice called, 'our quarrel is not with you, Bolt-Commander. You're a hero. Starbeck needs to leave. We need peace, but there can never be peace when you are led by a man of war.'

Floré grimaced and leaned in to whisper in Starbeck's ear. 'You always told me,' she said, 'there is no peace...'

'Only the next war,' he said hoarsely, but she was already sprinting down the corridor to the split junction. *They'll be right at the corner.* With an overhand lob she threw the heavy ewer of oil she'd found in the niche behind the doused lamp. The ewer exploded and she heard screams and then her hand was on her sword and she slid to her knees and exploded up in an arcing backhand, the blade igniting red-hot on City Watch blood even before it left the scabbard. One arrow went wild above her as an oil-soaked steward realised how utterly dead they were, and another was running. The steward burst into flame, their tunic sodden with lamp oil, and the blue-garbed lancer to their right blocked the swinging sword with their bow, managing to lock the blade in a tangle of wood and bowstring and arrow and arms, and then those arms were burning.

Floré dropped her sword and rolled back and watched the scene for a moment. The lancer and the steward were both screaming, one's chest ablaze, another's hands. At the far end of the corridor, the door opened and Tomas was there with a commando and another lancer. The steward fleeing towards them holding a bow opened her mouth to yell something, but Tomas jerked his hand and the steward slammed upward, their whole body flying into the stone ceiling of the corridor. The corpse hit the floor, and Floré scooped up her sword and stepped back as the lancer and steward ablaze in front of her were cut down methodically by the commando and lancer who came with Tomas. She pointed her burning blade at the lancer who had just arrived.

'I don't know you,' she said, and the man took a step back and raised his sword.

'Steady now,' Tomas said. 'Steady steady steady, Floré. *I* do know him. He owes me six gold from a game of cards in the summer that he thinks I've forgotten, and he was born in Fallow Fen. Steady, Floré.'

Floré nodded and lowered her blade. 'They tried to get Starbeck,' she said, and the knight-commander emerged from the darkened passage behind them and gazed down at the dead – two of his stewards, one of his lancers.

'This seems to be their big move,' Tomas said, nudging the dead steward, whose tunic was still smouldering, with his toe. 'Castrum reinforcements are on their way. We can trust any commando who has seen the rotstorm, I'd say. Never met a commando who doesn't love you yet, sir. Beyond that, everyone needs someone to vouch for them.'

Together they went to the commanders' corridor, and Floré

led them to the rooms she had been given a few hours before. As soon as they got in she began to strap into her armour, leaving the lancer and commando at the door.

'Benazir is fetching the children,' Tomas said, 'and Voltos is being *diplomatic* with the Orubor. We should leave – this mission can't fail to infighting.'

Floré nodded and went to pull on her boots and then saw the state of her socks, lamp oil and blood and filth. With a sigh she pulled them off and rummaged for another pair in her kit. As she was pulling them on and reaching for her boots, Starbeck sat down at her table.

'I need Inigo. The field commanders. I need my assistant and my lancers. I need the head of the castle stewards. What's left of the commandos.'

Floré pulled one boot on.

'Sir, that can wait ten minutes. We are leaving now. You said to me: wood, water, wool, and wine. They want peace. Are we giving them the marches? Piss, isn't that what the reformists want as well? This is madness!'

Watching them, Tomas smoothed his moustache with his thumb and blew out a sigh. He looked worn out. Floré knew something as intense as throwing a human body with enough force to kill it on impact was an immense feat for a skein-mage. *Most would knock an arrow from the sky and be panting on the floor. He's getting stronger.*

'They sent good wood and clean water, thick wool and rich wine,' Starbeck said. 'That's not all they sent. They sent the twisted bough of a rotstorm birch, a bottle of red water from the marshes under Lothal's bones. The skin of an albino crocodile, thick and rough to the touch. A wineskin of liquor fermented from whatever poison grows there, a wineskin not one of us would drink from.'

Starbeck sank his head into his hands and Floré saw he was

not the wolf he once was. He was lean and grey still, but there was a stoop to him – a fatigue down to his bones.

'They sent us everything the Northern Marches provides them, and showed us what they were fleeing. They will die before they go back. They would die, but I don't know if we even have the strength to kill them. It must be peace, Floré. Peace at any cost. Too many are dead. The reformists want the Stormguard to step aside, but without our strength the rust-folk could take the entire protectorate if they have a fancy. With One-Eye with them, even we can't stop them.'

Floré stood and flexed her toes in her boots and swung her cloak over her shoulders, and then reached down for the last item. Gauntlets of steel, polished and scratched and misused. Mended and repaired, supple red leather gloves under thick metal. Stormguard commando gauntlets. The gauntlets you wore when you went to war with the storm itself.

Floré pulled on the gauntlets and cinched them tight, and turned and touched her forehead in salute.

'Suffer no tyrant; forge no chain; lead in servitude,' she said, and Starbeck drew himself up and returned her salute.

'We'll kill the mage,' she said, 'and do our damnedest to save Anshuka from whatever he has planned so she can send the wolf back to its grave. Peace at any cost.'

'Peace at any cost,' Starbeck said.

She left the room with Tomas, stopping only to put a hand on the shoulder of the commando and lancer at the door.

'Keep strong, brothers.'

She'd made it ten steps before Tomas called out to her.

'Floré!' he said, and he was smiling. She frowned.

'We need to go, Tomas.'

'I know Floré,' he said, and with a bow he pointed in the other direction down the corridor. 'But Benazir and Voltos are meeting us *this* way.'

Floré marched back up the corridor and past the two guards and kept walking, but she heard what Tomas said and the smirk in his voice when she was a few steps past him.

'Keep strong, brothers.'

The lancer and the commando laughed, and Tomas laughed, and Floré shook her head and gripped her gauntlets tight, felt the lancing pain of anxiety spiralling up the scarred nerves of her right arm. Wood, water, wool, and wine. A world where nobody needed to be sent screaming back into the rotstorm, where no goblins tore through the night, where no mages rained fire and death. A world where Marta could live.

Peace at any cost.

5

A Spider of Glass and Gold

'Mistress Water left a book of parables and a few scant proclamations for her whitestaffs. She was not a stateswoman or a politician; she sought no crown – though surely she had the power to take one. She was a survivor, a woman who looked around and wanted better for her kin – her family, her friends. The revolutionary council made their choice when they renamed themselves. They cast off their old Undal names, clans and tribes and houses with histories dating back to when humanity first landed on this continent. They took simple names, and claimed no dynasty. None is born above another, she said. How to reconcile this statement with the power she wielded, both in magic and influence? Perhaps none is born above another, but some are set above by their actions.' – **History of the Revolution**, Campbell Torbén of Aber-Ouse*

Brude watched the reeve and the one-eyed mage talk in a bubble of summer, and she shivered. The Claw Winter was bearing down hard on the Northern Marches; snowdrifts taller than a man blown by a tempest of grey cloud and howling wind.

When the snow had stopped, the temperature fell even further until the fresh powder froze. Rust-folk had spent the morning shovelling the snow clear of the hilltop where the mage had requested the meeting – *nobody except the reeve,* his message had said. They had set up a canopy and six braziers, more fuel than they could truly spare, a table of more food than she could justify wasting from their meagre rations. *All to impress the mage.* Brude sneered. *The mage who won't even meet me.*

'Commandant Jehanne,' she called, and her adviser from Cil-Marie broke away from her conversation with one of the squad leaders.

'Have you ever seen magic such as this?' Brude asked, and the woman peered up through at the calm atop the hill. The snow there had melted away, and the braziers were extinguished. Tullen One-Eye and the reeve sat in an oasis of calm air, hoods down on their cloaks, hands bare.

'Never quite like that,' Jehanne said, and Brude sniffed. 'The Sun Master can control the weather, at a grand level. But not so focused, I think. Though I suppose all of Cil-Marie is as they want it to be, so why would they need such a... local effect?'

Brude gripped the wand of starmetal in her belt. *If Tullen chooses to kill the reeve,* she thought, *there is nothing I can do. He could kill us all.* The reeve was a plain-looking man, someone you would walk past without ever considering, but in him were the hopes of her people. Brude kept her gaze firm but felt her resolve wilting. *What is the point?*

Jehanne was staring at Brude, careful Jehanne with her tactics and advice, her fleet of ships and the hammer in her belt.

'There is no point us guarding,' Brude said at last, and gestured to the cottage and windmill at the base of the hill. In the snow against the windmill a dozen rottrolls and trollspawn were huddled, snoring, indifferent to the cold. Brude led her adviser inside and together they found a space in one of the upstairs rooms, what might once have been a bedroom. Brude squatted on what was left of a straw-stuffed mattress, her legs bending thrice as she tried to find some semblance of comfort. Decloaked and inside, Jehanne sat carefully on an overturned chest and waited with her infinite patience. *Does anything rattle the soldier?* Brude was a tempest of emotion, the storm in her heart matching the storm of magic in her soul. *What must it be like to be so measured?*

'Wine!' she yelled, and from outside the room there was a scurry of steps. A few moments later a girl in layers and layers of stolen clothes stepped through the door, an Undal bottle and two clay cups in her hand. She set them down and Brude waved her away and then rubbed at her face with her crooked fingers, rubbed at her eyes. *So tired.*

'You do not trust Tullen One-Eye,' Jehanne said, and poured them each a glass. 'I thought he was a hero to your people?' Brude took a sip of the wine and tried to picture the Northern Marches in summer, green grass and flowers and blue sky. *We must survive the winter first.* This Claw Winter was a brutal thing. There were seasons in the rotstorm, seasons of warmth and cold, but all were simply layers beneath the incessant acid rains and funereal gales – they were never the focus. Here, winter was like Jehanne's hammer – beautiful as anything Brude had ever seen, intricate and wholly its own thing. *And deadly,* she thought. *Still, the winter is better than the storm.*

Without a word or motion Brude fell into the tempest within herself and found the chaos, and called to it. The hearth sparked into flame, as did the four candles scattered half-finished around the room. As a final touch she sent a stir of heat into her wine, feeling her energy sap a little. *As if I could be more tired.*

'Do you want your wine warmed, Commandant?' she

asked, and Jehanne nodded demurely. Brude sent a spiral of heat into the woman's cup as well and then slowly let the chaos drop, let the layer of connection and disconnection and abstract potentials fall away from her vision. They both drank and watched the hearth.

'A legend can be a hero,' Brude said after a long silence. 'A man is something else. One-Eye has wandered the rotstorm oft these last three centuries. Mute. Invincible. Something between a ghost and a memory, a silent witness wandering untouched and untouching as all around him, only death. I do not trust him, Jehanne, because I do not know him. What is his mind, after three centuries of this cage? Reeve says he escaped Anshuka's bonds; he delivered us the wolf – where is the wolf, Jehanne? It does not do my bidding. I reach into the storm and I howl when it is close as he bid us, and sometimes it comes. Not always. Sometimes it does violence. It killed a patrol of our own, east of Port Last. Do you know why? I do not. I do not think he does, either. I think he is powerful enough to end this war in a day, and yet he has not. *Why?*'

Jehanne drank her wine and gazed at Brude. They had spent many long days and nights together, marshalling forces, planning attacks. Brude still did not know how the woman thought. When she learned of the ships lost at Riven in a skein-battle, she simply sighed and shook her head as if the loss of three great warships and the scores of sailors crewing them were a minor inconvenience. When Jehanne learned of new deployments of lancer legions at the border of the Marches, she squinted and perhaps the ghost of a smile touched her lips. *What are you thinking, soldier?*

'My name is Jehanne de Thibault du Cilcan, Commandant-arc du Fantôme,' she said. 'You are *Ceann Brude*. The form of my name, in Cil-Marie – it has meaning. My name, child of the most influential parent, of a place. A rank and a role, and where you serve. So, it is Jehanne child of Thibault of the city of Cilcan, scout commander of the legion of ghosts. Do you understand?'

The legion of ghosts. Brude nodded and shifted on the broken bed, twisted her right arm to alleviate the pains in the joints and ligaments running up it.

'I would be... Brude, daughter of Rol of the town of Pertcupar. War-leader of the rust-folk.'

Jehanne smiled and refilled their wine cups. 'Brude de Rol du Pertcupar, Ceann du Ferron!'

Brude returned her toast and eyed the hammer on Jehanne's belt – the black metal of the haft and head inscribed in silver and gold.

'I am tired, Jehanne,' she said, trying for the first time the commandant's name without its rank. 'What do you mean by this, the names?'

Jehanne met her eye and nodded. 'Very well. What I mean, Brude, is that you know who I am and who I serve. You know what cause I follow. It is not the same as yours, but you know it and so you can understand it – you can understand my motivation and my action. In turn I know your aim; I know your war. Tullen One-Eye is legend – he is madness. He is outside of the rules of war. Legions and tactics scarce matter when a skein-wreck is involved. I do not know the name of his ancestor – I do not know his rank. I do not know what land or cause he serves. I had thought him a weapon returning to the fold of Ferron, but he is... distant, the reeve says. Odd. What does he want? As you say, surely he could end this all. He will not meet with you, or I.'

Brude flexed her fingers. 'We are agreed, it seems,' she said, voice hushed, and Jehanne leaned back against the wall and finished her wine.

'There is another thing,' Jehanne said, and this time she did not meet Brude's eye. 'I have seen a dagger the same as his. The dagger your old ceann, Varratim, wanted to use to kill a god. The dagger this Tullen claims to have used to slay the great judge Nessilitor.'

Brude dropped into the storm so she could better see Jehanne, so she could see the trailing light and heat and vibration, the chaos of pattern at her core, her mind. *I see you.*

'Where was the dagger, Jehanne?'

Jehanne rubbed her hands together and her lips parted and closed and for a long moment she was silent, and in the chaos of the skein, Brude could see lines wavering, minuscule connections breaking and reforming and changing every moment. She could not read the woman's face, but could see turmoil in the storm of thought in her head, a dancing array of lights twisting around themselves.

'In the palace of Cilcan,' Jehanne said, and Brude could not picture it – a city across an ocean, a land she'd never dreamt of. 'It was in the belt of the maître du soleil – the Sun Master.'

~

Yselda waited in the stables for the rest of them to arrive. Cuss was fussing with a chestnut horse, stroking its cheek and patting its neck as he quietly chatted nonsense to it. Benazir was pacing up and down the stable, a dagger in her hand, huffing in the cold. Yselda pulled her own cloak tighter and stamped her feet. The stable was warmer than outside, the heat of two dozen horses and their mess filling the air with a must. She kept her hand on her sword hilt. *Reformists attacking the castle.* They had seen no reformists, only confused guards at their post looking for direction. Benazir had been unequivocal in her orders.

'Kill any traitors. Any steward with a weapon, break their arms before you ask any questions. Anyone look at

Knight-Commander Starbeck funny, cut first and ask later. Eyes sharp.'

Each group of guards they had left stood with bare steel in their hands and an anxious shuffle in their feet, but no question remaining.

'Tomas will bring Floré,' Benazir was saying, and the door to the stable swung open. It was Voltos, leading the ancient Orubor Highmother Ash. The Orubor was as tall as Yselda once perhaps, but now stood crooked and peering up at her. Her skin was an unmarred blue, lustrous white hair spilling down her shoulders. She was clad in a simple tunic of deerskin, and a cloak of undyed wool dusted with snow. Her feet were bare despite the cold. Her face was lined and her eyes surrounded by the wrinkles of age, though the iris and pupil and sclera were all a deep whirled gold, as if a molten coin was about to set. Voltos closed the door behind them, huffing, and when Highmother Ash saw Cuss and Yselda she smiled. Her teeth were serrated, a row of neat triangles that looked sharp enough to rip and tear.

'The little guardians,' she said, and came forward to look at them both closely. Cuss grinned at her but Yselda just held her gaze. *They saved Cuss,* she made herself think. *Even if they look like monsters, they saved Cuss.* As the Orubor gazed at her, Yselda found herself glancing at the tips of long ears poking through the thick tresses of white hair. Ashbringer had been lithe and deadly, but this old woman was winnowed and wizened. *I wish Ashbringer was here.*

'So you would have me ask favours of the gods, as Ashbringer once did?' she asked, and Yselda shifted uncomfortably. Ashbringer had taken them from the wilds south of Ossen-Tyr to the heart of Orubor's forest in a single step, calling on a doe spirit. The bogle had opened a portal of some kind, a circle in the meadow linked to a circle in the forest. Yselda did not pretend to understand it, and when they had asked Tomas and the whitestaffs on Riven none had heard of such a thing, save perhaps in old folk tales, and even those were unlinked to the savage Orubor. Cuss's plan needed access to the same magics if they were to wake Anshuka.

'We must wake the bear,' Benazir said, and Highmother Ash turned and gazed at her.

'You, you I've not met.'

'Bolt-Commander Arfallow,' Benazir said with a perfunctory bow. 'We must wake the bear, Highmother. We must wake Anshuka to face Lothal – it is the only way.'

The old Orubor considered Benazir for a long moment, and then turned to the horse nearest her and peered up at its face.

'We do not ride horses, in the forest,' she said at last. 'I have lived many years but it was not until this summer when we came south that I was able to spend so much time with them. They are magnificent creatures.'

Yselda watched as Benazir folded her arms and rolled her eyes just out of eyeline of Highmother Ash. She felt her face going hot. *They need to get along,* she thought. *We all need to get along.*

For a long moment they stood in silence, Highmother Ash staring up at her horse, and Benazir, Cuss, and Yselda staring at the Orubor. 'I told you in the summer,' she said at last, 'waking Anshuka is no simple thing. She has slept three hundred winters. She has slept through war and plague, fire and frost. She has slept peacefully, under our watch. You are not the first to ask us to wake the mother.'

Benazir pressed the side of her hook to her temple and rubbed, and her mouth twitched.

'Lothal is back,' Yselda said quickly, just to jump in before Benazir said something hot-tempered. 'And Tullen One-Eye, with the dagger he... you... with the dagger. Can we wake her? There seems to be no other hope.'

Highmother Ash nodded. 'In dark times when all is black, there will always be a mote of light.'

Slowly she raised her palm and from the sleeve of her tunic a spider crawled – a spider with legs of perfect spun glass, a plump black body studded with whiskers of gold. Its eyes were orbs of glass, each filled with a mote of dancing red smoke. Yselda's breath caught. *A bogle.*

'How...?'

Highmother Ash stroked the spider's back and it shivered and raised its front legs.

'When dear Voltos told me the plan, I knew what must be done. I have been a season in this keep – did you not think I would find its gods? There are many gods, across this world, even in the least likely places.'

Yselda leaned forward to look at the spider. She hated spiders – alien and crawling, their webs catching her face as she ran the forest paths. Her father had always laughed at it, had always told her – *better a spider than a dozen midges, little deer, and that's your choice.* She shivered and shuffled away from the unnerving Orubor and the little god.

'Ashbringer is captured,' Yselda said, and the old woman nodded. At her shoulder Yselda felt Benazir's presence behind her, and the older woman's hand on her shoulder, stopping her retreat. The chestnut horse breathed a wet fog out as Cuss patted its cheek, and Highmother Ash turned her hand over as the little spider god crawled and explored the gaps between her long fingers. 'Tullen has done something to her... blocked her from helping us. He took her.'

'So Voltos told me,' Highmother Ash said. Her voice was a rustle of leaves in the high canopy, her speech carefully articulated. 'I'll speak to your mage about it. Ashbringer is bound, it seems, or cut away. In either case, she will persevere. If Deathless walks unbound from the great mother, then he is perhaps vulnerable at last – she will find that vulnerability. It is who she is – it is all she has ever been fated to do.'

The stable door swung open hard and Floré and Tomas were there, cloaked, heavy packs on their backs. From the keep a scream. Floré glanced at them all, dipping her head to Highmother Ash.

'You understand the plan?' she said, and one by one they assented.

'Wake Anshuka,' Highmother Ash said, 'and take your swipe at the Deathless one. Ha!'

The old woman crouched in the centre of the stables and began to sing softly, and Yselda could see Floré shaking her head in the dim torchlight. *At least she didn't try and stop me joining this time,* she thought, and then gave a start as a horse shuffled in the stall behind her. She clutched the hilt of her sword and felt the cold of sweat at her lower back. Her heart had not stopped racing since Benazir had come for them and taken them through the dark tunnels of the keep. *I'm not a soldier.* When she had cried on Cuss's shoulder, it was because she did not know how to tell him she wanted to leave. *I don't want war,* she thought. *I don't want violence.* The sickness in her heart when she was firing arrows, even into that monstrous trollspawn. *A child, once. I'm not meant to be a soldier.* She was happy that Floré had not tried to stop her joining, had not tried to leave her behind, but the idea of more violence made her stomach flutter. She looked at Benazir and Floré, both so sharp-edged... *I'm not like them.*

The spider danced in a circle in the dark of the stables, raising its forelegs, twisting, crawling, and ever Highmother Ash sang and the screams from the keep grew louder. Yselda went to Cuss and Tomas and stood close to them.

'We must rest,' Highmother Ash said. Her voice was thick and strained. 'A single night, and with the dawn I will take you to Anshuka. But I cannot go all at once. It is too... too far for me. Something is wrong with the webs, the currents. We will travel and rest and travel. Do you understand? The knots that hold us all in place are fraying... *frayed*. I cannot go far.'

The spider finished its dance, and a circle of glowing silver light in the centre of the stables held steady. Within it, dark snow half-trampled to mud.

Floré drew her sword and beckoned them in. Behind, the stable door opened and there were three men with swords, no tabards, streaked in ash and gore. They stared at the sight before them – Cuss and Yselda and Tomas and Benazir and Floré and Voltos and Highmother Ash, huddled close in a circle of silver light, a spider of glass and gold dancing at their feet. The men yelled but then there was only the noise of rustling branches and Yselda blinked and then the dizziness was over her and she was crouched in the trampled snow and mud, Cuss groaning on his knees next to her, Tomas standing stock-still. They were surrounded by towering pines, the close walls of the stables having disappeared in a heartbeat.

'Interesting,' Tomas said, and she saw him reach a hand into his cloak to a cloth bag slung below, a hand to the head of the black kitten Jozenai who was mewling in confusion. Sixty days at the Riven citadel had put meat on the little kitten's bones, but her paws were still outsized compared to the rest of her.

'You took the cat?' she said, and he looked down at her and gave a sheepish smile – the most sincere emotion she'd ever seen him show. The kitten mewled.

'I thought she might be killed by reformists for her conservative ideas on parliamentary constitutions,' he said, and Benazir slapped him on the back of the head.

'Where are we?' Voltos was saying, and Floré was laughing.

Yselda looked ahead and realised exactly where they were and felt her mouth open wide as a shiver took her from head to toe. *Hasselberry.*

Home.

~

'This is where I was drawn,' Highmother Ash said, and Floré stared at her and clenched her fists. *Bullshit.* All around them the pines were tall, their upper boughs thick with snow. They were at the west edge of Hasselberry, where the forest road left the village, and another path wended through the trees to Floré's house. *To what's left of my house.*

'What is the game?'

'No game, Floré Artollen. There are many paths to the Orubor's forest. I sought the least resistance. This was your home?'

Home. Floré looked to Yselda and Cuss, both of whom were staring at the lights of the Goat and Whistle Inn. Snow coated the village green, and someone had long ago pulled the tables from the grass and leaned them up close to the inn wall. She could see the whitestaff Izelda's house thick with snow, stone and timber charred and broken. The mill was intact as were the inn and the provision house, the old Forest Watch barn. Tyr's house had a torch lit outside. *Who lives there now?*

'So... where are we?' Benazir asked, and Cuss turned and smiled at her.

'Hasselberry!' he said.

'I must rest,' the Highmother said, and Voltos went to her and supported her arm. 'I must find another little god, somewhere. There is always one near.'

Floré went to Yselda and stood with her and the two of them turned north. Loch Hassel was frozen, thick sheet ice with a dusting of snow that danced as the night wind pulled at it. Thick cloud above, but the few lights from homes in Hasselberry cast a faint glow on the edge of the loch.

'The old man of the loch,' Cuss said, but Floré held a hand for calm. Her gut was aching, and she couldn't bring herself to look at the broken shaman tower and the gutted temple below it. *Where I left Janos for dead. I was a fool.*

'Into the inn,' she said, and without waiting to discuss she led them across the village green and into the familiar comfort of the Goat and Whistle.

The talk all stopped as they entered, and then she saw Essen – red-haired Essen from the lumberyard.

'By the bear – Sergeant!'

He leapt up from his table and crushed her into a hug and then seemed to remember himself. Half the tavern was clamouring with chatter at once, and Floré recognised so many faces. Sandy the miller, Essen. Someone new behind the long wood bar. Nods from so many people, those who worked the trees or held their outlying farms – all would have drawn close for the season, for the Claw Winter.

'We need a quiet table,' she said, and Essen nodded. Within a moment they had a booth in the corner. He lingered for a long moment and looked as if he wanted to say something, but Floré could not be the returning hero for him.

'I'll get you some drinks,' he said, and headed over to the bar. A gaunt man was wiping at the dark wood of the bar, eyes intent on their group. Shand and Esme who had run the inn for all the years Floré had lived there had been killed when the orbs of light attacked the village. Shand and Esme who had been Yselda's adoptive parents. Floré threw the girl a glance – Yselda was looking down at the worn wood of the table, sat quiet between Tomas and Benazir. Next to them Voltos and Highmother Ash were drawing the stares of the whole inn, but none dared approach their table. Almost all talk had silenced, as even with her hood raised it was clear that Highmother Ash was an Orubor.

'Cuss,' Floré said quietly. 'I think you should go and show Essen your new axe, and give him our tidings. If you'd be so kind.'

Cuss beamed and then he was up with his axe gripped by the neck, and a pockmarked man leapt up from a table by the bar.

'Baal's spit!' he yelled. 'Cuss bloody Grantimber?' With a laugh he rushed across the room and clapped the lad on the shoulders and the loggers were laughing and yelling. The spell of silence cast by Highmother Ash's presence was broken, and quiet conversation slowly began to build again. *Nash,* Floré remembered. *I gave him a gold piece to ride to Undal City with news of our mission.* She wondered if he had ever made it down there.

The new innkeeper introduced himself as Marten, and she gave him gold for rooms worth silver. *Money doesn't matter now.*

'How soon?' she asked the Highmother.

'In the loch, the lad said? Dawn. At dawn I will be ready.'

Tomas and Voltos and Yselda took the old Orubor upstairs, and Benazir and Floré were left alone.

'This is the place then?' she asked, and Floré smiled. 'Where was your house?'

Floré drained her glass of ale and grabbed the bottle of wine Tomas had ordered and left unopened and slipped it into her cloak.

'Cuss!' she called, and when he looked she pointed at their bags and pointed upstairs. He nodded, face flushed and brown curls matted to his head with nervous sweat from the attention. One of the loggers asked something, and when Cuss turned away Floré grabbed Benazir and pulled her from the bar and back into the cold.

They traded swigs from the wine.

'Why Hasselberry?' she asked, and Floré shrugged.

'No threats, no skein-mages. Fresh air? In the summer the whole forest is flowers, in the autumn the ferns and bracken all turn brown and red. Even in the dead of winter the gorse flowers bloom, deep yellow. Like nothing you'd see in the city.'

She didn't say, *like nothing you'd see in the rotstorm*. She didn't need to.

They trudged through the snow to the forest road and took the fork down the little lane. Janos had kept the hedges trimmed back, but a season of freedom and brambles reached out to snag at trousers and cloak. Both moved through it easily – no bramble could compare to the grasping vines and thorns of the rotstorm. Every step was a battering ram to Floré's calm. There was the path where Marta collected blackberries, the patch of nettles that once stung her ankles so badly the little girl had sworn vengeance and thrashed them all with a stick. There was the pile of worked stone Janos had ordered to wall the back of their garden in the same manner as the front, though he had never gotten around to it. Floré was so sick with the anger and the sadness. Anger at Tullen One-Eye for taking Janos from her. *How could I lose him again?*

In silence they walked. *Is Marta sick, tonight?* She had spent so many nights nursing Marta's endless fevers and shakes, the nightmares as the girl saw things a child's mind could never comprehend after reaching for the skein. *Where are you, little chick?*

'You know,' Benazir said, 'I once jumped into a wyrm's mouth with nothing but a dagger. And even *I* think this plan is crazy.'

Floré clapped her on the shoulder and took them round the

final twist in the path. It was calming to have Benazir beside her. If she had been alone, the sight of the cottage would have broken her, she knew. With Benazir, the ache was still so potent, but she could lean on her friend. The cottage was still there, the outline of it. Hints of charred beams broke through the drifts of snow. Floré leaned on the front gate. The lilac bush that grew up next to it was frozen, blooms caught in jagged crystals of ice. She snapped one free and felt it in her fingers, cold and sharp and brittle. In that moment she didn't feel anger at Tullen One-Eye, at *herself* for all her failings and brutalities and endless mistakes. In that moment as the scent of cold lilac filled her she didn't feel the pulsing anxiety for Marta that kept her nerves firing and her eye twitching. She felt stillness, a millstone under deep water.

In her mind she went to the place where Janos was, her Janos, her image of him, and there was something like a smile there. A figure who had just left the room. *But they'll be back someday, maybe.* She knew it wasn't true, but it was nice to think so. She closed her eyes and thought of Marta and didn't picture her sick or afraid or alone – she pictured her held close, dancing by firelight and singing together, the three of them. She felt the anger in her melt for just a moment and instead the warmth of her love for her family filled her. *I'll protect her, my love.*

'It was a good life, Benny,' she said, and Benazir took a swig of the wine and put an arm around her shoulder.

'He was a nice lad, Janos,' Benazir said, voice solemn. '*Terrible* poetry though. Gods.'

Floré's laughter carried across the frozen snow, and through the ruins of her home.

6

ICE FISHING

'The dryad sickens. I do not know what ails him – he speaks no tongue of man nor beast. He tills the endless fields and wanders the edge of the desert, and behind him the valleys are thick with life. But he sickens. I can see it in his walk, the way his eyes stop and gaze at the horizon. I do not know what is wrong with him. I sent you north, but now I call you south. Berren is dying, and if he dies then so too will the dream of Ferron. A god my father tamed to walk this arid land and from it draw forth green and water and all that we might need. If he dies, we are lost.' – **Private letter,** Empress Seraphina of the Gilded Spire

Ashbringer pressed at the confines of her cell. It was not a physical cell – there were no walls to bind her, no shackles cutting into her wrists. *But where would I go?* She could find no melody, no rhythm, no *pattern*. Tullen came to her and then left, and then found her again. He took her with him for a day, a span, and then forgot her and left her alone and abandoned in some far-off place. He seemed to want something from her – someone to hear his confessions, his thoughts perhaps. But ever she would push back at him in the small ways she still could, and eventually he would leave her to fend for herself.

Silent and alone she felt the pattern and the pattern below, felt the song – and saw only herself, curtailed. Everything outside of that was as through dim glass, sound through running water. She reached into the patterns stored in the scars on her skin and felt familiarity, but she could not manifest them. Each of them was a pattern that linked to the world beyond, and she was utterly apart.

'I once travelled the length of the world in a heartbeat,' she said to a tree. 'I asked the little gods for their favour, as my mother taught me. I asked and received and went from beach to mountain, from glade to forest.'

Ashbringer brought out her stub of sword and tested her thumb against the ragged inch left of its blade, but something made her pull back before the blade pierced her skin. *Deathless.* He had put his spell on her. Cut her from the skein, and put a weight on her mind, a weight that kept any thought or action that would move against him, or herself. She could not even conspire against him.

'He promised to free me,' she said, again to the tree. The tree did not answer. It was a dead tree, leaves long lost, branches brittle. Ashbringer left it and went to the broken wall of the homestead. Tullen had brought her here and they had eaten dinner together by firelight, and then he had grown distracted.

'Wait a moment,' he had said, and he had risen to the sky and then with a flurry of his cloak he was gone, flying south. That had been three days before. She knew she was far in the north, likely in the Northern Marches themselves. She had spent the day before hunting rabbits – her beautiful bow was lost, lost on the island of Iskander, but she fashioned a simple sling from a strip of her cloak and by mid-afternoon she had two of them. There was a satisfaction to sending the stones spinning with her sling. Now she found them where she had left them, strung from a broken beam. She took off their heads with a wood axe she found behind the tumbled barn of the abandoned homestead, an axe slick with ice. With the heads gone she gutted them with her broken sword, the sword that was meant to kill... *no, never mind that.*

She had lost her dagger on Iskander as well. It was a foolish job for a blade so fine, the stub of it still etched in runes of magic, the blade itself imbued with silver and the blood of those who had smithed it, imbued with a hundred songs.

She wrenched out their guts and threw them to the snow where they steamed. The clouds had pushed back at last, only a few remaining dancing across the sky. The wind was brutal, but she was on the east side of the barn where the sun found her and the wind did not. Crows came fast for the guts, three of them with grey backs and black wings and heads, and she watched them and shivered as they ate. *I've grown indolent,* she thought, *and stupid with it.* For the last decade as she had hunted Tullen One-Eye across the protectorate, through Isken and Tessendorm, she had kept herself warm with the skein – it was a little trick, a stirring.

Now she shivered, and curled her toes in the boots she had stolen from a dead man two spans past. A man dead by the road, his head caved in, his coin and steel taken. The fact his murderers hadn't bothered to take his boots was indicative of just how poor the boots were. She skinned the rabbits, jerking back their fur and cutting at fat and sinew where it stuck, cutting around their feet so the skin would tear free.

Ashbringer built a fire and it did not light, and she threw the flint she had found away and into the snow and then spent frantic minutes searching for it as the sun began to dip. Finally, she found it. Finally, the fire lit. Her hands were so cold that when the flint slipped and cut a bright line of red into her finger she did not even feel it. She set the rabbits on spits of green wood and washed her hands in snow she had collected in an old tin bucket.

She ate her rabbit, tearing chunks of flesh with her teeth.

'My goal in life is to do a thing I cannot now do,' she said, to nobody, just to hear a voice. *Just to not be alone.* 'Hunt the Deathless mage, and bid him come to the mother for judgement. Kill him if I can. What now?'

Ashbringer ate her rabbit and stared at the firelight, the hand not holding the rabbit clutched tight to her stomach for warmth. The night birds were quiet in the cold, the whole world seeming frozen to a perfect stillness.

The snap of a branch pulled her from her reverie. They were coming through the woods – two, at least. She grabbed the rabbits and with quick leaps and one hand pulled herself up to the top of the homestead wall below which she had set her fire. The wall had once had a roof of thatch above it, but half of it was burned back and the other half collapsed into a mess of beams and frozen heather and dried straw.

'Where are we?' a voice said, and another shushed it. *They are speaking old Ferron.* She had learned it as a child, but did not know if her tongue could still speak it. Two figures stepped into the clearing surrounding the homestead, moving cautiously towards the light. Each wore a heavy cloak of patched leather, layer upon layer of leather and wool beneath. Their heads were wrapped in thick pelt hats and scarves of wool again. She saw a band of red cloth pulled over their clothes, the red catching on the firelight.

Both carried spears, and slowly they stepped towards the fire. They whispered to each other. *Rust-folk?* Ashbringer chewed on her rabbit and scratched her head, felt the stubble of hair that was growing out. *A decade of a shaven head, a glistening blade, and a mission. And now I chew burnt rabbit*

in stolen clothes, aimless. No magic, no blade, no mission.
She closed her eyes for a long moment but could still hear the
two figures moving forward, stepping carefully in the snow.
Highmother, help me.

Are you a blade? a voice in her head said, so soft.

Ashbringer blinked. It was her own thought, not some spirit
or ancestor guiding her.

Am I a blade? Am I my magic? Am I my mission?

'Assassin,' she said, softly. All her life she had trained to kill.
Before she was grown she could use every weapon the Orubor
had. *Trained for one mission. Be the claw of the Highmothers.*

The mission was to kill Deathless Tullen One-Eye, but
she could not do that. *What else is there?* Obeisance to the
Highmothers. Obeisance to the forest. Obeisance to the
mountain. At the heart of her forest, at the heart of her people,
was Anshuka.

Ashbringer leapt from the wall and landed in the snow,
clutching her rabbits. The two figures wrapped tight scrambled
back, one of them letting out a scream.

'You come from the storm,' she said, her Ferron halting, and
one of them threw its spear. With the hand not holding her
rabbits, Ashbringer snatched it from the air and spun it. The
weapon was poorly made, a rough iron blade at the end of a
bowed shaft of weak wood. She threw it down and took a bite
from her rabbit, stared at the two.

'You are one of the bear's guardians,' the spearless one said,
voice deep. From under their cloak they drew a blade of curved
steel. 'Ceann Brude will want your head!'

'Ceann Brude,' Ashbringer said, and nodded. With four steps
she was on him, and she let him swing at her. She spiralled
around the swinging blade and with a motion drew her broken
sword and slashed up, under his extended arm, up where the
blood flowed so strong. The second spear-wielder jabbed at her

as she ran past, but the man she had cut stumbled and dropped his sword, swayed, gripped at his arm.

'Sister!' he said, and then he fell to his knees. Ashbringer cocked her head at him. The blood was pouring fast through his clothes, billowing steam. *He is dead already.*

The other figure – *sister* – jabbed again and again with her spear, and Ashbringer danced back and back across the snow and rough ground, and then she leapt forward, inside the woman's reach, and slashed down with her broken sword into the woman's hands. The woman dropped the spear and clutched at the fountain of blood pouring from the stumps of two fingers, and she fell back into the snow. Tucking her sword back in her belt, Ashbringer kicked the spear from the snow and caught it with her free hand. She spun it around and pointed the tip at the throat of the woman below, and behind her the man finally slumped to the snow, dead.

Ashbringer took another bite of rabbit, stringy and lean. *Obeisance to the mountain.* She leaned down and saw her reflection in the dark eyes of the woman below, the blue of her skin marked with red rune scars, the points of her teeth, the pure gold of her eyes. *I will serve, Highmothers,* she thought, *even if the song is held from me.*

'Where are we?' she asked. 'Who is Ceann Brude? And where do they sleep?'

~

'I hope we aren't transporting to my childhood home this time,' Tomas said. 'The food is terrible, for one thing.'

Cuss didn't laugh. His head was aching from the ale and the mead he'd consumed with Nash and Essen and all the lads from the mill who used to take the piss, all the lads who'd had no time for him. Suddenly he was their height, had muscles on his arms and an axe with stains of trollspawn blood on it. He had a red tabard, not for show, not some piece of dress uniform or something given to a cadet to teach them to be part of something. His was used, had been used, had been worn fighting the enemies of the protectorate. *They actually respected me.* One of the lads whose name he couldn't even remember had tried to take the piss but Cuss had met his eye and the other man had backed down with raised eyebrows. They'd all bought him drinks and now it was the next morning and he felt like nothing but a lump of cold coal. *Baal's spit,* he thought, and took a swig of his water. *Why does ale taste so bad the next day?*

They were standing at the edge of the loch in the light of dawn, if you could call it dawn. *More like light grey.* There was no sign of the sun – cloud covered the sky utterly. Cuss kicked at the snow where the land met the ice of Loch Hassel. In summer there would be beds of reeds here. He smiled as he pictured sword fighting with Petron with broken reeds, dragging their little rowboat out to fish for trout and pike. *Did it sink?* When the orbs came and took Petron, Cuss remembered waking in the reeds, soaked in blood. *What happened to the boat?*

While they waited for the rest of them to arrive he left Tomas and wandered the fishing docks and inspected the upturned rowboats. He had already walked behind the inn and seen the row of houses buried in snow, where Ma and Jana were resting. *Don't think I have any more tears, today.* He gripped the head of his axe and kept walking.

He found the boat just as the others were arriving back at the loch edge – it was turned over in the open shed where a bunch of the fishermen kept their little rowboats. Someone had painted the bottom blue, but the rest of it was as he remembered. He knew it was his boat the way he knew his own hand, or the face of his mother. The oarlock on the right side was bent, and it had the snub bow that made no sense if you thought of it. The little fix of wood to tie their lines to when they were night fishing was there near the prow. *Da made that.*

Cuss ran his hands along the little boat and smiled. *Blue, Petro. Brilliant. You'd love it.* How to put into words what he had lost when he lost Petro? He couldn't begin. But he knew Petro would love seeing the boat like this, and that was enough.

He was smiling when he went back to the others. Floré stamped on the ice at the edge of the loch and nodded. The ice was rough and thick with frozen rushes and grass, and the snow on top of it hid where small stones jutted free. Past that edge, Cuss could see the wider expanse of ice dusted with snow. There were no tracks of people – everyone knew a story about someone who had died, falling through the ice. Cuss shivered at the thought of that black water, and no way out of it.

'It'll hold us,' Floré called. Cuss thought she looked worn this morning, angry. 'The old man stays near the centre – we head out, Highmother Ash sings her song, and we're away.'

She stepped out and Benazir and Tomas followed, the latter extending an arm to help the old Orubor Highmother Ash down the snowy bank. Voltos leapt down after them, and Cuss looked to Yselda. She was whiter than the snow, her face pinched. Cuss knew about the wolves, the last Claw Winter. Her family had lived north of the loch, and the wolves had taken them as they tried to flee across the frozen surface. Only Yselda had survived, her brothers and mother and father all lost.

'Hey,' he said, and she blinked and looked at him.

'Did you find it?'

'What?' she asked, and he put his axe to his shoulder and waved back at the inn.

'Last night, you mumbled something about finding something. Something you left.'

Yselda nodded faintly and gazed down where the others were slowly stepping across the ice. She reached her hand down her tunic and pulled out a locket of carved wood. The wood was simply carved with a stain of black char running across it.

'Wood from a lightning tree,' she said, and he nodded and peered close. 'My mother gave it to me. I wasn't sure it would still be there, in the inn.'

Cuss gave her a smile and gestured at the loch.

'We've got the commanders with us,' he said, 'don't worry.'

Slowly she nodded and descended gingerly onto the ice and Cuss followed, keeping ten feet back in case their combined weight was too much. He looked wistfully back at Hasselberry – in the snow, from this angle the scars didn't look too bad. *They'll be okay.*

He wished then he had a locket from his mother, not just memories. Something to hold on to. Instead he gripped the axe and decided that when this was done, he would get his rowboat. *I could put a sail on it, Petro!* He didn't know how to sail, really – on the ship to Riven, he had watched the sailors on *Basira's Dance* as they worked their ropes. It was too complicated. But the idea of their little rowboat with a single sail, cutting across the loch... *I like that. I can figure that out.*

The walk across the loch started to panic him after only a few minutes, when he realised that they were so far from the shore that if the ice broke there was no way they'd get back without freezing to death. The air was so cold little crystals were catching the light in the wind, but the snow was holding off. The ice was a mixture of impossibly slick and then rough, and it groaned as they walked. Twice he fell, fists and knees impacting heavily on the ice, but it did not crack, only groaned and whispered. His hands and feet were freezing, even with his gauntlets and the gloves beneath pulled tight, even with two pairs of socks on.

'Step soft!' Floré called back at one point, and Cuss walked as carefully as he could but every step felt like a hammer.

Yselda was in front of him, and she was fussing with her bow and her sword. She'd walk ten steps with her bow and then unstring it, and stow it and grab her sword, and then twenty steps later she'd grab her bow again. Her head never stopped moving, scanning the horizon. Cuss closed the distance between them a little.

'Yselda,' he called, voice low. 'It's okay, Yselda. Stow the bow. We're almost there.'

She glanced back at him with wild eyes and grimaced.

'You can't just say it's okay, Cuss,' she said, voice low. 'That doesn't make it okay.'

Cuss didn't know what to say to that, but then ahead a few hundred feet he caught the singing of Highmother Ash. *She's calling the old man.* He couldn't make out the words of her song, but soon he and Yselda had caught up to the rest.

'I don't like this,' Tomas was saying, and Floré, Benazir, and Voltos were spreading in a loose circle around the Orubor, facing out. Benazir had a dagger in hand, and Voltos had his own obsidian-bladed dagger in hands that were cossetted in wool-lined leather gloves that were exquisitely embroidered. Floré was looking at the treeline.

Yselda drew her bow and began to string it again and Cuss scratched his chin with the blunt side of the axe-head. The steel was freezing.

'What can hurt us out here?' Cuss said, and Yselda glared at him.

'Wolves,' Floré said, and he tried to catch her eye.

'You mean they might come out onto the ice?'

'No,' she said, and with her sword she pointed at the tree-lined bank to their north. From it a dozen grey shapes emerged, each with a shoulder as high as his chest, each thick-furred. Yellow eyes staring. They padded forward to the shoreline.

'I mean that in a Claw Winter,' Floré said, her voice steady, 'the hunger and the cold drives the wolf packs from the Cimber hills west, down to Hookstone forest. They wait at the edges of the loch for anything stupid enough to come for water or to leave the safety of the trees.'

An arrow flew high and cut through the air towards the distant wolves and then slammed down to the ice, skidding and bouncing. It was a hundred yards short easily. Yselda swore and drew again.

'Hold on, girl,' Floré said, and Yselda ignored her and fired again, straining to pull back her shortbow. The distance was too great.

'Yselda!' Cuss said, and Yselda swore and threw down her bow to the ice. She pulled her sword and he could hear her breathing from ten feet away.

'We have to run *now*,' she said, and none of them responded.

'Trust, Yselda,' Tomas said, and with a solemn face he stepped between Yselda and the northern shore of the loch and raised an empty hand towards the wolves. 'Stay close to Floré. They will not reach us; I promise you that. I have not lived this long to die to dogs.'

Below the ice under the hands of Highmother Ash, something was glowing. Cuss stared down between his feet. *The old man.* He had only seen him once before, late at night as his father slipped coins down into the water in offering, muttering wishes as the huge eel snapped its jaws lazily and writhed below them, mottled yellow body sparkling, black pit eyes and teeth that shone with green light. The bogle of Loch Hassel, a great eel of gold and green. Below him under the ice there was a green and yellow colour to the glow.

'It's here!' he said, and they all glanced down.

'Hold, Yselda,' Floré said, and Yselda next to him was shaking as the wolves stepped forward onto the frozen loch. They broke into a loping run across the ice but Yselda held her sword straight, even as her arms trembled. Cuss moved to her shoulder and hefted his axe.

Tomas closed his hand violently into a fist and the wolves shrieked as below them the ice splintered. More than half fell into the icy water, writhing, and the rest were in disarray, still a hundred yards away. One of those not in the water howled long and high, and Cuss felt his heart quicken more than he thought it could.

'*Hold!*' Floré said again, and Highmother Ash raised her voice, her song using no words that Cuss could guess at.

A howl answered the call of the wolf on the loch. A howl deeper than the biggest bell Cuss had heard, thick and rich. A howl that made his breath catch. A howl that broke across them like a crashing wave. A howl that was thunder incarnate; a storm given form. Highmother Ash stopped singing.

'The wolf,' Highmother Ash said, and below them the ice glowed gold and green – but all their gazes were locked on the treeline.

The pines to the north of Loch Hassel were mature, growing straight and true – not like those twisted trunks south of the loch where the gales from the Wind Sea bent and warped the wood. The trees stood from knee high to thrice the height of the shaman tower. *Must be a hundred feet,* Cuss thought.

The wolf that stepped through the pines had to shoulder its way through the narrow gaps in the trees, pushing past bough and branch, pausing a moment to lean its shoulder into a young tree that bent willingly away, roots ripping from earth. It was at least half the height of the tallest tree at its hunched shoulders, its jaws open and waiting. Cuss fell to his knees and next to him Yselda was scrabbling on the ice on all fours for her bow. *Lothal.* Tomas lowered his fist and gripped the satchel at his waist where Jozenai the cat was held, and he began to back up with small steps.

Lothal. Cuss felt sick, felt his blood freeze. Black fur streaked in glowing silver, eyes like pits of pure darkness. Teeth like swords as it huffed and snapped its jaws and stepped from the trees to the short snow-lined beach. From the rent in the ice the wolves that could clawed themselves out of the water and ran to their master's feet. A few remained, desperately scrabbling for purchase. Floré grabbed Cuss by the collar and pulled him up. *When did I fall?* He blinked and grabbed his axe, which was somehow on the ice next to him, and he threw a glance over his shoulder across the ice to Hasselberry. The town was quiet under the blanket of snow, a few wending smoke trails drifting from chimneys.

'*Now*, Highmother!' Floré yelled, and next to him Yselda drew back her bow and fired a shot.

Cuss could hear his breath, hear the low murmur of the Orubor's song. Yselda screamed with rage and dashed forward ten feet, drawing back her bow and sending arrow after arrow through the air in high arcs. The arrows fell short and scattered and slid on the ice, or the whipping wind blew them off course and they flew far wide. One looked as if it struck true but the great wolf Lothal did not flinch or move. *What good is an arrow against a god?* At the foot of Lothal, more wolves were massing. Dozens of wolves. Cuss gripped his axe.

'Hasselberry,' he said, but didn't know what to say next. *We have to save them. We have to get them out.*

'We can't fight this,' Tomas was saying, and Benazir was dragging Yselda back by the shoulder, back to the circle of light, a circle of silver that lay beneath them in the black water below the ice.

Cuss could only stare at the eyes, black orbs that ate all light, black as the bottom of a well at night. The great wolf huffed and a cloud of hot breath spilled from its mouth, a tongue of dark meat red slavering behind teeth black as coal. *What does it want?* He couldn't bring himself to move.

'Are you ready?' Highmother Ash asked, and Floré pulled Cuss in close to the others.

'We have to help them!' he yelled, and pulled free from her grasp. *Doesn't she see? Hasselberry has no defence!* 'I'll lead them away, to the woods. I'll...'

Floré pulled him close and he didn't hear her words, he only saw the wolf Lothal pounce up and land on the ice, its front paws together slamming down. Across the loch the world groaned as cracks bounded outward faster than he could think, faster than he could understand.

The wolf howled, its front legs half sunk in the water, and the ice across the lake danced and reverberated and shook and bucked with the sound, and Cuss fell to his knees and as he went to stand he was in water – water so cold his skin burned, so cold his breath blew out of him in an instant. He could feel himself slipping lower into blackness, the only light a burning circle of silver. He gripped the haft of his axe as ice hit him, in the head, the back, the legs. He was tumbling, lost in darkness and then a hand grabbed him by the tunic, and even in the water in the deep black he could still hear the wolf howl reverberating, could feel the churn as the world itself tried to kill them all.

Cuss closed his eyes, and the world began to spin.

INTERLUDES: EYES SHARP

THE UNNAMED KNIGHT

> *'The broken claw!*
> *The blooded eye!*
> *The deep below!*
> *The burning cry!'*

Tullioch battle chorus

The flight from the great mountains of the Blue Wolf down to the Tullioch Shardspire was easy – Ruemar had adrenaline, had a *need*. The little Antian children she had called Jurren and Gellen, the humans Bullitar and Bollitar – she had flown them south, south and away once she had discovered how to open the orb of light left abandoned by her captors. She had planned on taking them to a village or a town, but the first she reached in the mouth of a wide valley was burned and buried in snow. The second was at the edge of a small forest and the people there fled from the orb until she landed, and then when no fire or force flew out they charged with axe and pitchfork as the ramp descended.

Ruemar was so tired, so weak, and she did not speak their

tongue – and so away she flew. That first night she set the orb down in a silent valley far from any settlement, next to a single tree that grew tall and proud. The rest of the valley was rock and heather, cold and dark and silent save for herds of antlered beasts that roamed the steep hillsides – deer, she thought they might be. She had heard of deer. They all slept together, wrapped in the blankets they had taken from the cavern in the mountains – the orb was so cold, and the smaller of the Antian coughed all through the night.

Ruemar was already tired then, and she decided not to risk any more missteps. She rested the day in the silent valley and then when night fell again they flew south above the clouds, and she had navigated by the stars as her father had taught her. They danced over clouds, and dipped below to see when they reached the sea. It would take many days to sail from Undal south and east to the shardspire, that great edifice that all their people had hoped. When she arrived, it was to a clamour of great horns blowing, a night of strong wind and a swell crested in white that broke on the coral walls of the reef city. In the traders' dock, ships from around the world bobbed in the swell, and the people came out and stared up.

She waited, and waited, and waited. The Unnamed Knight did not come. A line of Tullioch current dancers lined the top of the shardspire, still more below. Ruemar dipped and spun, tried to show herself as no threat, and slowly lowered to a courtyard at the edge of the city, ever so slowly. The little Antian Gellen and the two humans were crawling at the seats, trying to better see through the vista of hazed glass.

The shardspire was a hundred and fifty foot of coral, a tower with a base a hundred feet wide. It had been crafted a millennia ago by her ancestors, and generations of current dancers had worked at it, shoring it up. Living veins of coral pumped water from the sea to the peak, and back down it trickled inside and out, keeping the coral alive. The spire was cut through halfway towards a promised peak – *where Tullen One-Eye killed the old Unnamed Knight, and cut the tower in two.*

Ruemar had landed the orb and when the light dimmed and the ramp extended, she walked down slowly, the children behind her. She did not recognise the faces that met her, faces full of fear and focus. She fell at the bottom of the ramp.

'The little one is sick,' she managed to say, and remembered little more.

It was days later she had woken, woken to a thousand questions. The Unnamed Knight was hunting Cil-Marie incursions to the south with the fleet. *You must show us how it works. You must tell us all.*

Ruemar had asked for her father. Ruemar had learned that Heasin, the great warrior who had saved them all in the caverns, had died fighting to save the Undal god-bear. Ruemar had slept, and when her brothers came to her she had pressed her head tight to theirs.

A current dancer tried to take her wands, and she left them with scales scored by claw and tooth. When her father's guards returned from their mission and requested a ship, a rescue – humans stranded on Iskander, a battle between great mages, she had not asked permission. In the night she had descended the shardspire and stalked the coral streets until she found the courtyard where she had left the orb. There were guards, of course, but none could open the impenetrable stone of the orb, and so they were lax. They squatted around a little board, muttering to each other as they moved game pieces she did not recognise. Ruemar had walked past them and ignored the first query.

The ramp lowered and the query turned to a yell, but then she was running and the ramp was already raising, and she leapt inside and turned to ensure they did not reach her in time. The ramp closed, and she was alone again – a bag of food, a cloak.

It took her a day of flying to find the island of Iskander, and three days of rest before she could transport the Undal and their white-robed servants north across the ocean. Ruemar was shaking by the time they brought the orb to rest in the reef city of the shardspire. She had found the great monastery at Riven coated in snow, a fat barrel drum of a castle perched in the shadow of a mountain. Her father was there, on the rooftop looking north towards open water as if he was waiting for her. The man who had thrown her the keys and set her free so many spans before had been there. *Tomas.* She owed him her blood, but he only asked this simple task.

Flying the orb left Ruemar feeling broken, mentally and physically exhausted – she felt as if she'd spent a span swimming against the currents of the low shelves, out where the kelp farms met the open water. She was so tired. When the lightning of the brutal rotsurge sent them crashing to the ground in Undal City at the entrance of their great stone castle, Ruemar had felt a rib crack as she slammed into her restraints. *What is another wound?* She was too tired to feel pain. Some of the Undal had asked her to help them in their fight but she had told them she must do as the shardspire asked her. *Whatever that may be.* Really, she just wanted rest.

Her cargo set down amidst the lightning and raging storm in Undal City, Ruemar had left with her father. *Home.* She was so tired already, and the last stretch flying over open water had her eyes closing, her breath coming in pants. It cost her to fly, sapped her strength, left her weak and shaking. Her father Leomar had examined the weapons, the great wands of black iron tipped in gems as big as her foreclaw. She knew his mind – he loved his clan, and wanted them to rule unquestioned.

'We could go to the Deepfarrow and rest there,' he said, and Ruemar did not respond or relent as he continued to put forward his case. 'The Unnamed Knight does not have the mind for this. We could unite our people.'

Even as she was shaking with exhaustion, on and on he badgered her. *So good to find my father,* she thought, and in truth there was a dependable nature to his grumbling. Always he would have a complaint against the shardspire and the Unnamed Knight, always there was some reason why the Deepfarrow were being held back. Glad as she was to see him, and glad as she was to see the sea beneath her spreading out wild and free, she was too tired to keep arguing. When for a third time he suggested the Deepfarrow holds instead of the shardspire, she snapped at him.

'It is my orb,' she hissed, feeling the bright pain in her rib, the dull ache in her head. 'My energy. My choice. My crest has faded, father. I am no juvenile.'

~

Leomar stood next to her stool, watched as the helmet and its wires and threads melded to her skull, watched as she pressed unmarked points on the black stone and metal in front of her and the orb responded with movement and flight.

'Let me fly,' he said, ignoring her words as he always had ignored anyone's words but his own. 'The strain on you... you are too young!'

Ruemar batted away his hands as he reached to touch controls he did not understand with the insistence of an old warrior used to his commands being followed.

'My crest is gone,' she growled, and her father looked at her, gaunt and scarred, a knife of steel and three wands of starmetal in the belt at her hip. He dipped his head and stood back.

It is my miracle.

They were flying south and south, and from iron waves finally she saw it – the broken stub of the shardspire and the dull hint of the reef city below. Ruemar felt herself as a mote in the sky, a lost cloud. Closer they grew and the spire grew and grew until she was coming again towards the courtyard at the end of the reef city where she had first taken the orb – where she had stolen it back. This time the sunlight was casting across the waves, clouds scudding high above.

'You rescued young ones,' her father said, staring across the city and the seas beyond, 'and now you have done the Undal a great service. I am proud of you, daughter.'

Ruemar only felt tired. She remembered the day after she woke when she asked after the little ones. They had all been captive, abducted by the orbs to fuel the strange ritual of the demon Varratim high in the Blue Wolf Mountains. She had spent long moons in those mountain caverns before she understood how to fly the orb, and the little Antian and human children who had been with her had been sick. Jurren especially, coughing, always cold.

'Are there Antian here?' she had asked when she woke on the shardspire after that first desperate flight. 'Humans? To care for them? Is Jurren well?'

The Tullioch who had been nursing her, bringing her thick soup of kelp and crab and hot pepper, did not meet her eye.

'There are people to care for them, and a ship to take them home.' The Tullioch paused and gathered its loose robes and went to the door. She turned her head half back, still not meeting Ruemar's eye. 'The little one was weak. It died in the night.'

It died in the night.

Ruemar pushed the orb to descend to the courtyard at the edge of the reef city, and with a thought the lights dimmed and whatever strange thrust was keeping it aloft fell away and the orb settled onto its spindly metal legs. She closed her eyes and slipped the helmet from her head and breathed out a sigh.

'What is wrong, daughter?' Leomar said, and he put his hand on her shoulder. She pressed her face to it, the hardness of his scale and talon a reassuring strength. Through the haze of the crystal strip bisecting the orb, she could see sunlight dancing in the courtyard.

'I did not save all the young ones,' she said, and felt such a twist in her heart she could speak no more. *The little Antian was not weak,* she thought. *It was only a child.*

The ramp to the orb lowered, and she reached for her blade. *I did not do that.* She went to jump from her chair but her leaden legs would not obey, and she fell to the deck, straining to pull herself up to a crouch, to be ready. Leomar stepped in front of her and spun his spear of dark metal and hissed.

'Calm,' a voice said, a voice muffled by metal, and from her knees Ruemar saw the Unnamed Knight. A Tullioch clad only in a simple loincloth and belt and a helm of unadorned metal, featureless and smooth and close-fitting around his skull. He was muscled and tall, his scales a mottle of black with yellow at the joints and hands, a patch of yellow at his chest. Behind him she could make out more, many more Tullioch standing ready, but the Unnamed Knight climbed the ramp alone. In his hand he held a simple spear of black metal, metal that matched the wands at her hip. It had no head, but at one end it tapered to a wicked point. There was always an Unnamed Knight – faceless and clanless, a skein-wreck to lead the Tullioch. She knew that when he died another skein-mage would take up the mantle. Not every Unnamed Knight was a true skein-wreck – but the enemies of the Tullioch could never be sure.

Leomar bowed, and Ruemar dipped her head, felt a groan escape her lips. She was queasy with the fatigue.

'Easy, now,' the knight said, and he walked to her and her

father stepped aside. Lowering to his knees, he cupped her face in his hands and Ruemar felt herself fall into the true current – the eddies and whorls of connection. She saw *him*, the Unnamed Knight – like the columns that dotted the outer reef, that dropped from shallows all the way to the benthic depths where no Tullioch could dive, where no light went – where deep currents still pulled, forever down. He was a depth, a whirlpool, a reef, he was…

Warm. From him, she saw ribbons of connection reaching out to her and she did not fight them. Warmth and strength and power flooded her. With a blink the current dropped from her eyes, and she looked up to see her own reflection staring back at her in the shining helm.

The knight spent the day examining the orb alone, and Ruemar spent the day resting in the infirmary, though with his benediction she felt far stronger than she had before – after her previous flights in the orb. She had a room alone, and lay on the low nest nook and stroked the four wands she had taken from the demons. Each had an identical handle, ten inches of dark black metal – *starmetal*. Starmetal rocks dotted the southern coast of Undal, and the seabed and reefs of the Wind Sea. Strewn there on a night of fire so long ago it was known only in song; a night when the stars themselves fell, scattering across the Wind Sea and the wider world.

Ruemar inspected the gems one by one visually, and then within the true current. Runes she did not recognise, runes wrought on and *within* the crystal, together forming pattern. A red gem that would bring her flame, blue that would cut fine like a blade. The purple gems pushed a wall of force outward, like a gale, and the green sent any waking in its path to sleep. Ruemar had not long studied the true current with her broodmother when the orb had taken her – she had looked, and touched a little, but always held herself back the way she had been told. Long after dark she was still nestled in her nook, when the door opened.

The Unnamed Knight was there, a cloak of black sharkskin covering his shoulders with the hood raised over the smooth metal of his helm. His spear was slung at his shoulder in a leather harness.

'I would have you fly me, Ruemar daughter of Leomar. If you are willing.'

Ruemar nodded her assent. Together they descended the quiet spiral of the shardspire, damp coral underfoot. The knight asked a stream of questions, pausing after each that she might consider her answer.

'Must the light shine for it to fly? The field of silence that surrounds it, can you adjust its strength or diameter? How high have you travelled? How fast? Have you fired the weapons? What other abilities do you suspect of it?'

Ruemar answered as best she could. *She did not know; she did not know. Above the clouds, faster than any bird or ship. No, she did not know.* She felt a fool. The expression of the knight was unreadable behind his helm, and as they crossed the reef city together Ruemar felt a strange sense of calm descend in the long silences between his questions. The city was empty so late at night, quiet and dark. Red crab scuttled amongst the leftover mess of the street vendors, and clicked their claws in challenge at the passing Tullioch with utmost bravado.

The guards bowed to the knight when the two of them reached the courtyard, and inside the orb sat still and dark, black stone and hazy crystal on spindly legs of metal. The walls of the reef city held back the wind, and above Ruemar could see only stars – it was a clear enough night that she could see the great current cutting behind and through the stars, that band of light pressing ever on through the blackness above.

'Come, daughter,' the knight said, and together they walked

up the ramp. He gestured for her to take the pilot's chair, and he took the chair next to it, marvelling as it and the wand attached to it swivelled around the strip of crystal, the metal of the chair attached to a strip of metal circling the inside of the hull just below the crystal. All of it moved so smoothly, with no clear mechanisms.

Ruemar held the helmet of the orb in her hand and stared down at it.

'Will we help them?' she asked, and the knight stopped his play and turned to her.

'I would give you the power to fly, if you would take it, daughter.'

Ruemar nodded, and as the strange metal of the helmet folded and melded itself around her skull, she dropped into the skein and felt the power flowing from the Unnamed Knight into her. She shivered and let her connection go – she did not need it to fly, needed only thought and her hands, her eyes. The light flared on, that bright white glow suffusing the courtyard, and through the crystal strip Ruemar looked at the guards and willed the ship to move upward. She still wasn't sure if it was her hands on the slick metal controls or her mind and her will, but the ship did what she wanted. The controls were intuitive, like guiding a child by the hand. There was the softest clunk below as three metal legs folded softly into the light-infused stone, and then they were rising into the night sky.

In starlight the reef city was a wonder – the walls of it were patterned like waves, and as the orb rose higher and Ruemar looked down, the city looked like the mouth of a great clam, rippling streets keeping direction with the waves around. The shardspire was unlit save the occasional dim flicker where perhaps a candle or a bulb of luminescent plankton glowed through the slit of a window, the tower blocking out at first half the sky and then less and less as they rose, and Ruemar ran the orb in a wide circle around the spire, upward and upward, stopping to hover at its sheer top – the wound had long since been scarred over and shored up with new coral colonies, grafts of polyps from the sunlit reefs – the flatness of the shearing slice that toppled the tower slowly turned into something more natural with the accretion of more coral, of *more life*.

As she flew close around, the glow from the orb cast shadows on the endless intricacies and mottles of the coral tower, tiny shadows combining and moving. There was only a hint of the wonderful colour that one could see in daylight, brief glances of variegated red and yellow and green. Glancing down she could see where the broken shard had fallen so long before, scars still clear in the rippled topography of the city streets below – those shards were part of the city now, integrated as tunnel and wall and home. The scars were as much a part of the city as any wall or strut or pillar.

'Take us up,' the knight said quietly, and Ruemar smiled at him and clicked her teeth. It was so much easier with whatever he was feeding into her – the orb still took, she could still feel it wearing on her, but she was bolstered. *I could do this forever.* She began to rise gently, but then as they picked up speed she upended the orb so she was facing upward, the weight of her own body pressing back into the chair. There were little straps that could be secured, and she had tied two loosely around her waist. She used the speed of the orb itself to keep her pressed to her chair, up and up and up again, up towards the stars.

There were no clouds. Finally she levelled out and looked out across the Wind Sea – in every direction, the waters spread, the reef city a point of pale shadow in the darkness below them. The orb held its place in the sky perfectly – it was strange to not feel the push of the tireless winds. She could not see the coral caverns of the Deepfarrow in the west, or the other clan holds across the reefs. Everywhere, waves were breaking, breaking on those intricate wild reefs that gave them shelter and food, keeping them free. She spotted a mote of light and squinted downward. *A ship's night lantern, maybe.*

'Our oldest tales tell of swimming wild seas and journeying far,' the knight said. She looked at him, trying to read his expression, but there was only the shining metal. His face was turned upward to the stars, and following his gaze she looked at the firmament and let it wash over her.

'Take us to the water, Ruemar.'

She flew them down in a long series of spirals until they were skimming over the water, and the knight held out a hand. She brought the orb to a stop.

'Turn off the lights, if you will.'

Ruemar reached and found the little switch she knew controlled the glow of the orb – it seemed to fly slower with the lights off, though she did not understand why. There was so much she did not know. Clearly the orb was deeply connected to the true current, and the stone and crystal was all worked by no tool she knew of. She did not even know if the field of silence surrounding the outside of the orb persisted when its light was dimmed – *how would I have even tested that, alone with four children?*

Even the thought of the children made her jaw clench and her claws flex. *Weak,* the nurse had called little Jurren. They hung in silence and darkness above the water, stars above and waves below, waiting at that juncture between two infinities.

'The Antian was not weak,' she said at last. 'He was a child. Are we going to help them? My father said...'

The knight put a hand on the back of her neck, the way an elder would when comforting a juvenile. Ruemar did not protest.

'Your father said, this is not our war,' he responded, and she nodded. He gestured at the black water through the crystal strip. 'Take us under, Ruemar, and turn on the light.'

Ruemar hesitated, but he did not speak again. She stared at him for three breaths and then turned on the glow, and willed the ship to lower itself down, down towards the black water.

The moment of impact was jarring, a little jolt, but then they were down and down again. Ruemar could see no reef, no seabed, only black water in every direction, only visible so close with the glow of the light.

'Open yourself to the current, daughter.'

Ruemar fell back into the current as the orb cut through in the churn of tides, passing unfazed through the grip of the great channels of water that crossed the ocean. As with the sky above, it held firm to where she had piloted it – only the slightest shake and tilt acknowledged the great pressures beyond. Around her, she could see the current – the true current, the current below all others. The orb was a mix of utter simplicity and confounding complexity – its stone was flat, flat in a way nothing else she had seen appeared to be, in the current where everything always had another layer, another angle. Pushing outward she felt the ocean around her – a fish, the dance of plankton, the little beasts too small to see that thronged everywhere. She could see past the glow of the orb another twenty feet in the darkness. The knight next to her reached his hand and in it was a ribbon, a ribbon of vibrating light that danced from his chest to his hand. She reached for it and then she saw everything.

The Unnamed Knight shared his sight with her, only for a moment, and she saw hundreds of feet – *further than my eyes in the clearest water*. There was a shark, shoals of fish, each of them intricate and strange in the abstract of the current – she could see the shark's skin and stomach at once, its brain, where it had been, its intention and its possibility, could see the pressure pushing on it and the soft buzz it sensed from other creatures in the tip of its nose. Below the shark there were stands of soft coral, and each one of them was a joy to behold – every coral was a hundred thousand polyps linked so intricately, and as she stared, the knight stared with her. She saw one polyp alone, the connection within it.

'Something is wrong with the currents, daughter,' the knight said, but he did not withdraw her from his sight. 'Across the ocean floor there are stones, great black pearls – points of connection across the world. Anchors. They are broken, daughter. I have been to see the Whale, and she wanders far – further than I have ever seen before. The world is changed.'

Ruemar felt her sight drop back in scope until it was only her own sense of the true current. She rose from that, brought herself back into the physical, and turned off the light of the orb and stared out into the darkness. *All to black.*

'Are we going to help them?' she asked again, and the Unnamed Knight pointed through the crystal to her right, and far in the distance she saw a mote of light – a spark, like a tiny fire under the water. *Blazefish.* The light would lure some foolish little fish, and the blazefish would feast.

'They took our children, Ruemar,' the knight said. 'They took them from home and clan, and in the dark they killed them. They cast fire down on our walls and our roofs. There are only five, that I know of. Five creatures like me in all the known world this side of the endless seas that I have ever even heard rumour of – a sorcerer king in Caroban; a hermit in Lello; the Grand Sun Master in Cil-Marie; the richest man in Uradech. Those and Tullen One-Eye.'

Ruemar gripped at the hilt of her knife.

'Are you afraid of him?' she said, and the knight nodded.

'He killed the last Unnamed Knight who fought him, more than four centuries ago. He broke the shardspire, our greatest monument. He killed the owl Nessilitor, by all accounts a power as great as our Bird and our Whale. There is something... We do not seek each other, people like me. Knights, skein-wrecks, magi – whatever we are called. We do not *occur* near to one who already *is*, and we do not seek. There is a repulsion. Perhaps fear is the word. But I'd not risk our world for war with this mage. The one who took our children is dead. This is not our war.'

Ruemar pictured the little Antian Jurren coughing on the cold floor of the mountain cavern as the snow flurried past the cave entrance. She pictured rows of chained children, and rows of watching mages clad in black, throngs of goblins at their beck and call. She felt a hot itch under her scales at the memory of the sacrificial altar, the glowing runes inscribed upon it.

'I'll go alone if I must,' she said, and the Unnamed Knight put his hand on the back of her neck and together they stared out at the darkness, the light of the blazefish long faded.

A PRIVATE CONSTELLATION

'The girl is a mess, Salem. She has no discipline, no respect. Whatever rule we set for her she breaks. Whatever teacher we find for her, she scandalises. She flirts with the maids and steals from the cooks. Anshuka, save us from our children. I had thought to send her to the lancers or the City Watch, but she is dissolute. An embarrassment. Every night, another war to be fought over dinner. I can indulge her no longer. I think Undal City or Aber-Ouse would only give her outlets for her recklessness – I remembered you've a cousin in Port Last, administering the keep. Might they consider taking her in? I would pay handsomely, and surely there is less trouble to be had that deep in the north.' – **Private letter to Salem Starbeck,** Commander Hallfast of Fallow Fen

Benazir and Guil were lying over the blankets, limbs and fingers and lips entwined. Through the narrow window of the Stormcastle tower, the distant thrum of thunder reverberated across the sky.

'Enough, Commander,' Guil said, and extricated herself slowly, over the course of a dozen kisses, each shorter than the last. She sprawled over the bed and grabbed her cup of wine and drained it, and then rolled back onto the twisted sheets. 'It's too bloody hot.'

Benazir moved one hand to Guil's leg, the other running through the tufts of her red hair, feeling the shape of her skull beneath. It was dim in her chamber, but this deep in summer the sun ran high in the sky, and over the rotstorm to the west the last orange hues were fading, leaving only the purple and red aching pulses of light from the roiling black and grey clouds.

'The wine should be chilled,' she said, and Guil passed her the cup back and stretched out. Benazir watched Guil's long limbs stretch out, the flex of muscle under pale skin dotted with a thousand freckles. She sipped at the wine. It was warm and sour.

'I thought as our newly appointed commander, you'd have better wine. I think it was chilled when you got it, but it's been a little while.' Guil crawled up the bed and nestled her head into Benazir's shoulder. 'But then perhaps command isn't all chilled wine and dalliances with the troops.'

Benazir grinned and gave Guil a squeeze.

'Many a dalliance,' she said, 'but only one troop, so far.' She frowned. 'You understand we need to keep this discreet?'

She felt Guil nod, but then she was biting the flesh just below her collarbone, biting hard, and Benazir gasped and bit her lip to not scream out. Guil let her grip slacken and grinned up at her.

'I can be discreet.'

They stayed in bed, and as the last of the light faded Benazir pulled on an old cotton smock and lit a candle. Guil was still lounging. Benazir knew she would stay until the night was darkest, and then Guil would slip back to her room. As a sergeant, Guil had some privileges. *No sneaking out of the privates' barracks for a tryst behind the storerooms.* Cupping the candle with one hand to protect it from the breeze, Benazir grinned. She'd experienced enough of that, years living in Stormcastle XII as a private, a corporal, a captain. It meant that now, as commander, she knew which corridors and old classrooms to avoid. *Best let them have their fun.*

Back in bed Benazir read the daily reports by candlelight. Always, more reports. Reports on stores, reports on coin reserve, on troop deployment. Skirmishes along the Stormwall, which section needed work. Where the summer work camps were set up, how many horses lost to crocodiles, how many trainees lost to the rotstorm. *Too many.*

She moved her lips when she read, the occasional word slipping out loud. It was an old habit, one her father used to berate her for. Eventually she waved a hand to Guil and she retrieved parchment and quill, lighting her own candle but retrieving no clothes. She lounged naked, and Benazir's eyes kept flicking to the constellation of freckles lit by dancing candlelight. Guil was lanky and sinewy and scarred, like most of the commandos, but the candlelight cast dancing shadows across every curve.

'Focus, Commander,' Guil said with a grin, and Benazir felt her face flush. *Focus.* Guil's quill began to scratch as Benazir called out her notes. The sergeant had come to take notes, the way she came every night. And every night for the last season, she had stayed. Benazir forced her eyes from the stretches of bare skin, down to the reports. *Focus.*

'Tell Nostul he needs to get the apprentices out with the patrol squads this span,' she began. 'I need Voltos to look at the pattern of breaches north of Stormcastle XI – once or twice might have been chance, three times is enemy action. We need more arrows, up a third from our last order. The fourth and seventh patrols are below fighting strength – get temporary promotions from the most senior crop of cadets onto wall guard, and get the wall guard onto the patrols. There should be a lancer detachment arriving in the next three days from Bow, training on the Slow Marsh, but they want a look at the rotstorm – get Thom to set up barrack space, make sure the kitchens know what's coming, and I'll have dinner with the commander and Nostul the night they arrive. Message from Thum-Pho at XIII says a rotbud sensed to the north-west – have Yonifer put a patrol together.'

Guil scratched with her quill and then stretched out and placed the parchment and quill and ink on a side table. Benazir sat, eyes unfixed, and held the reports in front of her. She was running through each of those orders, second-guessing every one of them.

Guil slid behind her and put her arms around her. She kissed Benazir's neck, and Benazir felt a shiver run down her core.

'How do you always know what to do, Commander?'

Benazir squirmed and pushed the pile of reports off the bed, and set down the candle. She rubbed at her eyes, one hand for each eye.

'I don't,' she said quietly, and lay back into Guil, letting her shoulders relax. 'Don't call me commander.'

'Well,' Guil said, 'you certainly *seem* to know what you're doing, at least.'

Benazir closed her eyes and pictured her father yelling at her, the day he died. He was sick of her, sick of her stealing wine and gold, sick of her getting into fights and being rude to what passed as nobility in the protectorate – Stormguard commanders and their spouses, merchants, scholars. *Fat old fools more interested in lining their pockets than helping their people.*

'My father tried to send me away, the day Fallow Fen burned,' she said, pressing her head into Guil's shoulder. She did not open her eyes. 'We fought. Fallow Fen was rich, but the defences were a mess, the Stormguard undisciplined. Money to be made and corruption everywhere. With the utter righteous fire of youth I told him exactly how much of a despot and a disappointment he was. He said he was going to send me to Port Last, to learn the meaning of *duty*. I decided to run away and join the Chainbreakers.'

Benazir could almost *hear* Guil frowning. The younger woman ran her hands through Benazir's hair and then down to her neck. *Duty.* Benazir had first met Guil when she was in the blue garb of a cadet. *And I was a captain.*

'You know what duty means,' Guil said, and in the darkness they held hands. 'You saved me and Yonifer, my first mission into the rotstorm. You led the fight at Fallow Fen. Your plan ended Urforren, and has given us the years of peace since. You know what to do – how do you always know what to do?'

Benazir turned herself over so she was looking up at Guil. She could see the concern in the younger woman's face. *So much younger.* Guil was a fresh sergeant, trying to figure out how to command respect from her troops, attention from her officers. How could Benazir possibly tell her what it all meant? *You saved me and Yonifer.* She felt a twitch in her eye. *Myte and Frolley dead, Orun dead, Fingal dead. Floré and Janos abandoned.* What Guil saw as her moment of truest bravery was in fact anything but. *It was the moment I let the fear in.*

'I don't know what the right thing to do is, love,' she said, and kissed the inside of Guil's pale wrist. 'I know what I *think* is right, and I make that choice. I try to listen to Voltos. Before then, I listened to Starbeck, and Floré, and even Janos. Nobody knows the right thing to do, but indecision is itself a decision. My father wasn't corrupt, but he couldn't see a perfect path forward and so he hesitated. *Perfect is the enemy of done.* You do what you think is right, and if it was wrong, you do the right thing next time. You do the work.'

Benazir didn't know how to say that, when she was a girl, she was so certain of right and wrong that she burned bridge after bridge. That when she was a private, a sergeant, she was so scared of being wrong that she would argue with hell and fury rather than admit what she didn't know. That when she was a captain she was so afraid of failure she let that fear drive her choices. *Even when I knew in my heart I was wrong. What about now?* Benazir had learned so much. Patience, strategy. How to take the fear and hide it deep. How to take the anger and harness it. How to make the choice, and take the consequence. *But can I make the hard choices?* She should have sent Guil away, that first night, but she hadn't. *Still I put myself first, my needs, my wants.*

'You've done your hard yards in the rotstorm,' she said at last and felt Guil relax a little. *This isn't about me.* It was about Guil being unsure of her command, and Benazir knew the right things to say. She held Guil's hand to her face, felt the soft pressure of fingertips on her cheek. Guil wasn't some cadet being taken advantage of, wasn't some green private. Guil was a sergeant of the Stormguard commandos. *I love you,* Benazir thought, and she smiled. She said it again, silently but moving her mouth, and Guil smiled back.

'You know the right thing to do,' she said, and as the storm raged outside they held each other close in the darkness.

~

A different bed, a different time. Waking was not a simple thing. Benazir remembered the battle at Stormcastle XII – a knife fight in the village beyond the castle walls, crow-men and rust-folk and rottrolls assaulting the castle itself, hundreds upon hundreds. Always on the horizon, the rotstorm roiling. She dreamt of the rotstorm, of a purple bruise swelling across the sky, as if the sky itself were under attack. Dancing lightning like pulsing veins and capillaries just below the surface of the cloud, or forking outward across the sky. Beneath the cloud there was a haze of acrid mist, rolling motes of red acid cloud and a thicker haze and rain above.

When she woke, she knew two things: pain and loss. The pain was simple in its extreme – Benazir had leapt into the mouth of a wyrm, a mouth with three jaws and a thousand teeth. Even as her rune-dagger had caught on flesh and began to burn away at the beast, it had *chewed* her. Pain – right hand gone at the wrist, tendons and muscles flensed to the elbow. Ribs broken; how many she had no idea – it was a wet sharpness that came with every breath. Her left arm was cut with long jagged rents, and her legs and hips and chest and shoulders all cut deep, cuts that flared if she moved, if she so much as breathed. Across her face, thick slashes that burned with every breath, with every attempt to speak.

Benazir felt the pain acutely. Someone had given her medicine, but she did know what. *I am meant to be dead.* Pain and loss. The pain was something that could not be fought. It was the tide – you do not fight the tide. It will happen, and what it brings you must accept. Benazir looked up at a simple stone ceiling and did not hear thunder. It was dark. *I'm meant to be dead.*

Pain and loss. *Captain Guil fell to a rottroll.* Who said that? She remembered standing with Nostul and Lady Kelvin in the tower of Stormcastle XII, watching an impossible orb of light dance across the sky.

Benazir lost time. She had no account of days, or spans. She woke to moments of confusion, to pain. Screaming in the night. *Captain Guil fell to a rottroll.* Screaming in the day. *I'm meant to be dead!* She wept, and the tears ran into the healing wounds across her face and the salt stung and burned and she knew she was alive, and so she wept more.

'Rest,' Starbeck said. It sounded like Starbeck, but he wasn't meant to be at the wall. *You must keep the council in line,* she tried to say, but her mouth was a clot of blood. Her vision was a haze, light and dark.

'You bloody idiot,' Floré said, and Benazir laughed and clutched at her ribs with a hand that *wasn't there* and then she was screaming and strong hands held her down, and she curled in on herself and for a moment she remembered the battle at Stormcastle XII, the dead spread across the mire.

'Where is she?' she said, and she wanted Guil, but Guil was not there. *Guil is dead,* a voice said in her head. *Guil can't be dead.* Benazir knew it to be true, knew somewhere in her heart. *I didn't see a body. How many times has a commando been dead and showed up? Guil isn't dead.*

Guil is dead.

Once, she woke and she was still. The pain was there but there was a haze over it all. She was in a room of high stone walls, arching windows with panes of thick glass through which she could see sky, blue sky with scudding white clouds. A gull crossed the sky, a shadow far above. She was alone in the room. Mutely she held up her right arm and stared at the thick wrap of bandages around the stump on her wrist. With her left hand she traced thick stitching and scars that covered her face, her neck. *I'm meant to be dead.* She tried to picture Guil, crooked teeth and toned arms and the burst of freckles across her nose and cheeks.

When Floré found her that day, Benazir had stopped weeping.

'Hey, sis,' Floré said. Benazir had no words. Floré was older, a few strands of white in her ashen curls of hair, a few new wrinkles at the folds of her eyes. Her cheek was an angry red around a geometric scar, a handful of sharp lines that cut deep into the flesh. Her nose looked fresh broken, one eye bruised and swollen, and she was walking with a limp and a crutch.

Benazir gestured to her with her left hand and Floré came and sat on the bed and they pressed their foreheads together the way they had when they were cadets sharing secrets after lights out.

'You look like shit,' Benazir said, her voice a thick and wounded thing. Floré shook her head.

'Janos?' Benazir asked, and Floré's shoulders dropped.

'Dead,' she said. Benazir gripped Floré's shirt at the shoulder and fell back into her bed, the room swimming. *Janos, gone. Guil, gone.* Floré did not ask her about Guil. *She doesn't even know about Guil.* Benazir felt sick.

'There's someone you need to meet,' she said and limped from the room. When she came back in, Benazir stared at the little girl trailing her. A girl with ashen hair cut short, skin the colour of deep red clay after it had been fired. *Floré's eyes,* she thought, *Janos's nose.* The girl looked up at her and gave a little smile, and Benazir made herself smile back. *Crooked teeth.*

'I don't know what to do,' Floré said to her, hours later. Marta had fallen asleep on a chair.

Benazir stared out of the window, at the dark sky beyond.

'Suffer no tyrant; forge no chain; lead in servitude,' she said at last.

'Simple as that?' Floré asked, and Benazir frowned, feeling the scars at her jaw split and tingle as she did. Guil had died for those words, Guil and Lady Kelvin and Myte and Frolic and Fingal and Orun and a thousand since then. Every soldier lost patrolling the walls of Stormcastle XII and the Stormwall around. Every soldier dead on the march to Urforren, at her command. Every civilian dead at the hands of a rottroll or goblin burst from a rotsurge because her commandos didn't stop it, every farmer killed by a rust-folk raid because her border patrols were too predictable.

'What else is there?' she asked, and she looked at Marta, asleep on the chair. 'They've taken so much. We have to fight. We have to keep her safe. There is nothing else for us.'

Floré had no words. In the silence, Benazir thought of Guil standing on the Stormwall with the wind tussling her hair, one hand on a sword hilt and the other on a wineskin. Benazir looked at Marta and felt her love for Floré growing to encompass this new creature, this little child. There were no children at the wall. *How long since I saw a little child? Not a cadet, a true child?* Benazir felt the pain, knew she was meant to be dead, and reached for Floré's hand.

'I'll keep her safe, sis,' she said, one-handed and emaciated, broken in every way – Floré laughed so much it woke Marta.

SHRINEKEEPER, SLEEPING FOX

'*Why have the Judges and the greater spirits of Morost been utilised so infrequently in the realm of warfare? There is no clear answer. We know that these creatures exist on a spectrum, from the bogle by the well in a village right to the great mother Anshuka herself. The Judges are set apart by their scale, and worshipped accordingly, but in essence our shamans, whitestaffs, and mages largely concur they are simply greater spirits. At the order of Tullen One-Eye, Lothal the wolf led the armies of Ferron in their conquest, and at Mistress Water's plea Anshuka rose against him – note that each request came from one truly mighty with power – a skein-wreck far beyond any normal mage. Unprompted, do Judges ever fight? No records of this have been found – they keep apart, each to their own place. Perhaps this is inherent to their nature, spirits tied to a place and a people. Perhaps only a skein-wreck or the great Mistress of Riven herself could rouse them to war. Yet the world is wide – should we fear skein-wrecks afar leading the great spirits of Ona or Caroban to war? In this we are protected by reputation at least – Anshuka watches over us even as she sleeps.*'

– Memorandum to the Grand Council on the question of extant threats, Commissar-Mage Inigo

Torrenda crashed through the wayhouse door without slicking the rain from her coat or stamping the mud from her boots.

'I need the witch,' she said, breath ragged, and Taaveti – the tender of the wayhouse – stuck out her bottom lip and cast a glance over the growing puddle at Torrenda's feet and the storm beyond the door.

'You all right, Shrinekeeper?' she asked, and Torrenda closed the door with a jerk and threw her pack down from her shoulders.

'The witch, Taaveti,' she said, and the woman finally put down the clay cup she was wiping and headed further into the back to the wayhouse. Torrenda took sharp breaths, her lungs still burning from the final climb up the rock spire. Three days without sleep she had been marching through the canyons of Ona, trying to reach the town of Laitila. Three days of rain, and a turn of the moon since the world started going mad. Torrenda finally slipped off her waxed jacket and ran rain-slick hands through sopping hair. Rubbing her hands dry on the thick wool of her jumper, she felt the heat of the smouldering peat brick held close to her stomach, separated from her skin only by the treated leather of its pouch.

'Welcome, Shrinekeeper!' a voice called, and she started and clutched at her stomach. The wayhouse was empty save a handful of rope weavers who were taking up a corner, fingers never ceasing as they wound and wove, both smiling at her. She nodded back but did not trust her voice to speak.

Shrinekeeper. The idea of it made her start to tremble. *Am I still a shrinekeeper?*

Looking down at the water and clay and mud pooling at her feet Torrenda couldn't bring herself to fix it. Never had she dragged such a mess into a wayhouse, but her arms felt like lead. Half a moon ago she had been at the crossroads shrine two dozen miles south of Tarran Point, a few hours west of the bogs at Laitila. She had brought her ever-burning brick of peat through the wet air of Ona's rock stacks, wending through valley and canyon until she came to the shrine. All the shrines were the same – a hollow cairn of stone built over the rare slick black dragon rocks that dotted the land. In each cairn, peat bricks for the wet and weary traveller that they might know the father dragon's warmth even as he twisted his way through the clouded sky far above.

As shrinekeeper, Torrenda would fill the cairns with fresh peat, and where she could she left one brick half soaked and half lit, like the one she carried close to her skin – so close she could feel it burning at her thick-scarred stomach, through its leather pouch.

The shrine at the crossroads had split – the immutable black stone suddenly gouged with cracks of glowing silver. The tulka, the little canyon fox spirit who lived at the crossroads, had come to her in fear.

And now I am guardian to a guardian.

From her pack, a whimper.

Torrenda rubbed her eyes and patted the pack, and made a shushing noise.

'Not here, little one,' she said. *What would the weavers think of a tulka in their wayhouse?* She did not know, did not have the energy to find out.

Taaveti the wayhouse tender, returned and called for her, eyes twitching as Torrenda trailed rain and mud across her clean floor. Her expression shifted from annoyance to concern as Torrenda reached her. *I must look as bad as I feel.*

The wayhouse at Laitila was like so many others – a single-storey building that sprawled across the top of a rock chimney, and a few rooms dug down tight in the core of the rock itself. It was down a set of carved stairs that Taaveti led her, and then left her at a doorway hung with a simple woven door.

'Witch?' she called, pushing through the door. 'Sami? I need help, my friend.'

Torrenda drew up short. There was a witch in the room, but it was not big Sami with his beard and his smile; Sami she had known twenty years or more; Sami she had shared a glass and a bed with on so many nights when her path passed through Laitila. In the low-ceilinged room a woman sat on a stuffed cushion, tending a candle. Torrenda slumped. *Woman! How old is she? A girl!*

'Where is Sami?'

The girl smiled and gestured Torrenda to sit, and so she dropped her coat and gently placed her bag next to the cushion and sat. Her legs were aching – even after twenty years of walking good miles every day through Ona's canyons and gullies, the last three days had been more than she thought she was capable of.

'I am Aida,' the girl said, and gestured at the amulet of the dragon around her neck. 'Sami has gone to Wasserchild for a season to teach plant lore to the students. I am here in his stead.'

Torrenda shook her head. The girl barely looked old enough to marry, let alone serve a town as a witch must. Lank brown hair and long bones with no padding on them. *A sparrow where I need a hawk.* Torrenda found herself too tired to even swear and rally.

'I can go no further, Aida,' she said, 'though I don't know if you can help me.'

Slowly she unclasped the straps on her bag and from the nest of clothes within removed the tulka. The young witch's eyes widened. The tulka had lived in the little forest behind the crossroads dragon shrine. It had the shape of a small canyon fox, but its fur was matt black streaked with whorls of shining silver, the claws of its feet a shining onyx, and its eyes were orbs of perfect pearl.

'How?'

Torrenda sighed and gently placed the tulka down. It gazed at the witch for a long moment and stretched its legs out, first forward then back, and then climbed up into Torrenda's lap.

'Tulka don't leave their place,' the witch said at last, lighting a second candle from the first. The little fox closed its eyes and pressed closer to the smouldering peat under the frayed yellow of Torrenda's woollen jumper. She stroked its head and back and tried to keep her eyes open.

'The dragon rock underneath the shrine at the crossroads south of Tarran Point cracked,' she said, and the relief of telling someone who might understand how impossible that was filled her eyes with tears.

'I lit the shrine, and a moment later it cracked. Then the fox found me, and followed me. Half a moon I've travelled since, and three shrines I found. All were cracked, all the same – glowing silver seams marring the rock. No tulka to be found, except this one at the first.'

The witch crawled around the candles and sat cross-legged on the carpet in front of Torrenda, slowly looked her over. *Soaked,* Torrenda thought, *she sees a tired soaked woman, panicked and half-mad. She is not wrong.*

'Half a moon you've travelled,' Aida said, and Torrenda nodded and drew the little fox closer.

'The last three days I've had no sleep. I've not stopped. The last shrine…'

Aida reached a hand down and tentatively scratched at the top of the fox's head, and it clicked its jaw appreciatively.

'What happened at the last shrine?'

'I was coming here to find Sami anyway, to ask his advice. To tell the caravan leaders, or the witches in Wasserchild. Tell someone who might *fix it*. But the last shrine… the tulka there is a scorpion. I have never seen it before, but a local told me so. The shrine was as the others are, cracked with silver. The scorpion. When I went close to the shrine with the fox, it attacked. Attacked me, attacked us both.'

Torrenda shut her eye and pictured it, the dragon stone slick black in a field of dusty brown boulders, the shrine on top of it dark and empty of peat or flame. The shrine was a few canyons over from a group of farms that called themselves Onen Marja, *lucky berry*, after the brambles that wove through their paths and around their rock chimneys. Torrenda had approached the shrine, the air thick with mist around her, the fox at her heels. Then it was chaos. A scorpion the size of her arm racing at them, its pincers and stinger flashing gold, its carapace a dull white limned in a faint blue glow. It ran at them, tail raised high, and Torrenda fell back to the ground and then it was jabbing at her feet with its tail and claws and she was scrabbling and…

In the witch's room beneath the wayhouse in Laitila, Torrenda told Aida of the attack. She managed to get through it, but her jaw ached and her head pulsed.

'The fox saved me,' she said at last, her voice so quiet. 'It killed the scorpion. It ripped off its tail and tore it to pieces. *It killed it.*'

They both sat in silence for a long moment, and Torrenda slowly gestured to the fox's cheek, its back leg, as it lay asleep on her lap. Each was scarred, fresh wounds scabbed and healed. The witch Aida went back to her cushion and rubbed at her hands.

'A tulka cannot be harmed by any human or beast,' she said quietly, in the tone of one repeating a phrase from a book or a childhood classroom. 'And a tulka will never attack any human or beast.' Even as she said the words she was staring into Torrenda's eyes, and Torrenda knew what she wanted. *She wants me to tell her it will be okay.*

Slowly, Torrenda rolled up her sleeves and began unpeeling the thick bandages over her right arm until the jagged wounds were visible, inflamed and wet and only half-healed. The witch lifted her candle and stared at the wounds.

'Something has happened to the dragon shrines,' Aida said, and drawing a small chest close to her began to rummage through pouches and boxes of vials. 'The tulka are fighting, and loose from their places. Attacking *humans.*'

Torrenda felt her head nodding in agreement, but she was so tired and her arm ached so much, and the burning peat at her stomach was so warm. The little fox lifted its head and began to lick at the wounds on her arm.

'We must check the shrine in Laitila,' she said, and felt her head nodding forward. The woman Aida was suddenly at her side, a thick salve in hand she spread across the oozing pincer cuts that screwed their way up Torrenda's arm. The salve was cool and Torrenda let Aida lower her down to the thick carpet by the candle, let her pull off her boots, let her gently lift her head and push a cushion below it.

'Sleep, Shrinekeeper,' she said, 'you have done all you could have done. In the morning, we will seek answers.'

Torrenda felt sleep take her, her uninjured arm wrapped close around the little fox.

'Don't worry, little one,' she said, and then she slept, and dreamt of the great father dragon dancing through cloud above, fast and frantic.

ACT 2

THE PATTERN BELOW

'The war of insurrection is fought by few, but supported by many. Each act of solidarity is a blow against the oppressor. Each gifted loaf of bread or pair of boots a blade at their throat as they sleep.'

Four lessons in revolution, Knight-Commander Jozenai

7

FIRE AND SNOW

'The Stormguard have offered us protection, where it has
been asked. Some are grudging, through the fear those orbs
have brought or through a hatred born of the memory of
the war we fought. War leaves a stain. The Stormguard
would not break the armistice – our information and
intelligence networks have spread across the northern
continent. Our advisers have made themselves ubiquitous
amongst those that govern in Undal, in Tessendorm, Isken,
Kelamor, Cinnae, and Uradech. They assume we spy, and
they assume we serve some greater goal – but what do they
care what happens far below the earth? A small cost, when
in return they get the ore we mine. What do they care of
deep gods and hidden councils? Their deepest mines are
scratches. It is for this I write to you. I am a criminal and
an exile. I bake my bread in the shadow of their keep, and
I save what coin I can to return to my family. I write to
you because never have I seen them pressed as this. Not
in our war, not by the barons of Tessendorm. Not in their
histories of the corvus epidemic or their violent reforms.
The Stormguard have no allies. This is the time.' – **Letter**

to the Hidden Council of the Undal Redoubt, Bellentoe
Firstclaw

Floré coughed and then spewed water so cold it made her
throat ache. *So cold.* She rolled onto her knees and her hands
were pressed wrist-deep into snow. *Judges' spit. So cold!* She
spewed another lungful of black water and closed her eyes a
long moment, felt the dizziness slowly pass. She tried to blink
the water from her eyes as she gulped deep at frozen air. She
could hear groaning around her, but before she could open
her eyes to check they had all made it she felt a familiar sharp
pressure at her throat, right on her jugular vein. *A sword point.*
Floré kept entirely still and opened her eyes. She could see
leather boots in snow.

'They are with me, children,' Highmother Ash's voice called,
weak and frail. 'We need fire – and quick about it. The girl is
dying.'

The blade left her throat and Floré rolled to her back. They
were in a wide meadow coated in snow and surrounded by
towering oaks. Above her the branches of the oaks danced in
the wind, bare fingers of wood reaching out to one another.
Benazir was laid flat on her back next to Floré, staring up at
the sky breathing in deep huffs. Next to them in the snow
Voltos was curled in a ball and coughing. Tomas was rubbing
at his face and wringing his hands. All of them were drenched
through in the ice water of Loch Hassel. Cuss was... *No.*

Cuss was gripping Yselda close, his mouth opening and
shutting but no words coming out. Yselda with her eyes wide
but unseeing. Yselda not breathing. Cuss was shaking her, his
hands gripping at her cloak and tabard, and all around them,
wherever they were, a dozen Orubor were staring, save two
who had pulled Highmother Ash to her feet.

'Fire!' the Highmother called again, and the Orubor at last

began to move. Floré rolled to her feet and rushed to Yselda's side. She pulled her from Cuss. The boy was frantic. *Not breathing.* Floré grabbed the girl and pushed at her chest. She laid her flat in the snow and tilted back her head, and a slick of water poured from her mouth. *Not breathing. Not breathing.* She ripped the gauntlet from her right hand and pressed her fingers to Yselda's neck. *No heartbeat.*

Floré pushed her other gauntleted fist into Yselda chest over and over. '*Breathe*, damn you, girl.'

Highmother Ash came to her and crouched and held her hand over the girl. The old Orubor was as soaked as the rest of them, the strain clear on her face. Her skin was sallow and there was a thick smear of blood beneath her nose. Closing her eyes she flexed her fingers over Yselda and began to sing, a low throaty rhythm. Floré sat back in the snow and gripped at her knees, and next to her Cuss was weeping. The old Orubor gasped, and with a sudden convulsion Yselda was spewing black water and bile and oats, gasping for air. The Highmother swooned, but with a swish of leather through snow an Orubor was there catching her before her head hit the ground, lifting her frail form up into his arms. Cuss went to Yselda, cradled her head as the girl pulled in weak breaths, eyes fluttering.

'That was Lothal!' Tomas said, his teeth chattering. He was gripping something in his hand and pawing at it desperately. *Is that Jozenai?* Floré felt as if she'd been punched in the head, a thick stabbing skewer of pain in the back of her skull breaking through the numbness and the cold. She reached her hand to her scalp and her fingers came back wet with water tinged pink with blood. The broken ice had battered her as she tried to reach for Cuss, for Yselda, for Benazir, for Voltos... She forced herself to look around at each of them. *Alive.* She gripped her knees again and stared at Tomas, at Jozenai. The little cat was wet through – after six spans in Riven never leaving Tomas's side, it had doubled in size from the scrawny lump it had once been, but soaked as it was it looked so small. *And cold.* Floré watched Tomas holding it in one hand, and with his other he drew the starmetal wand from his sleeve. No flame threw from its tip, but it began to radiate red light and heat, a heat she could feel hints of even half a dozen steps away.

She fell back in the snow and shook, shook down to her core. High above, the skies were clear, nothing but a blue so pale. Hands were pulling at her, Orubor hands thin and slight but strong. Between the dozen Orubor they began to pull Floré and her companions to their feet, and two lifted Yselda. Silently they guided them to the edge of the snow-packed meadow. Set back in the woods a few dozen yards from the meadow's edge was a hall of some kind, swooping arcs of wood seamed together tight, the architecture an echo of the vaulted eaves of the trees above. The roof was steep, coated with a thick layer of snow. The Orubor led them through and there were pallets, fires being lit. The Orubor carried Highmother Ash through a narrow doorway and out of sight – Highmother Ash seemed unable to stand after whatever aid she had given Yselda.

'That,' Benazir said, wiping snow from her face, 'was Lothal the fucking god-wolf. Lothal – *the Lothal.* Lothal, march beside me and grow claws and sharp teeth and big muscles Lothal. Berren's black blood we are utterly, utterly screwed.'

It took them hours to get warm. The Orubor brought blankets and fresh clothing, breeches and shirts of tanned deer hide. Floré realised her pack was gone, everything she'd taken to prepare for a winter campaign. All she had left was one sodden set of clothes, drenched boots, her tabard, her sword, Tyr's old knife, and her gauntlets. *What the hell happened to my cloak?* She remembered the churn of black water, a flash of yellow as the old man of Loch Hassel spiralled past, a cold beyond anything she had ever felt – then a flash of silver and a dizziness that still had her blinking, nausea raising hot bile into her frozen mouth.

A younger Orubor brought them tea, cups of carved wood and a pot of cracked clay. It was sweet and pungently floral, but it was hot and that was all that mattered. Before squaring herself away, Floré had stripped Yselda from her sodden clothes and wrapped her in a dozen blankets, and then dragged the girl to the blazing hearth. She was pale, eyelids fluttering, but she was breathing. Tomas made Jozenai the kitten a nest of blankets and set her next to Yselda, and Voltos laughed so hard Floré thought he was breaking into hysterics.

The Antian was swamped in the clothing of the Orubor – his pack was gone too. Nothing they were given would fit him save a huge overshirt, meant to be worn over many smaller layers. His proportions were all different to theirs, short where they were long, broad where they were slight. He fashioned himself a toga from a blanket and pulled on the overshirt, rolling up its sleeves over and over again.

'Would it attack Hasselberry?' Cuss asked, when they were all huddled around Yselda and the fire. Of them all, only he had managed to keep his pack on. Glancing back at where he'd laid the contents out to dry, Floré smiled when she saw his axe. *Lad didn't even drop his steel.*

'You can tie a sword-knot to an axe handle,' Benazir said, working at the leather of her arm-hook with a scrap of dry cloth. 'I saw a lancer do that. They tie sword-knots to all sorts, lancers.'

In the loose tunics and breeches of the Orubor, Floré could see the scars spiralling up Benazir's arms and chest and neck, the marks of the wyrm's teeth. She smiled at the attempted distraction, though Cuss just stared into the fire. Floré knew that if Lothal chose to attack Hasselberry, then the village had no hope. She gazed at the door where the Orubor had taken Highmother Ash. *She saved Yselda. She helped us get this far.* Floré had been curt with the Orubor. *I've been curt with everyone.*

She looked down at where Yselda slept, and stroked the girl's hair. *I'm sorry, kid. Why do I keep bringing you into hell and trouble?* Floré knew the answer to the question, even as she asked it. Yselda was her cadet. Yselda was lost. Yselda was the same that Floré had been, when she was a little girl before she found the Stormguard. Floré only knew one model to shape a life – service and discipline. Yselda stirred, and Floré pressed her hand against her forehead and shushed her, the way she soothed Marta. Her hand faltered for a moment as she thought of Marta. *Would I want this for her, this life?*

'How does this change the plan?' Cuss asked, and Tomas pulled out his pipe and began searching the pockets of his wet clothes for tobacco.

'It doesn't,' Tomas said. 'Plan is the same. We need to wake up dear mother before that wolf rips the whole protectorate apart. We need to kill that git Tullen. You should start smoking, Cuss.'

'What?'

Tomas sat back and threw down his pipe, and rubbed his hands over his scalp. He pointed at Cuss's things spread out and drying.

'You have an uncanny ability to get through anything, and everything, with what looks like a wheel of cheese wrapped in a handkerchief. If you smoked, I could borrow some dry leaf.'

The morning passed, and the Orubor moved swiftly through the room when they appeared, but offered no conversation or answers. They would not meet Floré's gaze, and when questioned simply ignored her. The floor was jointed wood covered in thick hide pelts, and there was no furniture save for the low wood pallets. Floré sat with Yselda and rubbed at the joints of her gauntlets with the cloth from Cuss's weapon kit. She'd dried the cloth by the fire first, laying it next to the dozing kitten.

'It's just going to keep happening,' Yselda said at last. Her eyes were open, staring into the flame. Floré put down her gauntlets. *How long has she been awake?*

'What is, Yselda?'

The girl squirmed in her blankets. 'Wolves on ice. Beasts come to kill everyone we love. As long as the rust-folk are out there, they'll send orbs, rotsurges, they'll send mages, they'll send *Lothal*. We'll never be safe.'

Floré itched the scar on her cheek and sighed. 'The wolves that killed your family were not sent by rust-folk,' she said. 'They were sent by their own hunger. Hunger driven by the Claw Winter. Anshuka brought that on us, the same as she brings the rotstorm to the Ferron. The rust-folk are trying to flee hell itself – we would do the same.'

Yselda pulled herself up and Floré saw the anger in her eyes and held up a hand for peace.

'They sent the wolf. They sent the orbs. They *took Marta*, Yselda. I've no mercy in my heart for what we must do next – but they are not the author of every ill in this world. There will always be someone who wants power, or what little resource we have. We will kill the mage. We will wake Anshuka and let her deal with the wolf. But if I could have a word with her, the madness of the rotstorm and the Claw Winters would be high on my list.'

Yselda settled back and looked again into the fire and Floré reached a hand out to her but drew it back.

'If you could change the world,' she said, 'how would you change it? That is what we must ask ourselves. Not where we've been. Where we are going now.'

The girl did not answer, but closed her eyes and clutched

at the locket of wood around her neck. An Orubor stepped through the door at the end of the cabin where they had taken Highmother Ash and Floré appraised him carefully. He was clad in the same cured hides as the others, his shining white hair braided tight to his skull. The orbs of his eyes were green, a dazzling green, and the skin of his face and hands were scarred in an intricate web of geometric red, a pattern of triangles and squares and curving lines.

'Floré Artollen,' he said, 'the Highmother is dying. She would speak to you, before the end.'

~

'You cannot see him,' the reeve said, and Brude tried to bite down her anger.

'I am war-leader, Reeve,' she said, careful to keep her voice low. 'I command our troops, our goblins, our wyrms. *Ceann* is the rank you gave me. I listen to Amon as he talks of logistics, I listen to the other crow-men as they talk of hunting more rotbuds deep past Lothal's bones. I listen to Commandant Jehanne on tactics and I listen to you as you talk of *our people*. Yet I cannot speak to the One-Eye. Why?'

'He will speak only to me,' the reeve said, and he tried to reach out a hand to comfort her.

Brude stalked away to the window. They were in one of the captured houses in Dun Fen, the market town they'd taken as headquarters for their occupation of the Northern Marches. *Occupation*, Brude thought, and chewed her lip. *Residence*. Through panes of thick glass rimed in snow, Brude watched as, in the street outside, a troop of goblins tried to haul the carcass of a horse. They'd looped a rope around under its front legs and there were twenty of them, but they made no progress. A rottroll who could have moved the horse in a moment watched lazily from the shadow of a building opposite. No rust-folk or crow-men were on the street – as night began to fall, it was too cold. They huddled together in houses, and by day dismantled their abandoned neighbour's walls for fuel.

Even with this cold, she thought with a faint smile, *it is calmer than the calmest day in the rotstorm.*

'We must be smarter than this,' she said, long hands gripping at the window frame. 'We are here to *stay*, for far more than a season. I need you to organise the workers and the farmers – get official lodgings set, ration the food and fuel we have.'

The reeve came to her and offered her wine but she did not take it. He was a plain-looking man, utterly innocuous and unthreatening in countenance, but he was the leader of all those in the rotstorm who wanted *out. He was born in the rotstorm,* Brude thought. *I must not forget that. Our weakest farmer is harder than any Undal warrior.*

'I do believe you killed him,' he said, 'but a skein-wreck is a difficult monster to put down. The words of Deathless have the ring of truth about them – you put the Salt-Man as close to death as perhaps any of us could. He simply finished the job.'

Brude did not look at the reeve – instead she caught her own reflection, the tattoo around and over her eye that once honoured and now mocked her: Ø. The rune for salt.

'We have lost another patrol to the east,' she said. 'I'm going to hunt down the Undal responsible. There must be rebels hiding in the high moors. One or two patrols might be chance, but a third is our foes.'

The reeve sighed and rubbed at his face. He finished his cup of wine. Setting it down he went to the door and lingered. Brude did not look to him – she looked to the goblins in the street, their team broken down into arguments. One of them was gnawing on the hide of the dead horse.

'The Stormguard responded to our message,' he said at last. 'They will meet us for peace talks, in Ossen-Tyr. Will you join me there? I thought we could go together. If we take an orb, and a dozen crow-men...'

Brude turned to him and flexed her hands, cricked her neck. The cold was making the ache in her bones worse.

'The wolf will not come to my call,' she said. The reeve stared at her. 'Your mage said he would come, but he only came a handful of times. Now he ranges far, and follows no order of mine. What does the mage want, Reeve?'

The reeve shrugged and opened the door.

'He is an army, Ceann Brude,' he said. 'He has killed a god before. He wants to succeed where Varratim failed. Do you understand what that would mean?'

Brude grimaced. *I will not hope.*

'When you kill a Judge,' she said, tasting the words, 'their work is undone.'

The reeve nodded.

'We have been down this path before, Reeve. Kill the bear and end the storm, turn those of us the storm has touched back into what we were, perhaps.'

'Yes,' he said, 'but not with the deathless mage and the wolf. It costs us nothing. If he succeeds, it gains us everything. The war will continue – you will win a peace for us. At Ossen-Tyr they will see you, and the power of the orbs. They know their skein-wreck is dead, their fleet is shattered, their armies scattered and battered by the winter. They will take the peace and they will surrender to you the marches – and if they do not, we will hold them through the winter, and sow seeds in spring.'

Brude tried to imagine digging in soft earth and placing a seed, but she did not picture herself as a beast – *a demon*. Instead she pictured herself as she might have been, a woman whole in body, unmarred.

'I would help him kill Anshuka,' she said, and that old hope of absolution was there again down in her gut – the hope she had tried so hard to kill. *I could be free.* The reeve shook his head.

'He wants no help,' he said, and with a smile he left her, closing the door behind. Brude was alone in her room. Maps scattered across the table, maps and reports hastily scrawled from distant sentries and troop leaders. An empty bottle of wine and a full ewer of water, hard black bread she had not even begun. *When did I last eat?* Brude set the latch on her door and hung her cloak on the peg, kicked off her boots. Grabbing the most recent map Amon had passed to her, she stalked to the bed and settled down onto it, the lumps of the straw mattress rearranging beneath her as she sat cross-legged. She stretched her arms and shoulders, twisted her head, flexed her spine as much as she could. Her bones were strong – *too strong.* She thought human bone would have more give in it, perhaps. She felt like a suit of armour locked together, with a layer of wizened flesh atop it. The skin of her hands made her sick, so she did not take off her thin leather gloves.

There was a knock at the door and then Amon was there, a tight grin on his face. Brude did not meet his eye, and forced herself to stare at the map. *I will not hope.*

'I brought dinner,' he said, and not waiting for a response he brought in a tray with two steaming bowls. 'Soup, with chicken and barley and some potato, too. Even found some *pepper*, and a red powder that tastes like smoke. You need to eat, Brude!'

Brude unfolded from her bed and went to him, and together they ate the soup in silence. As he ate she stole glances at him, the smiling lines around his eyes, the set of his jaw. She knew she could not have him. *Not as long as I'm still a monster,* she thought, and she dropped her spoon into the bowl and put her hands below the table where she didn't have to look at the twisted long fingers, the stretched and scarred skin. There was nowhere she could put them where she would not *feel* them, though.

'Tell me of your travels, to find Jehanne in Cil-Marie,' she said, and he smiled indulgently.

'Again, Brude? I have told you this. The smugglers' roads to Isken, passage on a ship to Kelamor. A real ship! I've never been so sick in my life. I had to convince the Cil-Marie embassy in Kelamor that I was legitimate, which was no easy thing – but the reeve sent me with many artefacts dug from the storm, and eventually they took me past the Crown Islands to Cil-Marie itself. What is there to tell? It was incredible.'

Brude had been holding her spoon as he talked, as he gesticulated with his perfect hands, but she had not eaten a bite. She smiled at him.

'Tell me about the ship, then,' she said, and together they ate, and Amon spoke, and Brude did not think except for him and his words.

After the soup, she told Amon all that the reeve had said – that Tullen would kill Anshuka, and reverse the changes to Brude, to the other crow-men, to the goblins.

'If I am human again... I... Well.'

Brude stared down at her bowl and grimaced, and then Amon put his hand on her shoulder, slowly. She raised her eyes to meet his.

'You are Brude,' he said gently and smiled at her. 'If he gives us a miracle, we will thank him. But we will not wait for miracles, hey? There is life to be lived, here and now.'

Amon's hand lowered from her shoulder and sought out her own but Brude snatched her hands back and turned away. She felt sick, sick at the idea of him touching her hands, her body, twisted as it was. She wanted him to hold her hand; she wanted to kiss him and draw him close. *No, I can't hope.*

Amon drew his hand back and blew a breath through his nose. And they sat in silence a long moment.

'The soup was good,' she said, and he nodded slowly and gathered the bowls onto the little wooden tray.

'Sleep well, Brude,' he said, and as he left her she heard him sigh. Brude sat at the table and felt tears come, but they did not fall. She blinked them away. She felt the ache in her gut and her bones, the burning in her sinew, and with it, rage. Tullen claimed he had killed Janos the Salt-Man, not her. Tullen claimed he would kill Anshuka and lead them to freedom. Not Brude and her war – Tullen and his miracles. *Tullen who won't even see me.*

Brude did not hear the assassin, did not hear so much as a movement. She could hear the wind and snow outside, but no footstep betrayed the killer who had secreted themselves in her room. The first she knew was a flit of darkness over her eyes as a garotte slipped over her head and then someone was behind her, heaving with all their might to strangle her as a short blade stabbed at her back over and over – *a blade of silver*. Each wound burned like acid, a spreading pooling pain that sent muscle twitching. Had she been human, her kidneys or liver might have been skewered – but Brude was not human.

Slamming herself backward so her assailant was crushed against the wall, she did not try to pry the garotte from her throat. She could hold her breath well enough – a lifetime in the rotstorm had taught her that to breathe was to die if the wrong cloud was passing. Bending her arms back on themselves she managed to grab the arm with the blade, the skewering arm, and *grip*. The assassin drove their weight and strength, but Brude was heavier – *I am stronger*. Closing her eyes, she felt the tempest within herself, the storm that made up every cell of her body, every sinew. Her blood began to sing as she called on that invisible chaos that suffused the world and sent energy crackling through it. From her pores, lightning sprang – ten thousand sparks, like an eel in the mires of Hop Vasser.

The assassin spasmed and groaned, and then collapsed. Brude let go of their arm and launched herself across the room, twisting as she went, gravity having no hold on her. She brought up her hands, each clenched fist wreathed in roiling black flame, but the assassin was unconscious or dead. Brude glanced up at the shadows high above, the beams and rafters below the tiled roof. *Is that where they hid?* She had been hours in the room, with the reeve, with Amon. *How could they have hidden so long?* Slowly she moved closer, her toes trailing the floor as she floated. The assassin was not human. Blue-skinned and pointy-eared, tall as a human but thin and sinewy like a stretched goblin. White stubble covered her head, and she was dressed in rust-folk garb – she even had a red sash across her chest. Brude licked her lips. The assassin's mouth was open and slack, showing serrated teeth behind thick dark blue lips. *Blue skin, jagged teeth. An elf of the bear's forest.* Red scars of pattern were cut across all the skin that Brude could see, ear and scalp and neck and face and hand. *Do they use the pattern?* Brude had never seen an Orubor before – none had ever been seen in the storm. They stayed in their forest, across hundreds of miles of hostile territory. *A forest of ghosts that none leave alive.* That was the story her mother Rol had told her.

Allowing herself a breath of freezing air, Brude darted forward and pulled the weapon from the assassin's hand – the garrotte was flung to the floor, but the Orubor was still holding a hilt of antler with a jagged inch of silvered steel above it. The wounds in Brude's back were screaming as the tempest tried to piece her back together, but she ignored them. *I know pain – pain is nothing new.*

'Guards!' she yelled, and the sound of footsteps running greeted her. *An Orubor assassin.*

Brude gripped the antler hilt and stared down at the strange beast, and grinned.

8

ORUBOR'S WOOD

'*When Mistress Water met Jozenai, leader of the rebels hiding deep in the great glen of the Brek, she bore another name. Jozenai had spent a decade at war in secret, terrified of incurring the wrath of the skein-wreck Tullen One-Eye. Jozenai's band of fighters lived in the wild, supplied by the villagers of the Brek and Hookstone forest. To move openly against the Ferron was to incur terrible repercussion – not on the fighting band themselves, who knew the hills and forests better than any Ferron, but on the slaves left behind. The atrocities of the Ferron overseers are well documented later in this treatise – suffice to say, when Mistress Water found her army the only thing greater than their anger was their fear. She took their fear, and let their anger burn bright.*' – **History of the Revolution**, Campbell Torbén of Aber-Ouse*

Highmother Ash lay on a raised pallet of wood, her frail form covered in pelts. The geometrically scarred Orubor with the green eyes and tight braids waited at the closed door, watching Floré, but she paid him no mind. The room was empty save a low table with a tea set, the bed, and a hearth that blazed merrily. High windows with sills of wood and panes of thin glass let in the afternoon's sun, but the Claw Winter was still bearing down and the light in the woods beyond was cold and dim.

'The girl lives.'

The Highmother's voice was weak, but there was no hint of question.

'Thanks to you,' Floré said, 'though I've no idea what you did. I owe you a great debt for that, Highmother.'

She flexed her fists awkwardly – she had no gauntlets, no belt, no hilt – nothing to hold. She went to the bed, barefoot over pelts of deer and bear and wolf and more. The fur was luxurious under her feet.

'In the summer, after the orbs of light… you told me you could not help my daughter.'

The Highmother blinked up at her and gave a little gasp of pain, her mouth opening to show the pink of a tongue, the yellow of old teeth. Once-jagged spikes worn down to something gentler. The unmarred whirling gold of her eyes met Floré's, and Floré did not allow herself to break from that alien gaze.

'I did what I could, then, guardian,' she said, and Floré nodded in response. 'Your daughter has a touch for it beyond what I've seen in the forest. We are closer to the song of it all, do you understand? The great rhythm and chorus – we can find a melody. We understand the boons the little gods might give, and know how to ask. But we are still so weak, and so few. A thousand years we have lived in this forest – when Anshuka was a little god, amongst the trees. When she left us and joined Ferron, and became a Judge. When she finally returned, she slept. These last three centuries we have guarded her. What is your plan, child? You wish to wake the mother and have her fight once more?'

In the firelight Floré gripped the hem of the deerskin tunic and felt the nerves in her right arm tingling as they always did when she grew anxious. She glanced back at the muscular Orubor by the door. *A thousand years…* She did not know any history of the Orubor, only that they guarded Anshuka as jealously as any treasure. They did not leave their forest, and suffered none to live who entered. Rumoured to read minds, to eat the flesh of the humans they killed. *Savages.* Floré could not balance those ideas with what she had experienced – the Orubor knew magic, magic that made the skein-mages and whitestaffs of the protectorate look like clumsy children. They had weapons of great intricacy and craft. She stared down at the dying old woman and thought about ore and forges and the ringing of hammers. *This forest holds many secrets.*

Highmother Ash coughed and shivered, her whole body convulsing for a moment, and then she was panting, her hands gripping at the heavy pelts that lay over her.

What is my plan?

'My plan is peace,' Floré said at last. 'Peace at any cost.'

The old woman closed her eyes. 'Would that Ashbringer were here, so that she could aid you. Three centuries we have hunted him – what makes you think you can kill Tullen One-Eye?'

Floré grinned, a true smile. Her cheek was still tight on one side where Varratim's rune-wand had cut it deep.

'It's the boy's plan,' she said. 'A good lad, Cuss Grantimber. He stood by your Orubor, he stood by Anshuka against goblin and demon and orb of fire. He saw a path. Why do our skein-mages fear the crow-men?'

The old woman did not open her eyes.

'The skein-mages, the skein-wrecks – they draw power from the pattern,' Floré continued, and she stared at the old woman, willing her to listen – to *understand*. She could feel the green eyes of the Orubor standing guard at the door boring into her, but she did not turn to it. 'When we fight Tessendorm or bandits, a skein-mage is worth a legion against any force. On a naval ship they are prized beyond even a skilled captain. But in the rotstorm? It is the commando who hunts the crow-man, Highmother, not the skein-mage. Why? The crow-man is *chaos*.'

The Orubor by the door moved forward and frowned at the old woman, and began to mutter something, over and over, fast syllables repeating, a language full of sharp edges. Highmother Ash stirred.

'She gave too much, trying to wake that girl,' the green-eyed Orubor said, breaking his song. His accent was clipped and precise. 'It is a gift, a gift she has given you. I do not understand why she has brought you here. I do not understand why she would give her life for a human child.'

'We are allies,' Floré said, reaching for the Highmother's hand. 'We protected Anshuka from the rust-folk when the summer was high. Allies help each other, even when the cost is great.'

The young Orubor turned his gaze to her, mouth downturned.

'Peace, Rowan,' Highmother Ash said, her voice barely a whisper as her eyelids fluttered open. Gently she squeezed Floré's hand. 'Floré Artollen. Finish. How do you kill the Deathless man?'

Floré breathed deep. *I have to make her understand!* Without the Orubor, there was no plan. *Without Highmother Ash's help, I have nothing. I can't save Marta.* Floré felt the shaking begin, the pain in her wrist and arm along the lightning scars, and she tried to keep her voice steady. *I must show her I am strong, that she can trust me.*

'Tullen One-Eye is invincible,' she said, 'because of the magic he wields – the pattern he holds close to him. It keeps age from him; it shields him from fire and blade. But no magic works in the chaos around a crow-man, save their own bastard arcana. Do you understand? We will find him, and we will bring a crow-man. His magic will fail, and I'll put a knife through his heart.'

Highmother Ash held Floré's gaze and reached out a hand to the young Orubor. He took it gently and spoke to her softly in their own tongue, and she nodded. Outside the cabin there was a rustle as a breeze cut through the tops of the forest and set the trees swaying, dancing with each other. Glancing through the window Floré could see treetops bending, branches reaching high in the pale light of winter as snow tumbled from them. *Please,* she thought, and she closed her eyes for a long moment and fell into a black pit of the future. *If she doesn't help us, how do I get to Marta? How do we stop Tullen?* For a moment she allowed herself to picture a horse, just her and Marta riding east from the Antian redoubt, towards the Isken border. *I could leave it all,* she thought. *Leave Tullen, Lothal. Leave the winter and the storm. We could go somewhere new...*

'Deathless comes,' Highmother Ash said. 'He comes, and he bears the blade that killed Nessilitor the Lover. We have trained you for this, Rowan. You and your sister must be brave. You must fly the orbs, for Floré Artollen. She will kill him for us. You must tell the others to gather our warriors in the meadow of the bear. We must wake the mother, or the wolf will bring silence to the forest.'

Floré felt the dream of escape crushed by the certainty of duty. With the orbs, there was a chance to fight Tullen. *And I swore an oath.* She opened her mouth to thank the Highmother, but the old woman's eyes closed and Highmother Ash fell slack on the bed.

'No,' she said, and next to her the Orubor Rowan clicked his teeth and bowed his head. Together they sat for a long moment with only the crackling of the hearth breaking the silence, each holding a hand of the Highmother. Rowan gently placed the hand back on the Highmother's chest, and Floré did the same.

'*Give* you our greatest weapons,' the young Orubor Rowan said, and Floré licked her lips. She had told the Highmother half of the plan, her half. The gauntlet, to strike down Tullen One-Eye. But she had not told her Benazir's role. *If we have the orbs,* she thought, *there is still hope. I can save them all.*

'Every flight of the orbs is a year of life, an effort that saps and breaks the strongest-willed,' Rowan said, and with his long fingers he stroked the blue skin of Highmother Ash's face. 'She would have my sister and I give you years of our lives, Floré Artollen. Perhaps more.'

Floré rubbed her nose, felt the bend of it where it had been broken who knew how many times. She dipped her head in recognition of Rowan's words.

'The Highmother trusted me,' she said, and sat as straight and as steady as she could. *Do not waver now.* She pictured Marta, deep in the north with Antian and lancers, deep in the strange world of those mole-dog scholars. Marta sick, Marta dying. *I need these orbs. I need this Orubor.*

'The cost we ask is great,' she said carefully, and she could see how *young* this Orubor was. She took him in. She had seen this before, had *done* this before. He was not angry, or doubtful of what the Highmother had asked him. *He is afraid to die.* 'Better to die protecting Anshuka, than live to watch her downfall.'

She did not believe the words, but she did not need to. *I need him to.* Floré hated herself for saying the words but the anxiety was rising in her at the idea of the Orubor not holding to Highmother Ash's words. *I don't have time!*

Slowly, the Orubor nodded, and Floré felt sick. *I'm sorry,* she wanted to say. *I don't want you to die.* It was a cold calculation, in the end. Tullen had to die, Anshuka had to wake, and Marta had to be safe. *Peace at any cost.*

'Can we leave within the hour?' she asked, and the Orubor blinked and turned to her. *Do not give them the chance to reconsider.* 'We will take the orbs, and hunt the mage. You must tell your people to try to wake Anshuka, and gather your warriors to defend her.'

Floré put a hand on the Orubor's shoulder, and then she rose slowly and left the room, bare feet on soft fur, and returned to the others. They were eating from plates of roasted venison, thick cuts of meat barely braised and dripping blood. The venison was set amidst dark red apples, as if the Orubor were unsure what humans ate. Yselda was dressed but still wrapped in many blankets, sallow-faced and hunched close to the fire. *I should send her home,* she thought, but where was home? Hasselberry, where all Yselda's family were dead and gone? A cold barracks in Undal City? Floré closed the door behind her and sighed. The girl had been quiet when they were stuck on Riven, quiet and sad, and Floré did not know how to help her. *And now the Highmother is dead, likely from the effort of saving her.* More guilt to add to whatever else was weighing on the child.

All of them turned to her, expectant.

'The Highmother is dead,' she said and bowed her head. Inside, she was so relieved that the Highmother had granted her the orbs that she wanted, she could have kissed the ground, but the woman deserved respect. She had saved Cuss from his wounds in the summer, had tried to help Marta, had taken them all so far. She tried to swallow down the excitement and pulsing call to action in her heart.

'They will give us the two orbs they have, and Orubor to pilot them. The orbs are to hunt Tullen, while they try and wake Anshuka. You all know the plan. I'll hunt us a crow-man; Benazir will find Marta.'

It pained Floré to even say that out loud. Every inch of her screamed to fly straight north, to find Marta and then safety. In her heart she knew – *there is no safety while One-Eye lives.* She felt the frozen fire inside her, her anger, her rage, every moment of her life becoming a weapon. *I can be a weapon.* The years in Hasselberry were a dream; Marta was a dream. If she wanted Marta to be safe, Tullen One-Eye had to die. *And who else can kill him but me?*

'I'm no use against crow-men,' Tomas said. He was sat near the fire, little Jozenai curled in his hands. 'But they won't be alone. There will be beasts from the storm, and problems we can't foresee. I'll join you, Artollen, if you'll have me. I owe you that and more.'

Benazir skewered a chunk of venison with a long fork from the platter on the floor between them all and started to chew on it.

'I'll ask one last time, Floré,' she said. 'Let me hunt the mage. You should go to Marta.'

Floré kept her mouth tight, chewed on her cheek. She couldn't say, not even to Benazir, what she was really feeling. *I can't go back to her after what I've done. Not yet.* Every time she thought of Marta now, there was an after-image. A goblin, on the end of her sword. A goblin, under her boot. A thousand little children dead at her hands. The blood on her soul was thick and scabrous, and she needed to do something to fix it. Below that, the urge for violence was still throbbing in her core. Tullen One-Eye had killed Janos, and she could not walk away from that. She wanted to be with Marta, she wanted to avenge Janos, and she wanted desperately to be a mother and not a monster. Floré just shook her head, and Benazir did not press her.

'I'll take Voltos and head to the Antian Redoubt,' Benazir said. 'Get Marta, and back to Undal City. With a few dozen whitestaffs they should be able to stave off the worst of what's getting her, until we can find a skein-wreck who isn't insane. We will ask the Tullioch about their Unnamed Knight, head to the Uradech if we need to. Someone somewhere will be able to help. When Marta is squared away, we'll return here and guard Anshuka.'

She did not mention the true plan, the mission Floré had spoken in her ears alone, but they held each other's gaze for a heartbeat. Before Benazir sought help for Marta, she had another destination that Floré had made her swear to.

Next to Benazir, Voltos was nodding animatedly.

'My people may have managed something, already,' he said. 'Our link to the skein is not quite the same, our practices different. There are many roads to the same destination.'

Tomas held his kitten up to his face for a long moment, black fur and white chest patch pressed close to his skin, and then handed her to Voltos. The Antian held the little beast tentatively as it stared dumbly up at him.

'For the little girl,' Tomas said at last. 'I don't think she will be safe with me. I've already half-drowned her today, and it's not even dinnertime.'

The kitten mewled, and Cuss coughed awkwardly.

'Sir,' he said, and Floré held up a hand to stop him. She opened her mouth to say, *You've done enough, Cuss. You've lost enough.* But then she saw that his pack was already set, his clothes and boots lined up ready to jump into. His axe blade gleamed in the firelight, leaning against the wall, and at the neck where wood joined steel a sword knot of bright green with a streak of white down the centre was carefully tied. She looked him in the eye and did not see anger. She saw determination. She remembered his face in the rotsurge at Undal City, pure anger as he fought falling away to calm resolve the moment the violence ended.

Floré nodded. 'With me, son,' she said.

Benazir threw an apple at Yselda, who flinched as it struck her on the shoulder. She had not even seemed to notice it coming towards her.

'That means you're with me, Private. First lesson of the day?'

Yselda opened her mouth but had no answer, and she looked around, confused. 'Sir?'

Benazir skewered another piece of venison. 'First lesson,' she said, chewing and grinning. 'Keep your mouth closed when you're underwater.'

~

There was nothing to their farewell, no embraces or poignant words. Floré gave Benazir a nod, and Benazir hustled her team together. Cuss and Yselda were leaning close and Benazir went and grabbed the girl by the shoulder.

'No goodbyes,' she said, and pushed Yselda forward down the path. 'No need for goodbyes when we will be together soon.'

The lie of it burned in her throat, and when Voltos and Yselda and their Orubor guide could not see her she glanced back, and caught Floré doing the same. Benazir smiled and tried to say without words – *I will find her*. Then Floré was walking away through the trees. Benazir bit her lip and forced herself to move forward.

They spent three hours traipsing through the forest to reach the orbs, and every step Benazir cursed the bloody Orubor. Her clothes were still sodden, so she was dressed like a mad cannibal elf. She had resolutely packed all her gear, wet as it was, but the Orubor clothing she had been given was overlong in the limbs and close everywhere else. She wore her belt and daggers and boots, but the rest of her gear was a cold lump in a bundle of deerskin, being dragged on a sled across the uneven snow by two Orubor who did not speak or even meet their eye, but fingered the long knives at their belts whenever they thought they were unobserved. *Excellent. Mad bloody elves with knives.* Yselda and Voltos followed behind her, both silent, and ahead of them the young Orubor, who had been introduced to her as Hawthorn, led the way. Floré, Tomas, and Cuss were headed off in the other direction – the Orubor had split their orbs, one with Anshuka for defence, one with the weapon-smiths of somewhere called Elm. *How many tree names can there be?* The Orubor made no sense to Benazir – one moment they were ancient unknowable mystics, singing magic and chattering away about gods, the next they were utterly practical.

'How much further, Hawthorn?' she asked, and the young Orubor grinned at her. Her head was completely shaven, and her skin was covered in intricate curving scars of red that stood out starkly against the blue of her skin. Her grin was disconcerting, perfectly white teeth that came to jagged points.

'A few more moments, *Benazir*,' Hawthorn said, lingering over Benazir's name as if it held some exotic meaning. Benazir flexed her left hand.

'It's Commander Arfallow, if you please,' Voltos said behind her, and Hawthorn laughed and kept walking.

'We are to fly orbs of fire and death together, no?' she said, stepping lightly over a fallen bough. 'I thought it might be nice to be less formal, if I am going to die for your plan.'

Benazir chewed her lip. 'As I said before, I can fly the orb if you show me how. I'll take the cost.'

Hawthorn only shook her head and walked on through the silent forest. Benazir had spent years at the Stormwall, and before that had grown up in Fallow Fen far to the west where the rotstorm was an ever-present threat on the horizon. Never had she seen a forest like this, ancient and tall. The occasional young trees had burst through where an older had fallen, but in the hours they had been walking almost every tree was ancient, tall and reaching to the sky. Trees of every kind, trees she had no idea the names for. Beds of late-autumn ferns were frozen on the cusp of red and brown, frozen before they could die and turn to mulch. The paths they followed felt like trails for deer, but there was no game in these woods to Benazir's eye, no birdsong. *Only silence.*

'When we see Anshuka, is there a mode of respect we should show that is appropriate to your people? I do not wish to offend.' She glanced back at Voltos, and he smiled at her question. The Antian looked even more foolish than she, wrapped in odds and ends and folds of Orubor clothing that was utterly unsuited to his physiology. Hawthorn hesitated and turned back to them, huge blue eyes seeming to take them all in at once.

'She is a god,' she said at last. Her grasp of the Isken trade tongue seemed complete, and Benazir could not tell if her hesitation was a pause for translation, or a pause for consideration. 'What could you possibly do to offend a god? Do as you will. We are here.'

Benazir rubbed the bandage-wrapped stump of her right arm against her chest. *Here* seemed to her to be more woods, the same as before. She fell back to speak to Voltos as they kept walking, through trees and more trees.

'If the plan works, and One-Eye is killed,' she said, 'and Anshuka awakes, and defeats Lothal once more... the last time they fought, the stories tell of calamities, Voltos. The first Claw Winter, a storm of ice and death trailing Anshuka as she went to find her sleep.'

It was not a question, but they had spent years working

together and had discussed this matter a dozen times or more when marooned at the island citadel of Riven. Voltos rubbed at his eyes with the heel of his palms and shook his head.

'We are not in the realm of the known, Commander,' he said. 'This is gods and great magic. You are a soldier. You must do the same as ever – what you can, with the tools provided. Marta may be the key to the protectorate's future – there are skein-wrecks across Morost, but they rarely fight one another. They have nothing to fear but their own kind, and there is something… I do not know. It is strange. They keep to where they *become*, if that makes sense. The Unnamed Knight does not travel beyond the Wind Sea, the Lord of Caroban and the Sun Master of Cil-Marie stay in their own realms. It is perhaps fear, it is perhaps only the knowledge that even victory would cost them much, and risk more, should they face one another. With Janos dead, we are at the whim of any who have this power. Marta could be our shield.'

Benazir pulled her borrowed cloak tight.

'Nobody carries only a shield,' she said. 'In the other hand, there is always a blade.'

Floré had told her, quietly in the keep back in Undal City when she gave Benazir her mission. *Don't let them make her a weapon.* Benazir narrowed her gaze and felt the scales in her heart, the weights that might tip them – her thirst for revenge, her love for Floré and little Marta, the need of the people of Undal. She did not look too closely at those scales, did not let her thoughts linger. Floré had given her a mission that she would trust to nobody else, and Benazir meant to see it done. They emerged past an oak with a trunk wider than any tree Benazir had ever seen, onto a meadow. The meadow was knee-deep in snow and ringed on all sides by towering trees, their branches naked save for layers of snow or delicate leaves entombed in ice, red and brown and even some still green – the

Claw Winter had come fast and early, and leaves that would have fallen were now frozen, a million delicate ornaments ringing the meadow.

The north end of the meadow was blocked off by a rocky outcrop, towering even above the trees, but Benazir ignored it. In the centre of the meadow was an orb of black stone bisected by a crystal strip, standing on three legs of spindly metal. It sat above the snow, and next to it in the meadow a stone of slick black rock poked up from the sheet of white. The black of the rock was marred by seams of silver that seemed to glow and burn.

'What in the hells is that?' Benazir asked, and when nobody responded she turned to the others. All of them were staring north, Voltos wide-eyed, Yselda clutching the pendant she wore at her neck. Hawthorn and the two Orubor pulling the supplies all had their heads raised and the palms of their hands on their chests. Confused, Benazir looked north again at the rocky outcrop. She tilted her head, and *saw*.

Anshuka.

Higher than the tallest tree, a true hill of stone and tumbled rock. Within it, *of* it, Benazir could see the shape of a great bear. Her head was the size of a barn, each folded paw larger than the largest lumber cart. Large beyond measure. Large beyond anything Benazir had ever seen. Snow did not settle on the rock – the whole of it was free of snow and ice, and tufts of grass and fern and even a little tree grew green and bright on the slopes of the sleeping god.

'Judges' spit,' she said, and Hawthorn laughed and gestured at the orb resting silent and still in the meadow.

'Come,' Hawthorn said, 'waking her is not our job, thank the ancestors. Night is coming – it is a good time to hunt.'

9

HUBRIS

'Tullen – we must speak. They are trying to turn us against one another. I hate the base nature of these politics – I am empress; you are my consort. You are more powerful than any alive. You have my love, and I have your allegiance. Six times the Talpid houses have sent dark figures for my blood, and once they drew a cut before my Tullioch cut the assassin down. Enough, I say. They try to turn my love against me, and I am sickened to be away from you. Come with me and we will end this chapter with an example – we will begin again anew, as we always do.' – **Private letter**, Empress Seraphina of the Gilded Spire

Ashbringer paced the walls of her cell and tried to keep warm. The cell was deep in what was once Dun Fen's Stormguard garrison, where City Watch and lancers once organised and trained. *Grey tabards, blue tabards.* She knew them so well. She had thought she knew all the world so well – Ashbringer, the wandering claw of Anshuka herself. The eye of the council of Highmothers, their blade in the dark to move beyond the home forest and keep them all safe. She knew it now for hubris.

She had fought goblins before, when she had come across a rotsurge deep in the north of the protectorate that had seeded the ground with dozens of the beasts. She had fought them in the meadow of Anshuka herself, when the crow-man Varratim tried to kill the great god-bear. She thought she understood the children of the storm.

Hubris. Varratim had struck her down with barely a thought with his wands of steel and gem, in the shadow of the god-bear. And now, with a fraction of her power and with the tumult of the last season fraying her senses, she had thought she could kill another crow-man. So easily this war-leader Ceann Brude had shrugged her off, had shocked her like a lightning strike and left her convulsing on the floor. Ashbringer remembered looking down at the pale face of Ceann Brude from the rafters, this woman seething with anger who was clear in every step.

To find her place in those rafters she had spent days hunting rust-folk across the Northern Marches, killing them only after she interrogated them. Most shared no language with her – those who did, she tried to scare with her jagged teeth and orb eyes, the way she had scared humans across the protectorate on the rare occasion when it was necessary for her work hunting Deathless. It did not seem to impact on the rust-folk. One, a man bearded and strong, she had lost her temper with and she had begun to beat, to cut, as if she might find truth in his screams.

'Why don't you fear me?' she had said, panting from the effort of her torture, and the man had spat blood in her face.

'You're just a goblin,' he said, 'a blue goblin. Another of the bear's toys. Do what you want. I'll tell you nothing. We'll not go back to the storm.'

The man said no more, but he did scream, and then he did die. Ashbringer had repeated the process another four times before she learned of the war-leader Ceann Brude taking counsel in

Dun Fen, and then spent long days marching through the snow and long nights crawling across the rooftops of the town until she found her quarry. She had stopped reaching for the skein by then – all it brought her was sorrow. But she could still trust the sinew in her arm, the focus of her eye.

Killing the war-leader seemed as good a thing as any to fill her time, when she could not sing, could not look at the grass or the trees. Could not hunt Deathless. She had spent every moment since her birth training to kill him – endless hours practising the blade, practising combat with muscle and steel and silver and rune and magic and song.

'And now look at me,' she said, just to hear a voice again. She had spent so long travelling alone in her life, but always she had the skein, the songs of the little creatures and plants to keep her company. Now she found herself muttering, conversations half-formed and half-forgotten even as they passed her lips. She stopped pacing and sat in the corner of the cell and stared at the bars. They were thick bars of steel, and the walls were cold stone. There was no window, and the dungeon her cell was in stank. She could hear humans talking in other cells, someone crying, but couldn't bring herself to care.

She stared at the bars. Even as a child, she could have escaped this place. Could have sung to the chorus of the world and changed it, imposed her will. Broken the bars, twisted the lock, eased stone from stone. *Something*. Her hand flexed and she pictured the broken hilt of her sword, the antler of a little god that had been killed centuries before. The crow-man had it now, Ceann Brude with her strange long limbs and fingers like the willow's dangling tendrils.

Late in the night, Ashbringer found comfort in the fact that Tullen would come for her, eventually. He would not be killed – *could not be killed*. He would grow bored of whatever scheme he held and would look for her in the skein and come to her, for someone to talk to, to boast to. The sorrow that followed that realisation was a pure thing, the understanding that she wanted to see him again, if only so she could speak to someone who might understand. *Is that what he wants from me?* In that moment, in the back of her cell in the cold and filth, she understood why he had chained her. *Three hundred years,* she thought. *If I were like this for three hundred years, what would become of me?*

It was not the same, of course – Tullen had severed her from the skein, put a wall of nearly opaque glass between her and the world, and with it a command that she would not think of harming him. Anshuka had done far more to him – he had been compelled to watch the ruin of his people, compelled to think on his crimes, compelled to aid no Ferron in word or deed. Wherever he fled, he would be drawn back to watch the rotstorm ruin everything he had built.

Ashbringer stared at the wall of her cell and tried to think of Anshuka doling out commands and edicts. The great bear was a force of nature, a waterfall, a mountain. She was not one for intricacies and cruelty. The punishment of an animal was never cruel – it was swift justice, complete and barbarous and true. *Why did she do that, and why command my ancestors to then hunt him?* The contradiction and the intricacy made no sense.

A door opened and closed, and down the hallway there were footsteps and the dance of flame. Ashbringer gripped her hands around her arms. There was nothing in the cell that could be used as weapon, nothing that could save her. A woman arrived – the adviser she had seen in Ceann Brude's room. Long black hair and a scarf of intricate weave surrounded a smiling face, intense eyes staring. She wore the same heavy cloak lined in fur and complexly patterned dark leather armour Ashbringer had seen her in before. A metal hammer incised with symbols hung at her belt. In one hand she held a lantern, in the other a little stool. She set it down and sat, legs crossed, and placed the lantern carefully down next to her. Ashbringer judged the distance – the woman was beyond the reach of her arms.

The other cells had been quiet before save the snores and occasional weeping, but now they were utterly still. *Everyone is listening.* Ashbringer stared at the woman.

'Hello,' she said, 'I am Commandant Jehanne. I advise Ceann Brude. Do you understand Isken? I do not prefer it, but few here speak my tongue, and I am afraid I do not speak Orubor.'

Ashbringer drew herself forward from the back of the cell and forced herself to sit, back straight, cross-legged, presenting a façade as calm as she could manage.

'None speak Orubor but Orubor,' she said eventually, and Jehanne nodded.

'I wanted to talk, before you leave in the morning. Ossen-Tyr will certainly be exciting, but I fear we would not have a chance to talk, just the two of us. Tell me... does Anshuka sleep deeply?'

The question threw Ashbringer. She licked her lips and squinted at the strange woman. *Military adviser from across the sea.*

'What do you care of the gods of others, Commandant Jehanne?'

'*Gods,*' the woman responded, lingering over the word. 'We do not use this... term. Spirits, we say. If everything Tullen told the reeve about you is true, you have encountered a certain dagger. A dagger that eats power and pattern, or spits it out in a terrible torrent. That is correct, no? The dagger he wears at his belt. I've not spoken to him myself, but I've certainly seen it. And now this chain of whispers, Tullen to the reeve to me...'

Ashbringer held herself still. She would not ask if Tullen was here. *Has he abandoned me?* The thought made her sweat, even as she realised how ridiculous it was. He was to be her victim, not her saviour. She did not respond, but instead waited and stared at the woman. Jehanne removed the small hammer from her belt, one hand on the handle and the other tapping the gold and silver symbols that cut across the black metal of its head.

'That dagger was a gift,' she said eventually, and grinned. 'A gift from Cil-Marie to Ferron nearly five hundred years ago. A gift to Tullen One-Eye, skein-wreck of the Ferron Empire. It was the tooth from a spirit – a great shark who hunted the waters south of Cil-Marie. Ihm-Phogn, the first Sun Master, hunted it down, and from it forged a great weapon. His descendants offered it as a gift of *respect*. Power recognising power. That is what we do, in Cil-Marie. We do not worship little gods and greater gods – we hunt spirits, and we harvest their power to enhance our own. We recognise other power, and it recognises us.'

She tapped the hammer on the stone floor below her, and where it struck the stone fractured, a web of cracks spiralling outward in a moment. The flagstone was split into a dozen pieces with that single tap. Jehanne slipped the hammer back into the loop of her belt.

'All this to say, Orubor... *Ashbringer*. Ashbringer, Tullen told the reeve your name was. Fascinating. All this to say, Ashbringer, that if your bear is asleep, perhaps she is ripe for harvest. One blow with the ur-blade by Tullen and your god will die, and I will harvest her bones. How does that make you feel?'

The woman was staring at her intently, trying to gauge her reaction. Ashbringer did not give her the satisfaction. Inside her heart was racing, and she felt a burning rage. Anshuka was mother to the forest, a heart of calm and peace and strength. They did not war, did not seek empire or ruin. All they wanted was the forest.

'Why fight one who does not fight you?' she asked, and Jehanne snorted.

'Resource? Renown? Revenge? Seven winds, Orubor. Just for the sheer challenge of it. To kill a spirit is no easy thing. To kill one such as this is to make history. And, of course,' she continued, waving her hand upward at the garrison above and beyond, 'that is just my personal perspective. Your *god*, at the behest of some long-dead skein-wreck, holds half a continent under an endless storm of nightmares that transforms children to monsters. She makes the rest live in something as close to hell as I've ever seen across all Morost. If I were what you would call an ethical or moral person, which I assure you I am not, the idea of doing anything other than trying to kill your god seems inexcusable.'

Ashbringer did not answer. Her tongue felt thick in her mouth.

'What do you mean, at the order of a dead skein-wreck?' she heard herself ask. Tullen had told her that the storm turned children to monsters, that Anshuka's ghost hunted children through the night. She did not believe Tullen. He was a liar and a murderer. *I will not be tricked.*

'Mistress Water,' Jehanne said. 'The hero of the protectorate. The skein-wreck who woke Anshuka and gave her the orders, three hundred years ago. Anshuka is just a spirit, little Orubor. Why would she raise a storm and keep it burning? What did you expect? She is just a tool someone has used for revenge.'

Ashbringer rose to her feet and went to the cell door. She pressed her face between the bars and stared down at the woman. Jehanne lifted her lantern and rose to her own feet, staring up into the Orubor's eyes.

'I can trust nothing you say,' Ashbringer said. 'Tullen is a liar and a murderer. Brude is a twisted monster. Varratim was a madman who cut down children.'

Jehanne smiled up at her and gave a comic frown. 'Come now, Ashbringer! Who of us hasn't killed children? Any who enter your wood are sentenced to die, young and old – is that not right? I've done my studying. You are zealots, guarding a god who barely knows you exist. What were you, before she got to you?'

Ashbringer blinked and snatched a hand out to grab Jehanne's cloak close, to smash her head into the cold iron of the bar and then break her arms, but the woman was out of reach. She did not flinch.

'Think on it, Ashbringer. I enjoyed this. I would certainly like to speak again. It is so interesting to meet such a rare creature – I've asked the reeve to request of Tullen if we could have you, for the Sun Master. A gift – power recognising power. I do hope he agrees.'

Jehanne bowed her head and strode away down the corridor, and as the flame of her lantern dimmed and the door shut behind her Ashbringer was left alone in the darkness, the cold iron bars pressing at her face. More questions came to her than answers, endless questions. Closing her eyes she reached for the song and the pattern, that great relief of the skein, but still it was like a haze of frozen smoke. She could see nothing, touch nothing.

She was alone.

In the cold of the cell, Ashbringer retreated to her corner and tried to sing, but no melody came to her, and so she wept in the darkness.

~

Floré knew that the orb was killing the young Orubor Rowan. It would take from him, as it had taken from the Tullioch Heasin, as it had taken from young Ruemar who escaped the caves. As he flew she watched him grimace and she offered him the little solace she could, a gentle hand on the shoulder, a word of thanks. There was nothing more she could do, but it was one more burden to add to all the others, another stone in the cairn of guilt that filled her heart. Floré set her jaw and did not let her upset show, did not let anything through the façade of strength. When the guilt and the fear were too much, she turned again to her anger and focused upon it. Best not to think about Marta. Best to think of Tullen One-Eye, her blade in his chest, her hands around his neck, her boot on his spine.

Up they flew in the orb, up from a glade hidden deep in the Orubor forest – a glade that bordered their village of Elm. Floré spared a glance through the crystal strip as they flew, having buckled herself into one of the seats that hung suspended by thin metal rods from the centre of the strange craft. From there, sat alongside a huge wand of steel tipped in a faceted ruby the size of her skull, for a moment she could see the village of Elm below as they rose into the sky. She saw steep-roofed houses of thick timber, and a column of smoke from what must be a smithy – three buildings facing onto each other, each an elaborate construction built around a central tree, beneath which a forge and smelter stood. Lithe Orubor worked bellows and tongs, fuelled the flames, and tended their work with focus.

Rowan did something on the central surface of the orb in front of him, the slick metal of the captain's helmet snug around his skull. It was connected back to the orb by a series of cables, tubes, intricate chains. He flexed a hand and outside the crystal the world shone white for a moment as the glow of the orb activated, and with it their propulsion.

Floré turned back to the view below as the crystal strip darkened, counterbalancing the glow. She stared at the little village. *What would Hasselberry look like, from above?* She pictured her house, before it was destroyed – the thatch of the roof, the crooked chimney, the little garden. She wiped the tears from her cheeks quickly, closed her eyes and breathed deep, focusing again on the frozen ember of rage she carried within her, lest her sorrow drown her.

Cuss was in the other wand chair, and Tomas stood next to Rowan, following the movements of the young Orubor's hands over buttons and knobs and switches of metal and glass and crystal.

'Ossen-Tyr,' Floré called, and below them the forest grew wide as the orb shot upward. Floré caught a glimpse of the forge workers of Elm ceasing, staring upward at the orb as it shot towards the banks of heavy grey cloud above. Rowan had been insistent that they go straight to the orb and not tarry. She stared at him as he flew, the red geometric scars or tattoos that stood out stark against the blue of his skin. His green eyes were beautiful. Highmother Ash had clearly trusted him, and Floré had to have faith in the Orubor. Even now a runner was sprinting through the forest below somewhere, trying to find the Highmothers – to convey Highmother Ash's final decree, that Anshuka must be woken.

They crested upward in a slow arc, and Floré could see the strain on the Orubor's face, the grit of his teeth. She had wondered at the wizened features of the crow-men they'd fought in the Blue Wolf Mountains in the summer, but since flying with Heasin and then Ruemar, it was clear enough. Tomas agreed – the orb took energy from the pilot, as did the wands. To use either, one did not need the skein, though it would certainly make it easier.

'I'm sorry,' she said, bringing her chair close to Rowan's. He did not look at her, kept his gaze focused outward. 'I'm sorry for this. I know it is hard.'

She reached her hand to his shoulder and he did not flinch away, but did turn to look at her.

'I will do my duty, Floré Artollen,' he said. 'It is all any of us can do. I have no gift for the skein, or the sword, so I never thought I would leave the forest. Perhaps I should be thanking you for all I might see. You say Ossen-Tyr – this means nothing to me. You must guide me, once we leave the mother's wood.'

Tomas leaned close and began pointing the way, and Floré watched the Orubor's hands dance over the orb controls.

He has no gift for the skein, she thought, *does this mean any of us can fly the orbs?* Floré had always thought of the skein as something *not for her*. It was the same way she felt about watching someone play an instrument, or singing a melody true and clear. Inaccessible, utterly different. Watching Orubor's forest spread below them she saw a hundred thousand trees capped in white snow, broken only by the stone hill at its heart – *Anshuka*. In that moment she closed her eyes and tried to reach, tried to feel the world around her the way Janos had described it so often – patterns and layers, connections and possibilities, reality and chance and all of it. She could hear a faint hum, Tomas asking quiet questions of their Orubor pilot. Cuss was silent. She did not feel the skein, or any pattern. She felt sick at the sudden movements and acceleration; she felt an ache like a cold knife at the idea of sending Benazir to fetch Marta rather than doing it herself.

'Let me kill him,' Benazir had argued, back on Riven when they came up with their plan, but Floré had shaken her head, resolute.

'I need you to help me, Benny,' was all she had said, and Benazir had nodded and not pressed further. Benazir understood. Some people needed to be killed, but some people needed to die by your own hand. Floré had watched Tullen sink a knife into Janos. She had watched helpless, unable to move, or speak or scream. Unable to hold him. They had only a few moments together from finding him alive to Tullen tearing him away – *how could I ever forgive that?* As much as she was afraid of finding Marta, and her daughter just seeing another blood-drenched soldier, as much as she believed that she was best suited to hunting the skein-wreck over any other available after her years hunting crow-men in the rotstorm, all of it was secondary. The core of it was a simple fact. He had killed Janos in front of her, and Floré would not stop until she killed him.

In the orb, as they broke into the bank of dreich grey cloud, Floré did not picture Marta, saving Marta, holding Marta again. Instead she pictured Tullen One-Eye standing over Janos, a bloody knife in his hand and a smile on his lips.

'Sir?'

Cuss was next to her, a hand on the back of her chair. They broke through the cloud and suddenly there was no wind, no grey – night had fallen as they marched to Elm, and as the orb cut through the last of the cloud, suddenly Floré could see every star in the sky. Rowan held them level for a long moment, and he and Tomas spoke in hushed tones.

Floré held her breath a beat and blinked away tears. Her anger and her fear and her love were all wound inside her, snakes wrestling each other, sinuous and indistinguishable.

'How do you do it, Cuss?' she asked, and he tilted his head and smiled.

'What, sir?' Floré put a hand on his cheek.

'I've seen you get angry. Seen how much anger you had after you lost Petron. Your mother, your sister Jana. I was worried about you, before we went to Riven. Worried the anger was all you had left. But you seem to have control of it. How have you done it?'

Cuss looked increasingly embarrassed as she went on, and glanced behind to check that Tomas and Rowan were not listening.

'It's what Captain Tyr taught me,' he said in the end, and

Floré widened her eyes. 'After Da left. I used to get angry, really angry. Even yelled at Ma. Like it was her fault. I'm not good with words, Commander. Can't say what I'm feeling, most times. Do you understand? There aren't proper words, for feelings. But Captain Tyr, he took me out around the loch, almost to the eastern end. Ranging, he said. When we stopped for lunch he told me about when he was in the Antian war, up in Aber-Ouse. He said, you can hate all you want, but if all you do is hate then they've won. Live well, keep who you are, and all your enemies will be sorry for it.'

Floré gazed out at the stars and flexed her hands, gripping the gauntlets hooked on her belt. The steel was cold.

'I still hate them,' Cuss said, and then he leaned up to squint out of the crystal strip at the stars. 'I won't change who I am, though. Petro wouldn't have liked that.'

'What if who you are is the problem?'

Cuss shrugged at her and produced two wizened apples from the pouch at his belt, incongruous as it was, wrapped around the leather tunic the Orubor had given him. He passed one of the apples to her.

'Be better, I guess,' he said, and took a bite of his apple. 'I normally just think, what would Sergeant Floré tell me to do?'

The orb began to pick up speed heading west and south, and Floré bit into the apple. It was floury in parts, bruised in others. *What would Sergeant Floré do?* She smiled. Sergeant Floré trained the children with the bow. Sergeant Floré baked bread with Janos. Sergeant Floré took Marta walking down the game trails of the forest, Marta's little legs so slow, stopping at every flower and singing as they went, pockets full of berries. In her mind she reached for Janos, the last little gift he had given her in the skein – a kindling within her mind where her memories of him lay.

I need to remember who I am. I need to get back to Marta.

Floré ate the apple down to the core, and then threw it at Tomas. He dodged it and rolled his eyes.

They dipped back below the clouds once every ten minutes, seeking landmarks. Cuss spotted the wend of the Unerdan river below, and from there Tomas was able to navigate based on guesses as to the identities of the towns below, motes of light that they were. Floré was sorry for the fear the sight of the orb would bring to those people, but they were right to be afraid, and she had work to do.

Within an hour they were descending towards the mountain town of Ossen-Tyr, and she could see what remained of the stone walls that ringed the city – the orb assault in the summer had burned many buildings and broken many old walls. But she could see timber and scaffolds, piles of fresh worked stone at every wound, ready to build back. The town was nestled amongst hills of red and grey stone, in a high range of steep mountains. Conscious of the panic they would bring, she had Rowan dim the lights and move slow, and they settled in a passing place a half mile down the mountain track. There were no carts on the road, though Floré was sure the progress of the orb would have been tracked with watchful eyes.

'I'll wait here, Floré Artollen?' Rowan asked, and Floré lifted the sack with her kit and gripped him on the shoulder.

'Rest, Rowan. Thank you. Remain here. We will return with the weapon we need to kill One-Eye,' she said. 'Raise the ramp behind us and let none enter. If we aren't back by tomorrow sunset, head back to Anshuka and protect her as best you can.'

The young Orubor nodded dolefully, his mouth turned down into a grimace.

'If you all die, your plan dies with me,' he said. 'Tell me – how would you kill the Deathless man? If you die, I will take your plan and we will try it again and again until we succeed.'

Floré glanced at the ramp opening down to the dark and

cold beyond. Rowan was right. *If I fail, perhaps they will succeed. Perhaps someone else will keep Marta safe.*

'We will kidnap a demon,' she said, 'and with it break his pattern. And with his pattern broken, Deathless Tullen One-Eye is just another man. I've killed enough men – one more should be easy enough.'

The Orubor looked confused.

'Why here, then? Do we not need the storm, for a demon?'

Floré smiled. 'Peace talks,' she said, and beside her Tomas blew a breath through tight lips.

'Peace talks,' he echoed, and gave Rowan a wry look. 'And we intend to take at least one of their envoys.'

Rowan opened his mouth and shook his head slowly in amazement as they left the orb. When she reached the bottom of the ramp Floré breathed deep, the freezing air of the Claw Winter even purer and colder up in the mountains if that were possible. The road was lined with thick heather coated in thicker snow, and beyond the heather and boulders were copses of trees that had grown huddled together for shelter against the wind.

Floré looked back at the inert black stone of the orb looming over them as the ramp raised, and she pulled on her gauntlets. She gripped the hilt of her sword and worked it in its scabbard, making sure it was loose and ready to draw, and without a word she turned and began the climb to the mountain town of Ossen-Tyr. Tomas and Cuss fell into step, Cuss with his axe on his shoulder and his Stormguard commando tabard worn proud over the leather tunic the Orubor had given him. Tomas was eying the road behind them.

Floré's last visit to Ossen-Tyr had ended in fire and blood, and she set her jaw as she marched. She thought of Benazir, far in the north hunting for Marta, and allowed a brief smile to break through her grim expression. There was nobody else in the world she would send in her place to find Marta. *Benny will help*, Janos had told her when Marta was first taken. Benazir was her sister. Benazir was her friend. Benazir was a sharp blade and a cold eye and heart warmer than any other Floré had known. Floré knew that in all the world, if there was one person she could trust to know what Floré wanted it was Benazir Arfallow.

10

CHICKENS EAT SCORPIONS

'The Stormguard have no allies. Reformists seek to topple the council; wyrms and goblins block the seas to the south. To the west they are besieged by the rotstorm, and the Northern Marches have fallen to the rust-folk. Isken have no interest, for the Undal have no goods to trade save wool and ore that can be gotten cheaper elsewhere. Tessendorm want only warm bodies for their fiefdoms, to work and be worked until nothing is left. Never have I seen them so weak. This is the moment we must stand by our bond. The armistice must hold. If we do not stand by them now, then what was our word worth?' – **Letter to the Hidden Council of the Undal Redoubt,** Bellentoe Firstclaw

'Voltos, is this… normal?'

Voltos did not respond to Yselda. Instead he stared down at the Antian Redoubt below them. A single flame from a burning brazier was glowing from the tallest tower, but aside from that brazier the redoubt was utterly unlit. All of them lined up against the hazed crystal of their orb and stared down. Hawthorn was holding them steady, five hundred feet from the ground, their orb drifting slowly through the sky with its glow and its propulsion both minimised – they should have appeared as a speck of black against a black sky. Yselda had felt sick for the first hour of the flight, her head spinning as she tried to reconcile the horrible distance below them, but she was steady enough to take in what she now saw.

The Antian Redoubt was built through a fist of rock that split up from the wild moors, vast plains of rolling heather and wending streams now coated in snow. It was a clump of a dozen towers, each circular and unconnected from any other – at least, unconnected above ground. They jutted outward from the rock promontory at odd angles, one straight up, one nearly horizontal to the west and another east, and many more at odd angles. As they had headed north the clouds had thinned, but what little starlight there was did almost nothing to reveal the truth of the redoubt to Yselda. It was utterly dark, a shadow against the pale snow beyond. The snow seemed to gather starlight, reflecting endless points of light and contrast, but the redoubt was a shape and nothing more. *Except that one flame.*

Yselda tried to breathe and be calm. *Marta needs you.* She still felt cold, and couldn't help but keep her fists in her gauntlets clenched at the hilt of her longsword. Whenever she closed her eyes she saw the wolves on the ice, those from her childhood and those from the morning, all of them mixed together. Her brothers and her mother and her father, dying then. Lothal the wolf staring down at them this morning, eyes impenetrable. Every resolution she had made to leave Floré, to leave the Stormguard, to find some place she could serve without violence… Yselda could hold nothing fast. *How can we fight the wolf?* She knew in her heart only Anshuka could. *It's too big for me.* She would not say it aloud, but she wanted nothing more than a quiet room. The redoubt was meant to be a fortress of stone, home to the Antian realm in Undal. It would be safe, there. She let herself hope for a moment. *If Marta is cured,* she thought, *we could stay there.*

'What should we be seeing, Voltos?'

Benazir's words seemed to snap the Antian from a daze.

'My apologies, Commander,' he said. 'I... The redoubt is what remains of another age. Our tunnels and mines cut below the northern continent, the southern, even the eastern – all Morost is woven through with them, an intricate series of connections. Some are lost, whole cities forgotten or broken off by earthquake or flood or war. Bad blood. Some have been connected since before humans came to these lands. We live in the tunnels and cities below, which are far more temperate and far less *changeable* than the surface. Fewer predators than above ground, in the upper levels at least. The redoubt is one of our outposts – a tunnel once ran from the heart of Ferron to here, and then on to our holdings beneath Tessendorm, which connects to Isken, and so on. The Ferron tunnel is abandoned now.'

Hawthorn took the orb in a long loop around the rock promontory, and Yselda stared at the towers. Each was a hundred foot long at least, jutting from the stone at angles where they should have fallen without arch or pillar to support them, and in the darkness they watched.

'This is our watch post, our trading post with the Undal Protectorate,' Voltos said, and he took a pair of eyeglasses from a pouch at his belt and perched them on his grey-flecked snout, peering down through the crystal. 'A place for a sunken kingdom to trade for what we might indulge in. Those of us... oddities who prefer the open sky to the tunnels below, we leave as emissary or trader, and so on. What you should see is a mound of rock, stark white and worked smooth. And from it, a dozen towers, one for each holt. Each should be lit, a thousand candles in a thousand windows. Never have I seen it dark and silent as this. You should be seeing a wonder, the great reminder of our stonework, our mastery of the elements. Our mastery of the world. Instead, there is darkness. I do not know, Commander. I do not know what we will find.'

'Take us to the light,' Benazir commanded, and Hawthorn lowered them slowly. The young Orubor was sweating with the exertion of flying the orb, of channelling whatever arcane energies held it aloft. She gave no word of complaint, and slowly they began to approach the signal fire. The light was atop the most vertical of the twelve towers, and as they lowered Yselda realised her scale had been all wrong. The redoubt was *huge*. She had taken the towers as spindly things, but as they grew closer she realised their true scale – each was different in size but the tower top they approached was at least the size of the pentacle courtyard back in Protector's Keep.

She clutched the talisman at her throat as she tried to make out what stood next to the huge burning brazier – a dozen short figures, *Antian*, wielding spears and staring up at them. All wore heavy cloaks over silk robes woven through with decorative and protective ceramic plates, a heavier version of Voltos's usual garb. All but one wore helms, ornately worked, steel-lined and padded and wrapped with long scarves that fluttered in the wind. As the orb grew closer Yselda saw them shuffle back and fall into defensive postures – the field of silence that surrounded the vehicle must have enveloped them.

'Land us slowly, Hawthorn,' Benazir called, adjusting her cloak and checking the set of the hook on the end of her right arm, 'and as soon as we are off, raise the ramp and lower the field of silence. Let none aboard but us. If we die, your mission is at its end.'

'*Benazir*!' Hawthorn called, and laughed through clenched teeth, and Yselda could see the strain on the Orubor's face. *It's killing her.* She shivered at Hawthorn's forced cheer. *How long can she fly us?* 'Your optimism is a balm to my nerves,' the Orubor continued. 'Bring me back some Antian food!' Benazir shook her head and straightened her still-damp tunic, and Voltos stepped in front of them. He was holding the little basket he had found for Jozenai the kitten, back in the Orubor's lodge. It had been full of fruit they had tipped into their makeshift packs, and Tomas had folded up a blue scarf of his, once it had dried, and padded the bottom of the basket. Yselda had watched Tomas stroke the cat gently under the chin and murmur a goodbye to it, when he thought none were watching. Always she did not know what to think of him, in turns so brash and cold and arrogant and wry. *But he stood between me and the wolves.* Voltos fiddled with the folded leather shirt he was using to keep the kitten under cover, and Yselda smiled at the mewling cat within.

'Does Marta even like cats?' Voltos asked, and then the ramp was lowering and Yselda could not think to answer. She followed Voltos and Benazir down onto the tower top – there was no rampart, only a sudden edge and then hundreds of feet of blackness, and ragged stone below. Yselda felt sick. The wind was pulling at her, as if the world itself was trying to force her to the edge of the platform, and she braced herself and bit her lip. It was utterly cold, a cold that seemed to rob whatever mote of warmth she had found since the frozen loch. Worse than the cold was the silence that emanated from the orb as soon as she stepped onto the ramp, the silence of a noise too loud for ears, a pressure in the chest.

They had been flying slow and without lights for their final approach, so the sickly brilliant white sheen was at least absent, and as the wind pulled at her she gazed off to the edge of the tower, away from the waiting Antian and their spears. She remembered that same pressure over Hookstone forest the night Hasselberry was attacked. The night her second family had been taken from her. *What would Shand and Esme think of this – Antian and flying orbs and all sorts?* She tried to smile at the thought of them, sweet Shand and stern Esme, but the smile died on her lips as the image came to her mind unprompted of their daughters Nat and Lorrie, little girls. The rust-folk had killed them all.

Yselda closed her eyes, and after a moment the oppressive silence lifted and the wind was a howl ripping at her ears. The Antian were all yelling, but did not approach. One stepped forward and said something in the Antian tongue. She did not try and listen or watch as the dozen Antian bearing spears yelled at Voltos in a tongue that rolled, guttural and thick – Yselda did not know if it was one language the Antian spoke, or many. *I don't know anything.* They had to yell to be heard over that cutting wind, the wind that seemed to reach the edge of the tower top and then batter against it, eddying and hurtling itself across the flat of the stone.

The one with no helmet raised a hand and the rest fell silent. Voltos approached them, and Yselda felt her chest heaving with the panic of short sharp breaths. *They'll kill him too!* She closed her eyes again and tried to breathe deeply, but it was too cold, the wind was too strong, and she felt herself shaking. Her eyes squeezed shut and she was back in the black water of the loch and the wolf was at the shore and no arrow would pierce it; *nothing would stop it—*

'Calm, Yselda.'

Benazir's hand under her arm, Benazir's voice in her ear, close and quiet, barely audible over the tearing winds.

'I need you. Floré needs you. Marta needs you. So take three straight breaths and stand to attention, or you'll be spending the night cleaning out whatever passes for a latrine around here.'

Benazir pulled herself straight, but didn't let go of Yselda's arm, and she leaned gratefully onto the slight commander. Voltos turned to them and gestured at the brazier where a metal hatch was being pushed up from the stone. The Antian guards had turned their spear-points to the sky, and were staring hard-eyed at Benazir and Yselda. She stuck next to Benazir and followed Voltos numbly, and together they descended the short staircase that had been revealed. All of it was worked impeccably with intricately decorated masonry, every stone etched with some embellishment – a curving sign, a symbol, a shape, an abstract animal. The moment her head ducked into the tower it was so much warmer, so much *quieter*. They descended perhaps a dozen steps and walked into a wide room arrayed with low chairs and tables of dark wood. Tapestries hung on the walls, tapestries that depicted faded scenes of Antian figures, of storm clouds, a snake, a great dragon – other images she couldn't make out in the near dark of the room.

The only light was a candelabra with four fat candles sat on the central table. Behind them the Antian guards stepped in, spreading around in a loose rank by the door. Yselda could feel Benazir tense next to her, and Voltos was smoothing his whiskers. He looked nervous. She had never seen so many Antian – only Voltos, and a handful in Protector's Keep or in Undal City itself. One of the bakeries near the keep, Bellentoe's, was run by an old grey-furred Antian who baked delicious bread and always gave Stormguard cadets extra rolls. The variety amongst them surprised her – some were a little taller, nearly five and a half feet, and others a foot shorter than that. Most were stocky, but a few looked lithe and skinny, their silk robes baggy over them. In coloration many were as dark as Voltos, but some had brown fur, and one was a pale golden colour, a gold so pale it was almost white. All of them were silent and staring, and finally the one with no helm stepped forward and gestured at the table.

'Voltos Thirdskin, you name yourself. You are in Holt Varsi. Your means of arrival raises many questions. I am Pekka Secondclaw.'

Voltos bowed low and placed the basket with Jozenai inside onto the table. In vain he tried to smooth the silk of his robes – the soak in the dank waters of Loch Hassel and the subsequent drying by the Orubor fire had left them wrinkled and stained. He wore a short cloak the Orubor had given him, and he licked his muzzle and scratched at his chin nervously.

'I am Voltos Thirdskin, adviser to the Stormguard, emissary of the Hidden Council. I claim no holt, and bear no arms but the dagger my mother gave me. I bring you Commander Benazir Arfallow of the Stormguard commando, and her attendant Private Yselda Hollow. We must speak to the Hidden Council at once – we bring news from Undal City.'

Yselda did not think Pekka looked impressed by their titles. The Antian had a deep brown fur, and looked much younger than Voltos – there was no grey in his muzzle, and he was heavily muscled beneath close-fitting silks. The ceramic outer panels of his armour were intricately decorated with swirls and motifs painted in red and blue over a black backing. Slowly he went to the table and sat, and from the shadows an Antian clad in simple cloth brought forth a ewer of wine and a single cup. Pekka poured himself a cup of wine and sipped from it, staring at them. Voltos made no move to sit, and Benazir stood stock-still, so Yselda held herself back as well. She could feel the tension in Voltos's stance – the usually calm Antian was leaning forward, gaze locked on Pekka.

'Why are the holt towers dark, Pekka Secondclaw?' Voltos asked, and Pekka set down his glass. He turned his gaze to Benazir, looking her up and down, staring openly at the hook attached to the stump of her right arm. Yselda he spared a glance, and then he turned back to Benazir.

'Do you know we keep chickens, Commander Benazir Arfallow of the Stormguard?'

Benazir smiled, but it did not reach her eyes.

'I did not, Pekka Secondclaw.'

'There are tunnels all through this world, deep below the surface. We live in many, and have no interest in what goes above. But sometimes, there is value. Centuries and centuries ago, someone thought, could they raise those little chickens you humans love down in the dark. There are plenty of grubs to be had, worms and centipedes and spiders. Do you know what we found?'

'Pekka Secondclaw, I must insist,' Voltos said, but the other Antian held up a hand to silence him and did not bother to look at him. Instead he continued to stare at Benazir.

'There are scorpions, in the deep. Did you know that? They are not so common above the ground, not in Undal. Scorpions with a sting that hurts like a dagger thrust. Scorpions with a venom that will leave a child twitching and frothing, and dead the next day. A fortunate thing – it turns out, chickens eat scorpions. Their sting doesn't bother beak or talon, and the little terrors will gorge themselves on the flesh of something that appears far more deadly than they.'

In the darkness of the tower, Yselda tried to keep still and tried to force her eyes to adjust to the shadow. With only the four candles burning, the wide room they were in was dark, and she could not see the faces of the Antian who stared at them with spears in hand – only the shape of them, the shuffle of their feet. *What on earth is he talking about? Why are they being so strange?* She forced herself not to grip at the handle of her sword, instead resting her gauntleted hands at her belt and squeezing the fingers within as tightly as she could.

'Why are the holt towers dark, Pekka Secondclaw?' Benazir

asked, and gestured around. 'I was expecting welcome, light and warmth, the embrace of an ally. What has happened here?'

Pekka swirled the wine in his cup and looked down into it as if it held the answers. His ears drooped, and he clenched and unclenched his jaw. Yselda could see long teeth, white and strong behind black lips.

'All have retreated to the city below, for safety. The Claw Winter is brutal, and strange enemies abound. The wolf Lothal has been here himself, sniffing at the base of the redoubt. Orbs of light, the same orbs that took our children in the summer, have been seen. Worse, something is wrong with the deep below. Those who pray to the ones chained in darkness murmur that bonds are broken. The earth shakes as they rouse from a slumber that has lasted since the first dawn.'

Pekka peered forward at them, and Yselda saw the feverish intensity in his eyes. *He's insane.*

'Have you heard them, Voltos? The deep gods? They whisper to some, in their sleep. I have heard them. I have been blessed. The witches and the council are there now, in the deepest tunnels below the city. The anchor stones are all broken, molten silver cracks across stone that has been unmarred since the world was built. What do you think that means, Voltos? I think it means old gods are rising. I think it means old alliances don't mean the same thing anymore. Old ways of being won't work for us, when the deep ones wake.'

Pekka drank from his wine, and Voltos carefully took a half step back. Yselda moved her hands below her cloak – she pulled the strap at the wrist of each gauntlet tight. There were eleven Antian between the three of them and the stairway back to the orb, as well as Pekka at the table, and the servant lingering in the shadows. *This doesn't feel like a safe haven.* She tried to picture Marta here, somewhere warm. She had no idea what he was talking about. *Chained ones? Deep ones?* Next to her, Benazir was utterly still.

'I am an *ambassador*,' Voltos said, his voice suddenly strong and deep. 'I report to the council and the council alone. I bring to you an emissary from our allies. Take us to the Hidden Council at once – rumours of deep gods and broken stone will have to wait.'

Pekka shook his head slowly and raised a hand. The Antian behind them as one levelled their short spears. Each spear was five foot of straight wood topped with a shining blade of obsidian, flaked and knapped so that each blade caught the candlelight and reflected a dozen jags of deep yellow on black across the curved facets of its surface. Yselda went to pull her sword free but Benazir's hand was on her arm, and the commander just shook her head.

'The redoubt is *under my command*, Voltos Thirdskin,' Pekka said, snarling. 'You have an orb – an orb of the rust-folk, an orb of *Ferron* – I will take it. The council left us up here to die by wolf or magic, to hold this shell as if it were an honour. Holt Varsi, who despise the open sky and worship the old gods, left to fester above. So be it. It shall be a weapon in our hand.'

The muscular Antian rose and drew from his belt a long dagger of obsidian with a handle of twisted white wood wrapped in leather. Languidly he pointed it at Voltos.

'You will give this orb to me, and tell me all you know, *Ambassador*. Take the others and put them with the rest of the humans.'

Yselda did not fight the strong hands grabbing at her wrists. *The rest of the humans – Floré needs you. Marta needs you. Did Nintur and the lancers make it this far?* She understood none of the Antian discussion that erupted around her as Voltos protested in his native tongue to the encroaching guards, but even in the common tongue she had followed little of what passed between Voltos and Pekka. Deep gods and witches, a hidden council and a buried city. *I need to find Marta.*

She felt the fear then, the usual fear, that familiar companion since the summer; the same fear that had haunted her dreams since she lost her mother and father and brothers to the wolves on the ice. It turned her guts to water and her blood to a shivery tang. The Antian took their weapons – Yselda's bow was sunk in Loch Hassel, but she had kept her sword. An Antian pulled her sword belt from her, the longsword she had been given when she became a commando, and the antler-bladed dagger with its burning rune and silvered blade. From Benazir they took six daggers, and all were piled onto the table.

'Voltos,' Benazir said, ignoring the Antian who pawed at her, checking for hidden blades, and Voltos broke from a snarling argument and turned to her. Two Antian were attempting to take his obsidian dagger and he spat and growled at them.

'Cultists and fools!' he spat, and then threw his dagger down to the table and let his shoulders fall. 'But they should not harm you. Even they would not be so mad. Let me sort this out, Commander. Give me time.'

Two of the Antian grabbed him by the shoulder, and then at spearpoint Yselda and Benazir were forced from the room. She managed a last glance at the room before she left, Pekka and Voltos still snarling at each other, Jozenai's basket forgotten on the floor. She felt helpless without her dagger. She had worn it at her hip every day since Floré had given it to her, back in Hasselberry. *What if they don't give it back?*

At spearpoint they travelled down and down again, down stair and ramp, lit only by a single torch. Benazir was next to her, and as they walked the commander slipped her arm into the crook of Yselda's elbow and gave her a squeeze.

'I'm afraid,' Yselda said at last in a whisper as the Antian in front of them paused to unbar a heavy door of stone.

'Be afraid,' Benazir said, her voice low and strong, 'and do the work anyway. Marta needs us. Follow my lead, and when the time comes don't hesitate. If they have her, we'll get her out and we'll get her up. Understand?'

Yselda nodded in the darkness. Her hand went to go to the antler hilt of the dagger Floré had given her – *Benazir's old dagger*. A dagger wielded by Benazir, wielded by Floré, wielded by Yselda. But her belt was gone, her dagger was gone, and her tunic fell loose around her waist. Yselda clenched her fists inside her gauntlets and forced herself to breathe as they descended, down into dark and stone, but she could not stop the tears running down her cheeks.

11

NOOSE

'*With the coming of Mistress Water from the mines, Jozenai called what we now name the first revolutionary council – in truth this was not the first, not even Jozenai's first. Every successful revolution is built on the bones of those that failed before. Jozenai had escaped his bondage in the chaos of an uprising a decade prior and had tried and failed to overthrow the Ferron garrison in the Cimber Hills five years before the council with Mistress Water – an attempt that left the revolutionaries bloodied and harried for years to come. The first revolutionary council took its members from escaped slaves, from what remained of the free Undal, and even supposed heirs of the old Undalor nobility. The mines had taught Mistress Water the skein and the meaning of suffering – now she had to learn the brutal art of politics.*' – *History of the Revolution*, Campbell Torbén of Aber-Ouse*

'What in all the hells are you doing here, Artollen? I thought you were on your way to Orubor's wood to get us an orb, to hunt us a demon, to *kill us an unkillable man*?'

Starbeck was pale and pacing in the darkness of Ossen-Tyr's

Stormguard barracks. Floré cinched her sword belt tight over the fresh commando tabard she had taken from the barracks stores, and breathed out a deep sigh at the familiar weight of her blade at her hip. She grabbed her gauntlets from the table and slipped them onto her belt. The last day had been a nightmare. *Magic and nonsense.*

'Sir, that is still the plan.'

With a smooth movement she drew the sword and checked it over. The black steel blade was unmarred by the fighting in Undal City and she could read clearly the dual line of runes that echoed each other, running up the blade on either side of the fuller that ran down its core: ᚷᚦᛖᛚᛚᚦᚷ ᛈᚱᛗᛏ ᚠᚾ ᚠᚤᚩᚷ ᚷᛖᛖᛖᚷ.

Starbeck stopped pacing and walked over to her, gripping her by the shoulder.

'Commander, what the hells are you thinking? I need you to focus. Debrief.'

Floré sheathed the sword and rubbed her eyes. They had arrived at Ossen-Tyr half frozen, and a hook-nosed City Guard sergeant had refused to believe who she was.

'Artollen? You can't be Artollen,' he had said, over and over. 'Last Artollen from the commandos who came through here I heard about, was the night everything went to hell. That you? Lost a lot of people, that night. Lot of people. Can't be Artollen.'

Floré had only glared at him, until Tomas stepped past and with all of his usual tact demanded immediate entrance for Bolt-Commander Artollen, her steward, and the Primus of Stormcastle XII. They had been escorted through the deserted streets of Ossen-Tyr to the looming black of the old Ferron overseer fort, where a hundred torches and braziers blazed. The city was cold and empty, burnt and broken stone homes and stores shored up with temporary wooden fixes. Compared to those empty streets, the garrison was an oasis of life. There were dozens of lancers and City Watch intermingled, on patrol or standing guard, all of them with hands on weapons.

The stables were a bustle of movement, but finally the City Watch patrol escorting them managed to get the attention of a steward and they were taken to rooms in the barracks and told Starbeck had been informed. Floré had sent Cuss to get them both fresh clothes, armour, tabards, to replenish their packs, and Tomas had disappeared saying he was going to make enquiries. When Cuss returned she had sent him to get himself fed, and then Starbeck had arrived flanked by no less than six City Watch.

Now the two of them were alone as she finished checking her gear, and she could barely focus. *Marta. The plan.* She could feel herself swaying, gently, so she sat down, and Starbeck poured her a cup of water and pushed a heel of bread at her. They were in a commander's room, so there was a little table and some chairs as well as a single bed and a chest. The steward had brought fresh water, but she had no idea how long the bread had been sat there wrapped in cloth.

'Eat,' he said, and she fell on the bread as he spoke. It was hard and chewy, and tasted of nothing more than yeast. 'I only arrived two hours ago. The reformists killed at least two dozen back in Undal City. They were targeting those in office. We put them down, perhaps for good this time. There were enough loyal soldiers there for that, at least. I left the next dawn to come here, for the peace talks. The Grand Council are trying to root out whatever is left of them. What are you doing here? Did the Orubor fail?'

Floré shook her head and drank the water.

'Sir. No. We had to go stepwise, so we stopped in Hookstone forest. Lothal was there.'

Starbeck leaned back in his seat and rubbed at his eyes.

'We have two orbs,' Floré continued and forced herself to

swallow the stale bread down. 'Benazir and Voltos have gone to the redoubt. They'll get Marta, and get her back to the whitestaffs in Undal City. We are still on mission, sir. We need a crow-man. That's why we're here.'

Starbeck shook his head slowly and then began to laugh, a chesty laugh that was almost a wheeze as he understood. He smiled at her. Floré frowned. In twenty years, she had never seen him laugh.

'Peace at any cost, I said, is that right?'

She nodded.

'Peace at any cost, even the Northern Marches themselves, even Fallow Fen. Peace at any cost, and you think the best place to grab the crow-man you need is… from the peace talks?'

Floré grimaced and rubbed her eyes. *So tired.* And it was so *tiring. Why can't he see?* She let the cold burn of anger swell up inside her, let that familiar rage she had carried all her life rise to the front. She kept it so controlled, always chained and in check, always a tool at her disposal. Now, tired and afraid and so far from Marta – her own daughter she was afraid to face, afraid to find a girl too sick to cure – Floré let the rage take over.

'There's no peace while that bastard Tullen One-Eye is still walking, *sir*,' she said, clenching her teeth. She could feel the heat rising in her cheeks. 'The man can level a city in the time it takes you to put on your boots. He can command Lothal the pissing god-wolf, who I just saw in Hookstone toppling century-old pines like bullrushes. We don't know his plan, but he has had three centuries to think on it. You've seen Tollen's folly, the old tower? I grew up in the village outside of Tollen. We used to climb the ruins. An old Undal chief's castle, and he upset Tullen One-Eye at a dinner party and so One-Eye turned the whole place to stone, every room and every window spilling over with stone. If you climb what's left of the outer wall and up to the second level, there's a way into what was once a courtyard. Every door and window opening onto it, full of stone. In one of them, reaching out from the window is a hand. It's under cover from rain and wind in that courtyard, and more than four hundred years since One-Eye killed that Undal chief you can still see the fingernails on that hand. Stone. This isn't war against the rust-folk, this is everything we have against *him*. Would you rather I risk the orb in the rotstorm? Would you rather I take *any chance* at all? There will be crow-men here, and we need one. If it costs us another year of war but kills this fucker, it's a price I'll pay.'

Floré was standing. *When did I stand up?* Starbeck stared down at his hands.

'Peace at any cost,' he muttered. 'You were always the heavy hand, and I made you that. Take off the tabard, Floré. They arrive at dawn. If you can do this without bringing down hell on us, I'd be grateful, but do what you must. Anything you need, you have it, but if you fail, then you will not fail as Stormguard.'

Floré stared down at him and her hand went to her chest, to the lightning etched there. She had been a Stormguard cadet since she was an orphan too small to lift a shortsword. She had worn the cadet's training tabard, the commando tabard, the Forest Watch tabard. Her anger was ebbing, slowly fading down to a simmer, cold and hot all at once. *My whole life I've served.* Slowly her hand unclenched from the fabric of the tabard, and she nodded. Starbeck went to leave but he paused at the door.

'The runes on the sword are the same as all of it,' he said, staring back at her over his shoulder. 'They don't mean anything on their own. They mean what the person who made it thought they meant, or wanted them to mean. No rune has power on its own. No symbol has power on its own. You are not Stormguard because of a tabard, Floré.'

Starbeck left, and Floré bit her lip. She undid her sword belt and pulled off the commando tabard, the rank slides that showed her as bolt-commander. Underneath the tabard she wore a tunic of cured leather and, below that, utilitarian wool and cloth dyed black, all of it found by Cuss in the Ossen-Tyr armoury. Looking down as she tied her belt back on, she saw the figure of a bear embossed and moulded across the torso of the leather. It was the same colour as the armour, and in the candlelight the bear moved as she breathed, the flame highlighting claw, eye, open mouth.

Mother, she thought, *I hope you're waking, you bitch.*

A knock at the door drew her from her reverie. She slipped Tyr's old knife into its sheath at her left hip next to her gauntlets, and opened the door wide, expecting Cuss. Instead, it was the hook-nosed City Watch sergeant who had met them at the city gates. His steel cap was gone, revealing a thick head of wiry hair held back in a loose knot behind his head. He scratched his nose and nodded to her.

'Bolt-Commander Artollen, your presence has been requested. You've a messenger.'

Floré frowned. It was near midnight, or past it.

'This way, if you please.'

The man didn't wait for an answer, but turned and headed down the corridor. The corridor outside of the room was freezing – the old Ferron overseers' forts didn't hold heat well. Floré grabbed her green cloak from the peg by the door and hurried after him.

'Wait, man! What messenger knows I'm here?' she asked as she caught up, and he shrugged and kept walking, face sour as ever. Floré blew out a breath and followed, fastening her cloak. The news of her arrival would have gone to Starbeck, but who knew who Cuss and Tomas had been speaking to since they arrived. *Don't those idiots have the sense to stay quiet?* The garrison was quieter – still there were guards on every wall, and torches blazing high. They marched down three more corridors, and Floré had completely lost her way.

'Where in the hells are we?' she asked, and grabbed at his shoulder to stop him. The man drew up short and turned to her. 'What in blazes do you think you are doing?' the man snorted. 'In there, Commander.' He gestured to a closed door.

'Messenger in there. Said it's about your daughter. Morta – that it? Wants to talk private, like.'

Floré stared at him, but the man only scowled, and as soon as he said Marta's name, mangled though it was, Floré's heart almost exploded. *Who knows about Marta, here? Who even knows I'm here? Is it Benazir?* She tried to think quickly. Could Benazir have already found Marta and returned? Could it have been so simple that Benny had decided to meet her here? *But why the secrecy?*

'Who is this messenger?' she asked, and the sergeant just shrugged and opened the door, and Floré pushed her way in. *Marta.* The room beyond was a storage room stacked high on the left wall with barrels and casks, and against the right wall heavy crates of wood and cloth sacks. A single torch forty feet away, at the far end of the room, cast a dim light. There was a figure cloaked in black with their back to the door halfway to the lit torch.

Floré stepped forward into the room, and her hand went to her belt. She pulled her gauntlets on and cinched them tight. *Is that Benazir?* The figure could be. *Benny, I'll split your head if this is your idea of a joke.* She was so tired, and her head was beginning to pound, a creaking ache behind her eyes with every heartbeat.

'Judges' spit,' she said, 'I don't have time for this. Who *are* you? What is this?'

Behind her the door slammed, and she heard a click. Floré backed up and drew her sword, and with her left hand tried the door. It was locked. *Shit. Ambush. Of course it's a bloody ambush, Floré. Of course it is!*

Weaving her sword in a loose circle, she rolled her shoulders and took a step from the wall. *Marta and Tullen.* That was all that mattered: that she could save one and kill the other.

'You don't have time for this,' the figure said, turning. Floré couldn't see her face but a voluminous blue dress flashed from beneath the dark cloak. 'You don't care. You said that to me before, you know. *I don't care about your parochial bullshit,* you said, and then you rather ruined my day.'

The woman lowered her hood, and as she did, from the shadows between the barrels, a dozen torches were struck up with scraping sparks of flint, and the room filled with flickering orange light, each held by a man or woman, all of them staring at her. As her hood fell, a cascade of red hair tumbled down with it to her shoulders, and the Hanged Man of Ossen-Tyr smiled. The head of the Ossen-Tyr gang Floré had decimated to reach their failed whitestaff, so she could use him to find Marta. Floré pictured her sword-knot, returned to her with a tiny noose of string in the autumn. She had wondered at the time – the sword she had been using had been left in a midden, behind the burning remnants of the Hanged Man's hideout, amidst a dozen corpses. *It was a message.*

'Now,' the woman said, her voice mellifluous and smoky, 'you caused me all sorts of trouble, Floré Artollen. You killed my people, and because of *you* I have had to rebuild from dirt and ashes. But war is a time for profit, to be sure. I can be patient. I knew you would roll through town, one of these days. Perhaps not for a span or a season, perhaps not for a year. But I've been waiting.'

Floré tried to keep track of the figures. There were none behind her, but at least a dozen of them throughout the room, each wielding a torch. All were cloaked but beneath the cloaks she saw patches of leather and steel. *Armoured.* In the hands not holding torches, she saw a meathook, cudgels, daggers. Hard eyes and fixed gazes, scarred faces and hands. *Professionals.*

'What do you want?' she asked, and as she spoke she unclasped her cloak and let it fall to the dusty floor. She felt a spike of fear. She couldn't fight a dozen criminals, alone. If she fought here she would die, and Tullen would turn all Undal to ash. *And Marta will never pick berries in Hookstone forest.* 'I can get you whatever you want. Money, whatever it is. Please. We can't do this now.'

'Oh, I want nothing special,' the Hanged Man said. 'Just you.'

~

Ashbringer had thought she could not sleep in the filth, but she must have dozed because when she woke he was there. *Deathless.* He was standing at the bars to her cell and smiling, clad in dark shirt and trousers and high boots. The dagger was tucked in a simple belt, obsidian blade out and open for any to see, and even in the dark of the dungeon the green gem on its pommel shone.

'Good morning, dear Ashbringer!'

She did not respond. She was rancid, days of sitting in her own filth with no water to drink, only a bowl of thin porridge to eat each day. She felt sick, her guts roiling and her head muddled. She gripped at her arms and leaned back hard against the cold stone of the wall. With a wave of his hand, a dozen torches lining the corridor blazed into light. Muttered voices from the other cells rose for a moment and then fell as the prisoners saw Tullen One-Eye, tall and straight-backed. He had shorn his head since she last saw him, and though his moustaches were still long, his beard was cropped close and thick, peppered with grey as it was. The eyepatch he wore was a simple strip of red cloth. He smiled at her, showing all his teeth.

'I've been neglecting you, my friend. I am sorry. Much is afoot! Come now. It is time to eat and be clean. We have a way to go.'

Tullen walked away and then there were attendants, a woman and a man dressed in rough-spun tunics who dragged her from the cell. She did not resist. She considered ripping out their throats, but Tullen would only make her comply eventually. *There is no resistance I can give.* They dragged her along a corridor to a room with a tub and threw her down.

'Wash,' one said and threw her a cloth. On a chair there was a set of clothing. The attendants didn't leave. They stood at the door and watched her as she stripped from her soiled and torn clothes and sank into the tepid water. Ashbringer cleaned herself, and as she did another attendant brought a tray of food – a bowl of thick stew, the meat cooked until it was grey and all the flavour boiled from the carrots and potatoes. The three of them stared at her and whispered in their own tongue, and she ignored them as best she could. Stepping from the tub of now-filthy water she rubbed herself down with the cloth they had left her and pulled on the clothes that had been left on the chair. It was a pair of trousers and a tunic, both dyed a garish red. Neither came close to fitting her, but there was a simple rope belt beneath and with that she could at least make them stay on.

She ate the food slowly, hating how much she needed it. How much she needed *him*. When the last morsel had been licked from the plate, she held it. The plate was a simple piece of fired clay. *I could break it, cut down her, then him, and the third with my teeth...* Ashbringer set the plate down and ran her hands over her scalp. What had once been assiduously shaven skin was now thick white stubble.

'Where is he?' she asked, and the attendants stared. Finally, two stood aside and gestured for her to follow the third. The two who had stood aside fell into step behind her, and she curled her lip. *Children of the storm.* Her muscles felt weak; she did not have her weapons or her magic. *This is what I have become, prisoner to children.*

Tullen was in a chamber at the top of the fort in Dun Fen, sat in a high-backed leather chair by a fire. When she was shown in he waved away the attendants, who bowed fearfully and carefully closed the door as they left. The room was high-ceilinged, with huge windows on three sides giving panoramic views of the town below and the moors beyond. Even with the leaden cloud above and the faint flurries of snow spiralling down, Ashbringer could see moorland, a little lake to the south, a forest at its edge.

'So you decided to hunt rust-folk,' he said at last and put down his book. It had a blue cover, but Ashbringer could not quite read the title. 'Why, pray tell? Were you bored?'

Ashbringer paced the room. The wall with no window was lined with bookshelves, and the floor was covered in thick woven rugs with bold sygaldry – a lion, a dragon, a towering tree. She went to the books.

'It seemed something to fill my time, since you hold me from my purpose,' she said, and trailed her finger across the spines. She heard Tullen sigh.

'Do you read much, Ashbringer?'

She shook her head.

'We have no written language,' she said after a long pause,

and left the books to stare out of the windows. 'Our history is story, told and told again. Our tongue is a song – how could you write a song? I can read Isken. I prefer to *be* than to think away my life.'

Tullen laughed at that, and on the little table by his chair a bottle raised itself into the air and poured out thick red wine into two cups. As the bottle settled down, he gestured to the second chair in the room across from him. Ashbringer sat and drank from the wine. It was sharp and rich. She had had no clean water for three days, and knew if she quenched thirst with this it would cloud her mind even further.

'You would rather be,' he said, sipping his own wine, 'but *be* what? You are a weapon. An assassin. Trained every day, all of your life. Trained to hunt and track, swindle and murder and bribe and cajole and intimidate. *Find the Deathless man.* And why? To fulfil the wish of *Anshuka*. She is a mirror, Ashbringer. She reflects what those who pray to her hope and fear. They fear the monsters of the storm, and so she makes the monsters of the storm. They hate themselves for the hell they call down on the ruins of Ferron, and so she sends the Claw Winter as punishment. The goblin, the crow-man, the rottroll, the wyrm. Each and every one you will find hidden in some Undalor folk tale from aeons back. They are the deepest fears of the people – the slavering beast, insatiable and stupid; the twisted creature with no morals, only power; the brutality of strength unchecked; the horror of a beast beyond all ken, which consumes without thought and takes without feeling. Do you understand yet?'

'Why not ask her to stop?' Ashbringer said, her voice so quiet. The crackle of logs burning in the fireplace was the only sound as Tullen stared at her, until she broke his gaze. *Break the bottle, take the jagged edge and… no.* She could not think of harming him. His bonds on her were too tight.

'What would you do, if you were me, Ashbringer?' he asked. 'The woman I love is dead, ripped to pieces by her own people in their fear when the storm came. I have sired no children. The empire I built is gone – these rust-folk are just some little mess. They mean nothing to me. Revenge? Mistress Water is dead three hundred years. Anshuka, oh I hate her. I love her, though. She was a Judge. We raised her higher than any other little god. There are so few, Ashbringer, so few true Judges, gods of great power in this world. With Ferron we made *more*. She was glorious, walking the plains of Ferron. Flowers bloomed wherever she stepped, and none felt fear. She was so delicate. The mistake was ours, giving our intention over their own. Instead of chance and fate guiding their character, we stepped in. Prayer. Focus. *Influence*. This is what I have done with Lothal, this new Lothal. I have raised him, but I did not press him. He will be what he will be – a wolf. There is beauty in that, isn't there? A purity in a creature unfettered by intellect. There is no evil in a wolf. There is no good. There is only its nature.'

Ashbringer placed down her glass of wine and pictured taking a burning log from the fire and setting it to the rugs, the hangings and tapestries, the wooden beams. Burning the whole fort to the ground. She took pleasure in the image of Dun Fen ablaze, until she thought of Tullen inside the flame, and then the thought died.

'You could be yourself, Ashbringer, without a pattern laid upon you,' Tullen said, and she turned her head to look at him better. She blinked, and he frowned.

'If I were you, Tullen One-Eye, slaver, murderer, war criminal,' she said, 'if my hands were so drenched in the blood of innocents for so many centuries, I would not allow myself the luxury of death. Death would perhaps be best, but I would use the power I had to make this world a better place. I would stop the rotstorm. I would heal the sick. I would build roads. I would sit in a room at the Undal City docks and turn dust to gold coins and hand them to the beggars. I would forget my petty vengeance, my dead woman, and I would think about the generations who suffered because of *my* crimes, and the generations who still suffer because of *my* crimes. I would do good works, or have the decency to die. I would realise I was a man and not a wolf. That with my intellect came a capacity for good and for evil.'

Tullen looked out of the window and poured himself more wine, by hand. He did not fill her glass.

'You won't do that though,' she said, 'because in the end you care only for you. Other people don't matter.'

Tullen drank his wine and shook his head.

'There are no other people, Ashbringer. I am alone.'

12

BLOOD AND BRANDY

'Your excellency, with my greatest feeling I must apologise. You know of course of the reparations we have sent, and the shame I have decreed. Tullen is our burning sword, but he is in the end a sword. There is a time for the sword, and this negotiation was not it. He has erred, and forgotten his place. Rest assured he will learn, and for now you have the sorrow of all Ferron. Please, accept these gifts – from the hives of Talpid, honey that you might remember our sweet past. From the laboratories of Jurron, one of Nessilitor's own light-sculptures – it will shine as long as the great owl lives, a symbol of our eternal fraternity.' – **Private letter**, Empress Seraphina of the Gilded Spire

They had descended until the tower sank into the fist of rock that was the Antian Redoubt, and suddenly the stone around them had opened into a warren. Grand chambers connected to storerooms connected to long corridors of sleeping chambers, a mixture of worked stone and blocks and almost organic white stone that curved smoothly. The only other Antian they saw were occasional guards who nodded with deference at the patrol leading Benazir and Yselda deeper and deeper into the rock. Their guards wound them downward until they came to a set of double doors where more than a dozen Antian were sat around. The doors were barred, and after a brief growled conversation the Antian picked up their spears and slowly opened the door.

Inside was a long low chamber, and from it many doors and corridors spread. It was full of people – hundreds of humans sat in clumps and huddles, old and young, all of them clad in layers and layers of clothing. There were piles of clothing, bundles, bedding, pans. *How long have they been here?*

The Antian gently pushed Benazir and Yselda in.

'Please!' a woman called, pushing towards the doors. 'Please, we need more food, and the water is running low. Do you have any healers? The children…'

The doors closed behind Yselda and Benazir with a heavy *thunk*, and then there was the grating sound of the wooden bar being dropped behind. All eyes in the room were on Benazir, and she breathed deep and held her left hand up in welcome.

'I am Commander Benazir Arfallow, of the Stormguard commandos. Who leads here?'

The woman who had yelled to the Antian came forward. She was perhaps in late middle age, Benazir thought, blonde hair braided down past her shoulders and a face worn by the sun. She wore a simple dress and shawl.

'You want Captain Nintur,' she said, and already the throngs of people sitting around were whispering to each other. 'He took charge after he came in a few spans back; he's been organising and keeping the peace.'

'Fascist!' a man just behind her said, and hawked spit at Benazir. She didn't flinch. The spittle landed on her boot, and she glanced down at it. 'Antian got us locked up in here, still better than facing the damn Stormguard. Cutting up folk just because they think they got a bit of rust in their blood. Killing rust-folk so much they took the whole bloody marches in revenge. Could have let them through to Isken, but no, no. Starbeck and his cronies need their war, and their wall. You one of his dogs, eh?'

Benazir breathed deep and looked around. Everyone was silent, watching. *Waiting to see how I react. How the Stormguard reacts.* On the wall it was all so easy.

'Any who kill without merit will meet the justice of the Stormguard, or one of the independent houses who deal with corruption,' she said, and held up a hand to stop him jumping in. 'I'll happily debate policy another time, but right now, I need to talk to Nintur.'

The man sniffed and stalked away, three others following in his wake, and Benazir was left to a muttering crowd. *That could have gone better.* Shaking her head she put her hand on the arm of the blonde woman.

'Nintur,' she said, and the woman nodded and began to lead them through the crowds. Many were wounded, most were sat by some bag or sack that was surely all their belongings in the world. A man was heaving, weeping next to a fireplace – one of the few in the long hall that was lit. The others were dim, even though fuel was piled high.

'Why not light more fires?' Benazir asked, and the woman shook her head. She didn't look back. Yselda followed at Benazir's shoulder, silent and pale. The girl looked so afraid, but Benazir could only push forward. *I'll chivvy her up when we have a minute that isn't absolutely bloody stupid.*

'You're here the day after fresh wood arrived,' the woman said. 'Last time we burned through it in a few days, and the next supplies still weren't for a span. Have to try and ration it, take turns by the fire.'

Benazir shook her head and scratched the scars on her chin.

'The Antian are our allies,' Yselda said. 'Why would they do this? They won't let you leave?'

The woman paused and turned to them. She squinted at Yselda and then at Benazir, who shrugged. *Let her explain it.* It was clear enough to Benazir. As the woman spoke to Yselda, Benazir looked around, counting the refugees.

'Leave to go where, girl? Aber-Ouse is a span or more on foot, in good weather. It's a Claw Winter. More than half would die on the road, and those who made it, you think it's going to be any better up there? They haven't let us out into their city proper, but they don't hurt us. Any who want to leave can leave, but they can't come back. They keep us locked up so we don't wander round their home. I don't know what they're about, but they haven't hurt none who didn't need hurting. Food is meagre, but meagre is better than none. We want more, course we do. But I'm not for knowing they have more to give, right now.'

Yselda grimaced and gripped the locket around her neck, but didn't respond. The woman led them on, through the hall, and whispers followed them. Benazir held her tongue and tried to keep her calm. *Fascist.* She'd lost her love, lost her arm, given her whole life to keep these people safe. *And they call me a fascist.* She breathed deep and let the anger sink down inside her into that black pool where all of it, the hate and pain and rage and fear, lived. She pushed it down, and the pit roiled but her face remained calm. *What do you want, Benazir?* Nobody asked her what she wanted. They just expected her to serve and serve and serve. *Even Floré...*

The blonde woman showed them to a side room, a barracks lined with small Antian beds where a dozen lancers were lounging. Some played dice, others were cooking over a small fire in a hearth in the wall, and a few were wrestling, slick with sweat. She could tell they were lancers. Even the women were tall, all of them heavily muscled. A few wore tabards, but only one of them could have been Nintur. Benazir knew he was in command before she saw his rank badge – he was a tall man, hatchet-faced and grim, hair cut back into a utilitarian buzz. As the others lounged, he was at a table inspecting a map by candlelight. He looked up when they entered; they all looked up except the wrestlers. The wrestlers continued for a long moment in the silence and then one of them slammed the other down hard, driving the wind out of her.

'Ha!' he said, out of breath. 'Ha bloody ha, did you see that, Garren?'

The wrestler looked up and realised Garren wasn't watching – nobody was watching. All of them were staring at Benazir, tabard blazing red emblazoned with a golden bolt of lightning that shone in the faint candlelight. She raised her hook and pointed it at the man at the desk.

'Captain Nintur. I'm Bolt-Commander Benazir Arfallow. Starbeck sent me. Where is the girl?'

Nintur set down his map and stared at her for a long moment, and then turned to the back of the room. Every eye followed his gaze. In an Antian bed, pushed close to the cooking hearth, Benazir had thought there was a pile of old blankets and clothes, but as she stared she saw a mess of ashen curls slick with sweat. *Marta*. In ten quick strides Benazir was at the bed, and she heard the scrape of Nintur's chair as he stood but no lancer made a move to stop her. Yselda was with her, and they both knelt at Marta's bedside. The girl was thin, her breathing rapid, and Benazir felt a fever on her brow when she pressed her hand to it. She cupped Marta's chin and gazed at her a long moment, and Marta's eyelids fluttered.

'Benny?' she said, and Benazir leaned down close and held her tight. Marta blinked and crinkled her nose, smiled up at Benazir. 'I rode a horse, Benny. His name was Bubbles. Is Mama here?'

'I'm here, love,' Benazir said, and Marta closed her eyes as Benazir pressed her hand to the girl's head and gently stroked her hair. 'I'm here. You'll see your mama soon. Rest, little one. Rest.'

She held Marta tight for a long moment until she felt the girl settle, and then with her good arm lowered her back to the bed. She stood and locked eyes with Yselda, the girl's face stricken, and then she turned and nodded to Nintur. All through the room the lancers stared at her with bated breath.

'New mission,' she said quietly. She didn't want to wake the babe. Slowly she scratched at the scar on her chin with the dull side of her hook and took in the soldiers in front of her. 'Get your shit, get squared away. We need to have a chat, or do some violence.'

~

Floré flexed her forearms and wrists and fingers, her gauntlet segments cracking together. The blade in her hand was a familiar weight, and all her scheming and planning stopped. All her worry and fear for Marta stopped, the worry that had blinded her so far as to let her wander into so obvious a trap. All of it was gone, and there was the fury, that beast that lived inside her chained – but now the chains were broken. She let the fury fill her, and she didn't think about picking berries in the forest, or the press of Janos's hand against her own. Those thoughts were buried by the beast, the burning creature that rose inside her.

Floré looked around the locked room and spat on the floor. There was a single exit, behind her. The left wall was stacked with barrels, the right with crates. Thirteen enemies, armed with fire and steel. Armoured and angry. She didn't need to think about crow-men, didn't need to think about the morality of killing goblins and their kin. *These people made their choice.*

'Thanks for returning this,' she said, and raised her sword, the sword-knot dangling from the hilt – red with a white stripe at its core, damp forever with the arcana of the founder of the realm. The Hanged Man stared at her, and the twelve thugs began to spread in a wide semi-circle. Half of them slotted their torches into wall sconces, and a few slipped off cloaks and rolled their shoulders. Floré took two steps forward rather than stick with her back to the locked door, her eyes darting at the newly illuminated room for any advantage. 'Do you know the significance of it?'

The Hanged Man shrugged. Floré breathed in three sharp breaths, getting as much air in her blood as she could, and began to stretch out. The old scar up her right arm was tingling, the lightning-burned nerves singing as she prepared to act.

'Some Stormguard thing,' the Hanged Man said. 'I care not. I only wanted you to know you were not forgotten. Actions have consequences. Respect is due, and revenge is necessary. You kill my people, there is only one ending.' The Hanged Man went to the right and leaned against a crate and pretended to inspect her nails. *Bitch.* 'Kill her. Make it hurt.'

The nearest two moved for her, but Floré was already running hard right. *Respect is due, and revenge is necessary.* It was a good line – she was sure the woman had practised it. As they began to close on her Floré felt a sickening wave of fear, but she instead let her anger overpower it. *How dare they?* If she died here, they would leave Marta an orphan. If she died here, Tullen One-Eye would burn Undal to the ground. *If I die here,* she thought, spiralling her sword with her wrist, *I'll never be able to make it right.*

The man on the outer right of the circle had a shortsword and a torch, and as she ran at him he pulled the sword back and pushed the torch forward. *As if I would stop.* A sensible warrior would dance and parry, would keep their distance and hope for help. Floré could not afford sense. *I won't die here!* She didn't swing her sword, didn't give him that beat to bring his own to bear. She kept her blade close to her chest, diagonally up to deflect his own if it happened to land, and barrelled into him. They went down in a pile, the torch between them, but Floré's sword blade was pressed in a line across his chest and she jerked the blade to the right, digging into his neck. She ignored the burning at her chest and gripped the upper end of her sword blade with her gauntlet, trusting the steel to protect her fingers. Gripped like that she could swing it around over his neck, just as the runes across it tasted blood and flared with heat and light.

His torch was dropped, his sword waving ineffectually. The sword pressed across his whole neck with a wet explosion, and his blood sprayed up across her face. Floré let out a yell as it filled her mouth, her eyes – a yell of pure rage and frustration and hate. *You won't keep me from her!* The blood and meat below sizzled and boiled as the blade grew white-hot.

Floré spat the dead man's blood and scrambled up, and it was just as she thought. They thought he'd kill her, and they'd held back. *If you were Stormguard, I'd be dead already.* Drenched in blood, sword aflame, Floré pointed at the room and screamed again with every ounce of rage in her soul.

'You won't take me from her!'

There were three in the next layer, and they were reeling from the flame of her blade. She could taste iron in her mouth, and she blinked the blood free. She spun the burning sword in a series of twirls in her left hand as she advanced, but that meant none were watching her right fist as it flicked forward underhand, moving from hip to shoulder in a heartbeat. Tyr's silver blade sank into the gut of a woman who collapsed to her knees, and then Floré was stamping forward, a series of brutal chops batting aside the defence of one and cutting deep into his chest, and a backhand with the gauntlet slapping the other to the ground after she parried his long dagger.

Those behind them were quick to dart in but a long sweep of the flaming sword kept them back, and she finished the sweep by burying her sword in the back of the head of the kneeling woman with the dagger in her gut. The woman pitched forward dead, and Floré held her sword firm.

'She isn't paying you enough to die,' she roared, and to emphasise her point skewered her blade into the stunned man she had backhanded who was starting to regain his feet.

Suddenly she was on the ground with a brutal slam as a figure darted from the darkness to her left and tackled her. She didn't feel a stab or a cut – he'd taken her to ground and was scrabbling back, hips over hers pinning her down on her side. He struck down twice, thrice, with his fists on her head and then reached back for his weapon. Floré still had a grip on her sword but couldn't bring it to bear so she dropped it and grabbed a burning torch dropped by the man she'd killed first. She flailed it with her left hand and the man on top of her leaned back for a second, but that was enough. Kicking and scrambling herself free she pulled back.

There were still eight of them – two hung back next to the Hanged Man, but the rest spread out wide. Floré pulled herself up and backed up to the left of the room, back to the rows of barrels small and large that lined the wall.

'You can't fight eight people with a torch,' the man who'd tackled her said, and from the back of his belt pulled out his weapon – the meathook she had spotted earlier. One of the others darted forward and retrieved Starbeck's rune-sword from the debris and blood, then yelped as the blade caught flame. The handle would be unbearably hot without armour.

Floré met the eyes of each of her attackers, one by one. She saw resolve, and she saw her reflection – blood-drenched, lightly armoured, unarmed save for a guttering torch. Floré threw her torch to the floor at the feet of her nearest foes and raised her hands, and the thug with the rune-sword picked it back up, his hand wrapped in rags. He stepped forward and pointed it at her, and Floré grinned.

'Ever heard of *eyes sharp, blade sharper?*' she said, and with a twist she grabbed the small barrel from the rack next to her at head height and sent it spinning at the big man with the meat hook. He didn't dodge it, but leaned his shoulder into it and the cheap wood cracked, covering him in liquid. He snorted.

'It'll take more than a barrel of wine to—'

Whatever he was going to say was lost in a scream as the torch at his feet caught the liquid and a trail of flame burned up him, coating his arm, his shoulder, his face. He began to career around the room screaming, and Floré picked up the next barrel.

'Brandy!' she shouted over the screams. 'Fucker should have said *brandy*!'

She threw the second barrel but the remaining thugs were already scrambling back, and the one holding the flaming sword threw it down with a shriek and ran for the door. The burning man collapsed, and the second barrel landed and rolled away, unbroken. Floré stepped forward and scooped up her sword, and wiped the blood from her nose on the back of her wrist, feeling the heat from the blade.

Two of them were at the door, the others huddling at the back of the room around the Hanged Man with their weapons raised. She turned from them and fell on the two wrangling with the door, skewering the first even as she shoulder-charged the second, and then impaling her too as she fell, pushing the blade deep past batting hands. The woman had lost her steel.

Amateurs. I won't die to amateurs! She had a deathless man to kill, her daughter to save.

Floré turned back to the remaining thugs and flourished her sword. There were still so many of them, but beneath her boiling blood there was an iron certainty in Floré's heart. *They will not keep me from Marta.* Behind her the lock clicked.

'Commander!'

Cuss burst through the door with Tomas and three others clad in City Watch grey. Floré smiled, teeth sticky with blood, and turned back to the Hanged Man.

'I've got things to do,' she said, and spat a mouthful of blood to the floor. 'But they can wait a moment. No, no. No. Pick up your knife. We aren't done.'

INTERLUDES:
BLADE SHARPER

THE POWER OF THE SUN

'The ruins of Ferron and the rotstorm are our most pressing threat. Tessendorm have increased their slave raiding from the north-west, but with three lancer regiments on rotation there is little to fear. Isken have a small standing army but enough coin and favour for every mercenary in Carob's Strait to come calling. Kelamor, Uradech, and Cinnae will trade with us through Isken, but beyond that are not worth focus. Similarly, the savage lands of Ona and Siobh are known to us only through the Caroban ports, but there is little trade and less risk. The pirate kingdoms of the Crown Isles make any sea trade past Kelamor a risk, and as ever Cil-Marie blocks the south, impenetrable and inscrutable. There are rumoured trade routes south of the Crown Islands, but every tale tells of a different world. The Antian and Tullioch have each made their separate peace with us. The protectorate can flourish if we keep the rust-folk and monsters of old Ferron in check, the pockets of the Isken traders full, and our border with Tessendorm strong.' – *Memorandum to the Grand Council on the question of extant threats,* Commissar-Mage Inigo

Jehanne de Thibault du Cilcan, Commandant-arc du Fantôme, was meticulous. When the boy came for her she was already in her dress uniform. Her page had picked the dust from it piece by piece, and the black silk was immaculate. The gold trim at her collar was no less than she was entitled, and as she broke her fast with fresh fruit her page brushed her hair, over and over and over until it was thick and magnificent. He did not raise his eyes as he worked, and he took great care to be quiet and unobtrusive. *A good boy,* she thought. The messenger also did not look her in the eye, and waited for her to wave him in. Arnoulet wanted her – she had waited three days for this summons, three days thinking on her mistakes.

She did not glance at herself in the mirrors lining the Sun Palace as she walked to her appointment. She did not need to. *You are the daughter of great men. You are the daughter of great women. You are the daughter of soldiers, diplomats, wizards, and royalty. You are magnificent.* She repeated the mantra over and over, the mantra she had been taught as a child so she would understand her place in the world.

It was the height of summer in Cil-Marie, but Jehanne did not sweat. She did not *allow* herself to sweat. She had spent months in the jungles of Siobh and Caroban, had spent a year at court in Kelamor. She had done her time in beautiful Cilcan as well, of course, three years of courtly intrigue, murder, and the purging of dissidents. She was master of her own body. She had earned her hammer. *You are a faithful weapon,* she told herself, once again. *You could not have known. You were betrayed.*

The Sun Palace was a huge complex, sprawling over many buildings. The buildings where Cil-Marie was governed and the Sun Masters ruled were protected by no wall, only a row of flowers meticulously tended. To step across the flower wall without invite was punishable by banishment, death, disfigurement – all of the usual. Jehanne stepped over it, as she always did, without hesitation. She did not need an invitation – her rank was her right. The gardeners of the Sun Palace who were tending to the flower beds bowed in deference.

When she reached his offices, the door was open and Arnoulet was drinking tea. She waited until she was bid enter, and when he finally noticed her in the doorway he lazily waved for her to sit. In court, rigid rules must be followed, but they had campaigned together, hunting dissidents in the south of Cil through the dark forests. Arnoulet would not stand on formality. His office was panelled in light wood, a warm space lined with books and filled with chairs and low tables and desks. Every desk and table was piled with maps and reports, cluttered and utterly opposite the careful decorum of the rest of the Sun Palace.

'Tea?' he asked, and she shook her head. He shrugged and poured himself another cup from the pot on his desk, spilling drops on the immaculate paperwork all around. In a land of perfection, Arnoulet was the ragged edge. Jehanne smiled. *Sometimes a ragged edge is needed. A tidy mind misses much.*

'It is faddish, I admit,' he said, 'but I have to say I rather do find myself actually enjoying it. Now. Jehanne. We must speak on your next mission.'

Jehanne sat poised and still and watched his face intently, looking for any expression that might hint at his true meaning.

'I had thought we might discuss my *last* mission, Colonel Arnoulet. I am glad to see you in good health.'

He shrugged and leaned back in his chair, and put his cup

down on a map of the Crown Isles carelessly. Jehanne leaned across and took up the cup and put it back on its tray.

'Someone spent many hours drawing out that map, Colonel,' she said, and he laughed.

'By the time I need a map of the Crowns, enough will have changed that I'll commission a new one from the library. Do not worry, Commandant. I have read your report, I have spoken to the survivors. I have spoken with the other colonels. None blame you. The first lesson of warfare is how to *lose*, not how to win. Ihm-Phogn said – *if you are not prepared to lose, do not even begin*. Do you want to talk about it?'

Jehanne forced her hands not to clench into fists. In her mind she could picture the faces of the three men she had left behind. Could taste iron, water, and blood. *Dead, or worse*.

'You were meant to be supporting those rebels who fight against the mage-king of Caroban, establishing a web of informants, all of the usual. You spent a year in the jungles, built a network, kept your head down and your profile low – and then you show up at our embassy in Uradech, a few hundred miles in the wrong direction, fevered and wounded and, by all reports, wild-eyed, even. Most of your team still in Caroban. What went wrong, Jehanne?'

In the calm of Arnoulet's study, Jehanne could taste the humid air of the Caroban jungle, could hear voices in the trees.

'The rebel cell was betrayed,' she said, carefully clinical in her tone. 'Someone in our network was breached. The mage-king did not come himself, but sent the equivalent of two legions. They burned the jungle ten miles in every direction, a great circle closing in on us. By the time we knew we were surrounded, there was nowhere left to flee.'

'Yet flee you did, and with half your team alive. How? I have read the report. I want the story.'

Jehanne frowned. *He has been too long behind a desk*. Her

love for Arnoulet ran deep, and he had taught her the brutality necessary to their work, but still an ember of rage seethed in her. *The story. As if it is just another report on his desk.* Of course, it was. She knew that.

Jehanne could not bring herself to lose decorum, and so rather than clench her fists and blow a hot breath through her nose, she clenched the toes on her right foot, hidden beneath the table. She clenched them until her foot ached and then let them go, and smiled at Arnoulet. *Composed. You must be composed, if you are to serve.*

'I lost three of my team in the initial confusion,' she said. 'One was elsewhere in the camp, the other two were at secondary camps to the north and east – rumour in the city afterward leads me to believe these camps were targeted in a similar style, on the same night. They are dead, or captured. The others stuck close to me. We spent a night treading water in the waste pit of one of the mines as the jungle around us burned. A handful of rebels with us. I lost another two in there. If they had the location of our camp with enough notice to organise such an attack, then the network was compromised. Without the leadership, this iteration of the rebellion was doomed to a slow death. I thought it prudent to withdraw, and so when the fire had passed us we trekked through the jungle to Caroban city and stowed away on a trader heading to Uradech, and then found our way to the embassy there.'

She did not tell him about the leeches, the junior officer who was killed by a jaguar as they slept, her neck snapped. How they woke to see her wedged in the crook of a tree high above, staring down, the great black cat next to it utterly unafraid, its eyes assessing them lazily. She did not mention the rebels she had killed herself, the three who had stayed with them in the slurry pit all through the night, who had marched with them from jungle camp to jungle camp for the whole year before

– who had carried out a dozen raids at her suggestion, who had treated her with respect and friendship and had shared bread and wine and more with her.

She had broken them one by one with her hammer, unsure if they could be trusted. She did not tell him about the stinging flies, or how when they reached Caroban, the mage-king's agents were searching every ship and the only way aboard was packed in great crates below endless green bananas, spaces that cost her every promise and coin she could scramble from the hidden caches in the city. The summary was in her report, but the report did not tell of the spiders large as a hand that crawled across the fruit, or the first mate who wanted to be paid double once they were out of sight of land. *I kept my hammer,* she thought, and she did not tell Arnoulet about the nightmares.

'I'm sorry, Colonel,' she said, and he shook his head.

'No apologies, Jehanne. You are a ghost – this is the work. They had a year of your advice, and their cause was stronger for it. You taught. Those who survived will heed those lessons. Every revolution is built on the bones of the one that failed before it. Caroban will weaken, and Cil-Marie will stay secure as the mage-king's gaze turns inwards instead of out.'

Jehanne bowed her head in deference. Arnoulet refilled his tea, and again gestured to offer her some, and this time she accepted. It was bitter and lukewarm, and tasted like flowers. She forced herself to take long sips, matching his own. *A stupid fad. Give me a cup of wine any day.* Since she was last in the capital everyone was suddenly drinking tea, comparing blends. Jehanne thought it gauche, to embrace some foreign drink so eagerly. But the upper streets of Cilcan thronged with new teahouses.

'The next mission, sir?' she asked, and Arnoulet shuffled through papers on the low table until he produced a map of

Morost, from Caroban in the east to the rotstorm in the west. It cut off at the southern border of Cil-Marie, not showing the wild lands beyond in all directions, those distant islands and continents that were a mixture of guesses and hysteria. Arnoulet tapped the Undal Protectorate, that little strip of land between the rotstorm in the west and the powers of the merchants of Isken and the savage 'barons' of Tessendorm.

'There are disturbing rumours from Undal,' he said, 'lights that travel across the sky. Our records show Ferron was using great orbs of light to transport people, livestock, all sorts in the final years before his sudden disappearance. If this technology has been found, it is of vital importance we retrieve it. This is your primary goal. Second to that, these last ten years you have excelled – wherever there is an insurgency, we send you, and you fan the flames. One of those who live in the rotstorm has come to us – *rust-folk*, they call themselves. His name is Amon. The remnants of the Ferron Empire that survive beneath the rotstorm are desperate. They've schemes and magic, but no standing army. We'd send you there, as a lone agent. Foment a rebellion, keep Undal focused to the west, rather than the south. There are other rumours, of the bones of dead spirits... You know the Sun Masters would well reward any actionable intelligence on such matters.'

Jehanne could not keep her face still. She had commanded a dozen agents and a hundred informants beyond in Caroban. She had advised armies, been spymaster to royalty and great power. *A lone agent?* She grimaced fiercely before managing to control her expression, but Arnoulet saw it. The Undal were a backward country at the edge of the world – they hardly posed a threat to Cil-Marie. *A backward country,* she thought, *and children's tales of dead spirits and flying orbs. Sun preserve me!*

'Commandant,' Arnoulet said, and he set down his tea and leaned forward. 'Listen to me close. The orbs could change everything, if they are real. Your role advising the rust-folk is simply our easiest access. In Ferron, beneath the rotstorm there are the bones of spirits, Jehanne. Lothal the wolf. Berren the dryad. The Sun Masters have spent long centuries mining power from the bones of our own spirits. The orbs would be a great boon. Any trace or remnant of fallen spirits would be an even greater one. We hunt the little spirits, Jehanne, but there are no great spirits left in our lands, and the bones grow sparse.

'This is not a demotion. This is a mission I trust only to you. Bring us an orb, bring us the location of the bones of the dead Ferron Judges. This *rotstorm* has lingered over the waters to our north-west for three centuries, and not even the Sun Masters have been able to shift it. They want support. You are a lone agent, Commandant, because I am not sending other agents. I am sending you a fleet. If you need more, we will send more. Nothing is of higher priority.'

Jehanne's face flushed and her hand went to her belt, to her hammer. The hammer she was given when she attained her rank. Her badge of office, the weight and trust that the Sun Masters held in her. She felt the cold metal of its head and her fingers traced the arcing grooves and glyphs incised across its face. *A fleet. The bones of a Judge. Orbs of light.* She nodded to Arnoulet and allowed herself a smile.

'I have a research dossier,' he said, 'and then this afternoon, if you are ready, you can meet their messenger. Amon, he is called, as I said. Tomorrow the fleet commander awaits your inspection and briefing. This is not going to be simple, Jehanne. This rotstorm is hell itself, and we are talking of the bones of their gods. For the bones of a Judge of Ferron, no price is too high.'

Jehanne sipped her tea. *Is it jasmine?* She was starting to taste different notes in it, as it cooled.

'There are no gods, Arnoulet,' she said, and he raised his cup in agreement. 'There is only Cil-Marie, and we must stay strong.'

THE DRAGON ABOVE, THE SNAKE BELOW

'*The castrum has received a strange report from the village of Auchenbelg, near Laga, south of the Slow Marsh. A bogle has been killed. This report was verified by a skein-mage on secondment with the City Watch in Laga. Castrum records indicate that this bogle has been known since before the founding of the protectorate. No recorded cases of the death of a bogle or place-spirit are accompanied by a physical corpse, save the death of the Ferron Judge Lothal, whose bones remain within the rotstorm. The bogle of this glade outside of Auchenbelg was an otter of a remarkable living stone, with flesh of sinuous granite and claws and whiskers of shining iron. Its eyes were said to be green glass. Accompanying the report, the ossified corpse of the otter – the eyes are dun and grey. Any malleability the stone flesh may have had is lost, and it resembles a statue in death. Where it was wounded, organs and vessels of stone can be seen of workmanship impossible by hand – indeed, our skein-mages have agreed that based on inspection within the skein, this was indeed a bogle.*' – *A note on the otter of Auchenbelg,* Primus Thum-Pho

Torrenda awoke in the witch's room carved deep in the rock beneath the wayhouse in Laitila. It was warm, and she could hear the pounding of rain on the distant roof. A blanket was over her, and the little fox tulka pressed its warmth against her chest. *No.* She realised at once what was wrong. The peat brick in the pouch cinched tight at her waist was warm, but the usual flickering pain of its heat was dulled.

'No no no!'

With one hand she scooped up the fox and placed it down on the rug, where it blinked up at her. After stripping off the heavy woollen jumper, she reached under her tunic and found the twisted knot holding the brick in place. With the bag removed she felt the usual odd lightness and flexibility around the waist, and the coolness on her stomach, its skin filigreed with broken veins from the constant burning heat for so many years now.

Torrenda opened the pouch and stared down at what remained of the peat brick. There was no spark or flame – *not that there should be* – but also no curling smoke that might hint of the slow smoulder she was meant to maintain.

'Dead,' she said at last, and closed the bag. There was a single candle burning low in the room, sat in a saucer on top of the rug. She did not have any urge to try and relight the brick – it was meant to be lit at a shrine and carried to the next. An act of worship. A practice of meditation, walking flame so far in the cold and wet for the service of others.

Torrenda scratched at the fox's head, tilted its chin to check the wound on its cheek where the scorpion had struck it three days before. The wound was sealed, but still swollen. *Tulka striking tulka,* she thought, *tulka wandering the wilds, following shrinekeepers as they walk in the rain.* Nothing changed in Ona – the rain fell, the shrubs grew, the father danced in the sky above. Peace and stillness. A house might be built, when another tumbled. A child would be born. *But nothing like this.*

Torrenda pulled her jumper back on and slipped the peat brick and its pouch into her backpack. The truth she knew was that nobody needed a shrinekeeper. She was a relic of ancient days when fire was so hard to find that the hardiest would wander the wilds, bringing the spark to those who needed it, who would in turn guard it as long as they were able. Ona was wet, always wet, wet underbrush and wet kindling and wet fuel, as the storms that grew over the Crown Isles crashed on the barrier mountains that protected Ona from strangers, from war, from trade, from everything except the rains. *Nothing changes.*

Generations ago they had started building better, had started cultivating the little shrub-birch betulac with its oily bark that lit even when soaked, had learned to stock fuel under oiled skins or in dry caves carved from the rock pillars themselves. *They haven't needed someone like me in three generations.* Torrenda didn't carry the spark for utility's sake – she did it to worship the father above who had given it to them, who had raised the barrier mountains and kept them safe with their fertile canyons and protected pillars. *I do it because I don't know how to do anything else.*

Wincing at the pain in her wounded arm, Torrenda left her bag and her jacket and mudded boots and climbed in woollen socks up the bare stone steps of the witch's room and into the wayhouse above. The rope weavers had gone, and there was only the stern face of Taaveti the wayhouse tender leaning over her low bar. She was deep in discussion with the young witch Aida, who was mixing a panoply of herbs into an old wineskin. The bar was littered with many more, pouches and bottles and sprigs tied tight, and the witch tore into them with a knife no bigger than her thumb, eyes tight.

'You're awake,' Taaveti said, and actually smiled. 'Aida told me what is occurring. I've soup for you, and a fresh loaf. Fresh clothes in the dry room, and hot water for a bath.

When the fox peered out from behind Torrenda's ankles, Taaveti tugged at her braid and raised one hand shoulder high, palm upward. A hand supplicating to the great dragon above.

'Will it eat?' she asked, and Torrenda laughed and shrugged.

'You know as much as I, Taaveti. But if something could tempt a spirit to eat, it would be your bread.'

The fox stayed by the wayhouse bar curled on an old chair as Torrenda emptied her pack and boots and coat into the dry room and scrubbed mud from them. The bath was hot enough to prickle her skin, but after three days' walking her whole body was taut and when she emerged in fresh clothes to a fresh batch of salve on her arm and a bowl of hot soup she began to feel calmer. It was a few moments of peace, of stillness, and then Aida returned through the front door of the wayhouse, soaked with rain and swearing.

'Ash and piss!' she said, and Taaveti clucked her tongue at the young woman.

'Mind yourself!' she said, and Aida pulled her rain cloak free and hung it roughly on a peg, gripping it for a long moment and lowering her head.

'The shrine north of town is cracked,' she said. Torrenda carefully placed down her mug of sweet mead and pulled the little fox tulka close to her chest. It blinked up at her with its glistening pearl eyes and huffed a breath.

'Tell me,' Torrenda said, and the three of them sat. The hearth was burning low and the room was warm but Torrenda listened to the rain on the wayhouse roof and pictured the little shrine north of Laitila. It was the same slick black dragon stone as the other shrines. From memory you had to climb the steep winding cutbacks from the Laitila rock spire and then it was north a mile, where a crumbled rock spire had blocked a canyon centuries and centuries before. In the stump of that spire, buried in rock with only a foot of black peeking from the rough brown, sat the dragon stone. The rest of the rock was sheer and broken, and no plants grew on the bare stone. Over the black of the dragon stone a simple cairn was built with a hollow at its core.

'It is cracked,' the witch said, and Taaveti scratched at her chin and disappeared behind the bar, returning with three thimble mugs and a bottle of clear liquid.

'Sap leaf,' she grunted, and poured them each a drink. Before Torrenda had even reached hers, Aida the witch had drunk hers down and was rubbing at her eyes.

'It's cracked,' she said again. 'Cracks of hot silver. They are cold but they glow like molten metal. I looked, in the river below. I lowered my mind and I looked and where there should have been a knot, there was a... break. A break in the pattern. Great currents, the currents that normally fall beyond your eye when you swim the river – they were *wrong*. Twisting on themselves. Self-contained. A snake eating its own tail.'

Torrenda drank her shot of sap leaf, the only liquor brewed in Ona other than the sweet honey mead. It was sharp and tasted thick and grassy, and the warmth spread through her chest. With both hands she held the tulka close, pressed her fingers into its black fur, felt the beat of its heart. *You are alive, little spirit.*

'I have not swum the river,' she said, and Aida nodded. Few had. The river below, the river that all things were in whether they knew it or not. *A river that joins the world.* Sami, the old witch with his beard and his smile who had been a constant in her life whenever her feet took her to Laitila had told her it was a river of connection, and when you were in it you could see the streams and currents that reached everyone and everything and drove everyone and everything onward.

'The river takes us from birth to death, from what is before to what is after,' Aida said, and the three of them sat in silence for a long moment. Torrenda knew it was the way of it – you would live and you would die, and perhaps would live again. Water fell from the sky and into the river, and the river flowed to the sea, and clouds grew and then the rain fell again. All was cycle, all was current. It was as simple as breathing.

'What can we do?' Taaveti said, and Aida drew from her bag the wineskin she had been preparing earlier.

'I want to dive,' she said.

Torrenda licked her lips. With no boots and no cloak and no brick of burning peat, she felt naked and weak. *What am I doing?*

'That is dangerous, no?' Torrenda asked. 'We should tell someone, no?'

Aida shook her head and unstopped the wineskin. 'Tell who, Shrinekeeper? Wasserchild is weeks away. We'll tell them, but I have the herbs and I've done it before. I want to dive into the river deep, and see all Ona. I'll keep the shrines in my heart and see what I can see.'

Aida sniffed the wineskin, and Taaveti slugged back her sap-leaf spirit and thumbed at her nose.

'How does it work?'

'I can swim the river,' Aida said, 'but the herbs let anyone touch the river, with this mix. They let you dive. You've had them before a little – it's what is in the mead the witches give on your name day.'

Torrenda remembered her own name day – fifteen flood seasons old, standing with Karle and Jussi. The witch then was a man with hair braided to his chest, a short man like a barrel who wore string after string around his neck, on each string some totem – a lizard's foot, a fox's tooth. She had drunk her wine and spoken her name for the first time – *Torrenda*. Before fifteen flood seasons you were a child, but after that you had choice and responsibility. Your first choice was your name.

What will you be, Torrenda? the witch had asked, and she had looked at the floor when she said: *Shrinekeeper*. Not out of shame, but because the press of people was too much. She had drunk the mead, and seen the river for the first time – currents of light and sound and sensation, feelings she had no words for linking her to her brothers, her village, her world. It had faded fast, and then there was firelight and dancing and songs to be sung – but the memory of it was as clear now as it had been in the moment of experience.

'I would like to do it,' she said, and Aida and Taaveti stared at her.

'This is not your name day,' Aida said, 'and this will be deeper in the river than many ever go. It might wash you away.'

Torrenda shook her head and pushed her hair back, set her jaw.

'I know every shrine in Ona. I know two dozen tulka, and every pathway of the thousand canyons. We dive together, and I can hold them in my heart. Every last one of them.'

It wasn't true, but it wasn't a lie. *I know more than any who is not a shrinekeeper.*

'It might work,' Aida said, and Taaveti poured them each another shot of the sap leaf. Across the table they joined their left hands, and the fox tulka stepped delicately up to the table, its onyx claws tapping on the wood. It stood still and they stared at it, and then Aida drank deep from the wineskin.

'Hold them in your heart,' she said, and then Torrenda drank three swallows fast and blanched as the bitter herbs burned her throat. Squeezing her eyes shut against the pain, she felt Aida grasp her hand and then hearing fled from her, taste fled from her. When she opened her eyes all was colour and light, pattern and connection. Aida and Taaveti both collapsed into layers of light and tangle and pattern and chaos, the tumult of life. Next to them, the fox tulka stared at her and she saw that it was a fruit, a fruit grown from a million lines of thought that stretched hair thin through the air, each a different colour and strength and taste. Torrenda began to panic at the overstimulation, human senses overloaded with input from an infinite number of sources, every nerve in her body taut.

Keep them in your heart, she heard a voice say. *Aida's voice? My voice?* She closed her eyes and thought of the dragon shrines.

The crossroads.

The waterfall.

The broken pillar. The twisted birch.

The painted cavern. The chimney-top. The river's heart.

On and on she pictured them and felt her love for them. Pictured her journeys to them, her joy at finding them lit, her patience when they lay cold and dark. Torrenda could still feel the stimulus across her, her skin, her tongue, her ears, her fingertips, and when she opened her eyes she was below the clouds staring down at Ona, that labyrinth of rock chimney and canyon surrounded by the barrier mountains. All was abstract, but she could see the pattern of her land and knew it to be her land even though she had never seen it this way before, had never seen a map that came close to encompassing it.

Look.

Aida's voice. Aida's pattern, its hand in hers, staring down from the clouds through rain, each droplet with a path before it and a trajectory behind traced in light and heat and feeling. Torrenda pictured the dragon stones and with all her heart focused on the slick black rock.

Below, lights began to twinkle, lights of silver brighter than the surrounding pattern. Somewhere she felt her body burning with fever as she struggled to concentrate, somewhere she felt the twitch of muscles spasming as the dive took from her, took her energy even to perceive the river, even with the witch's herbs.

Look.

Across Ona, the silver lights – *dragon stones* – glowed, and as she stared she realised what the twinkle was – it was a break, like a candle flickering through a broken lamp. *They are all broken.*

Torrenda could see them all, all of Ona – perhaps three dozen dragon stones were twinkling, and in her heart she knew every one was broken.

Are they all broken?

Her own voice, and faintly, Aida yelling... *Stop!*

Clouds above turned to clouds below. Torrenda tasted blood at some level as she bit through her tongue, as her body jerked at the wayhouse table in Laitila. She was back further now. She could see Ona, could see land north, could see sea to the west and the thousands of islands of the Crowns. Continents and seas beyond. Back further, and she could see it all, all of it pattern and oddity, some close, some far and some sideways. Links and currents, a river churning over all of it – not a smooth river but the churn of rapids, of white water and chaos. Twinkling lights... the dozens of dragon stones of Ona joined by hundreds more across ocean and land and mountain and deep. Some buried deep below rock, but in the river she could still see them and feel them and taste them. Twinkling. *Broken.*

The first seizure almost pulled her from the river, and she felt a hand dragging her from the clouds but Torrenda pulled her own hand away. *If the dragon stones are broken...*

Father!

In her heart Torrenda was a shrinekeeper – she walked the valleys of sodden Ona with her ever-burning brick, and she brought cheer and light and heat and a reminder of the father dragon above to the people of her land.

Below her, in the morass of tangled connection that was the world, the lights of the dragon stones fell dim as her focus turned to the father dragon. From so high above the world she saw him, and knew him at once, a point of incredible complexity even within the multi-layered madness of the river, strings of connection pouring to and from him like endless silk ribbons. A lantern shining bright through the storm. There was the faintest silhouette of form to him from so far, sinuous and graceful as he flew through the raincloud.

Father. Torrenda did not feel her body failing as she stared at the dragon. She did not hear the screams of Taaveti – they were somewhere so far down the inputs coming to her mind that they did not even register. She stared at the dragon, the shadow she had seen once in the clouds as a girl running between rock chimneys on a bridge of rope, the presence who kept the Siobh afraid of invasion, who brought the rain that brought the life to the bare rock canyons.

She saw thick streamers of connection that flew out from him and… ended. Abrupt, and torn. Frowning, she glanced across the world and she saw them.

The dragon. The snake. The bear. The wolf. The whale. The gull. The lion. The spider. A whole southern continent where there were none at all. A northern continent thick with them. Deeper, somewhere deeper, more shapes under rock and earth and water, far below. Oceans further south than any maps she'd heard of, and islands and great lands beyond, shapes and colour and hints of more. Beacons in the darkness.

Wake.

She did not feel the sweat slicking her skin, the blood coming from eyes and nose and ears. *The father is one, but there are many.*

Wake.

A hand in her hand and then Torrenda was screaming on the floor of the wayhouse, Taaveti holding her head firm as she thrashed, Aida collapsed next to her still gripping her hand. Next to her head, its brow pressed to hers, the fox tulka, such a little thing. As the river dropped from her eyes it gazed at her. Torrenda pictured the father dragon and the broken dragon stones, the torn connections trailing from him. She grew still. From the tulka fox a sense of calm flowed into her, and she blinked until the tears drowning her eyes were just a little thing, just more raindrops.

'Shrinekeeper,' Taaveti panted, falling back from her crouch to sit on the floor, 'Shrinekeeper, what in all dry hells did you see?'

Torrenda held a hand to her face and felt the slick of blood on her lips already drying, heard the rain outside.

'I saw the gods,' she said, and with her bloodied hand she drew the tulka close to her and embraced it. 'They are unchained.'

DAUGHTER OF THE MIST

'Heed the story, hear her wail, see the croft in ash,
the daughter of the Mist alone, claws of iron a-flash;
Spare my child, the farmer cries; back, ye beast! the soldier.
Wail and woe the daughter brings, and takes the debt
that's owed her.'

Final verse, 'Three daughters of the mist,
unkind', *Undal folk song*

Floré and Janos left Protector's Keep before dawn, descending
through the labyrinth of passages in silence. They passed from
their rooms in the upper keep through halls wrought from
worked blocks of granite and cut with high windows down to
the smooth black remnants of the Ferron overseers' fort below,
and then out into the street. The gate guard gave them a nod
and Floré smiled at him, but felt a shiver cutting through her.
Winter was at an end and the night was still cold, but it was
not the cold that sent prickles down her arm; was not the cold
that had the scars all down her right arm twitching as they
always did when she was nervous.

We could have had a life here, she thought, and knew it to be true. Janos led them away from Protector's Keep and down the side street to Bellentoe's bakery. Even with the rest of the street shuttered and silent, there was light and warmth pouring from the back door of the bakery. Floré waited with her bag as Janos slipped inside, and she heard the gruff tones of the Antian Bellentoe and then laughter. She looked away from the pooling light and back at the looming shadow of Protector's Keep. *Rank. Respect. Purpose.* She clenched her fist to try and stop the ache in her arm. Starbeck had spent the last span pleading with Janos not to go, even had him summoned to a meeting with the entire Grand Council where they begged him to stay in whatever form he would. It was too late – the seed was sown in his mind and hers, and now whatever pains he felt in the city, surrounded by Stormguard, reminded every day of the hell he had wrought at Urforren, she would know they were perhaps preventable.

Have you thought about the Forest Watch? he had said all those spans ago. Floré blew out through her nose and licked her lips and shook her head. Another life had been possible at Protector's Keep – a soldier's life, a life of service. *What am I going to be without that?* Starbeck's hurried order to her in the corridor the night before – *you will keep him safe until he is needed.*

'Goat's cheese!' Janos said, and she blinked and smiled. He frowned. 'You okay?' he asked, and Floré made herself smile and stretch out her hand to his, holding the outside of his hand gently and then snatching one of the pastries away.

'Just hungry,' she said, and together they ate and they walked the silent streets of Undal City east, to the star gate. The mail coach was ready to ride as dawn came and there were three other passengers – Floré paid them no mind. The driver squinted to read their letter of passage in the pale dawn light and looked between them as he loaded their bags.

'Which one's Artollen, then? Sergeant Artollen, of the Forest Watch?'

Floré made herself smile again, and raised a hand to her chest. *Bolt-Captain of the Stormguard commandos,* she thought, but said nothing.

'Aye, well, I'm from Larchford myself. You've a nice assignment waiting. Best fishing that side of the Unerdan in Loch Hassel. Climb up and I'll have you to Hookstone Town by evening.'

Floré did not look back at the walls of Undal or the towers of Protector's Keep as they left, did not allow herself to. *Look forward, girl,* she said in her mind in her mother's voice. She could still remember her mother's voice, if nothing else. Together she sat with Janos and watched the coast roll by, fishing crofts and wash-houses where the washers were already arriving, laden with baskets of dirtied linen and cloth from the rich houses of the eastern half of the city. It was a clear day and already sheets were strung between the wash-houses, the wind blowing them in from the sea, blowing them north. They strained against their pegs and ties. Floré caught a line of a chorus sung high – *kiss your daughters, count their toes, hear the daughters, wail and woe* – and then repeated low, and the sound of laughter. Then the cart was past, and the smattering of crofts and houses began to give way to barns and fields and drystone dykes.

'Do you know that song, my love?' she asked, her eyes lingering on a flock of sheep held fast behind a fence of woven willow. Some of the sheep were on the wrong side of the fence. *How did you escape?*

'Three daughters of the mist, unkind,' Janos said, his voice low. The other three passengers were asleep or feigning it. 'It's an old Undal folk song. The three daughters are great bogles, relu, godlings – spirits. The song is about the last daughter. While she sleeps long seasons, her mother is killed by the Undal to protect their sheep. One sister flees to the north, and another spirit kills her to defend its territory. One sister tries to fight and is killed by the Undal. The final daughter wakes, and one by one she takes the children of the village as they play or work, until a man speaks to her and offers her a deal – a tribute of meat and flowers each Chainday, forever more, for her forgiveness and her mercy.'

Floré pushed her hand through her hair, feeling the curls untangle. 'Cheery stuff,' she said, and Janos smiled at her, eyes crinkling.

'The old Undal were not a cheery folk,' he said, 'but it's a hell of a song. Catchy. Remind me when we are off this blasted coach and I'll give you my best rendition.'

Onward they rode and the sun climbed high. The three merchants or whatever they were woke and demanded a piss break, and then they were passing through the village of Dal. The driver stopped at the eastern edge of the village by a Stormguard garrison and jumped down to deliver his mail and packages, and Floré took Janos to the top of a wee hill at the edge of the town. As she crested the hill she turned back and saw Undal City in all its glory on the horizon, the high walls and spires, the Ferron lighthouse standing proud in the water just off the harbour, slick black stone rising to an orb of hazed glass above, dim in the morning light. A dozen ships could be seen waiting their turn to dock, two dozen smaller boats rushing between them or out on their own quests. Floré felt a twist in her gut.

'It was a good year,' she said as Janos caught her up, out of breath. He followed her gaze and held her hand.

'Aye, love,' he said, squeezing her hand, and she felt his wedding ring touch hers. 'We'll have more to come.'

With a gentle hand he turned her, and Floré took in the sweep of the sea to the south, iron water and whitecaps, distant ships with sails catching the sun, bright and white. A matching lighthouse to the one at Undal City's harbour sat in the water just off the short cliffs to the south of Dal. He kept turning her, and Floré allowed herself to be turned, breathed out and put Undal City behind her. Facing east with the sun high above, she could see the Star Coast. *I've never been this far east before.* Floré had served a year in the bogs east of Aber-Ouse, up near the Blue Wolf Mountains working with the lancers fighting back raids from Tessendorm, but never had she seen this half of her country.

Ahead of her under blue skies the Star Coast spread out, inlets and cliffs and sandy beaches, and within view a handful of black rocks ranging in size from a dog to a bullock – the fallen stars that gave the coast its name. Turning inland, rolling hills, herds of cattle and sheep, dozens of crofts and farms and groves of trees. The wind pulled at them both and Janos leaned into her and pointed to the north-east and she saw a distant blur of green, a green that spread up and back into hills, a green that ate half the horizon. Floré had ranged through the Slow Marsh in the west of the protectorate, fens full of streams and stunted trees and fields of bullrushes. She remembered the gorse and heather of Tollen, when she was a girl, and the bogs and lichened stone of the borders with Tessendorm. She'd travelled from the Stormwall down to the city and seen the farmland and tame orchards of the south coast. *Never something like this.*

'Hookstone forest,' Janos said, and she grabbed him around the waist.

Floré pictured the rotstorm, remembered the clouds of acid mist, the land barren except for hidden groves of twisted beech, rambling pepper-thorn that would skewer the thickest boot, rotvine twisting through dark peat waters to snatch at ankles to bite and chew. *No green in the rotstorm.*

'It can't all be forest,' she heard herself say, and she realised she was smiling. Janos kissed her temple.

'Let's find out, love.'

~

'Hands off, idiot,' she said, and she poured her flagon of ale on his head and then the man was up and the girl was on the floor and he loomed over Floré.

'Piss off,' he said, 'she likes it well enough. Maybe you'd like a taste, darlin'?'

Floré didn't even open her mouth to respond. She felt her heart beating fast. The man towered over her, and she heard a laugh from somewhere in the inn. The Goat and Whistle in Hasselberry was normally fine enough, but payday for the loggers meant a mighty piss-up. She could see the innkeeper Shand nervously eyeing the crowd. Most were locals, she reckoned, but every span brought some through to try and earn coin in the lumberyard. Some lasted a span, some a season. Floré felt the heat rise, a bloom up her gut and into her chest. *One,* she thought, *two. Count to ten before you act. Give them a chance. Calm.*

'Leave it, Cal,' someone called. 'She's Forest Watch.'

The big man sneered, not taking his eyes from Floré. *Three, four.*

'I don't see no tabard. I just see some girl who can't mind her manners.'

He reached out to push her and she let him. It was a gentle push to the shoulder, meant to intimidate. Floré looked past him to the girl who had fallen on the floor. One of the village girls, barely old enough to be courting, and this logger twice Floré's age had been trying to force his hand up her skirt and not taking no as an answer.

Five… ah, fuck it.

The first punch caught him across the nose, a quick jab and then another, but then he rushed her, and before Floré could land her heavy right cross, he was on her, a flail of limbs, reeking of the ale she'd poured on his head. No art to his fighting, but a big man, a man who spent his summer splitting wood and his winter splitting wood and probably his springs and his autumns splitting wood, and he had the corded muscle to show for it. He grabbed her, one hand on her shoulder and another round her waist, and with a wrench threw her across the room. She slammed into two of the mill workers and a table: the ginger one – Essen – and one of his pals. They pulled her to her feet. The logger was saying something to his friends, turned away and laughing.

'Want a hand, Sergeant?' Essen asked as he pulled her up and Floré shrugged his hand away.

'Not necessary,' she said loudly, and with a hand held high stopped Shand, who was coming out from behind the bar.

Glancing back to her table across the bar she saw Janos. He was sat, frowning. *Calm,* he mouthed, and she nodded.

'Stormguard Forest Watch,' she said, and the bar grew still. 'Sergeant Artollen, Hasselberry.'

The big man – Cal – turned back to her and snorted.

'Leave it, girl,' he said. Floré took a step forward.

'A night in the cells and a lash,' she said, and saw him twitch.

'Piss on that,' he said, and grabbed his ale from the table. 'And piss on you. I'm off.'

'That was an order, citizen. Not a request. You'll apologise to the girl, you'll come with me to the cells, and tomorrow you'll take a lash. If you've an issue with the sentencing, you can complain to the garrison in Hookstone Town. We clear?'

'Just a bit of fun out of hand,' one of the loggers at Cal's table said, and Floré turned her gaze on him. He held her eyes for a fraction of a second before mouthing *sorry* and looking down at his pint.

'*Preserve the freedom of all people in the realm*,' Floré said. 'That includes the freedom for young girls to not be groped by morons like you. Cells, lash. Your choice to say yes or no.'

The logger Cal drained his pint of ale and put it down. *Handsome enough,* Floré thought, strong-jawed and tanned from seasons in the woods, a tumble of brown hair streaked with silver. *Handsome asshole.*

'What happens if I say no?' he said, and Floré was aware of Janos watching her from their table, Shand the innkeeper, the other loggers. She had only been in Hasselberry a season, but she knew already that if things went south they'd be behind her.

'I break your right hand,' she said, 'and you spend the night in the cells, and you get a lash.'

Cal slammed down his tankard and made for the door, but Floré stepped in front of him. He went to step around her but she moved again, and then again, and then with a curse of frustration he charged forward, arms raised and reaching for her shoulders. Floré let him come. At the last second with both hands she grabbed his right hand and spun her whole body, and with a crouch and a push of her legs she sent him sailing over her back and slamming into an oak beam. With a huff he raised himself to his knees and Floré was there, a heavy tankard in hand.

Thrice she brought it down, once to the temple, once to the nose, and once a sharp straight shot to the cheek.

'Wait!' he said, a hand raised, and dropping the tankard

Floré grabbed his first fingers in her fist and with a jerk snapped them backward.

Cal's wailing filled the room, and Floré picked up the tankard and walked back to his table, slamming it down.

'You and you,' she said, pointing at the first two loggers she recognised. 'Get him in the cell in the barn.' They hurried to follow her orders, dragging the sobbing logger Cal from the bar.

'Rest of you, mark my words well. You fondle someone says no, I'll fondle you back, but I'll *put my gauntlets on first*. Apologies for the disturbance.'

'No disturbance,' Shand called out, his innkeeper's voice filling the room, 'just a job finely done. My thanks, Sergeant Artollen.'

'And mine!' Essen called, and then a chorus of thanks and a few slammed tankards. Sandy the miller was shepherding the young lass away to the kitchens. Floré caught sight of the quiet girl Yselda, Shand and Esme's adopted orphan, and her younger sisters. They were peeking through the kitchen door, but fled when she met their eye. She went to return to her table and saw Janos silently clapping her in mock earnestness, a smile on his lips, and she felt her cheeks flush.

'A word in private, daughter?' a voice said, and Floré blinked in surprise when she turned and saw its source. It was Izelda the village whitestaff, a woman with wispy white hair and wrinkled brown skin, stooped and ancient. She wore her Riven amulet around her neck, a green carved stone on a fine chain of silver, and wore a simple yellow dress with a shawl of black wool.

Floré nodded and followed the old woman, bristling at being called daughter. The air outside was fresh, and turning north she could see the starlight reflecting on the calm waters of Loch Hassel.

'I'm sorry to disturb you, Mistress Izelda,' she said, rubbing at the split skin on her knuckles. 'The loggers seem to be like this most paydays, though normally a wee bit more sensible.'

The old woman took a pipe from some hidden pocket and a taper from another. Lighting the taper from the small lantern hung outside the inn door, she lit her pipe and drew a few breaths. Floré itched her nose. *What in the hells does she want?*

'No disturbance to me, daughter,' Izelda said at last with a sniff, 'though I've no doubt the crew and Shand would have stepped in less dramatically had you not been here. No. I just wanted to warn you to avoid blows to the stomach, given your condition.'

Floré felt her mouth open, and she tilted her head slowly. 'My condition?'

'Aye, daughter,' Izelda said, a puff of smoke spiralling up from her pipe. 'You've not been to me for aserwort, and any you had from the city would surely be done by now. That, and your face, and your chest. And... well. I am a whitestaff – I had a wee look, to be sure, in the skein. You're with child.'

Floré leaned back against the walls of the Goat and Whistle and stared at the whitestaff, felt her right hand start to shake, felt the cold air blowing across the loch, sharp against open cuts on her knuckles.

'Truly?' she said, and the old woman nodded and blew another gout of smoke and then tapped her pipe.

'Come and see me tomorrow and we can speak on it more, Sergeant. A daughter, by my eye,' the whitestaff said, and then patted Floré's shoulder and went back inside the inn. Floré clutched at her stomach and imagined a fist, a sword. Imagined Captain Tyr the mutton-chopped commander of the Forest Watch in Hasselberry handling the logger Cal. *Would he have bloody knuckles now? I didn't even count to ten. Straight to violence. Always violence.*

'A daughter,' Floré said aloud to the night air, and she shook all over. As she stared out at the loch her eye caught the shadow of the shaman tower standing crooked over the village green. The shadow called to a memory, the memory of Lothal's bones looming over her in a storm of lightning and acid and monsters and hell. Violence being answered with violence, and endless chain. *I can be better. I can be better, for her.* Floré blew out a sharp breath and then she was smiling and laughing and crying and then Janos was there and she kissed him and moved his hand to her stomach, and they held each other close surrounded by the breeze from the loch, the smell of pinesap and fresh ale, the forest close around them so black and dark it turned back to green, and from inside the inn the sound of laughter and song, a dozen untrained voices hunting for harmony and unity: *three daughters of the mist, unkind.*

ACT 3

THE GAUNTLET

'There is a saying, in the Crown Isles – no gods, no kings, no laws. This is not the world we build. Anshuka will guide us. The Grand Council will guide us. Our precepts will guide us: suffer no tyrant; forge no chain; lead in servitude. We will err, but do not lose faith. We will face challenges none can foresee – but these words will guide how we respond, forevermore.'

The Way of Riven, Mistress Water

13

Hidden City, Frozen Sky

'*I can hear the voice of the Hidden Council even now.
"Bellentoe, you left us in disgrace. You broke our laws."
This is true – but I never betrayed our people. I committed
crimes of passion, but never did my heart stray from my
home. Spy, they have called me... I have been your spy. I
have reported for twenty-two years, information great and
incidental, and have carried your notes and your packages.
You ally with them, but even then you seek to always know
– so that if they betray you, the hidden blade will be ready.
I beseech you. In the name of my holt. In the name of the
deep gods we hold at bay, and the love you may once have
borne me. I beseech you – help them. They are brutal and
they are rash but they seek to be better – they deserve the
same chance they gave to our elders.*' – **Letter to the Hidden
Council of the Undal Redoubt**, Bellentoe Firstclaw

The fight went out of the hired muscle. Tomas did his usual
trick, wreathing his hands in green flame, and most of the thugs
lowered their weapons slowly to the floor. The smouldering
corpses, the blood-soaked woman with the burning blade

– *gold only pays for so much*. The Hanged Man simply shook her head in annoyance, and affected an air of indifference as they placed the shackles on her.

'I'll be seeing you,' she said, and Floré shook her head. *No you bloody won't.* The woman had almost killed her, almost left Marta with no mother and Tullen with no gauntlet seeking him. *She almost ruined it all.* Floré tried to quell the anger in her, tried to get those old familiar chains of control on the roaring flaming creature inside her breast. She clutched at her sword hilt and stared at the Hanged Man.

'Hang her in front of the garrison,' she said, her voice a hiss. 'No delays – walk there right now, string her up.'

One of the City Watch guards cocked his head at her.

'We don't just *hang*—' he started to say, but Floré met his eye. She could feel the blood coating her face, tacky and thick, and her lungs were thick with charnel smoke from the corpses smouldering on the floor. *They don't just hang.* This woman had almost ruined all of it, almost doomed them all to Tullen One-Eye's madness. Through her anger Floré felt the nausea rising, the swift sickness filling the backs of her eyes, her mouth. *I almost lost Marta again.*

'*Knife*,' she said, and held her hand out to him. The guard winced, and with the hand not clutching his prisoner he drew his blade and handed it to her, hilt first. It was a Stormguard Hawk knife, but the blade was not silvered – standard City Watch equipment.

'In the name of the Stormguard,' Floré said, sheathing her sword and gripping the knife hilt tightly, 'I sentence you to die.'

The Hanged Man smirked. 'I think you'll find I have many friends, Floré Artollen—'

The blade sank deep, up through her gut and under the ribs. Eight inches of steel tapered to a killing point. The Hawk knife was not a tool for other purposes, it was not for rope, or for wood. It was not for cutting meat at dinner. It was designed to slip through the gap in a person's ribs, to go as deep as it must. The City Watch guards held the Hanged Man firm, and she didn't scream – Floré had angled the blade to her left, and felt the slick resistance of lungs popping. She left the blade in the wound, and stepped back. The Hanged Man fell limp, red hair tumbling over her face, and Floré closed her eyes and felt the adrenaline coursing through her blood. Hands reached for her, and the next time she blinked she was in another room, Cuss and Tomas and a Stormguard medic. The medic was wrapping padding and bandages and muttering about the infirmary.

'She doesn't have time for the infirmary,' Cuss said, terse. 'Do what you can, here and now.'

Floré leaned her head back against the cool black stone of the wall and smiled at that. *Wee Cuss, barking orders.* Cuss and Tomas were removing their tabards and checking their gear, packs gone. Only weapons remained. Tomas looked tired. When the medic finally left, he came to her and sat close, and Cuss joined them. The City Watch were scouring the building for any trace of the sergeant who had sold her out, but Floré doubted they'd find him soon. *So much almost lost for vengeance.* Always the cycle of her violence came back to her.

'Well?' she said eventually, and Tomas laughed.

'A good warm-up,' he responded, 'fighting a dozen criminals in a storeroom. Luck alone brought us, Floré, luck and Cuss trying to find you. Luck and the screams.'

Floré nodded and closed her eyes again and waited. Her palms were scorched and tingling from the heat of the flaming sword's hilt, even through her gauntlets, and her right arm was aching and pulsing with pain, a dancing spiral that climbed and descended her nerves and set her teeth on edge. She pictured Marta, screaming at her in the orphan's barracks of Undal City when Floré left her. *Please, Mama,* she had yelled. *I need Papa!* Over and over and over. Two things Floré couldn't give her – a mother who was there, or her father back. Floré rubbed at her eyes. *Why didn't I go to her?* She could not let Tullen live, and she knew Marta would not be safe as long as the mage drew breath. She trusted nobody else to finish the job. *And I can't help her.* That was the awful truth of it. Marta was sick, and needed something that Floré could not give.

Benny will help, Janos had said as he lay dying. *Benny will help,* Floré repeated, over and over like a mantra. She could trust Benny to do the right thing. 'They are arriving at dawn,' Tomas continued. 'One orb, by their messenger's claim, but we'd guess the other will be close by. Ceann Brude, the war-leader, and someone called Reeve. Presumably some others. I'd assume us snatching one of their crow-men guards will lead to all-out war, Floré. The talks will be a disaster. You're sure this is the way?'

Floré leaned forward and reached up and gripped his arm.

'There is *no peace*,' she hissed, 'while Tullen is alive. Negotiations don't matter. They have the marches already, they have Lothal, they have orbs. They have Tullen One-Eye, and he can kill us all. All that matters is we get a crow-man. You head back down the hill, get the orb. Bring it now, before dawn, and land it in the back courtyard. They'll land theirs in the square out front. I'll have Starbeck leave the back courtyard unguarded, and leave what material he has, canvas from carts – get it up there over the orb so they don't see it when they're flying in. We grab a crow-man and we get out. Cuss and I have Orubor cloaks – the corridor from the front entrance to the grand hall has a dozen passages off it – one leads straight to the back courtyard. We'll be waiting there, and we'll grab one. Shank it with silver and pull it out of there, into the orb, up and away before they know we're even there.'

Tomas shook his head. 'And then we simply keep a crow-man under control, find Tullen One-Eye, and get the two of them in the same space fast enough he doesn't stop us, and long enough for you to beat him to death.'

Floré stared at him. She could see the resignation in his face. *He thinks it won't work.* Perhaps he was right. What else could she do? She'd already walked into one trap. Burn the peace talks to have the slightest chance of killing Tullen? Or risk the orb in the rotstorm for the same? *Peace at any cost,* Starbeck kept saying, and she kept saying it back as if it meant something but she knew it didn't. *I have to keep her safe.* She had told Janos she would find Marta and would keep her safe. She had told Marta she would come back to her. *How can I go back if Tullen burns it all? How can I live when the man who killed Janos still breathes?*

The weight of it all was too much. She broke her gaze from Tomas and stared at the floor. She had to save Marta. She had to kill Tullen, for revenge, to keep Marta safe – for any number of reasons. She couldn't risk the orb, but she shouldn't risk the peace talks. She shouldn't risk Cuss, and Yselda wasn't handling her new life. Benazir was so wounded – she needed Floré. Starbeck was so pressed – he needed Floré. Floré pressed the heels of her hands into her eyes. *I'm so tired.* She just wanted Marta, to hold Marta close, to be home.

I can never go home again.

'That's the plan, Tomas,' she said at last, lowering her hands and blinking away tears. 'You knew that coming in. It's not a good plan, but it's all I have.'

Tomas just nodded and ran his hands through his hair.

'I'm sorry to question,' he said eventually. 'You are right. As long as Tullen One-Eye walks this earth, none of us are safe.'

Tomas patted Floré on the shoulder and then smiled at Cuss. 'Your teeth aren't sharp enough to be an Orubor, so don't grin too much,' he said, and then stood and left the room. Cuss frowned at him as he left, and Floré tried to stop her fingers shaking. Desperate for something to occupy her hands she tried to clean the blood from her gauntlets and sword. The rag she was using was clotted, utterly black in the faint light of the candles, and she scrubbed but the blood wouldn't wash free. Dawn was coming, and with it the rust-folk. *They come seeking peace*, she thought, *and I'm bringing a blade*.

'I'll find Starbeck and get the canvas squared. You should get some rest.'

Cuss's voice startled her, and she looked at him.

'We have a few hours, Commander,' he said, and passed her a clean rag. 'I doubt we'll get another chance to rest. Get some sleep. I'll wake you well before dawn.'

Floré let her gauntlets rest on the table, and the sword next to her. The blood had pooled in the rune engravings.

'It has to be this way, Cuss. He won't stop. Nobody should have this power. Janos had it, and it almost broke him. It's too much, for one person.'

Cuss sat silent and still with her, and then laid a gentle hand on her shoulder.

'He could do anything, and he chose this,' Cuss said. 'We'll stop him.'

From a pouch at his belt he produced a handful of silver coins, and counted out four, placing them down by her gauntlets. Four more he clicked into the metal slots of his own gauntlets, the little metal ridges that looked ornamental flexing and then settling back in place over the coin edges with a click. The edges of the thick coins jutted out past the knuckle ridge of the gauntlets.

'Silver and fire for demons, Boss,' he said, and with a tight smile left her alone in the dark. Floré stared at the pile of coins, and then snuffed out the candle.

~

'Walk me through it,' Benazir said, and Nintur ran an armoured thumb across the table top.

'Three dozen in this tower, at least,' he said, and sniffed. His eyes kept glancing back to Marta, still asleep. 'This group have been left to guard the redoubt while the rest have retreated below – some internal machinations, something about a threat from below is all we've managed to gather. Refugees who've arrived since the Claw Winter started have all been taken here. There are more than three hundred – this is only one of six rooms, Commander. We've requested to speak to their council, but this Pekka from Holt Varsi just keeps us here. They've made no move against us, and provided us with fare and shelter. Obeying the armistices in word, if not in spirit. I've not pressed matters – we've shelter and warmth and food, and it's hell out there. And when we left Undal City, it was half on fire and besieged by wyrms. I'm glad they left, at least.'

Benazir closed her eyes and bit her lip.

'Berren's black blood,' she said. 'We got some whitestaffs back to Undal City, but we need to get Marta there soon. She's wasting away. How often does she wake?'

She did not mention the other part of her mission. *Is she strong enough for that?* Floré had been resolute, but Benazir had seen the fear in her eyes. *Peace at any cost, sister,* Benazir thought, but a wordless doubt hung heavy in her chest.

'This morning she woke for a little while. She was weak, but we managed to feed her some porridge. Commander, if I may... I know Starbeck said the girl is important. But there are three hundred people here. The Antian have not given us free rein, but they have given us shelter. Is violence the answer?'

'It's *an* answer,' Benazir said, but then she rubbed at her eye. *Three hundred refugees.* 'We have a captured orb, Nintur.

Atop the tower. The Antian on guard from Holt Varsi want it, accords be damned, and they've taken my adviser against his will. This girl has a role to play.'

Benazir lowered her voice and leaned in close to the hulking captain.

'She is a skein-wreck, Nintur,' she said, and the man went rigid. It spoke volumes of his loyalty that he had taken his men north through the hell of a Claw Winter for spans and spans on Starbeck's order without knowing even that. 'She is the daughter of the Salt-Man. She is a hammer that can change the world, if she lives. Lothal the wolf is out there in the snow and storm, and the Ferron have taken the Northern Marches. For a skein-wreck, or even the chance of one in a few years, it is worth any risk. I need to get her to the orb, and back to the whitestaffs.'

They both stood in silence and watched the lancers gearing up, buckling on armour. They had no weapons. Refugees were lingering on the periphery, quiet but watching. *We need to keep control of this situation.*

'The way up will be bloody,' Nintur said, and Benazir realised the solution and smiled at him. She waved to the lancers to gather around and cast a glance at Yselda. The girl was sat with Marta, holding her hand, speaking to her quietly even as the younger girl slept.

'I need to see the Antian council. We swarm the door guards, and then hold the doorway – you need to bar it from the inside until we come back. Three of you with Marta at any time – kill any who try to harm her. No hesitation at that. Arm yourselves as best you can.'

The lancers shifted their feet, and a young woman with a flame of red hair and a burst of freckles raised a hand.

'Sir, we can't make the top of the tower without killing, if we can make it at all.'

Benazir nodded and grinned. The girl looked like Guil, a little. The same hair, the same freckles. *But the nose is wrong, and the eyes are wrong, and the mouth is wrong.* Nobody else would ever look like Guil. *You'd like this, Legs,* she thought. Guil always appreciated a plan that wasn't just blood and violence.

'We aren't *going* up,' she said. 'Holt Varsi guard the redoubt, and Pekka Secondclaw commands, correct? I've no time for their politics, his deep gods. Couldn't give a shit. The council probably don't even know we're here. I'm going *down*, to talk to whoever the hell is in charge.'

They gathered by the door, and Nintur's lancers herded the refugees back. Some called advice and criticism, but Benazir didn't engage.

'Best fist?' she asked, and Nintur pointed to a hulking man with curling ginger hair, skin ruddy.

'Rollo.'

Rollo grinned at her. The hulking man was wearing a heavy chain shirt under his blue tabard, and when Nintur pointed to him he pulled on a steel plate helm with cheek and nose guard, and then cinched the ties on his gauntlets tight.

'Can't promise they won't die if I hit them,' he said, stepping to the door, and Benazir shrugged.

'We all make our choices, Rollo. They've made theirs. I'd appreciate it if you break a limb rather than a skull, but don't risk your life on it.'

Benazir turned a final glance back to doorway leading to Marta, and closed her eyes for a long moment before giving Rollo the nod.

The man marched forward, frowning, and pounded on the door, heavy hits. His gauntlets smashed against the wood of the door, over and over, and Antian voices began to yell questions but Benazir couldn't hear them over the pounding of steel on wood. The door opened a crack and she saw a flash of obsidian, and another – at least three Antian, spears drawn, faces worried.

Rollo hauled at the door and threw himself through, onto the spears of the Antian. He had at least two feet of height on the biggest of them, and must have weighed double what they did. By the time Benazir had stepped through the door with Nintur, two of them were already on the ground, dead or unconscious. The third was scrabbling away on the floor – Rollo had toppled into all of them, sending them into a writhing mass on the floor. He grabbed the fleeing Antian's leg and hauled him back across the smooth stone floor, and slammed his fist down on the top of its head. The Antian went limp.

In the dark of the corridor, Benazir held out a hand and a lancer passed her a torch from the refugees' hall. The three Antian were not moving. She listened hard, but she could not hear more coming down the stairs. Rollo pulled himself to his feet and flexed his right arm – there was a slowly spreading pool of blood at his bicep at a tear in the chainmail, and flecks of obsidian fell from the mail shirt down to the floor as he brushed at the wound. He nodded to her, and Benazir gestured back at the room and the lancers began to drag the Antian and their weapons inside, closing the door behind them. Benazir had a glimpse of Yselda's terrified face and mouthed at her: *Stay with Marta.* The girl nodded, and in her hand clutched at the locket of charred wood tied at her neck. Benazir smiled at her, and then the door was closed.

They found the nearest stairwell and moved down, and down, and down again. After a minute there was a noise from below and a querulous bark, and Rollo moved forward again, forward past the torchlight. A strangled scream and a brutal slam of flesh on stone, and by the time Benazir's torch illuminated Rollo again there were two Antian on the ground and Rollo was adjusting his helm. The big man carried himself as if every step was an effort, the weight of muscle and sheer mass above, a constant burden.

Benazir kept her breathing steady. She could have gone up, brought blood and the blade to Pekka Secondclaw and his scant troop. *I could have chosen violence.* A part of her wanted to. Why not, after all? They had chosen their path. When she had looked at Marta's sleeping face she had known she would do any violence to keep her safe. *But what else could I do?*

They carried on like that for what felt like an hour, but Benazir knew it was really a matter of minutes. When stairwells ended they moved horizontally until they could move downward again, ever downward. The passages were smooth, flat worked stone below what seemed to be naturally worn walls and roof, white porous stone that was dry and cool. The passageways and rooms were abandoned. Finally they found a sloping hall bigger than the others and emerged onto it. Benazir could see that a dozen stairs opened onto this one. *This is where the towers and holts meet.* She thought they must be at the base of the redoubt, down where the fortress above met the stone below.

At the lower end of the sloping hall was a great arch carved in stone, a huge fresco of carved Antian figures, each thrice life-size. There were dozens of them, some depicting scenes from what must be their mythology. *Their pantheon?* Benazir frowned at her own ignorance. She had treated Voltos like a person, always, but realised she had treated him as if he just came from another country – a land a few miles away, where customs might be strange and gods might be different to her own. *But people are people.* Now that she was standing in their halls, she could see in the stonework something inhuman – the imagery in their carvings was abstract and she could follow no narrative, no meaning. It was utterly different, and as Benazir's gaze lowered from the arching fresco to the great gates below, she shivered.

How similar are we? How similar can we be? She considered Voltos, all his long years of service. *How much of his manner is affectation to fit in with us, rather than truly who he is?* She was not sure what that difference could be, or if it even mattered.

'Halt!' came the call. At the great gates below the fresco, four Antian were standing guard. They had been sat on a low bench to the side, but seeing Rollo, Nintur, and Benazir, they scrambled to their feet and drew spears. Benazir strode forward and did not slow. They had gathered no weapons from the Antian they had subdued in their descent – she wanted to give no prompt for violence.

'I am Bolt-Commander Benazir Arfallow,' she said, and put steel in her voice. 'What holt are you? I need to speak to the Hidden Council at once.'

'Pekka said—' one of them started to say, and another shushed him.

'You are not permitted access to the city. You are to return under guard to the refugee quarters. Comply at once!'

Benazir sighed. She rubbed the flat side of her hook across her brow, feeling the release that pressure brought her. Sometimes when she woke she could feel her right fist clenching, but when she looked down there was only scar tissue and empty air. The weight of the hook was good – it brought her into balance. Benazir stared at the spear points and did not flinch. *Why does it always have to be violence?*

She could feel Rollo next to her rocking on his feet, ready to beat these four into a pulp if none of them got a lucky strike in. Nintur had his armoured hands balled in fists, looming and still. She had no doubt he would kill them all if she waved her hand. At her belt and at the top of her boots she felt an absence – the familiar weight of her daggers was not there, only leather and empty space. She flexed her left fist and took a step forward, forward, and forward until she was an inch from the points of their obsidian spears.

'Listen to me,' she said, and raised her hook to her rank badge and tapped it. 'I am Bolt-Commander Benazir Arfallow of the Stormguard commandos, Commander of Stormcastle XII. I am here on direct orders from Knight-Commander Salem Starbeck, Leader of the Grand Council of the Undal Protectorate. I come as an emissary to our noble and valued allies, the Antian. You will open this gate and take me to the Hidden Council, and then you will go back upstairs and find your man Pekka Secondclaw, place him in irons, and get him ready to face the consequences of his actions.'

She did not say, *The alternative is I will have these men beat you to death, and when I reach someone from a holt that actually matters I'll apologise briefly, and then do what I was going to do anyway.* She wanted to. She felt the words on the tip of her tongue, could see Floré smiling at that, Guil frowning in despair. She held her tongue. *Better they fill in those blanks themselves.*

'We are not your enemy,' she said, and one of them began to mutter in Antian to another, while a third held his spear straighter. 'The orb atop this redoubt is ours. Holt Varsi will not have it, Pekka Secondclaw will not have it for whatever cult he follows. This farce has gone far enough, but as of right now it has not gone *too* far. Do you understand? Now *open the doors.*'

Slowly, the spears lowered save one, and the Antian hung their heads. The Antian with spear still raised slowly circled them until he was behind, Rollo turning to face him with every step, and then he yelled something in Antian and began to run, back up to the tower of Holt Varsi and the endless stairs upward.

One of the Antian, red-furred with a scar at his brow and a wide muzzle, held a fist over his heart and bowed his head. The others went to the grand gates where a heavy steel portcullis was blocking their entrance. There was a sally port with a dozen heavy locks on it, and one of them worked at unlocking them with a huge loop of ornate keys as the other pounded on a metal slot until it opened, an Antian face behind. They spoke in hurried tones and, finally, the door opened.

'We follow the orders we are given,' the red-furred Antian said quietly, and Benazir nodded.

'None are dead,' she said quietly. 'Tensions are high. We must work together.'

The Antian nodded and bowed, and led them through the door. Stepping through, Benazir stopped suddenly, and felt Nintur and Rollo at her shoulders. They stood on an outcrop at the edge of a huge cavern of white stone, almost level with the ceiling. Every wall, the ceiling itself, was covered in intricately carved stone buildings, hangings, decoration. Below them, a city spread out – towers and forts, mansions and gardens and squares, a lake. The cavern was at least a mile wide, and everywhere there was dim light, a pallid green glowing from mushrooms that trailed along every pathway. Bridges of swaying rope or chain connected towers to caves and tunnels in the walls, and a dozen towers spanned the whole height of the huge space, great towers as grand as the shaman temple in Undal City, but never petering out – only rising and rising until the ceiling greeted them, the ceiling that was covered in hanging ropes and platforms – *homes*. Benazir watched, mouth agape, as a flock of bats flitted in front of them and then down, down deep into the city below.

The city was quiet, the streets near empty, but she could

see the distant motes of Antian walking, climbing, working, living. In front of her, four Antian armed with obsidian-bladed axes and dressed in ornate silk robes were standing, watching nervously. Their leader stepped forward and eyed the red-furred Antian next to Benazir warily, and then turned to her and bowed deeply.

'Welcome to Tuonela.'

~

Ashbringer clutched tight to Tullen. When he flew, he did not make her fly. Rather, he let her clutch to him in fear and desperation as gravity let him go, and every force that would normally hold a man to the ground *changed*. There was no thrust, no propulsion like the beating of a great wings. Rather Tullen changed the world around him so the sky itself pulled him through it. It was not the wind he changed, but something more primordial – the laws of physics bending to allow him to move as he willed, as he reached for their pattern and asked and tweaked, all with a smile. There was no change for her. The earth pulled her towards it, and the higher they flew the greater her fear. Fear of falling, a long fall to a short death. *Fear of wanting to fall,* she knew. *Of wanting it to be over.*

In the courtyard in Dun Fen he had thrown her a heavy cloak, and she had not hesitated to put it on. He could warm her, of course – could warm the air around them, could probably bring out the sun to warm the world if he chose to bend his will that way. *But he is a narcissist,* she thought, *and he doesn't want to be fussing with my pattern as we fly. He just wants me there to witness whatever end he has in mind.*

'Where are we going?' she said, and he had smiled.

'It was *your* idea. The reeve and his attack dog are off to negotiate, and then they will join us. Time for you and I to have some *impact.*'

The negotiations? She felt a heaving in the pit of her stomach as she stepped to him and gripped her arms around his back. She watched the sky for those first brief moments, but then closed her eyes and focused on her breathing, her memory of the wood, of Highmother Ash showing her how to hunt, how to kill, how to read every broken leaf and every tuft of fur in the forest. *There is always a trail,* the old Orubor had said. Ashbringer knew now that the Highmother had not been old, not when she taught Ashbringer as a child. But to a child, everyone not a child is ancient.

The queasiness was not from the unnatural flight. It was not from the cold, a cold so deep that she felt it in her bones despite the heavy cloak wrapped tight. It was not the hatred of Tullen One-Eye – that was a simmering heat behind her eyes that never dimmed, now. The queasiness was the question of what he would do next. She had watched him kill the Salt-Man Janos, pillars of fire, flight and magic and tricks and brutality. She had seen him topple stone a hundred foot tall, fly across the sky. *I am not sure there is anything he can't do.* Legend told of his feats back when his empire was at its zenith – the Tullioch Shardspire broken, and their own skein-wreck defeated. The Undalor chiefs broken – Ashbringer had seen the dozens of ruined keeps and castles that dotted the landscape, so many of them fallen at his hand.

She knew he was only limited by his narcissism and his imagination, the latter of which had been fettered these last three centuries. The caged beast had prowled these long spans, unbelieving that its chains were gone. The beast still feared the one who chained it, but every time she saw him he was different. More assured. *Are we going to the negotiations?* She remembered the story of the stone prince. She did not know how many he would kill, only that she could not stop him, and would go where he bid.

Hours, they flew. His body was warm against her and she clung to it, desperate for the heat, until she started to shiver and her arms began to spasm as the muscles lost their ability to make sense of her instructions. Finally, then, a rush of warmth as the air around her heated.

'You only needed to ask,' he said, yelling to be heard over the roar of the wind. She bared her teeth at his neck, willing herself to bite, but could not finish the thought. Instead her eyes turned up to the stars above, and then down at the heavy iron cloud below. She could see so many ancestors in the stars, the great river of souls and all those others who wandered alone. *If you walk alone, your soul will still shine.* She could not remember who had told her that. Her mother, dead all these years? Her father?

East, she thought, without realising why. She could tell from the stars, the patterns amongst the dead souls. *East and south.* Ossen-Tyr, then. Brude had spoken to her of the negotiations, Brude and the strange Jehanne who watched and always had a measured thought, never a word out of place. Ashbringer closed her eyes and tried to remember the words to the blackberry song, the song for autumn dancing. Without the skein, she could find no melody.

Every Orubor could touch the skein, though few could manipulate as skilfully as she. Most spent their days patrolling the forest, living, laughing, knitting, hunting. Some worshipped Anshuka and tended shrines to her across the forest, and others built and laboured for the comfort of the community. Only a chosen few dedicated themselves to the language of the little gods, the pattern and the pattern below it, recursive and deeper and evermore. She gripped one hand in the other behind Tullen's back and felt the scar at the hollow where her thumb met her wrist, a weak swirl that was raised. She could feel it, even in the cold. *My first rune scar.*

She had spent the night before the scarring meditating on the pattern it called, the pattern of a blowing breeze – such an indefinable thing, but she had captured it in her mind, understood it fully. That memory she linked to the simple sign, the simple sign she drew on her wrist with charcoal. Highmother Ash had wielded the blade deftly, cutting and then packing the wound with ash from a bough of oak in Anshuka's forest. It stood stark against her skin.

'You are Orubor,' Highmother Ash had said, still small then but not wizened, only wise. 'This pattern will always be there for you, should you seek it. You need only ask, and the mother will guide you to it.'

Flying high over the Undal Protectorate, Ashbringer wept silently as she reached for the skein and found the world beyond her fogged and distant, found even her sense of self skewed as through deep water. Long she sought the pattern, and did not find it. She turned on herself and found the pattern at her wrist, her first scar, and when she called to the pattern the call broke against Tullen's boundaries, broke and dissipated. When she had no more tears to give, she began to probe the edges of her bounds. She could not think of harming Tullen. She could think of an event that might harm him by chance, but not if she was conscious of that chance and sought it. It was a mental trick, to abstract the chance and the intention.

Every so often her mouth would open and the sharp tips of her teeth would close an inch from the flesh of his neck and the beating of his arteries below. Tullen paid her no mind, his eyes on the skies ahead. He did not speak as he flew, and seemed to forget her, limp weight on his shoulder that she was.

'Are you ready?' he said, and brought them to a stop, hanging vertically in the air. Ashbringer looked him in the eye.

'I have no choice, Deathless,' she said. 'You will do what you will, and I will witness. I will remember.'

Tullen held her gaze for a long moment and smiled.

'I really do think you'll enjoy this,' he said, 'overwhelming as it might be. Try to put aside what you have been taught, for a moment. Try to be like the wolf – truly yourself, without intellect, without thought.'

Ashbringer squirmed. She imagined pushing away from him and falling, falling until she hit whatever desolate mountaintop was below them. *It would be so sweet.* Her arms would not let go.

'The rust-folk and the Stormguard meet to talk of peace,' she said at last, blinking away thoughts of her own death. *He will not let me have that.* 'I cannot be enthused to watch you bring them back to war.'

Tullen laughed at that and held her closer still.

'Ashbringer, dear Orubor,' he said, 'you really don't know where we are, do you? You think I care about *peace negotiations?*'

With a wave of one hand, the clouds below them parted, pushing outward as if a great gale blew them from the central point that was Tullen One-Eye hanging in the air. Out and out the clouds blew, revealing the forest below. A dense forest topped with snow, ringed by steep embankments of granite cliffs. A river ran through it from north to the south-west, and Ashbringer knew it. She had swum in it often enough, had skipped stones. Had seen murder. It was the river Boros, running from the northern moors and the Blue Wolf Mountains down into Orubor's wood. Anshuka's forest. *Home.* Ashbringer went slack as her eyes flitted, and then she saw her – *Anshuka.* From so high the bear was the size of her clenched fist, an island of rock in a vast sea of trees. No snow lay on Anshuka, and the bare grey and brown of the rock was dotted with green, a green so dark it drank the starlight.

'Please,' she said, and around them the air was utterly still.

'Please don't. She is so beautiful. Please, Deathless, do not kill her.'

Tullen did not answer. Together they moved across the sky towards Anshuka, down and forward, forward and down. Ashbringer could feel panic in her fingertips, and she longed for a weapon. *Anything.* She bent her will on hurting Deathless, but the bond was too tight. Her mind slipped, and she was counting treetops, her eyes flitting to seek Orubor villages she could just make out in the forest, patches of faint light in the darkness.

'It was always going to end this way,' Tullen said, and at his hip she felt the weight of the Ur-dagger, the nexus. The god-killing blade. On they flew, down to Anshuka.

14

DAWN

'The heir to Ossen was the Longshank, descendant of the chief who Tullen had burned in his castle some two hundred years before. He wanted his land; he wanted to lead his people and to rule them benevolently. "I'll not trade one shackle for another," said Jozenai, and in this there was much debate – who would rule, for the safety and prosperity of all? War makes strange allies, and it was Mistress Water who found the path – when the Ferron were driven from the land, a council would be held and the will of the people followed. Those who came to the Brek fresh from the fighting, or newly broken chains, did not know what to make of this woman – with her grasp of the skein, she showed them her true power. They followed her, in hope.' – **History of the Revolution**, Campbell Torbén of Aber-Ouse*

Benazir had descended only three steps to the sunken city of Tuonela when the Antian guard held up his hand to halt her.

'None may enter, Bolt-Commander. Please. We will bring the council to you.'

'A witch if you please, as well,' Benazir said with a bow of her head, and beside her felt Rollo and Nintur's gaze drilling into the back of her skull. They stood in silence and watched the city below as a messenger ran. The red-furred Antian spoke murmurs to a throng of guards who were waiting inside the heavy doors, a dozen scowling Antian all armed with short spear or long dagger. They eyed the humans and fingered the hilts of their weapons, and behind her Benazir heard the stone doors grinding shut.

Benazir crossed her arms, and watched, and waited. *Pekka will know we are gone.* She could only hope Yselda and the lancers were holding the door so far above. Far below in the sprawling city she saw the runner make their way down and down, deeper and deeper, before disappearing into a squat stone building. Eventually there was movement, but the procession took an age to even begin to wend its way up from the basin of the city to the precipice gate where they stood.

Rollo and Nintur shifted next to her. When the procession was only halfway up, it seemed to cease completely, the figures disappearing into a little building attached to a higher wall by some chain bridge, but Benazir shook her head when that building itself began to move, the chains operated by some strange mechanism, a square box of worked metal and wood rising from the cavern floor and towards them. The chains ended at a wide ledge a few hundred feet from them, connected by a narrow pass, and slowly the box was raised and moved, chains clanking as they were pulled and manoeuvred by unseen means. Nintur coughed next to her and leaned down to her ear.

'Why *witches*, Commander?' he asked, and she spared their guards a glance to check if they were listening before she answered. She saw at least one ear twitch.

'For Marta,' she said, keeping her face stoic, 'as with it all.'

From the little room moved by chains, six Antian emerged.

Three were hooded in layered robes of silk and velvet, adorned with chains around their necks, chains worked with gems and intricate patterns. Their sleeves were long, and beneath the robes Benazir could make no sign of hand nor face. The other three were dressed much as Voltos always was, in simply cut but finely crafted robes and tunics of heavy silk, layered with other cloth. The lead Antian was grey-furred and wore a thick chain of silver around his neck – from it, a black stone dangled, delicately held in a filigreed mesh of gold. As they arrived, Benazir bowed low, her hook pressed to her chest. The Antian dipped his muzzle in acknowledgement.

'Bolt-Commander Benazir Arfallow,' he said, and licked at his whiskers, 'of the Stormguard. I welcome you to the sight of Tuonela, though no visitor is permitted to enter it true. Please, Bolt-Commander, tell me, what brings you to our gate, your companion bloodied? What is the problem that brings Stormguard to this gate, where none should walk?'

Next to Benazir the red-furred Antian of Holt Varsi who had been guarding the outer gate winced uncomfortably and stepped forward.

'If I may, Sage,' he said, and the Antian leader turned to Benazir as if for her permission. She opened her left hand in acceptance, and the gate guard continued. 'Holt Varsi has held the redoubt above, as ordered during the... problems, of late. As commanded by the Hidden Council, we have given succour and shelter to any Undal who arrived at our door – some three hundred now shelter in the redoubt above, as you know from the reports. Bolt-Commander Arfallow and her companions arrived short hours ago, but their means of conveyance was of concern to Pekka Secondclaw, and he wanted to interrogate their Antian adviser to seek truth before disturbing the council. Bolt-Commander Arfallow felt her suit could not wait, and as such she and her companions made their way to our gates.'

The old Antian frowned. 'What do you mean, means of conveyance? Who is your adviser, if you please?'

Benazir cleared her throat and tried to stand as straight as she could. 'Voltos Thirdskin has advised me since I took the mantle of Commander of Stormcastle XII from my predecessor, Knight-Commander Salem Starbeck. We arrived in one of the orbs of light the rust-folk have raided with this past year. It was captured by the Stormguard and is the property of the Stormguard. I believe your redoubt commander had intentions for its repurposing to better his holt's standing, and my adviser made intimations that Pekka Secondclaw may be a worshipper of... unconventional deities, by the standards of the Antian. Pekka Secondclaw made clear his intent to take our orb and refuse us access to the Hidden Council. You of course appreciate, given the treaties our two great nations have signed, that his... enthusiasm for this course placed us in a delicate position.'

The old Antian at the fore turned and growled at one of the others, a long and low speech, and at Benazir's side the red-furred Antian's shoulders slumped. Turning back to her, the Antian leader stepped forward and reached out his hand. Benazir held it with her own, and nodded to him.

'Your adviser will be released,' he said, 'with my apologies for the... mishap. You are quite correct that given our treaties, such an *enthusiasm* may be misread. Pekka Secondclaw will be educated. I am Sage Ilmari Secondtongue, of Holt Kivi.'

Ilmari bowed deeply to her, and Benazir forced herself to hold his hand gently, when all she wanted was to clench her fist. Already, bodies were moving, soldiers and guards conversing, and the great gates were opening.

'Why did you seek the redoubt, Bolt-Commander? We can offer you shelter and aid, as best we can in the redoubt above. Your ambassador left some spans ago headed to Aber-Ouse, and we were expecting her return any day. She has not been to Tuonela, Bolt-Commander. Few humans ever have been permitted. Our armistices are clear – the Stormguard hold no claim to the ground below the protectorate, and we hold no claim to that above. When you seek new mines, she speaks to us. When we must foray above, we speak to her. The balance is delicate, and dearly won by all.'

Benazir stared at the city below. It was a wonder. *All this time we thought them a forgotten people, a few thousand living in their redoubt. There are more here than the people in all Undal City.* She shook her head. She was painfully aware this first contact with the city below the Antian's public face should have been a diplomat, a politician, a trader – *anyone but me.* She was a sharp knife.

'I'd aid you with your ails, as an ally, Sage,' she said, hoping the form of address the guard used was correct. 'Secondclaw suggested you have woes, enemies in the below. The Stormguard are your allies in this, if ever you need us. But for now, I am here for a simple reason – to retrieve some individuals from the refugees at the redoubt, and to take them away. The other refugees we will send a force for, as soon as the weather allows, along with gifts and payment for the kindness you have shown them. The reason I requested the presence of your... witches, was to ask as to their ability.'

Benazir paused a long moment and stared at the strange city arrayed below her. Could she ask? She did not know how far to trust the Antian. If she took Marta to a thousand places in this world, how many of those would try to steal her away, keep the budding skein-wreck for their own? *What would we do,* she thought, *if on a raid we found some rust-child with gifts like hers?* She knew the answer to that. *We would never even know.* The Stormguard would drive them back into the storm, untested. *We must be better.*

'A girl is sick – skein-sickness,' she said at last. 'She is a child, but reaches and changes the skein more than most grown skein-mages. She does it in her sleep. It is eating her away. If there is anything your witches might do for her, before we take her away, you would have the gratitude of the protectorate. Our own medicine has failed.'

The sage bowed his head and let go of her hand.

'You have my sympathy, and support,' he said. 'There has been a… breaking in the skein. The ties that bind the world are broken, or at least fraying. There are great Judges above, Bolt-Commander – Lothal the wolf has been seen close at hand, and the rumour is that Tullen One-Eye is with him. We have long memories. When the orbs of light came, we heeded the old tales. *Orbs of light, dead of night, hide your eye, take your flight.* This was the rhyme I was taught as a child. The Ferron hunt, as they did before so many centuries ago. And now the ties that hold our world together fray. Strange beasts come to us from the caverns – bogles, spirits, relu. They have *attacked*, Bolt-Commander. There is no story of this, no history to learn from. We have lost many soldiers, many witches. Our city is an island, a mote of civilisation in the dark. Those who worship the old gods, the chained gods, call for us to return to ways long past – this *Pekka* appears to be one of them. You have done me a great favour in revealing this.'

Benazir nodded her head at the three hooded figures robed in silk and velvet.

'They may help us?'

Ilmari smiled, a grin that showed a great many teeth, and Benazir felt a chill in her blood.

'They may, Bolt-Commander,' he said. 'I brought them because three humans arrived at my gate with Antian blood on their fists, but they may yet aid you. My assistant will go with you, along with fifty men. Holt Varsi will be relieved of their command of the redoubt. Your refugees may of course stay, and will be cared for – I will personally attend them this day, and ensure they have food and warmth and what care we may give. You may leave, in your orb, and your passage will not be hindered. The Antian are your allies, in this and in all things. We will advise, but as per the treaty we will not move our forces past the shadow of the redoubt.'

Benazir bowed her head low and stared at the point of the hook strapped to her right hand.

'You have my thanks, Sage,' she said, 'and when the winter has passed, I am sure we would be delighted to visit your city and talk of how our relationship could deepen and grow. We go now to war with Tullen One-Eye. Should he bring down our protectorate, the fate of Tuonela and the wonders you have created here would be uncertain. Any aid you might send us in this fight would be something not quickly forgotten.'

The sage stood still for a long moment and then turned and stared at the city below. As he responded to Benazir, he did not look at her, but rather down across the subterranean city.

'You ask me to break our treaties, to send you what – witches, soldiers? Our witches are no match to him. Our spears will not make the difference. I am sorry, Bolt-Commander. The bond of friendship is one that grows slow, and has been poorly tended on both sides. We cannot risk drawing his eye. Come summer, a visit to the redoubt from your ambassador would be most welcome.'

Benazir followed Ilmari's gaze to the city below, and she felt her shoulders fall.

'We will stop him,' she said eventually. 'We did before. We will again. The bear will wake and the wolf will fall. She is a god, and Tullen One-Eye is only a man. We will stop him, and come spring the creatures that attack you from below may still be cutting deeply. You are an island, you said. Alone. Our bond untended. I am not a diplomat, Sage Ilmari. I am a soldier. Your witches may see something our mages do not. Give me their aid, and come spring I will bring you as many soldiers as you need to drive back your troubles in the deep.'

Ilmari turned to her and Benazir met his gaze.

'I have lost much,' she said. 'I've fought for revenge. I've fought for anger. I've fought for the joy of it, the song in my blood. I've fought driven by fear, and I've fought the honours violence brings. This is not that. This is survival. This is fighting to *live*. We will fight him, Sage – if it is only me and my one good hand, I will fight him alone. He cannot live – you know this. Your memories are longer than ours.'

Ilmari's nose twitched and he considered her a long moment.

'Have you ever been to the bakery of an Antian named Bellentoe in Undal City, Commander?'

'In the shadow of the keep,' she said, and smiled at him. 'Whenever my duties took me to the city. All the soldiers of Protector's Keep know Bellentoe.'

Ilmari nodded and turned to the Antian witches and spoke a few words in their native tongue, and then he turned and walked away without a backward glance, three silent attendants in fine robes following him. The Antian witches stood stock-still with their hooded faces focused on Benazir's – beneath those heavy cowls she could see only shadow. His aide coughed awkwardly and blinked at Benazir.

'Sage Ilmari has requested that these witches aid your young friend who is ailing, Bolt-Commander.'

Benazir did not take her eyes from the receding back of the Antian sage.

'Anything else?' she asked, and the aide scratched at an ear.

'They are to accompany you and advise you regarding the skein-wreck Tullen One-Eye. Our treaty insists we advise the Stormguard against all threats, that we act as a voice of warning and caution and cunning wherever we may.'

The sage Ilmari did not turn back, but Benazir smiled at him anyway.

It took barely a few minutes before fifty soldiers and the sage's aide were assembled along with the silent witches, and together they left Tuonela and slowly climbed the tower, Benazir's legs were aching already from the endless stairs. Holt Varsi gave no opposition as they climbed, and Pekka Secondclaw was nowhere to be seen, bound and dragged away by the soldiers that marched upward swiftly before her. By the time Benazir reached the refugee quarters the soldiers had already outpaced her enough that Voltos was free, waiting for her. The little Antian put his hand on her arm briefly and sniffed. His nose was caked in dry blood, and one eye almost swollen shut.

'I am sorry, Benazir,' he said, and she just shook her head.

'You've been nothing but true, Voltos. The orb?'

He blew out a long breath and gripped the dagger at his belt.

'It is still there. Hawthorn did not open the ramp, even when they had a knife to my throat. Her... dedication is to be lauded.'

Benazir laughed at that, and then Yselda emerged from the refugee quarters, carrying Marta. The girl was wrapped in a blanket, head on Yselda's shoulders. The witches went to her and circled around, and Yselda clutched her close.

'Mama?' Marta said, eyes opening blearily, and the three witches raised their arms and began to speak to each other. Benazir saw no light or sound, no hint at any magic, and then the witches' arms were lowered and they turned to leave. Benazir moved towards one but Voltos was there before her, bowing so low his muzzle nearly scraped the ground. He spoke quickly in his native tongue, and from the leading witch a short sentence was barked back, and then the three diminutive figures retreated a few steps behind Benazir and waited, heads bowed, to follow her.

Yselda hugged Marta close, and the little girl sniffed and looked around at the familiar and unfamiliar faces and grimaced. Benazir held a hand out and cupped her cheek.

'Hey, Benny,' Marta said. She rubbed at her eye. 'Where's Mummy?'

Benazir ruffled her hair. 'You'll see her soon, love,' she said, and then turned and bent low next to Voltos.

'They cannot help her,' he whispered, and Benazir fixed her gaze at the stone wall and kept herself steady. 'They said, only a skein-wreck could, if anyone. She is too strong. She needs to be bound, somehow.'

Straightening her back, Benazir sniffed once and then turned back and tousled Marta's hair.

'Fancy coming on an adventure, mate?' she said, and the little girl nodded warily, hand clutching tight at Yselda's tabard. Benazir nodded at her steward and Yselda began heading up the stairs, Voltos and the witches trailing her. Nintur tapped Benazir's shoulder as she went to follow.

'Sir,' he said, 'Knight-Commander Starbeck bade me to keep her safe. To take her here, far from where the rust-folk might come. Can we go with you? To keep her safe still?'

Benazir stared at the little girl being carried up the staircase, and slowly nodded.

'We've a stop to make, before Undal City,' she said, 'and I'd not say no to a lancer at my side. Take a squad – the rest should stay to organise these refugees and ensure the Antian keep the peace. Starbeck said he sent a mage with you – where are they?'

Nintur grimaced. 'Dead on the road,' he said mournfully.

'Horse caught a hole in the road, under snow, and threw her. Snapped her neck on the first day.'

Benazir blew out a long breath and left it at that. *So much for the mighty skein.*

When they finally reached the top of the tower of Holt Varsi, on the table in the final room before the summit, their weapons were all carefully arrayed next to Jozenai's basket. Benazir slipped her daggers into her belt and boots. The kitten Jozenai was wandering the room, trailed by an Antian, and when they entered the Antian scooped her up and put her back in her basket. Rollo the lancer hefted a war axe with one hand and then at Benazir's waved hand scooped up the kitten's basket.

'This is Jozenai,' she said, leaning down to Marta and pointing at the kitten. Rollo held the basket up. 'Your mum sent him to keep you company.'

Marta stared wide-eyed at the kitten, and Benazir waved for all to follow her. *Time to go.* Her heart was heavy with what had to come next. Marta was awake; Marta was well enough to talk. *Is she well enough to save us?*

Benazir squinted as she climbed the final steps with the lancers and Yselda and Voltos behind her, her hand resting on the hilt of her runed Hawk knife. A cold wind was still howling, but in the west a pale light was creeping across the sky, and the dark was beginning to fade. *Dawn.* Behind her the three witches stood, silent and inscrutable, dark robes catching in the wind.

Hawthorn lowered the ramp of the orb, and together they climbed upward, Voltos growling something back at the dozen Antian who watched them go, all of whom had their spears respectfully raised – none of Pekka's soldiers were there. These were from Tuonela, and they were not dressed for the cold. They shivered as they saluted, and Benazir returned a stiff formal salute of her own, turning and touching the claw of her hook to her temple before she entered the orb.

The ramp slowly raised behind them, and Hawthorn grinned at Benazir and then looked down at Marta.

'A little girl! Hello, little girl.'

Marta stared up at her and clutched the basket with Jozenai in it to her chest, and Yselda put a reassuring hand on the top of her head and scooped the girl up into her arms. Hawthorn was unbothered by the reaction. The brief respite while the rest were below in the redoubt seemed to have rejuvenated her.

'Where are we going, *Benazir?*' she asked, savouring the syllables of Benazir's name, strange as they were in her mouth. Her grin was full of jagged teeth, and Benazir's shoulders fell as she faced the next decision.

'We need to get Marta to Undal City and the whitestaffs,' Yselda was saying, but Benazir held up her hand. Floré had told her the orders – her and her alone.

'Lothal the wolf is out in the world,' Benazir said, and forced steel into her voice. 'Floré and the others hunt Tullen One-Eye, but only one thing can stop Lothal: Anshuka.'

Hawthorn was still smiling, but Yselda looked at her, confused.

'We have to help Marta,' she said, and Benazir tried to smile at her, tried to look calm and in command.

'We will,' she said, turning to Marta and stroking the ashen curls of her hair. The girl looked up at her, wide-eyed. 'But first Marta needs to help us. Marta, my love. You need to wake the bear.'

~

From a dark and silent corridor Floré watched the orbs of light descend over Ossen-Tyr. There was a window high in the corridor that overlooked the front entrance of the compound, so she and Cuss dragged a table down the long hall and stood upon it. Both of them were clad in only their armour with green Orubor capes atop – their tabards were folded and stowed. After Cuss had woken her with a whisper, saying dawn was near, Floré had smeared her face with ash from the dead fire. She did the same to him and together they went to the side passage that connected the main entrance hall to the back courtyard.

'Starbeck said they'll pass right by here,' Cuss whispered, and together they watched as, through a sky black with cloud, two orbs of shining white flew down from the west. Both glowed brightly, and as they grew closer they turned from motes to sparks to burning brands, until they were the size of clenched fists, that pale glow pouring off them stark against the clouds beyond. The snow that had been falling intermittently since they arrived was in one of its pauses, and when one of the orbs began to descend, its light reflected on a thousand white-coated surfaces. Floré had checked an eastern window as they ran down to the corridor – the sky was beginning to pale as the sun rose, but darkness still lay claim to the west. She flexed her knuckles and tried to steady her breathing.

'Knife work, for the corridor,' she said, and Cuss slung his axe onto his back over his cape. One orb lay high above, but through the narrow window Floré could see the other growing close. *How many am I killing, doing this?* She knew there would be repercussions, a potential treaty broken before it could even be spoken. A hundred times in the last few days she had thought about alternatives – hunting in the rotstorm itself. But the risks were too high. *Even if a thousand die,* she thought, *it is fewer than if we let Tullen have his way. He could kill us all.* She knew this would be no simple fight. Demons had magic, could heal nearly any wound, could fly through the air. They might be accompanied by rust-folk, veterans of the rotstorm who knew the brutality of combat for survival. There might be goblins, rottrolls, trollspawn. *We only need one,* she thought.

Next to her Cuss was muttering to himself, but before she could tell him to be quiet the silence pressed over them. As the light of the orb poured through the window of their passage and turned everything to stark hues of white and black, a familiar pressure settled on her chest and her ears as if she were deep underwater. *Silence.* Floré worked her jaw and swore and heard none of it. She had not expected the orb to fly so close, to land so near to the entrance of the old overseers' fort. *If the silence holds...* She knew this could change everything. If the silence held, their chances were a thousandfold improved. Rowan and Tomas were in their own orb even now, hidden beneath canvas in the back courtyard with the ramp already descended, ready to fly at a moment's notice. Floré pressed her forehead against the cold stone of the corridor wall and pressed until the pressure began to hurt, and she felt her right arm twitching even as it clutched Tyr's old silver dagger.

They killed Tyr. The orbs had come to his little village, *her* little village, and they had broken him. They had attacked, had stolen children in the night.

'I've killed no child,' Floré said, even though with the landing so close she could not hear her own voice – could only feel the pressure of the field of silence on her chest. It felt good to say it aloud, even if nobody could hear her. 'I've killed goblins and crow-men, rust-folk, rottrolls. I've killed none with their weapon thrown aside, and I've killed no child. I'll not let them make me the villain.'

She knew in her heart it wasn't that simple. As the white light pressed around them and seemed to fill the corridor, with it came a calm certainty. *I am the villain.* To some rust-folk child, growing up with an arcane storm on one side, a wall on the other lined with steel and knights. *Do they even know the Ferron had us enslaved for centuries, our families and histories broken?* The burn in her heart told her it didn't matter. The crimes of the dead could not be heaped on the living. She could not bring herself to think of Anshuka as some all-knowing deity. It was ever clearer to her that the god-bear didn't care, one way or another. *Just another beast, like the rest of us.*

Floré turned to Cuss and grabbed his arm.

'No matter what they did to us,' she said, in the silence, a silence that ate her words, 'no matter how bad it was. We *must* be better.'

She could see he did not understand, and so she just shook her head and pointed at the door. The aura of silence and the burning effusive light were both still present, though the light was no longer moving. *They've stopped outside.* Floré moved to the doorway and pushed it open an inch. The torches were blazing in the entrance hall. Starbeck was standing alone, hands clasped behind his back, sweating despite the cold, and ten feet behind him four City Watch Guards nervously fingered their sword hilts. The pale light of the orb filled the entrance hall – the front doors were open wide, and a freezing wind eddied around the entrance, sending the torches flickering even as their pale yellow light fought against the brilliance of the glaring orb outside. Floré squinted at it – three figures had descended. *Only three.* She knew the Stormguard delegation and presence was deliberately few, part of the negotiations before the negotiations. Floré pushed her fear down, and tried to harness her anger. She would do this, for Marta. No matter the cost. For a moment she allowed herself to think of Benazir and Yselda, far to the north. *Did they find you, little fish?*

The three figures stepped forward, and Floré blinked away her worry and took the measure of their outlines and then their detail as they stepped closer, the weight of silence still pressing in at her as she stared through the gap in the door. The silence gnawed at her other senses, put her on edge for a blade at her back, but she made herself focus. Two figures were human: a woman with lustrous black hair and a fur-lined cloak, and a thick-set man with watery eyes. Floré did not spare them her consideration.

She focused on the third figure – cloaked and hooded. It stood a head above the others even with the hunch to its back. From beneath the hood Floré could see no face, no expression to betray intent, but from beneath the cloak long hands clad in thick leather jutted outward on the ends of awkwardly bent arms. Its legs were similarly overlong and doubly jointed, and its walk was careful, as if every step was a challenge of balance. Floré could see a dagger of bare steel and three wands tucked in the crow-man's belt. *Wonderful.* The three of them stepped forward and forward until they were halfway to Starbeck and level with Floré's side passage. *Now or never.*

Floré grabbed Cuss behind her and looked him in the eye and he nodded. In the silence of the orb, they attacked. Cuss ran straight in, as they'd agreed, and Floré ducked left and sprinted a few steps before circling back. The three saw Cuss as he barrelled towards them, and hopefully didn't notice her. He shoulder-charged the heavy-set man, who went down like a sack of potatoes to the slick stone floor. The crow-man wheeled on Cuss and from her belt drew a wand of fire. The demon's hood fell back, and from behind Floré could see a shock of red hair, a pale face with a thick black tattoo surrounding one eye. Her face was a snarl, words being shouted in the silence of the orb, but Cuss managed to grab her thin wrist with his gauntlet and his other hand came up in a punch and then Floré was on her.

Through the heavy cloak she stabbed deep with Tyr's old lancer dagger, the silver blade punching through cloth and leather and piercing flesh beneath. The crow-man bucked backwards and her back slammed into Floré, sending her sprawling, but even as she scrambled to her feet Cuss was punching, over and over and over again, the silver ridge of his gauntlet raising welts and burns wherever it struck her face. The wand was firing a blaze of black and red flame, a cone of fire that shot up and around the room, setting tapestries ablaze and scorching stone wall. The rust-folk man was still on the ground, crawling to safety, and Floré didn't even check the other woman. *No time.* Starbeck and his guards were falling back. It was sickening not to be able to hear the fighting – she could not even hear her own heartbeat, the rush of breath in and out of her lungs. All she could sense was that pressure from the orb, the orb that was so close now – only ten feet beyond the open door of the garrison. *Full of rust-folk, or crow-men,* she thought, a staccato burst of fear in her as the melee turned her back to it. *I won't hear them come for me.*

Floré managed to keep her hand on the dagger and she went for the crow-man again, stabbing down into the shank of her leg, and the demon buckled. Cuss hit her again in the temple and the guttering flame of the wand stopped. The lanky frame of the creature sank to the stone, supported only by Cuss's iron grip on her arm. Floré stuck her knife in her belt and grabbed the demon's shoulder.

'Run!' she shouted, though still, everything was silence. Between them they hauled the demon up, its head a mess of blood and bone, and began to drag it to the side passage. *Not dead,* Floré knew. It would take more than a beating and a few skewers, even with silver, to put down a crow-man. The sickly light of the orb outside still saturated the room, and Starbeck and his guard had retreated back and out of the entrance hall. The rust-folk man Cuss had knocked to the ground was running back towards his orb, and the woman – *where is she?*

Floré had discounted her – she would be whatever the rust-folk counted as a diplomat, some leader or healer or whatever else. But Floré had survived a decade campaigning in the rotstorm. She'd survived crow-men and goblins and monsters, in a place where even the water and air around you wanted you dead. She'd survived because she didn't discount threats.

Her heightened paranoia saved her – as the hammer blow fell, she ducked low and threw up the crow-man's arm over her own head. She felt the arm break above her, and then she pushed her burden off and backed up three steps. The woman had let her hood down and her long black hair flowed over her shoulders, framing a face that was a mirror of Floré's own – grey eyes and amber skin. The demon fell fully to the ground, and as Floré unsheathed her sword, Cuss unhooked his axe and together they squared off against the woman. Floré threw a nervous glance back at the blazing orb just outside. The woman was armed with a hammer, black steel embossed with silver and gold, and the leather of her armour was finely tooled with intricate patterns. *She is not from the rotstorm – she is from Cil-Marie!* Floré drew her sword out and began to circle the woman, but the woman only smiled and lunged instead at Cuss.

The boy tried valiantly to block her with his axe, but she feinted high and then spun low and brought the hammer around in a swirling blow to his midriff. The woman was slight, but the blow sent Cuss flying ten feet across the stone slabs and crashing into the wall. It was impossible, but Floré didn't have time to process. The woman had spun to face her. In silence they duelled, Floré's sweeping cuts and probing stabs stymied at every turn by a twist of the hammer's head or a quickstep away. She could not see Starbeck and his guards, could see no Stormguard. Cuss lay senseless on the floor.

Floré slashed upward and the hammer met the rune blade

of her sword and instead of parrying the blade, there was an explosion of force. The sword ripped from her left hand and she barely managed to hold on, but then her arm stopped moving. The sword stopped moving. Floré was pressed in a vice of air, and she screamed but in the silence of the orb of light there was no sound – only pressure. From behind, long arms snaked around her. One hand reached down to her sword and plucked the blade from her gauntleted fist, and the other hand clutched her head, a palm at the base of her skull, long fingers reaching all the way up and over, their cold fingertips resting on her forehead. Floré stared at the woman with the hammer, who scanned the room.

Crow-men came into vision, five, ten, more than a dozen swarming from the orb and into Floré's view. The woman gestured at them and at the still form of Cuss, and Floré strained and screamed but her muscles would not listen. Her scream tore from her throat but there was only the silence of the orb. *Marta!*

The demon hand that clutched Floré's skull tightened its grip, and in the glow of the orb she saw nothing but white light, and then darkness.

15

Ephemeral Clouds

'Is this a joke to you? Am I some girl to be had and forgotten, some whore to be paid? I bid you come to me, with the wolf and the swords at your command. Do not think to defy me in this – remember from whence your power came. We will drive the slaves back to their mines, and water the fields with their blood. I will sow a crop of bones this season, and you shall be my farmhand. I am not angry about the girl from Hunesh – I have already forgotten her, and I have had her name stricken from all record and her family sent to the Undal fields. I am angry because there is a revolution, and my general is drinking and screwing his way across our empire instead of standing at my side. Come now. Your empress commands it.' – **Private letter**, Empress Seraphina of the Gilded Spire

In the dark sky as tendrils of dawn began to probe at the far horizon, Tullen One-Eye flew down to the god-bear Anshuka. For a mile around him the cloud and ice of the Claw Winter pushed out. Above Orubor's forest, Ashbringer could see nothing but clear air, air that was so cold and still that sparkles of ice hung in motes, as if the soul of every ancestor in the sky was falling.

They flew down to the meadow in front of Anshuka, and as they flew a brilliant white illuminated the snowfield below – one of the orbs the Orubor had captured, flooding the scene with a glow of eerie white. The orb began to rise towards them, sending dancing spears of light through the snow-covered pines, casting a pale glow over Anshuka herself, and Tullen stretched out his fist. In a moment the orb crumpled, its light extinguished, and from a hundred feet in the air a pile of broken stone and metal and flesh fell like an avalanche. Ashbringer let out a huff of breath. *Who flew, tonight? Rowan? Hawthorn? Juniper?* It would be one of the young warriors she trained with whenever she was back in the forest, young and lean and hungry to serve. *I see you, sibling.*

As they flew together lower and lower, slow and steady, Ashbringer could see firelight flickering in the woods, ringing the meadow. At the meadow's centre, the Highmothers were standing around the broken crúca stone – Elm, Oak, Rowan, Birch. She could not see Highmother Ash. *South, with the Undal,* she thought. From the treeline, a spark of lightning shot upward – one of the Orubor hiding in the trees reaching deep to the song and finding that spark. The lightning flew at them and Ashbringer opened her eyes wide, but she did not dare to hope. The bolt of crackling light flew true, but a dozen feet from them it crashed against an invisible shield, breaking like a wave against one of the great boulders of starmetal that dotted the coast to the south. Ashbringer was sick with the hate in her gut, the fear of what was to happen next.

Tullen landed them in the snow scarcely twenty yards from the crúca stone, and let Ashbringer go.

'Go to them,' he said gently, and she stumbled to her knees in the snow. Slowly she dragged herself up and trudged towards the crúca and the Highmothers, the mountain of Anshuka behind them silhouetted in starlight. Their hands reached for her and drew her close, and together they huddled, all of them facing him. There were no words to be said, at this. The crúca stone was broken, cracks of molten silver scarring across its surface. Ashbringer went to her knees and put a hand on it. *Mother, give me strength*. Tullen stood in the snow, clad in black. He wore no cloak, and was dressed for a summer's day in shirt and trousers, simple boots. From his belt he drew the dagger, and Ashbringer began to weep. The blade was chipped obsidian, a shard, and the hilt was twisted bone. At the pommel the great green gem, rough and unworked, shone.

She heard them running, heard the arrows cutting through the air. From the meadow's edge as the dawn light danced across the treetops, the Orubor charged in darkness. *Hundreds*. She had never seen so many of her people in one place. Balls of flame and crackling bolts of lightning, a hundred arrows shot and a hundred more in their wake. A hundred more swords drawn, swords etched in runes that glowed in the starlight, held in sure hands.

Tullen One-Eye smiled at her and raised his hand. The arrows did not reach him – twenty feet away, they stopped as if they had hit a castle wall and fell, broken or bent or simply spinning off. The lightning crackled and dissipated; the flame exploded. All of it at the edge of this wall, the translucent barrier where he had decided nothing would cross. The first of the warriors hit the sphere at a full run, and collapsed back in the dirt, face bloody and arm twisted. A dozen others suffered the same fate, until Tullen was standing in the snow surrounded by twenty feet of calm, and then Orubor five ranks deep, seething, testing at the boundary with flame and blade and whatever knack for the great melody they had. He took a step forward, and those directly in front of him stumbled and fell as the invisible wall forced them back. The wall tinged red, still translucent but *visible*, and the Orubor began to warily step back from it as it advanced, but Ashbringer and the Highmothers stood firm. Ashbringer felt it pass over her, a tingling sensation over her skin. *He is letting us in.* A few Orubor began to send arrows high over Tullen's wall to pierce him from above, but the wall swiftly grew to a dome and their arrows clattered uselessly away.

'I appreciate the audience,' he said, and the meadow fell still. Every Orubor stopped, breath ragged with rage to a soul. Ashbringer was crying. She could see the wreckage of the orb in the meadow beyond, and behind her the crúca stone was marred with hot silver scars. The stone was cold to the touch, but she could not bring herself to touch the veins of silver. *There is nothing we can do.*

'None of you need to die today, I think,' Tullen said. 'Shall I tell you why?'

Tullen raised the hand clutching the dagger at Anshuka, and closed his eyes.

'I travelled these woods before the Emperor Ferron raised the Judges,' Tullen said, his eyes still closed, his voice hoarse with strain as he concentrated. 'The Orubor called this place home. Humans. A clan of humans, whose ancestors had hunted and held this forest since time before time. Humans who gave honour to the bear spirit Anshuka that walked their woods, a great bear thrice the height of a man. At her feet, flowers blossomed, and in her wake berries ripened.'

Ashbringer stared at the great sleeping bear, the mountain, and pictured the goblins born in the rotstorm. Orb-eyed and grey-skinned and jagged of tooth, stunted where she was tall, broken where she was whole. *Are they my dark reflection? No!*

Tullen lies. She knew him for a liar. He would say anything, do anything – but she could not deny the truth in her heart that his words sparked. *What am I?*

As the first light of dawn began to play over the bear god's meadow Ashbringer heard the howl of a wolf, deep and resonant somewhere in the forest. *Lothal is here.* She stepped forward towards Tullen and he turned to her and opened his eyes, smiling.

'Do you see now, Ashbringer?'

She drew herself up straight, and eyes wide she drew the symbol of Anshuka across her chest – Ɏ. The symbol of protection, of community. *I am me. I am still me. I am, I am, I am.*

'What are you going to do, Deathless?' she asked, and Tullen lowered his blade and the corner of his mouth twitched. At the periphery of his dome of red force the Orubor stared inwards, hands clutching blade or bow, and behind Ashbringer the Highmothers clustered around the broken crúca stone. Tullen turned and stared west, and then north. He smiled.

'They are coming,' he said, and sat cross-legged in the snow, eyes closed. Ashbringer stared up at Anshuka, sleeping, and the tears on her cheeks froze as fast as they fell.

~

Yselda tried to wake Marta as the orb flew, but the girl would not wake. No matter what Yselda did, the girl would not wake. She gripped her, shook her, pleaded with her, but her eyelids would only flutter.

'We *have* to get to the whitestaffs in Undal City,' she said, but Benazir did not look back at her. Benazir looked out of the crystal strip of their orb as it flew south and east from the Antian Redoubt, her eyes scanning the horizon. They were up high over the clouds, Hawthorn leading them ever faster. The Orubor was looking wan and wizened, the glow of the orb outside washing back into the interior. Hawthorn had stopped joking, and Yselda could see from the strain in her jaw the effort it took her to move her muscles. *It's killing her!* Benazir didn't look at Hawthorn, either. She only looked forward. *How many have to die?*

Yselda stroked Marta's hair back from her face and stood, leaving her in the pile of cloaks they had made on the cold floor of the stone orb. Nintur and Rollo and the lancers were on edge, everything about the strange orb of light and the stranger creature at its helm setting them to mutter. They did not question Benazir.

Yselda went to Benazir's side and leaned in close.

'She isn't even awake,' she said. 'She can't speak to Anshuka. She's just a child, Benazir. We have to take her to get *help*.'

Benazir did not turn to her, just stared out of the crystal window and down – below them, thick snow clouds wound in spirals, and the odd patch of clear sky through to the ground showed nothing but snow. In the east the dawn had risen, and the topography of the cloud tops was highlighted in shadow and shades of brilliant orange. The sky above was still dark, but with every passing moment and mile it lightened.

'The Orubor will help her,' Benazir said. She did not break her gaze from the sky ahead. 'Have you ever seen something like this, Yselda?'

Yselda huffed and gripped at the amulet at her neck and looked at little Marta. She remembered the summer before, before the orbs. Mucking around with Cuss and Petron at the shoreline of Loch Hassel, the little beach north of Floré's house, Marta and Cuss's sister Jana sat in the sand under the watchful eye of Janos. He had packed them all a picnic. The sun had been hot overhead and they had spent the morning swimming. *I'll get you home, little one.*

'Lothal the wolf will not be stopped by you or I, little sister,' Benazir said, and Yselda turned and stared at the cloud tops. They were beautiful. The red and orange hues of sunlight lit the eastern slopes of the clouds, and cast long shadows towards the west. The clouds were mountains that moved, slowly changing, and Yselda's view of them changing as the orb flew on and on. The unnatural speed and smoothness of their flight had set her gut roiling as she tried to reconcile the dancing horizon with the calm at her feet, but now she was used to it she could see it for the wonder it was.

'Where did they come from, the orbs?' she asked, for something to say other than another plea.

Benazir shrugged. 'Tullen One-Eye and his empress broke old Undalor and built their empire, but long before that there was an emperor – *Ferron*. A man who never aged, who sought to answer every question. Where do we come from? There are many stories of Ferron, Yselda. The man is a myth. But a few tell of him travelling the skies in his orbs of light. I found one, in Riven as we waited over the summer. It said that he grew tired of looking for answers here and left, taking his orbs and his disciples to the stars.'

Yselda looked up. The dawn light was filling the sky, but she could still see the brightest stars high above in the washed-out blue. She thought she could see the tip of Char the Warrior's sword.

'What is in the stars?' she asked, and shivered. The old whitestaff in Hasselberry, Izelda, had told her stars were simply distant suns, and around each one, a world like their own might dance.

'The ancestors are in the stars,' Hawthorn said, voice hoarse. 'Look, *Benazir*.'

They turned their gaze from the stars above to the sky ahead of them. The firmament of snow cloud was broken – a clear line in the sky, a great circle twenty miles wide – below it, Orubor's forest. The orb pressed faster, lower, and all of them leaned forward to stare. Hawthorn growled, and Yselda gasped and felt her knees weaken.

At the heart of Orubor's forest, hundreds of little specks covered a meadow, breaking up the white of the snow. The mountain that was Anshuka lay still, uncovered by snow, but in the meadow below hundreds of Orubor were arrayed in a circle surrounding a single point, all facing inward. In that gap in the circle, she could see a few figures but make out no detail. *Are they looking up at us?* Hawthorn flew them closer, but as they reached the edge of the meadow the orb grew still.

'Take us down to them,' Benazir said, and Hawthorn grimaced.

'I'm trying!'

Yselda could see the strain on the Orubor's face, and then blood began to leak from her nose. Hawthorn gnashed her razor teeth and then she slumped back in the chair, and the glow faltered and failed and the orb began to plummet, twisting and twisting as it fell, and Yselda could not even scream. Benazir's hand gripped the pilot's chair and she reached her other arm to Yselda and she gripped on but then the orb stopped spinning. They hung in the air, silent and still, the glow of the orb dark, the lancers crouching low and gripping at whatever they could. Nintur was crouched low over Marta, his face pale, and next to him Voltos clutched Jozenai's basket.

Yselda breathed out and gripped tighter onto Benazir.

'Why aren't we falling?' she asked, and turned her gaze out

of the crystal strip. She could see the mountain, see *Anshuka*, and around her treetops swaying. From the meadow below a figure rose, floating slowly upward with arms raised, and she felt her breath catch. *Tullen One-Eye.* Head shaven, clad in black. He hung in the air in front of them and cocked his head to one side. He smiled, and with a hand he waved downward, and the orb began to descend gently to the meadow below. Yselda could see the Orubor now, hundreds of them armed with bow and blade. She could see a pile of broken black stone and metal – *another orb, crushed.*

As they descended she drew her knife and went to Marta and joined Nintur, crouching over the girl.

'Wake up, Marta,' Benazir said, quietly, but Yselda did not know if it was better to wake her or let her sleep. *Is it better for her to see her death and face it?* She had not been able to wake the girl throughout the hours of their flight from the north, and had no idea why Benazir felt she could wake her now. *Would I rather sleep now? Sleep, and dream of home?* She clutched the old antler of her knife hilt and ran her other hand through Marta's hair. *Sleep, little one.*

The orb settled roughly on the meadow below, burning white light extinguished, all inside silent save for Hawthorn, who was breathing in great heaving gasps. The ramp descended and a voice called from outside. *Tullen One-Eye.*

'Come!' he called. 'We have so much to do!'

They waited in silence, but there was no more word, and Benazir slowly shook her head and gestured for them all to rise.

Yselda scooped up Marta and held her against her chest. She followed Benazir down the ramp. Rollo and Nintur and the other lancers flanked her, every one of them clad in blue with the lightning bolt of gold across the chest. They all held bare steel, axes and swords and short spears, half of them carrying shields painted in blue and black, each with Anshuka's rune writ large over any other colour or sign: Y. Yselda felt Marta's weight and warmth, the faint movement of the girl breathing, and in her gauntleted hand she gripped her dagger tight. Benazir led them, a dagger in her own left hand, the hook at the end of her right arm extended and twisting as she slowly descended the ramp. She glanced back at Yselda.

'Keep her *safe*,' she hissed, her face a twisted mask of anger, and then she strode out of the darkness into the snow beyond. Yselda felt her breath catch. *Keep her safe*. As if it were that simple, as if Yselda was a mage or a hero. *I'm just a girl,* she wanted to say. Yselda felt herself swaying, and she breathed deep, inhaling the scent of Marta's hair. The dawn light tinged the snow with hues of pink and red and orange, and little shadows fells from every sweeping drift or footprint that marred the snowfield's smooth surface.

Above her, the mountain that was Anshuka sat implacable and still, asleep beneath stone and rock, and below it Tullen One-Eye stood in a circle of perfect calm, hundreds of Orubor lingering in the meadow all around, their gazes rapt. Yselda saw Ashbringer weeping on her knees in the snow next to a black stone covered in hot seams of molten silver.

'Suffer no tyrant,' she said quietly, whispering it into Marta's hair. She felt a hand on her shoulder, and Nintur stepped to her side.

'Forge no chain,' he said, and the other lancers echoed their words. Benazir moved her hand at her side at them – *stay* – and she stepped forward another ten steps until she and Tullen One-Eye faced each other, the mountain of the great god-bear looming over them.

'Some chains are more emotional, than physical,' Tullen said, his voice projecting across the meadow. 'There are the chains we impose on ourselves, those we craft for others through word or deed. I was so angry with her, for so long, but the truth is Anshuka has been chained – chained by your ancestors to a terrible fate. To incarnate the rotstorm, and take no part in history. To sleep. Did you think it was by choice? The bear is a bear, as the wolf is a wolf. There is no malice in a bear – and the rotstorm is a creation of malice if ever there was one. There has been so little choice, for all of us. Perhaps there is something there to think on.'

The Orubor stood entranced, bows bent and blades gripped in tense hands, and Yselda could see a faint haze of red between the Orubor and the heart of the meadow where their orb sat, where Tullen and Ashbringer and Benazir were arrayed. Benazir was staring past Tullen, up at Anshuka, but Yselda forced herself to keep focus. *Keep Marta safe. How do I do that?* She focused on the forest, the Orubor. Highmothers, warriors. The trees dappled in snow. She gauged the distance to run – she had been to this meadow before, in the summer when Varratim's orbs had come to kill the god-bear, and once only days before when they came to take their own orb. *To find Marta. To wake Anshuka.* She felt sick in her stomach every time her gaze locked on Tullen. She remembered the Riven citadel, the way he had killed Janos and left them to die in the snow. He had flown, thrown fire and magic easier than she could breathe.

'There has been no choice but war, and death, and horror,' Tullen said, and in his hand he held the knife with its blade of black stone, the green gem at its pommel. He held it before him, the hilt flat in the palm of his hand.

Benazir spun her own dagger blade in her left hand and spat in the snow. 'So what next, One-Eye?' she said. 'Kill the world and dance in the ashes?'

Tullen smiled. 'None of you understand,' he said softly, and then he closed his eyes for a moment and with a thunderous crack the dagger blade shattered into a dozen pieces, slipping from his open hand down into the snow below. Slowly he opened his eyes and dropped the hilt to the snow and dusted his hands together, flakes of obsidian falling from his palms.

'What next, Stormguard? She will dream, and then she will wake. The bear and the wolf have business, and then they are free to do as they will. No more chains. Only what the gods will.'

Across the forest a deep howl reverberated, and from the snow Yselda turned to the west, across the meadow. Lothal the wolf, blacker than the night, streaked in gleaming silver, stepped between trees and sniffed. Black eyes large as whole oxen stared at them in the meadow, stared at the stone mountain beyond, where Anshuka slept. The wolf prowled the far edge of the meadow, back and forth and back and forth.

Tullen One-Eye spared the wolf a glance and a smile, but then his eyes locked on Marta, and Yselda held the girl close as Marta moaned and wailed, her eyes fluttering, her limbs twitching as she convulsed. *She's in the skein. It's too much!*

Tullen strode forward and Benazir swung for him and then stopped, became a statue, utterly still. He glanced at her rank badge and curled his lip, and then turned to the lancers. With a wave of his hand they went tumbling, the dozen bodies including resolute Nintur and hulking Rollo spinning off to crash sickeningly into the snow fifty feet away. Voltos and Hawthorn had not descended from the orb above. Yselda flinched and fell back to the snow, still clutching Marta.

'I *thought* I sensed another skein-wreck,' Tullen said finally, standing over Yselda. 'But this is even more impressive. You were at Riven, girl. You and the other one.'

He inclined his head back to Benazir, but his eyes bored

into Yselda. *You saw him break Janos,* she thought. *You saw him stop time, you saw him tame Ashbringer, you saw him fly across the sky and hurl magic.* She knew what he was. *He is a wolf.*

Yselda raised her blade and got to her feet and pointed the tip of the knife at him, and held Marta close to her chest.

'You can't have her,' she said, and put every mote of emotion in her heart into the words, every ounce of strength into holding her arm steady.

Tullen One-Eye nodded, and then his mouth twitched.

'Always,' he said, 'people think they know what I want. Sit, child. Learn. The bear has had nightmares for so long, but the nightmares have focused where she was *ordered* to bring them to bear. I think I shall bring them here, no? Is that not righteous? I must whisper in the ear of the dreamer. Sit tight, child. Hold the little one close.'

Tullen turned from her and walked back to the centre of the meadow, and with a throbbing pulse, the dome of faint red light holding back the Orubor fell inward, surrounding his body, and then pushed outward even further. It pushed the Orubor, the Highmothers, the lancers. It passed over the orb of stone and metal where Voltos and Hawthorn still hid. All went tumbling back across the meadow until Tullen had a hundred feet of clear space around him, within it the broken black stone with veins of silver and Benazir, Yselda, Ashbringer, and Marta.

Lothal growled at the edge of the meadow and raked at a tree, bringing it crashing down to the snow with a slam that sent a tremor through the earth, but Yselda did not turn away from Tullen One-Eye. The man sat cross-legged in the snow and stared up at sleeping Anshuka, and Yselda clutched Marta close to her chest. The clouds that danced miles away at the periphery of the forest began to draw in closer to the meadow in a great rush, and they turned from grey and white to black and red as they coalesced and roiled above, titanic thunderheads meeting with a gale and a roar of air.

Tullen began to laugh as rain began to fall, and in the clouds above, lightning danced.

16

The Rotstorm

'*I miss you. I miss the tunnels of the redoubt, and the long deep road east. I have spent what coin and mind I have on rumour and word of the others – the Antian who are not bound by the northern continent. The seas here are wild, the reefs dangerous and full of violence, but ships do come. I met Antian who have sailed Carob's Strait and the Crown Islands. We have kindred in Siobh, hidden in the high places. We have kindred in the endless archipelago of the Crowns, and far below them. The word from the south is of chain and whip – the Cil-Marie do not recognise us as people worthy of honour or right. Why help the Stormguard? They will break the chains. If they are strong enough, they may break all the chains.*' – **Letter to the Hidden Council of the Undal Redoubt**, Bellentoe Firstclaw

Floré dreamt of the rotstorm, of acid mist. She'd dreamt of it ever since she was a little girl, sleeping sound with her brothers and sisters, her mother and father, all in one big room. She'd wake up scared by the rain, afraid that the rotstorm had come hundreds of miles across the Northern Marches and everything was flooded and lost. She'd dreamt of it when it was a presence at her window, at the Stormwall when she was training, when she was camping in the Slow Marsh as a cadet, when she was safe behind stone walls in her barracks. She'd dreamt of it when she was in the storm itself, of course – those fitful moments of sleep snatched on patrols and raids and missions, tucked up close to a bank of peat or thrown down to mulchy ground in one of the little copses of trees that grew so close, as if they were huddling together for shelter.

Floré dreamt of the rotstorm, and she was alone. Lightning and rain, thunder. Thunder. Thunder, deep and rolling, a splash of rain on her face and the sky above a bruise of purple and black and green and red, all of it dark, all of it churning. Lightning danced below the cloud and within it, black streaks and yellow and dazzling white, thin branching bolts of red that coated the staggering clouds above. Floré blinked three times and felt the rain burning at her face and realised she was not dreaming.

She was in the rotstorm. *No. No!* Her breath was ragged as she tried to draw in something, some fresh clean air but there was only rust and burn, and all around her the rain pouring hard. *Gods, no!* She could feel the rain burning her skin, could see the breaking bolts of lightning. *Death,* she thought, and could feel her heart beat so fast. *The rotstorm means death.*

With an effort of will she tried to shake the haze from her mind, to think clearly. Her eyes were streaming, but at least it was the weak acid of the rain. If it had been a blight mote, a red acid cloud that danced across the rotstorm marshes, then nothing would be left of her but gauntlets and rank buckle and sword.

Gauntlets. Sword.

There were many rules for a commando to survive the rotstorm, but paramount was keeping your steel. Gauntlets to protect you from the endless poison thorn and biting kelp and snaring rotvine, sword to kill whatever fresh hell the storm threw at you. Floré clenched bare fists, and felt no weight at her hip. Blowing out a breath, she shook rain from her face and opened her eyes again. Her hands were tied behind her back, around some sort of post. She was slumped in the peat of the rotstorm, and next to her a few feet away Cuss was similarly staked out. The boy was unconscious, one eye swollen shut. Floré gritted her teeth. *I'm sorry, lad.* She flung her head around, saw where they were, and slumped back against the post holding her up.

Fifty feet away to her right, Lothal's bones loomed through the pouring rain. Curved ribs as thick as tree trunks rising in rows out of the peat, a skull with teeth long as swords half buried in the rich black dirt. All of the bones were black, impossibly large, impossibly clean. The ground around was a peat bog, tiny canyons and gullies and thick grasses, little streams of ferrous water. At the base of Lothal's bones a great open-sided tent had been raised, and next to it an orb of stone sat on three legs of spindly metal, a band of crystal bisecting the orb horizontally.

Floré squinted in the rain and saw the shapes inside, tall yet hunched, spindly limbs trailing like afterthoughts. Crow-men. They moved between dozens of rust-folk, all of them armed and cloaked against the downpour. Outside of the tent, more goblins than she had ever seen before thronged and clamoured, all of them trying to see what was inside. *Ceann Brude.* The war-master of Ferron walked tall and spoke urgently, first to one group, then another. Behind her the dark-haired woman with the enchanted hammer followed diligently, and spoke little. Floré could not see the man they called Reeve.

'Cuss!' she called, but the boy did not answer. Floré strained at her bonds – they were rope or plant of some kind, slick and wet with the constant rain. She felt no give in them. At her feet, a wending rotvine creeper began to probe at her, its little fronded bud mouth opening and closing, lips of green petal revealing thorn teeth below. Satisfied she was food, the bud began biting, and from the swamp behind it, another dozen tendrils joined it, dragging themselves from the water and swaying towards her. Floré did not hesitate. She kicked to push them back and then stamped where she could, crunching her heel into the vine – but the peat below was soft, and the vines simply sank down and then lashed out again and again. Her trousers were thick cotton, but the thorns of the rotvine were sharp. She writhed to keep them from getting a grip or a hold, so each bite was only a scratch, but she could feel frenzy building in her chest.

Focus. She tried to pull herself upright, to slide her arms up the wooden pole, but the ground was wet with rain and the pallid grass that grew in patches over the peat was slick. She could find no purchase.

Floré screamed when the first rotvine bit down hard and true, and she wasn't able to shake it free. It clamped down on the outside of her left thigh, and then another was on the calf below it, biting but also winding around her lower leg, constricting and pulsing with strength. Floré thrashed her head and saw Lothal's bones looming over them in the rain, the crow-men and rust-folk under their thick canopy. Her eyes fell on the limp form of Cuss and she roared with rage.

'Cuss! CUSS!'

The boy's legs were already wrapped thick in rotvine, six or seven of the creeping vines twisting him tight. He was still unconscious, head slumped and mouth open as rain played over his face. *What's the plan?* Floré couldn't think straight. The gnawing of the little thorns at her legs, the ache in her head, the jittering scar tissue in her right arm that pulsed and ached and constricted. *This is where it happened.*

A decade before, Floré had stood beneath Lothal's bones and brought death to the rust-folk. She had stood with Janos, and together they had fought through rain and lightning to retrieve a rotbud, to keep the storm from the protectorate. *Is that what this is?* Floré desperately tried to twist and see the stake holding her firm to the ground. *Is it tipped in metal? Do they mean to bring down the lightning?* Floré had used that trick herself. It was one of the teachings of the balanced blade manifest – a sword can always be something more than just a sword.

Floré relaxed her legs and let the vines wrap closer, then strained them together and began to twist and thrash, feeling vines tear and thorns break off in her flesh.

'Brude!' she yelled, over and over. 'Ceann Brude!'

She wanted to yell more, but then her left thumb was engulfed in a burning pain utter and absolute. She could not look back, could only wrench her hands tight in their bonds, but she knew what had happened. A rotvine had her thumb in its mouth, had clamped down with its thorn teeth, and the brutal acid lining its throat was eating at the flesh. Floré clenched her hands into fists and screamed, and then made herself breathe deep.

Ceann Brude was walking from the canopy, flanked by her hammer-wielding shadow and three other crow-men, a dozen rust-folk. Together they walked through the rain under the shadow of the dead god and stood, looking down at Floré and Cuss.

'No trial for rust-folk,' Brude said in Isken, her accent thick. She had to yell to be heard over the thunder above, and the clouds shone red for a moment as somewhere deep within another bolt of lightning struck. 'Do you know where you are,

Stormguard? Assassin? Again we try and find peace, and again you prove yourself faithless.'

Floré forced herself to spread her fingers wide behind her back for a long moment, and then grabbed the rotvine creeper chewing at her thumb and *squeezed*. She felt that familiar tearing and popping of wet plant flesh and the creeper slipped from her thumb. As it fell back into the mud and peat behind her, Brude cocked her head and waved a hand. The rotvine creepers began to retract. Floré threw a glance at Cuss – he was still wrapped, his legs, his arms, his torso, every moment more rotvine wrapping closer.

'The boy,' she said. 'The vines. Stop them.'

'No trial for rust-folk,' Brude said again, and stared at Floré for a long moment. *She is so young.* Younger than Floré by a decade, perhaps, if the face she presented aged true. *The same age I was last time I stood beneath these bones.* Her red hair was plastered to her head by the rain, and around one eye and across the eyelid she had the old Ferron symbol for salt tattooed in a thick circle: Ø.

'He's just a boy,' Floré said, and saw the twitch in the woman's eye.

'That may be,' she said at last, and with a wave the rotvine smothering Cuss began to retreat and pull back. Through his rain-soaked clothes Floré could see rivulets of blood running from a dozen points. 'Perhaps he is just a boy. Perhaps he is a victim of your protectorate as much as the rest of us. We shall see. There will be judgement.'

Floré let her head hang. Lothal's bones were three days from the Stormwall. *Nobody is coming to help you.*

'The Stormguard want peace,' she said, at last, and the tears in her eyes were washed down her cheeks by the driving acid rain. *I'm sorry, Marta.* 'They will give you the Northern Marches. I wear no tabard. My mission is my own.'

Around the rust-folk and crow-men peering out from their canopy, dozens of goblins were gathering. A few of them ran through the storm, wind and rain lashing at pebbled grey skin, and they began pawing at Cuss, moving his head left and right. The boy was unresponsive. The woman with the hammer at her belt leaned in close to Brude on one side and said something in her ear, the gaunt and looming crow-man bending low to hear her, and then on her other side a rust-folk man with a pockmarked face pulled at Brude's arm and spoke to her. Their words were too quiet to hear over the storm. Brude was nodding and then she stepped close to Floré and leaned down. The brutal blows Cuss had rained down on her face and head had already healed, her skin unblemished and unscarred. She held out a hand to Floré and twisted it, as if to say, *go on*.

'Tullen One-Eye,' Floré said. 'There is no peace while he lives. He is too powerful. I planned to take you to him. A skein-mage cannot access the pattern if a… if one like *you* is close. You are chaos.' Floré leaned her head back against the wooden post and closed her eyes. 'Take you to him, kill him, and then give you your peace. He killed my husband. He has killed a Judge, broken the Tullioch spire, broken nations at a whim. You will not have any peace while he lives, Ceann Brude, except what he chooses to give you. Peace on the whim of a madman is no peace at all. Peace under the threat of a sword is no peace at all. Peace at any cost, for all of us – I gave myself this mission. He *must* die.'

Floré opened her eyes and stared at Brude as the demon flexed her overlong fingers, rain cascading from her cloak. She thought Brude looked conflicted for a moment, but then there was only rage in her eyes and her mouth set in a grim line, thin lips disappearing entirely.

'I flew with Varratim's orbs,' she said, 'and *I* killed the Salt-Man. Your skein-wreck. Your *husband*, you say? I found him, and I broke his pattern and I put my knife into his gut. I took his child. They say he returned to life and fought Tullen One-Eye – this was my mistake. I should have taken his head, and *I could have*. You think a skein-wreck has too much power? Tullen One-Eye will give us peace, or we will take his head. We do not need *you* to do this for us, Stormguard dog. You thought with one of us you could defeat him. Look around you – we are many, and we hunger for our freedom. Our freedom will be our own, not granted by *you*.'

Floré felt her hands shaking, felt the anger taking over her body, a white-hot rage filling her from her gut to the backs of her eyes. *You killed my husband. Killed my Janos. You took my daughter.* Janos's reprieve and brief moments of life at the Riven citadel were immaterial. This creature had driven a knife into the gut of her poet, had taken her daughter screaming to be sacrificed by a madman. Her eyes flitted to the crow-man's belt for a weapon, anything – there was a simple knife of dull iron, three wands of black starmetal ending in faceted gems of red and blue and green, and the hilt of a sword made from the antler of a deer. Only an inch of blade was left, a core of dark metal layered in rune-etched silver. Floré recognised Ashbringer's blade. *Has she killed you as well?*

Peace at any cost.

Starbeck's words echoed in her mind, and a few feet away she saw Cuss begin to stir. Floré knew she needed control, knew she needed to negotiate on behalf of her people, for Cuss, for Marta, but all she could feel when she looked at Brude was anger. She strained forward as far as she could and the crow-man jerked back and Floré clenched her jaw. Behind her back, her hands worked at the ropes binding her, and then she felt her wedding ring, Janos's below it, snagging on a rope. Floré stopped working her hands, and took a deep breath. Janos, holding a sprig of lilac and smiling at her as she turned to walk away. Janos, in their room high in Protector's Keep reading from a cheap novel he had bought at the market from Kelamor. Janos, holding Marta in his arms and speaking to her in a low voice as they walked the shoreline of Loch Hassel in the summer.

'Peace at any cost,' Floré said again, and let her anger slip away. Brude stared down at her.

'He has summoned us,' Brude said at last. 'You will die, I think. But perhaps not here.'

With a wave of her hand, crown-men and goblins swarmed around her and Floré closed her eyes, and then she and Cuss were being dragged through the mud to the orb of stone, leaving a trail of blood and crushed vine behind them.

~

Ashbringer could taste the cold of the forest in her mouth, and as she sat cross-legged in the snow of the meadow next to Yselda and Benazir and Marta she tried to sing. 'Run, run, towards the light; run towards the mother,' she said, monotonously, and then she fell silent. Marta was shivering despite all of their cloaks layered over her, lying across the laps of Benazir and Yselda. The rain was falling now, a steady haze, but there was no shelter in the meadow. Tullen sat and stared at the mountain, and Ashbringer sat close with the others, huddled by the crúca stone.

Voltos had dragged Hawthorn down from the orb of stone, but Tullen had paid them no mind. The Antian clutched at his dagger and stared at the skein-wreck and back at the looming presence of Lothal the wolf, who still stood staring at sleeping Anshuka from across the meadow. Ashbringer sang and sang, and ran her hand through Hawthorn's hair. Hawthorn lay breathing heavily, her beautiful skin wizened and wrinkled, her flesh worn away.

'You used to sing a lot better,' she gasped, and Ashbringer reached back her hand and held her friend tight. She had trained many summers with Hawthorn, young as she was. She had hunted in the wood, and told her tales of the world beyond by the light of the ancestors above.

Ashbringer did not look at her friend, wasted away, or the sullen faces of Benazir and Yselda next to her. She stared at Deathless.

'Do you submit to Anshuka's judgement for your crimes, Deathless?' Ashbringer called, her voice leaden, and the skein-wreck shook his head and snorted at her. He raised his face to the rain above, and a bolt of lightning broke down from the roiling cloud and smashed into a tree to the north of the meadow. The thunder rolled over them, and Tullen laughed. Standing, he walked towards them, by all appearances unstressed and unfazed by the storm above.

'I appreciate you not trying to stab me, in the last few minutes. You would have failed, and it would have made bringing the storm a lot less joyous. You are thinking, *What is he doing? Am I right? Why did he destroy the dagger?*'

Tullen shook his head, and Ashbringer saw the woman Benazir gripping her dagger hilt, looking at the man's kidneys.

'Anshuka sleeps. Do you think I am her focus? No. No. I was the focus of Mistress Water, three hundred years ago. A weight she laid on Anshuka's spirit. Like the rotstorm. Mistress Water laid down her judgement. The gods and spirits and relu and bogles and wraiths of this world do not judge. There is no higher judge than the beating red heart. We tried to shackle them, do you see? We tried to chain them, old Ferron gave Berren and Lothal and Nessilitor and Anshuka realms of the world to look over, ideals to live up to. They are spirits, children. They do not judge us, not unless we make them.'

'Lothal hunted us in Hookstone forest,' Yselda said, and

Ashbringer blinked slowly. Tullen glanced over at Lothal, and then turned to observe the girl.

'Wolves hunt, girl. It is his nature to hunt. It is Anshuka's nature to wander the forests, to sleep long. It was Nessilitor's nature to build great nests, beautiful nests, prisms of living light. Do you begin to see? Mistress Water chained Anshuka. I chained Lothal. Before then, Ferron himself chained all four Judges, gave them their purpose instead of *meaning*. There are other spirits, out in the world, unchained – the great dragon of Ona, the serpent of the Crown Isles, the bird and whale the Tullioch worship so fervently. There are spirits far below the earth that the Antian war with or worship. In Cil-Marie they harvest the bones of dead Judges to make their hammers, their great weapons. There are lands beyond these, worlds beyond this one. The great spirits can alter the world, but mostly they choose not to. Anshuka is the aberration in this, but it was not her doing. I think I have... fixed some of it. We have spoken, just now, in a way. Fixed, with a little vengeance. Do you want to know what I've done?'

There is no higher judge than the beating red heart. The man was almost giddy. Ashbringer rose from the snowy meadow and stared up at Anshuka.

'Can you help the girl?' Benazir said, and Tullen frowned and glanced at Marta.

'Probably,' he said, and then he locked his gaze to Benazir's. Ashbringer pictured reaching her slender hands up to his neck and twisting and... *No.* She could not picture harming Tullen One-Eye. Ashbringer lowered herself back to the snow, the cold ache in her legs, her heart.

They all sat in silence in the rain, and eventually Tullen blew out a long breath. Voltos was clutching a basket at his side, his eyes fixed on the ground. Ashbringer blinked at him and cocked her head, but the little Antian was lost in thought. *He listens.*

'Do you want to know what I've done?' Tullen said again, and Benazir spat.

'I know this rain,' she said. 'You've brought the rotstorm to Orubor's wood. Congratulations.'

Tullen shook his head at her sneer. 'Three hundred years I've waited, and this is my audience. Violent children. I've reborn Lothal to his power, but without the compulsion Ferron put on him for honour, loyalty, all that nonsense. He is now purely himself, with whatever hints or impressions those who worship him send his way. I've broken the ur-blade that was gifted to me so long ago by Cil-Marie – such a thing is not relevant to my wishes, and I wouldn't want it falling into the hands of someone who thinks Judges are there for *harvest*, rather than adoration. I have reached into the heart of sleeping Anshuka and found Mistress Water's compulsions – to use Anshuka's power to bind me, to use Anshuka's power to kill Lothal, to use Anshuka's power to raise a great storm unceasing over the Ferron Empire. The twisting of life to make *servants* for Anshuka, transforming the locals into savage guardians. The twisting of life to make *monsters* of the Ferron, taking those who had no say in war or empire and condemning them for generations. The Claw Winter is your own doing – the collective consciousness of Undal punishing themselves for what they know is wrong, the rotstorm they all wanted so much.'

Yselda stroked Marta's hair and Benazir chewed at her lip, and Ashbringer saw that Hawthorn had slipped into unconsciousness, or death. She pressed her hand to her friend's face, and then flexed her fingers.

'You say Orubor were *people*,' Ashbringer said, 'and Mistress Water made Anshuka change us to Orubor, to guard her better? That she raised up the rotstorm, and bade it transform the rust-folk within to monsters? You found all this. What did you do, Deathless?'

Benazir stood and went to the crúca stone. She was fingering the dagger at her hip and gazing sidelong at Tullen, but Ashbringer did not even begin to think any attack would be successful. Tullen turned his gaze out, and he pointed at the great sleeping bear.

'Bears fight wolves,' he said, and then chewed at his cheek. 'Everyone and everything I have ever cared for, save Lothal and Anshuka, are gone. I've lived too long. I want to take Berren the dryad's example – to die, to see what happens next. I just wanted to set things up for a little retribution first. I can't undo what has been done, but I have taken away their compulsions. Anshuka will no longer seek to punish Ferron with the rotstorm. She will no longer seek to kill Lothal. I've broken some larger chains, as well – ties that bind the spirits of the world to place and purpose. Things are likely to get a little messy, moving forward, but that is not my business. I spent a long time forging chains, and so I have spent my last day breaking them. The rotstorm will rage, but where will it go? That is for Anshuka to decide, or not decide. Perhaps the winds will decide. It may cross the Iron Desert west, or south to Cil-Marie. It might go north to endless ice, or it might hover over Undal City for the next three hundred years.'

Benazir drew her blade an inch and slammed it back into its scabbard with a huff.

'Why not end it, you bastard? You could end it. End it all.'

Ashbringer licked her lips. 'Will the Orubor continue? Or have you doomed us, Deathless? We are so close to the pattern. Our lives are so sweet. Our forest is so beautiful. Have you doomed us?'

Tullen's eyes grew hard. He did not look at Ashbringer, but kept his eyes fixed on Benazir. *He does not even hear me, anymore.* He had called her friend, but she knew it was a lie. *I am not him, and so I do not matter.*

'Nothing ends, Stormguard. Count yourself lucky I have not burned your entire land of jumped-up peasants to salt and stone. I've decided to forgo vengeance, and leave your fate to chance. You should be grovelling at my feet.'

Benazir drew her dagger and ran the blade across the hook at the end of her arm.

'Big man, with your magic,' she said, 'but at the end of it just another man. Weak and afraid.'

Ashbringer went to her side and gripped at her, pulled her back as the woman tensed, straining towards Tullen. *She doesn't know. He isn't a man.* Ashbringer had seen Tullen One-Eye in the skein, when she could touch it. She had seen him kill, uncaring; break, unflinching; exist, untouching. *He has spent three hundred years waiting to die.* Ashbringer knew Tullen One-Eye was not a man – he was a ghost.

'There are old gods,' Voltos said. His voice was hoarse, and he clutched to his stomach a basket of wicker with a shirt laid over the top, clutched it with both hands as he rocked back and forth in the snow. 'There are spirits who have slept since the dawn of the world, safely bound by the patterns. A spirit is alive. What lives may grow. What grows can be fed. You have no idea what you have done. If the Judges are truly unbound, nothing is safe.'

Ever has he lied to you, Ashbringer thought, *and ever is he playing some game. His words mean nothing.*

'There are only a few things left to do,' Tullen said, and Ashbringer saw that through the haze of rain, red mists were dancing through the trees of the forest.

17

DEATHLESS

'All of it was in vain – the attacks, the assassinations, the pressure political and direct. Ferron had the great wolf Lothal, and when he took the field the soldiers around him were wolf-touched: wild, full of bloodlust and power. Ferron had Tullen One-Eye, and when he waved his hands great nations bowed, and the most powerful mages were struck dead. What can an army do against a god and a skein-wreck? With only one soldier at her side, Mistress Water saved the cause when she travelled deep into the Orubor's wood – a land where none could travel and live. Fighting her way to the great Judge Anshuka, who slept beneath stone and bough. She touched the pattern and the pattern beneath and called to the great Judge, god of strength and community, and bade her feel our suffering and our anger. She bade Anshuka wake and fight for us, and the world was changed forever.' – *History of the Revolution*, Campbell Torbén of Aber-Ouse

Brude watched from her orb as they flew on and on, below the rotstorm, *within* the rotstorm. East. They crossed rivers, and hills, unperturbed by stinging pepper-thorn or lashing rotvine that covered the ground. It was strange to move so swiftly through a place that normally needed such consideration with every step. The horizon was always close in the storm, heavy mists and drenching rains circumscribing the world. She found herself longing for the Northern Marches where the horizon was a distant haze of moor and snow or rolling hill, or the view from the orb when they flew clear of the storm where she could stand and gaze outward at a horizon seeming to span half the world, and the stars above limitless in wonder. *The storm makes us small.*

Brude stood tall as she could amidst the cramp of the stone orb the stink of goblin and crow-men and rust-folk pressing close. The two prisoners huddled together at the back wall, watched by goblins and rust-folk.

On and on they flew, east and east again across the line of the Stormwall far below, the green and brown of the Slow Marsh. They crossed the mountains where Ossen-Tyr sat proud, and descended again and flew low across the river Undalor, frozen water over running water. Brude directed her pilot, and made no move for secrecy in their destination.

'Orubor's wood,' she said, again and again, and the murmur spread. Finally they flew high, high over Undal with forests and field spread vast below them, and Brude let out a slow breath when she saw it. Orubor's wood – she had flown past it dozens of times, as pilot, as war-leader. As scout for Varratim in the summer and as her own master. The ridges of brutal stone surrounding the wood were familiar, but the tall and ancient trees that she knew as a sea of tinted green were now white, snow on snow on ice. Every bough was frozen. The snow did not catch her eye, though – what she saw was the storm at the heart of the forest, where Anshuka slept.

The rotstorm. Brude laughed, and next to her Jehanne and the reeve shifted uncomfortably.

Amon sighed. 'We just left the storm,' he said, 'and the mage has brought it here? Where did he get a rotbud?'

Brude just shook her head. Over three centuries her people had slowly unravelled the secrets of the rotstorm, the wet-lightning, the rotbuds. *But,* she thought, *he is not like us.*

'Perhaps he does not need one,' she said, and Amon and the reeve stepped back, murmuring to each other. They flew slower, close to the treetops, until the edge of the storm enveloped them. The orb was not buffeted by the wild winds and rain, and through the haze of mist Brude could see the treetops of the forest swaying, some breaking, branches and boughs flying in the tumult of the arcane storm.

'I asked after the bones,' Jehanne said next to her, her voice a whisper. 'I did not hope to see a sight such as this as well. I told you, Brude – an orb of light and the bones of your dead wolf, and we will have a treaty that will never be shaken. What use are old bones, when flesh and spirit walk again?'

Brude did not answer. The woman from Cil-Marie was ever pestering her now, amidst her advice. Promises of *more*, of troops and magic and ships and whatever they wanted, if only she could have one orb of light. *As if I can spare one.* Brude had sent the other orb back to the Northern Marches to patrol. *To keep safe.* She knew how long and hard Varratim had searched, more than a decade to find the first orb buried in the ruins of old Urargent, deep in the storm. Years after that to seek the other orbs in the mountains of the Blue Wolf. She knew that the rust-folk had not the strength in arms to drive their own fate – only the chaos of their demons, the fear wrought by their monsters. With the orbs she thought they might be free. *If I give her one, how long until Cil-Marie have a fleet of their own?*

'Tullen One-Eye told us to come here after our treaty,' Brude said in reply, and then tapped the pilot on the arm. 'To the bear, brother.' Brude scratched at her back as she stared down across the forest. The crow-man piloting the orb made no sign of hearing her, but on and on they flew. Brude's arms and hands were so long and awkwardly bent it was easy to reach any part of her spine. The point where the Stormguard woman had stabbed her still itched, as did her face, even though she knew the wounds were already healed over. *Silver.* Trust the Stormguard, always there to ruin everything that could be good. 'It seems my decisions on orbs and bones are less important, Jehanne. The reeve listens to the One-Eyed mage, not me.'

The reeve was at the far end of the orb, speaking with Amon, standing over the Stormguard prisoners. *Always speaking.* Brude felt the itch in her back, the ache in her gut. In the rotstorm her bones hurt less, the rattle of thunder soothing the ache deep in the marrow, but still she hated it. In the cossetted silence of the orb, she could not feel the thunder that must be rolling around them in this little rotstorm over Orubor's wood.

'We spoke of this before,' Jehanne said quietly, and Brude simply nodded. *Tullen One-Eye can't be trusted.* The Stormguard woman had said as much, loath as Brude was to consider her words. Together they stared as the orb flew low, and then through rain and wind and haze they saw the meadow. They saw the wolf.

Lothal the wolf. Brude saw the mountain of Anshuka, still and silent, but Lothal was pacing through the storm, walking up and down the edge of the wide meadow. Lothal's pelt was soaked with rain and mist, and his coat shone with water and the faint glow of the silver pattern swirling through and under the fur. His eyes were a deep black that drank all light, and the lightning bursting through the cloud overhead did not even reflect in them – only darkness. Brude shivered. The black bones of Lothal half-buried in the rotstorm in the west were far bigger than the current incarnation, ribs as tall as the entire wolf standing, but it was still magnificent. It sniffed at cowering Orubor and paced, staring at the sleeping form of Anshuka.

Brude let herself fall into the storm within herself, and it came quick. The chaos of life, the chaos of the universe and the chance and wildness underlying everything. She could see pattern in it, and knew that to be a lie. *There is only chaos.* She opened her eyes and saw the rotstorm as it appeared in the chaos of her magic, a dancing and roiling mass of disconnection and chance meeting, explosions of light and sound and colour and taste, the acrid motes that hung in the air spiralling at random, pushed and pulled by unknowable currents and winds.

Brude breathed deep and clenched her fists. She turned to the wolf. The bones she had left behind were dead, inert things – patterns long settled, infinitely complex. Looking at them was like staring at the old altar up in the Blue Wolf Mountains, where the strange sharp runes incised on the black stone could hold your attention for hours, and the black of the stone hinted at depth below. In the chaos of the skein, that depth was even greater. Looking at the wolf himself, she allowed a moment to revel in the depth of his complexity. *Chance and chaos.* She wondered what Tullen One-Eye saw, what the Salt-Man saw that they could do so much. Brude was a font of storm, a chaos that could break the little patterns that tried to layer over every aspect of life and change it to her whim. Fire and lightning, wind and tempest. *Does Tullen see pattern even in chaos?*

She frowned. The wolf was howling, throwing back its head in the storm as lightning danced in the sky above, but she could hear none of it. Brude blinked.

'The stones and the bones are one,' she said, and Jehanne

next to her narrowed her eyes. Her hand went to the haft of her hammer, but she said nothing. 'Take us down.'

Her pilot lowered the orb at the southern edge of the meadow. There was already an orb in the centre of the meadow, next to Tullen One-Eye and a clump of cowering figures. She could see the strange Orubor she had captured. *The one Tullen stole from me.* With her was an Antian clutching a basket, a Stormguard commando holding a younger girl, another commando with a wicked hook where her right hand should be who stared at Tullen through the rain, unblinking. A dome of red light covered Tullen and the orb beside him, and as they descended the low dome of light spread out wider towards them, spread into a wall that pushed the snarling Orubor away from their landing spot. Brude cricked her neck and went to the ramp, but the reeve was there, crowding the ramp, a hand raised. The reeve and a dozen rust-folk.

'You must wait, Ceann Brude,' the reeve said, 'let me talk to him.' Brude snarled as the reeve bundled himself in his cloak and began to trudge down the ramp, into the storm. She followed him down, rubbing at her face and, standing at the bottom of the ramp, stared up at the bear mountain ahead of her. At the edge of the meadow Lothal howled and pounced, one claw pinning two Orubor who had approached him, the other claw swiping and sending other blue savages spinning into the snow.

Brude rubbed at her face and cast her eyes across the chaos. The Orubor were fleeing to the forest as the wolf began to kill in a frenzy, and through the freezing rain at the centre of the meadow she saw Tullen One-Eye, a hand raised in greeting to the reeve. As ever the man was clad in simple shirt and trousers, no cloak against the wind. The rain and wind of the little rotstorm did not seem to touch him, and Brude shivered as she watched him, and flinched as Lothal snapped another

Orubor in his jaws. She saw blue tabards amidst the fleeing Orubor in the haze and mist and rain, and above them a bolt of red lightning crackled across the sky and the world filled with thunder.

Brude stepped clear of the orb and her crow-men followed, along with Jehanne and Amon. Her dozen crow-men were waiting, tense, all of them hooded. *All of them hurting.* She knew they ached, knew their blood boiled as hers did. The hurt was less in the storm, but it was still there.

'He fears you,' Jehanne said next to her, so quiet, and Brude kicked a clump of snow and stared at Tullen One-Eye across the meadow.

'He should.'

The reeve was hurrying back to her, and four of his rust-folk sped up the ramp and dragged their two captives down. 'Stakes, for the prisoners,' he called, and the rust-folk exploded into movement.

Amon took charge, and within a minute the rust-folk had heavy boughs cut from the branches and were marching through the red light, into the dome where Tullen waited.

'Reeve!' she called, and he hustled to her side and averted his gaze from hers.

'You must wait!' he said, dismissing her without even meeting her eyes.

Brude spat into the snow, flexed her hands, and began to pace back and forth in front of the orb. The rust-folk worked swiftly, and soon stakes were driven deep and captives dragged and bound. Ashbringer did not fight, but the commando woman dragged from her own orb began to scream and strain when she saw those in the centre. One of the rust-folk levelled a spear at the little girl, and then the hook-handed woman was raising her hands for calm.

Amon picked up the little girl in one arm, and with a wrench

Brude realised who she was. She recognised the curling ashen hair. It was the girl she had taken from Hookstone forest, who she had fetched for Varratim to be sacrificed. *The Salt-Man's daughter.* She turned to stare at the commando now being beaten and dragged to her post, the woman with the same curling ashen hair. The woman was straining, screaming, fighting even as a dozen rust-folk beat her with spear butts. Brude furrowed her brow. *The mother?*

She pulled her hood back and ground her teeth, let the rain soak into her hair, down her face. Felt the tingle of its acid. The Antian was saying something, and Amon was returning to the orb, surrounded by goblins. In one hand he held the girl and in the other a little woven basket, covered in a shirt. He came to her side and his face was a grim mask. The girl was asleep or unconscious, and he sheltered her beneath the worst of the rain in his cloak. Brude met his eyes, and Amon shook his head.

'One-Eye says she is to be kept. The others are for the ghost-bear.'

'The ghost-bear hunts the rotstorm,' Brude said, and Amon shrugged and threw a glance back at the meadow where Tullen stood. His face was dark, brow furrowed.

'He says not, Brude. I… I do not like this, Brude. I do not like this.'

Brude turned her gaze to the line of stakes, four commandos and an Antian and an Orubor, all of them soaked in the freezing rain, all of them afraid. The wolf stalked around the meadow behind them, and then stepped close through Tullen's dome of red light to sniff at them. Part of her felt a thrill to see it, but another part of her felt sick, utterly sick. *What does this serve?* The commando had said the Undal would give them the marches.

'They'll give us the marches,' she said, and Amon shifted uncomfortably. The basket in his arms began to twitch, and through the scrap of shirt overlaying it a kitten's head poked out, mewling. Brude and Amon and Jehanne stared down at it, and it stared back at each of them in turn, crying for food. It tried to clamber free of the basket and Jehanne reached down and covered it back over, tucking the shirt tight around the edge of the wicker.

'I had a kitten, when I was a little girl,' Jehanne said, and Brude rolled her shoulders. Her back ached, her joints ached. She had a niggling burn deep in the soles of her feet, as if the nerves were constantly telling her she was stepping on a smouldering campfire. It was the usual, and normally within the storm the thunder made the aches ease, but right at that moment she could feel everything. She stared down at the little girl. Varratim had cut her hair short in her captivity, but it was thick now. *Daughter of the Salt-Man.* Brude had been ready to sacrifice the girl for Varratim's ritual. *I would have wielded the knife myself.*

She looked out at the rain. *They offer us the Northern Marches. No more dead children. No more goblins. No more wyrms. No more crow-men.* Tullen One-Eye was overseeing prisoners tied to stakes, overseeing bringing the ghost-bear. *If he can command the bear,* she thought, *and he has not already stopped it, then I will bleed him dead.*

'There are no cats, in the rotstorm,' she said quietly, and together with Amon and Jehanne they watched the rain and the wolf, and high above them thunder rolled.

~

Floré's wrists bled from the strain of pulling and jerking at her bonds – the vines or ropes binding her just seemed to pull tighter, and she slumped back. Her throat was ragged from screaming for Marta, but her little girl was unconscious in the arms of the rust-folk man with the pockmarked face and heavy cloak. He had sheltered her from the rain as he took her from Yselda, but Floré held no illusions. *They wanted to kill her before.* She had no idea what Tullen might want, but it might be worse yet. She could see him in the meadow so close, a scarce twenty feet away, more than a hundred feet away from the crow-men who seethed at the edge of the meadow. The Orubor had fled, and Lothal paced.

Floré forced her gaze downward, and then along the row of prisoners. She was next to Cuss, and then Benazir, and then Yselda.

'The rotstorm is unchained!' Tullen called, and his voice carried strong through the howling wind. *What does he mean?* 'The rotstorm is unchained, little children. It is loose. It will not fade, but it will wander the world and bring Anshuka's wrath to lands far from these. Ferron will grow green grass again. The ruins of your ancestors will be uncovered. Rejoice!'

There was no cheer from the rust-folk and crow-men, the goblins. They watched through the rain, silent. The living Lothal stalked around the meadow, quiet, circling the scene with impatient steps. Ever its gaze was fixed on Anshuka, the sleeping mountain. 'I give you this gift, children of the storm, but your fate is your own. I am leaving, truly leaving, and I will not look back. Just a little more, though – a score must be settled.'

~

Tullen One-Eye raised his hand and from the red mists of the rotstorm that seeped through the trees, the ghost of Anshuka walked. It was a bear of red mist, scarcely corporeal, thrice the height of a man. It's eyes and mouth and fur and paws and muscle, all of it red mist, the same acrid acid as the blight motes that wandered the storm unperturbed by wind or rain. Floré fell still and turned to Marta, and she saw the rust-folk standing with her beneath the rim of the stone orb, sheltered from the push of rain. *Marta*. The red ghost-bear of mist and haze was stalking ever closer to her and the others, staked in a row by the black luck stone with its molten silver cracks.

Floré kept her gaze flitting between the ghost-bear and Marta. She was going to die, and Marta was left in the arms of demons and rust-folk. She felt her muscles slacken at the thought of Marta in the rotstorm, Marta grubbing for roots and sleeping in filth. *What if it changes her?* Ceann Brude loomed over Marta, and the woman with the hammer was close, watching everything, unblinking amidst the lightning and chaos. Another burst of light ahead, black and gold and red. The spectral form of Anshuka stalked forward through the wood and Floré was pushing her feet back, anything to get away. *What if it takes her?*

In her mind she could see Hasselberry, her home, and sat in front of the hearth in Marta's clothes a goblin – a goblin with jagged teeth and orb eyes, no ears, a slavering tongue and a sickening propensity to violence. *What will I do if it takes her?* The panic consumed her, drowned out any anger in her heart, any semblance of control. She began to yell, over and over.

'Marta! Marta!'

She yelled until her throat was raw, and then she kept yelling, the strain of it sending her into coughing fits as acid rain soaked her face and acrid air tainted her lungs. *I'll kill her myself*, she thought, though she knew she couldn't do it. *I can't do anything*. Floré kept yelling.

'Anshuka's nightmare,' Tullen was saying, his voice clear and cold and cutting through gales and her own screams. He was walking away from them towards the slumbering god. The dome of red force and light trailed behind him, a dozen feet above him and a hundred or more wide. Floré felt a sizzle on her skin as it crossed her and she stared after him.

Yselda began to scream and Floré's head whipped around. The ghost-bear stalked towards her, staring at Yselda fixated. There were no words to the girl's terror, only fear.

'Floré!'

Floré whipped her head around. It was Benazir, Benazir wrenching at her arms, pushing back with her feet at the stake behind her with all its might. With a final shove she fell free, sprawling into the snow – her right hook hand had been left behind in the ties. Benazir pulled herself to her knees and scrabbled at her boot, pulling free a blade. She crawled through the snow and mud to the nearest stake – Cuss. She began cutting at his binds, yelling at him as she did. Cuss began to rouse only when she paused and slapped his face, and he gazed around the scene in confusion. Yselda kept screaming.

'Look at me, Yselda!' Floré yelled, desperate to calm her. Yselda caught her eye and for a moment she was calm, and the bear of red mist vanished.

'Look at me,' she repeated, and she tried not to picture Yselda broken, Yselda twisted into a rottroll or a wyrm. Floré's gut ached with guilt. *Why didn't I leave her in Hasselberry?* She threw her head around to check if Marta was safe. *Is that where the bear went?*

'Please, Sergeant,' Yselda was sobbing and Floré turned back to her and opened her mouth to say something, anything, but then she could only scream in horror as the bear reappeared, looming over its prey. *Yselda.* Cuss was screaming for Yselda as his bonds finally cut free, but Benazir tackled him to the ground. Yselda turned her head away from the bear, looking desperately for help, and Floré locked eyes with her, but then the girl was gone, shrouded in a boiling cloud of opaque red mist. Benazir pushed Cuss back to the ground as the boy strained to reach Yselda and she scrambled to Floré, cutting through her bonds with a single slice and running back towards Voltos without even pausing.

Floré pulled herself to her feet, and then fell to her knees in the slick of snow. Tullen was at the end of the meadow, a hand resting on the head of Anshuka. She turned and saw the ghost-bear dissipate into mist. Yselda was twitching on the ground below, and Floré dropped to her knees. *No.* Yselda the quiet orphan girl who practised with her bow and kept her uniform neat, who studied for the tests Floré made up and practised her knots. Yselda who had already lost everything.

Floré turned and saw Marta in the arms of a rust-folk man a hundred yards away, and she kept turning and saw Tullen One-Eye crouched by Anshuka's sleeping form, laughing at all of it, laughing at the chaos. *Anshuka.* A Judge's work was undone if it was killed. That was what Varratim had been trying to do all along. *I can still save her,* she thought, desperate, but she knew it wasn't true. *Would I kill a god, and leave Lothal free if it costs this?* Floré forced herself to her feet and scrambled through the snow and mud to Yselda's side. Benazir was behind her, Voltos and Ashbringer staggering free from their cut bonds.

Across the meadow the great mountain of stone began to crack.

'Time to wake!' Tullen called. The little trees and grass covering patches of sleeping Anshuka were buried in dirt and rock as first stones and then slabs began to tumble, thick slabs of brown stone that tumbled and slammed into the grass and flowers surrounding the sleeping bear, and then further to the snow beyond.

'No!' Floré cried, crouching low over Yselda's twitching body, but her scream was one of a hundred, two hundred, three hundred. At the edge of the meadow, she heard the wails of Orubor, and next to her in the snow Ashbringer was sobbing. There was another *crack*, a thousand cracks at once in a deep chorus of breaking, and the stone began to rise and suddenly Floré *saw*. The stone rose slowly in the air, and then began to fling itself, boulders and slabs and pebbles flinging themselves away, up and into the forest. Beneath, Floré saw Anshuka the god-bear, Judge of Ferron, god of the Undal Protectorate. The great bear was smaller than the mountain she had slept beneath, but only just. Matted fur of light brown was woven through with moss and vine, and great swirls of glowing green across her body and legs and paws and face.

'You are what she made you, Orubor!' Tullen's voice called, and above the cracking of stone and the breaking trees beyond, she could hear him clear. She heard Yselda sob, but Floré could not look away from the bear. *There.* Her chest was rising, her back rising, as great breaths came slow and steady. *There.* Her claws were the same glowing green as the swirls on her coat, mottled like jade. *Like the sea at night.* Anshuka stirred, her head moving to one side, one great paw sliding across dirt, raking a ravine in the snowy meadow. *This is your doing,* Floré thought, and her jaw clenched with hatred. *All of it. The storm. Janos. All of it.* If Anshuka had been stronger, had resisted whatever compulsion had been placed on her... Janos would be alive. Marta would be well. *Yselda would be safe.*

Floré pressed her hand on Yselda's brow and felt a brutal fever, and then the bear was rising up over them. Her sleeping head was taller than the tallest tree in the forest, and as she moved her head her mouth opened and Floré saw a glimpse of a tooth, a tooth black as coal, matte darkness against the greying pink of gum. Floré stared dumb at the sight of the god, awed and so small in its shadow, and she clenched her fist. *How many children has the storm taken? I should have let Varratim kill you when he had the chance.*

From the forest the Orubor ran, sprinting across the clear ground, howling shouts of denial, shouts of rage. They fell to their knees and wept at the edge of the red dome of light, or roared as they threw blade and arrow and magic against Tullen's unbreakable protection.

Anshuka opened her eyes, and there was no black pupil or black sclera visible. Floré stared into those pools of perfect swirling gold and pulled Yselda up onto her lap, held the girl close.

'You'll be all right,' she said, and beneath her felt Yselda buckle, her bones cracking and twisting, her muscles stretching and ripping and reforming. *Can I fix this?*

'Hello, little bear,' Tullen said, quiet, but she could still hear him over screams and crying and the scrape of rock and the breaking of bough and trunk as Anshuka pulled herself to her feet and stared down at them, stared far over the snow-coated forest, and huffed out a breath. Anshuka reared to her hind legs and reached her front claws up to the sky and roared, and all were forced to their knees in obeisance to the god-bear. The roar was thunder, was a wave on rock, was a storm at night, was a thousand bells of brass all beating at once over and over. With a brutal slam the bear fell back to all fours, its front paws breaking tree and stone as they came heavily down, sending up spumes of dust and rock.

Across the meadow, Lothal the wolf began to slaver and growl and then fled from the meadow into the high trees. Tullen began to laugh as Anshuka roared again and with a swept claw broke a dozen trees, and then began to lumber after the wolf, crossing the meadow over them in three quick strides. Where her paws fell, dozens of Orubor were killed, or huge craters were left in the meadow, and as she passed over Floré's head trailing dirt and rubble she heard Marta scream somewhere, and she gripped Yselda tight. She couldn't leave the girl. *I have to save her. I have to save Marta.* Anshuka burst into the treeline and followed the wolf, splintering old growth as fast as new, and the meadow had tripled in size – where once the bear had slept, only rubble remained.

~

Brude watched the gods and seethed.

'The orb, Jehanne,' she said, quiet. 'It is yours and you now know the location of old Lothal's bones. We will discuss access to the bones in future. For now, when this day is done, the orb is yours if I live. One-Eye must die.'

Jehanne did not say anything, simply nodded, mouth tight. Brude knew she understood the implication. *It is yours, if you help me do what I must.* They watched the treeline shake as Anshuka and Lothal slammed into each other, and in the centre of the meadow the staked prisoners cut themselves free, the ghost-bear gone. Brude knew it as Anshuka's nightmare. *I do not think it will return while she wakes.* She spat on the ground and stared at Tullen One-Eye, a man alone in a field of rubble, a hundred or more Orubor baying for his blood.

One of the prisoners was twitching on the ground, and chaos began to spread as in the forest Lothal slammed into Anshuka. The splintering of trees and the roar of thunder above filled her ears. Brude shivered at the noise of the warring gods, but the great bear simply shrugged a shoulder and sent the wolf spinning into a span of oaks that burst into so much wood. The wolf came back, jaws snapping, harrying at the bear's legs and paws, and Anshuka did not respond with her jaws. She simply heaved her weight at the far smaller god and sent it sprawling, again and again. Thick ropes of slaver hung from Lothal's mouth, but Anshuka seemed barely perturbed.

Rust-folk were running to the reeve, and those Orubor not clawing and slashing at Tullen's dome of light were engaging them with blade and bow. Brude's crow-men held back, close to her, and she could see blue tabards of Stormguard across the meadow moving between the trees. The twitching girl in the snow screamed, and next to Brude the little girl Marta screamed in unison.

Brude remembered her own transformation. She had been a girl of thirteen, and had thought herself perhaps old enough to be safe. *Safe from transformation, if not death.* She had been hurrying home to the shack she shared with her siblings and mother in Pertcupar, having spent the day at a neighbour's kelp farm helping pull in the crop. The night had fallen fast, and in the darkness the bear had found her. In an instant it was a figure at the edge of her vision, walking through the mist, and then it was next to her, sniffing. Anshuka's wrath. The punishment for all rust-folk, because of what their ancestors did. Under the shelter of the stone orb Brude bristled and drew a wand from her belt, the wand of flame. *For what Tullen One-Eye did.*

'The bear punishes us all because of him,' she said, and turned to her crow-men. There were a dozen of them, and all had the same visceral reaction as her to the ghost-bear. All remembered it. 'If he can summon the ghost, and wake the beast, he could kill it. The fact he would summon the ghost and not destroy it tells us all we need to know. The Stormguard would give us the north and peace. The fact One-Eye chooses to unchain the rotstorm rather than destroy it, that he would awake that monster rather than kill her, makes him my enemy!'

She could hear Tullen laughing as she turned, and then a roar split her ears and sent her to a defensive crouch. This was not Lothal's howl, low and melodic and thick and vibrant. This was a roar that shook the ground – thunder and bells, louder than any noise she had ever heard, a thick pressure pushing at her chest.

Through the rotstorm to the north where the wolf and bear fought, bolts of lightning burst downward, a staccato drum roll of a dozen strikes in as many seconds, all of them touching the earth with explosions of tree and stone and water. Through the haze of electricity and the pounding rain, the god-bear Anshuka reared back, eyes of liquid gold gazing at Lothal the Just. The wolf was cut and battered, bleeding silver light, but its jaws were slick with golden blood and Anshuka's legs and chest were cut and scored.

The lightning struck again and again, and the beasts threw themselves at one another, and in the explosions of colour and light the battle was lost to her vision. Brude twitched and forced herself to turn to her people, to turn to Tullen.

'This has to end,' she said, and her crow-men joined her. Together they stared at the deathless mage.

18

THE BEAR AND THE WOLF

'Dearest, the clouds are gathering. A messenger came bearing news – he has gone mad. Nessilitor was seen flying to the north, over the Storm Sea trailing blood that shone like starlight. The messenger claims Lothal is dead, claims you are dead. I know you are not. I know he is not. Clouds gather, my love, over Urargent – strange clouds of black and red, a lightning that does not cease. The rain burns the skin. What is this? I need you. There are riots in the streets as the workers panic. In the founder's square they killed Pelomar. They tore the stones from the streets and broke him. Pelomar, who has watched me these years when you have ranged. I need you, Tullen. Come now.' – **Private letter**, Empress Seraphina of the Gilded Spire

Floré pulled herself to her feet, and then fell to her knees as another roar from Anshuka melded with a howl of pain from Lothal, piercing through her skull and sending her crawling in the snow. She pulled herself to one knee and saw through the trees the great wolf pinned under one of Anshuka's huge paws, its ribs covered by an avalanche of muscle and fur and stone

346

claw as Anshuka pressed down and roared into the wolf's snapping maw. She felt sick. *I brought my child into this,* she thought. *What have I done?*

Floré darted forward through the slick of snow, grasping at Yselda's still form as she did. She dragged her through the snow away from the stakes, away from wherever the ghost-bear had gone, but the girl felt like dead weight. She had seen a blight mote of the same red mist strip flesh to bone, but Yselda was not bloodied. Floré threw her down and grabbed her and slapped her face over and over.

'Get Marta!' she yelled to Benazir, and then Benazir was running forward and pulling at the back of Cuss's tunic as he crawled in the snow towards Floré and Yselda, his legs bloodied. She hauled him up and pushed him behind her.

'I'll bring Yselda,' Floré yelled, and clenched her fists. 'Get Marta and get out.'

There was no time; there was too much happening at once. The gods were smashing into each other, the storm was everywhere, and now Orubor and rust-folk were cutting and fighting. Benazir was closer to Marta – Floré would wake Yselda and follow. *I can't leave her.* Every part of her wanted to sprint to Marta, to leave Yselda for the others to find, to look after. She wanted to do that because Marta was her daughter. Floré stroked Yselda's cheek and then slapped her hard. *Yselda is my daughter too.*

'Wake up, Yselda!' she yelled, and slammed the girl back into the snow. Yselda's eyes opened, and in them Floré saw the lightning of the rotstorm reflected, and she grinned. *Alive.* Yselda was sobbing though, immediately, and as she brought her hands to her face Floré realised why. The girl's hands covered her face, the fingers long enough to touch the back of her skull. The skin was red raw and split, and Floré let the girl slip from her grasp and stepped back. She could see the bends in her arms, too many joints. *Too many joints in her legs.* Her clothes torn and ragged under her tabard as her skin and bone and sinew had stretched, arcane growth pushing beyond anything a body should feel. Yselda began to scream, and Floré stepped in and pulled her close and stared back across the storm and meadow. *I'm sorry, daughter. I failed you.*

Anshuka had Lothal pinned where the forest met the meadow, the great wolf writhing beneath a heavy paw. Anshuka stared down at the wolf, golden eyes swirling with currents and pattern, inscrutable. Tullen's pealing laugh cut through the storm and chaos. Floré couldn't see Benazir or Cuss or Voltos. Tullen clapped his hands and then lightning struck, black lightning streaked with red, once, twice, thrice, a dozen times across the meadow. Floré hauled Yselda up to her feet and put her shoulder under the girl's arm. Yselda was moaning, eyes fluttering. *Where is my sword?* She had to find Marta. It was too late for anything else – she could do no more.

From the impact craters of the lightning, the goblins began to crawl. From each lightning strike hands clawed up through dirt and ashen snow, chittering voices shrieking as their little bodies shivered in the freezing rain. Anshuka roared again and Floré saw that Lothal had escaped her grasp and was running in the forest, dodging through the trees as the bear lumbered after him. Floré began to drag Yselda towards the nearest orb of stone, the one that was landed so close to the luck stone in the centre of the meadow.

Tullen was climbing the detritus left by Anshuka's wakening, slowly clambering up a pile of broken stone. None were near him, his dome of red light now thicker, a wall fifteen feet high that defended him like a rampart, open to the rain and brutal wind above. Floré saw crow-men in the crowd, and knew he was protecting himself from their confounding effect on the skein.

The goblins came for her, and Floré clenched her fist. They were a ragged line, running from the impact point of their lightning – some were leaping at Orubor, others were running wildly around, but at least a dozen were running at her and Yselda. Floré squared her shoulders and stepped in front of Yselda. She had no weapon, and their teeth were sharp. She resigned herself. *All you can do is all you can.* There were more of them, but she had the weight and the training. *Benny will get Marta.* Floré believed that, down to her core. The lightning dancing through purple-black cloud above reflected in the black pools of their eyes, and she could see teeth, so many teeth, rows and rows of jagged points in every mouth, tongues lashing and drool flying back as they ran towards her. She set her feet.

The ground in front of her erupted as goblins were engulfed in a column of purple light, and above her the world exploded in brilliant white and all fell to silence. Hanging over them, an orb of light circled tightly, pulses of purple force shooting from one of its great wands, over and over again at the approaching goblins.

The orb above them lowered and the ramp began to descend, and Voltos was suddenly by her side stamping through the snow, helping her grip Yselda as they stared up in silence at the orb of dazzling light. The Antian was bleeding, his face bruised, but he turned his head up at her and gave a tight smile. Through the chaos behind him three figures followed – Antian in heavy ornate robes. Ever before the weight of the silence that came from the orbs had been an oppression, an unnatural intervention, but for a brief moment as Tomas appeared at the top of the ramp, his hand extended to them, Floré allowed herself hope.

~

Cuss tried to breathe. *Dead.* Yselda had been covered by that red bear, and Anshuka and Lothal were fighting on the horizon. The wolf had wriggled its way free and had its jaw clamped on Anshuka's back leg, and the bear roared in pain. It filled Cuss's lungs and chest like a blacksmith's hammer, reverberating through him. Floré had thrown him back and yelled to get Marta, and as Benazir gripped him he spotted her. A hundred yards of meadow to the orb, and beneath it Marta was being held by some rust-folk man. He even had Jozenai's basket. A dozen crow-men loomed around her, rust-folk as well.

Cuss couldn't hear Benazir. Another orb was shining, and the dull familiar weight of the silence and pressure covered him. He blew out a breath and screamed, knowing nobody could hear him. He screamed for Yselda, for Petron, for his mother, for his little sister Jana. For Heasin. He screamed for his father, for everything in his life he had ever wanted and not gotten. A dozen of the rust-folk were running from the orb towards him. From the meadow around, scores of goblins were running through the snow. And explosions of dirt and ice where the newly arrived orb fired beams of force down into the meadow. *Chaos. All of it chaos.* He could vaguely see Ashbringer by his side, and Benazir, and he clenched his fists. He had no steel, no gauntlets or blade. *Get Marta.*

They met in a rush of violence. Cuss trudged forward, ready to die on the long spears of the rust-folk, but Ashbringer sprinted across the ice and mud of the meadow as if it was open plain and Benazir ran fast as a deer, faster than any of the rust-folk. Cuss trudged forward behind them one step after another, and when the first of the rust-folk tried to skewer him with a spear he twisted and gripped it, wrenching it out of the man's hands and sending him sprawling. Cuss stabbed him through the back before he could stand, and then they were in it truly. With a spear he could jab and prod at the next man who Benazir circled, and then she was on the man, ripping his throat open with her hook.

On and on they fought, each throwing bodies to the other, each supporting where the other was weak – suddenly the glow was still behind him but the intensity and pressure faded and he could hear, could hear screaming. Three goblins ran at him with their teeth bared but he focused on Marta, only Marta, and flipping his spear around he sent each of them sprawling with the butt end. Benazir showed no compunction. Her hook rent flesh and leather, and next to her Ashbringer was death itself. She had found a sword, battered and rusted, and with it she cut through rust-folk and goblin alike, twirling over and through the chaos.

Cuss spared a glance back. Floré and Voltos were dragging Yselda up into an orb of light, even as Tomas hopped down and began running towards Cuss and his fellows, long strides carrying him fast over the slick snow and ice. Cuss felt a grin spread across his face – they had left Tomas in Ossen-Tyr along with Rowan and the orb the Orubor had given them, before their failed attempt to kidnap the crow-man. *He came for us.* The tempest around them never ceased, and the rain stung at his eyes and his skin, but Cuss kept stepping forward, and fighting, every step another blow.

He fell to the ground with a crash as the earth below shook. At the edge of the meadow trees went spinning like so many reeds as Anshuka broke through the forest and returned to her meadow. She reared over them, a bear that was a mountain, fur woven with arcane green ley lines tracing muscle and spirit. It stared down at the meadow, eyes of pure gold gazing intently at the tiny figures below, and the hunch of its back hinted at muscle and power below. He could not see the wolf anywhere. Cuss found his feet, hands slick with blood, and using his stolen spear steadied himself.

Cuss flinched back as a spear almost took his throat, but then the woman wielding it screamed as Benazir skewered her gut from behind. With a wrench of her blade Benazir sent the woman falling to the swamp, and pointed her blood-slick knife at the crow-men who waited below their orb, watching.

'We get Marta,' she said, gasping, 'we get an orb, we get the fuck out of here.'

Tomas's arrival on foot next to them was heralded by a spume of flame thirty feet long from his wand, setting a dozen goblins alight and a dozen more fleeing.

'Sounds good,' he said, and then he was off running, he and Ashbringer pushing back towards the left as Benazir headed right. The man holding Marta had drawn no blade. He stared at Cuss, face grim, and Cuss stared back. Next to him was the woman who had hit Cuss with her hammer in Ossen-Tyr. His ribs were a mess from that single blow, still aching with every breath, and she smiled at him as he stepped near. In front of them at the bottom of the ramp to their orb, a crow-man. *The* crow-man, Ceann Brude. Cuss flexed his neck and rolled his shoulders. He dropped his spear so his grip ended right below its jagged point.

He rolled in fast, the way Floré had told him – *they always try to fly,* she had said, *but get a grip and don't let them think on their chaos.* With scrabbling hands he had her cloak and began to punch upward with the last foot of his spear, feeling its point connect with flesh below, but then he was sprawling back from a single backhand of hers. It felt as if he was hit by a rod of iron.

Slowly, Cuss pulled himself to his feet.

'We want the girl, and we'll be leaving,' he said, and all turned to Brude. Benazir's dagger flashed forward, a blurring arc of steel and silver aimed at the crow-man's eye, and with a hand Brude stopped it in mid-flight. Tomas and Ashbringer stood with wand and blade bare, ten feet from Ceann Brude.

'Tullen One-Eye has betrayed us,' she said, and with a hand gestured across the meadow. Atop his pile of rubble where Anshuka had once slept, Tullen was surrounded by a few rust-folk, but no crow-men or goblin could pierce the protection of the red wall around him. Cuss could see lancers in blue tabards fighting crow-men and goblins, Orubor with sinuous blades cutting down goblins with every step. 'It is chaos he has sown.'

A tree spun from the forest's edge, a hundred feet of wood and bough and ice and root that gouged a great rent in the snow of the meadow, and from the forest the gods came and all else grew still.

Anshuka and Lothal were both bloodied, deep cuts in the bear's legs and side bleeding hot gold that steamed, matched by a huge wound torn into the wolf's shoulders. Anshuka charged forward again as the wolf retreated into the meadow, the ground beneath Cuss rolling with the impacts, and with a stamp the bear brought both front paws down on the wolf. Lothal was too slow, too injured to avoid it. The orb Tomas had arrived in was circling high above them, bolts of purple force slamming down into rust-folk and goblins and crow-men, and Cuss shivered as Lothal howled and then *whimpered*. It was a pitiful thing, even loud enough to hurt his ears. The great bear huffed at the wolf and opened her jaws, teeth the length of spears made of black stone opening wide. She lowered her jaws to the wolf's neck and it arched back in surrender, and Anshuka's jaws clamped shut on empty air.

The meadow fell silent save for the falling rain, the distant roll of thunder. All the fighting stopped, every eye turned to the gods as Anshuka spared Lothal. Raising her paw slowly she huffed and snapped her jaws again, and the injured wolf crawled to its feet, head low, and ran into the forest without a backward look, ragged and defeated. Anshuka raised herself on her hind legs and slammed down, and when she roared it was a bellow of victory that sent Cuss and all around him to their knees, and threw goblins flying across the bucking ground, screaming and chittering and wailing.

Cuss stared into the golden eyes of the bear and saw no warmth, no compassion. It was utterly alien and animal. Turning from them, Anshuka began to walk away to the north, destruction in her wake as the forest parted to her strength. The rotstorm rain fell hard and lightning danced above.

'The other commando said you'd give us the Northern Marches,' Ceann Brude said, staring after the bear, and Benazir spat.

'Give us the girl, you'll have your marches. If that demon lets you keep them.'

Ceann Brude nodded slowly. 'Amon, give the girl to them. Take this orb, and leave. Jehanne – you have our allegiance, and the orb of light that remains settled in the meadow. If you can help us take it.'

Brude gestured first to the orb behind her. Tomas ran to it, wand out, kicking a goblin he passed on the way that tried to squawk and grab at him. Cuss reached his hands out, dropping his spear, and the pockmarked man gently passed him Marta. She was shivering. The man pressed the handle of the basket into Cuss's other hand, and gave a tight smile.

'Her cat, no?' he said, and then he stepped back into the shadow of the crow-men.

'Peace,' Ceann Brude said, and from the air she plucked Benazir's dagger and passed it to the commander hilt first. 'If there is war from this day, it is his doing, not ours.'

Cuss went to the orb, sidestepping the crow-men, holding Marta tight, his eyes never leaving Brude and the woman with the hammer and the pockmarked man. Behind them, a dozen other crow-men watched, and beyond them two-dozen goblins and the few rust-folk not crowded inside Tullen's wall of force.

'Tullen One-Eye has betrayed us,' Brude said again, louder, and she was turning to her people as Benazir gripped Cuss's shoulder and pulled him to the orb. Ashbringer made no move to follow – she just stared at Tullen One-Eye, and began to walk to him across the ruined meadow, stepping over the dead.

As Cuss reached the ramp he stared back once more. Tullen One-Eye's gaze flitted from them to the glowing orb hanging in the sky where Anshuka and Lothal had fought, and finally down to Ashbringer and Ceann Brude, who together with Jehanne and the rust-folk began walking towards his tumble of rock. He thought he saw the man smile. Cuss held Marta close as behind him the orb ramp closed, the tears in his eyes indistinguishable from the rain.

~

Ashbringer walked across the meadow to Tullen One-Eye, through his wall of magic. Behind her the crow-men and rust-folk and the woman with the strange hammer were stopped, a hundred feet away from the skein-wreck's perch. *Further than a crow-man's chaos can pollute the skein*. She picked her way over the burnt corpses of Orubor, twisted in death. Their ligaments and fibrous tissue had curled in on itself as it cooked, and the charred bodies were left in grimacing poses, fists raised like pugilists. Ashbringer stepped around them. She had not even seen him burning them, but she knew it would be him, bored, amusing himself as his gods fought.

'I can assure you, Tullen,' the reeve was saying, 'the crow-men do not speak for us. They are twisted, as you said. What place do they have in our new world? What place *could*—'

Tullen shut the man up with a waved hand that sent him flying in a huge arc, three hundred feet out and up. Ashbringer could not hear the impact of his body hitting the forest. Around Tullen the rain did not fall and the wind did not pull. There was only stillness.

'Ashbringer,' Tullen said with a sigh, 'it is good to see you. Ever there is trouble, eh? People cannot have peace.'

The rust-folk who had accompanied their reeve moved to attack him, and with a desultory wave of his hand Tullen turned all twelve of them to human pyres. Their screams lasted only a moment, and then they were ash and char and stink. There was no snow where they stood, in the rubble of Anshuka's den.

Ashbringer sniffed. 'You could end this storm, Deathless,' she said, and he did not respond. 'They want peace. Both sides. If the storm ended, the rust-folk could rebuild. If it does not, they will press out, but with the Northern Marches there is no need for more conflict. There is peace, Deathless. The only thing in its way is you.'

Tullen stared at her and shook his head, gestured at the chaos around them – bodies of rust-folk and crow-men, goblins. Great gouges in the landscape where Anshuka and Lothal had fought.

'They cannot abide peace,' Tullen said, and the orb in the meadow flashed with white light and began to rise, as rapidly as Ashbringer had ever seen one move. Tullen raised an open hand to it and sneered, made to close his fist.

'*Wait!*' she said, and before his fist could close her hand was in his. *Please listen, this once.* Tullen stood still and watched her.

'You called me your only friend,' she said, and hung her head. 'Why don't we leave this place? You have no tie here except revenge. If you won't end the rotstorm, let them fight amongst themselves. We can go. We can go anywhere, be anything, *do* anything. There are lands left to see, you said.'

Together they watched that orb cut fast up into the storm,

and then it was gone and Ashbringer felt her shoulders slump. The second orb followed it slower, climbing up and up until it was swallowed by cloud, and then it was only her and the crow-men. The Orubor and the lancers had fled into the forest. All of the crow-men were testing at the barrier wall of force, spreading out around the little rocky outcrop where Tullen had settled. Ashbringer held Tullen's hand.

'They are monsters, Ashbringer,' he said, slowly, staring down at the crow-men. 'Mistress Water bade Anshuka to make monsters, but the nightmares of the Undal polluted that scheme. What to fear more than a person who cannot die, a person who is not part of the pattern of this world? Someone *outside*. Anshuka made them chaos. I do not know. I do not know where the limit of their power lies, do you understand? When Anshuka bound me, the strength of her pattern overrode their chaos. But now... I have broken the chains, Ashbringer. The deep magic, the connection that binds all the world. How far will their chaos spread? The orbs and wands are untouched by it, but these demons are something beyond us again.'

Ashbringer stared down at Anshuka's meadow, and remembered it in flower, the wild flowers growing thick as the god slept in peace.

'They do not want us here, Deathless. Where would you go?'

Tullen stared up at the storm, and smiled at her. Suddenly the rain was falling on him, and from above, the wind was pushing down on them. In a few moments he was as drenched as she.

'I would go to Urforren, on a market day,' he said, and let her hand drop. 'I would walk the streets of Urargent, the university, and debate with the philosophers the meaning of truth, debate with the engineers how we can weave the skein into our industry. I would stare up at the stars from the gilded spire in Ferron's old palace, with its great telescopes, as Seraphina lay in the bed waiting for me. Can we go there, Orubor? Little blue goblin? You do not understand me. You never could. Chaining you was a mistake. I should have killed you like your mother and father and all who came before.'

Ashbringer looked down at the mud and looked inside herself, looked for the rhythm of the world, the music and melody of creation. She saw only a dim haze, if she looked at herself or elsewhere.

'The Undal skein-wreck Mistress Water made my people, you said. You said we were human once. I am so much more than that, Deathless. You should see. I can speak to the gods. Do you understand that? I travelled the land through their dancing portals, and sang their songs.'

Tullen shook his head and ignored her. He stared down at the rust-folk, all of them returning his gaze, unflinching.

'Is it death you want?' he called, and at the edge of his wall of light Ceann Brude flexed her fingers, her hands wreathed in flame. Tullen flexed a hand and the wall grew in opacity, but Ashbringer could still see the crow-men beyond. One leapt high and up, as if to leap past Tullen's defences, and with a flick of the wrist lightning struck down from the clouds and incinerated the creature, leaving only smoke hanging in the air.

'We live under the punishment meted out for your crimes, One-Eye,' Ceann Brude called. 'Our lands destroyed; our children corrupted. End the rotstorm, if you can. In either case, leave us. We do not want you here. You offer nothing but death.'

With a raised eyebrow Tullen shook his head. Slowly he raised his hands, and they began to crackle and pulse with electricity.

'I offer pain, as well, child,' he said, and through his wall of red light beams of burning white shot out, dancing over the rust-folk below, one by one. Ashbringer shut her eyes a long moment to the screams, and then looked up to the sky and smiled.

She went to Tullen and drew his hand down, and the beams of light ceased. She drew close to him and stroked his face, one hand cupping his head, the other his cheek. Gently she stroked beneath his eye.

'I cannot hurt you,' she whispered to him, and Tullen leaned into her contact for a long moment. *How long since you felt the touch of one who cared?* Tullen had bound her not to hurt him, to think of nothing that would cause him harm. Ashbringer gave one last glance upward.

'I believe something in my heart, Tullen One-Eye,' she said, and held him still. 'I believe that the only harm that could befall you, would be to live past this moment.'

With a single motion Ashbringer wrenched his head forward and plunged her thumb into Tullen's eye, felt it burst, and even as he screamed she felt herself burning, but she smiled, for she could see the sky.

~

Floré pulled Yselda into the orb and then it was all hell breaking loose. She left Voltos to care for the girl and then she was up in the swinging metal chair attached to the great wand of purple.

'I'm sorry, Rowan!' she called, but the Orubor just gnashed his teeth.

'It is a good death!' he responded, and then she let loose. Bolts of purple force flew from her wand as often as it would let her fire, once every few seconds. The wand was on some mechanism that let it sway and point at her lightest touch, and the ground was thick with targets. She sent her first shot down into the crowd of goblins, wincing even as she did it but clearing a path for Benazir and Cuss and Ashbringer and Tomas. They fought like demons, Tomas's wand of flame cutting swathes and pushing back rust-folk reinforcements, and Benazir and Ashbringer flowing like water through the ranks of the enemy. Cuss was stalwart, plodding forward through blood and blade, and Floré grimaced and bit her lip. *They'll get her. They have to.*

Like the rest of them she was slack-jawed and awed as Anshuka defeated Lothal and the wolf and bear disappeared into the storm, each in their own direction. She watched, bare knuckles gripping the control of her wand, as Marta was carried by Cuss into the orb past rows of crow-men, and she lined up her shot on Tullen. If he moved a hand towards it, she would shoot. It might be enough of a distraction for Marta's orb to escape. But then Marta's orb was up, fast and free into the storm, and Rowan followed it.

Suddenly they were in cloud, black cloud dancing with the light of distant and close lightning. She could hear Yselda sobbing. *My poor girl.* The wave of relief she felt seeing Marta fly free was tempered by a bone aching sorrow for Yselda, a darkness she could scarcely begin to realise. *I've doomed her. I've killed my girl.*

'Fly no further,' Voltos called, and Floré leapt down from her seat and rushed to Yselda's side as Rowan brought them to a stop deep in the clouds of the storm. The transformation was complete. It was undeniable. The girl was a crow-man. *Demon.* Her hands scrabbled at the stone floor and she retreated from Voltos and Floré, and Floré felt bile rise in her throat, an instinctive disgust. *Demon.* Short of killing Anshuka herself, there was no return from this. *What have I done? What can I do?* For all of her woes at striking down goblin and rottroll since she had discovered their origin, Floré had never truly considered the crow-men. They could think, and so were responsible for whatever they did. *If Yselda was left in the storm now, would she be responsible?* Floré stepped slowly towards the hulking form of the girl, her rain-soaked face now slick with fresh tears. A bolt of lightning crackled across the stone of the orb sparking from Yselda's hands, and Rowan hissed.

'Kill me!' Yselda said with a thick voice, and then she had her face in her hands again, sobs racking her body.

'Oh, my girl,' Floré said, and went to her. Next to them Voltos wiped his spectacles.

'This is the end then,' he said. 'A life well lived.'

Floré turned to him and glared. 'We can *fix* her!' she yelled, and Voltos flinched. He did not meet her eye, but shook his head.

'No,' he said, 'you can't. Unless you kill Anshuka, and we've no way to do that. Tullen destroyed the dagger. This is *all* our end, Floré. Do you understand?'

Floré sat back when she realised what he meant and felt panic spiralling over her. *No.* They'd escaped. Marta had escaped. *We all escaped.* The pure relief that had been washing over her was tainted, and her scarred arm began to twitch and writhe. *Yselda didn't escape. Won't ever escape.* She pictured the back of Marta's head disappearing into the orb, held tight in Cuss's arms, Benazir alongside. She nodded – she understood what Voltos meant. *I'm sorry, Marta. I'm sorry, Janos.*

'Yselda,' she said, and the girl managed to catch a breath, wiping at tears. Her brown eyes were bloodshot, her black hair soaked through, her face still the same girl Floré taught to shoot a bow behind the old Forest Watch barn in Hasselberry.

'You did well, daughter,' she said, and gripped the girl's hand tight. *How can I ask her this?* She fought down the shiver of revulsion at the odd angles, the endless bone jags of too many knuckles. She smiled and stroked a tangle of hair from Yselda's face.

'Do you remember the first orb we saw, in Hookstone forest?'

Yselda nodded.

'You were brave that night. It is time to be brave again. Do you understand what we need to do?'

Yselda stared at her, uncomprehending.

'Can we fix it?' she said, her voice so hopeful, and Floré felt tears sliding down her own cheeks through the muck and blood and grime. She shook her head, and Yselda reached up her hands to the locket at her neck, gripping it between overlong fingers. *How can I ask her to do this?*

'We can't fix this. We need to end this, Yselda,' Floré said, and she gripped Voltos by the shoulder and called to Rowan to catch.

'The plan was always to capture a crow-man, get it close to Tullen, then beat him to death.'

Voltos had taken off his spectacles and as she spoke he folded them neatly away. 'We have a crow-man,' he said, and stroked Yselda's face. 'Brave girl. It will be over soon.'

Yselda flinched as she realised his meaning. 'You want to go back?'

Rowan stared at Floré and she gestured at the stone around her.

'Take his magic,' she said, 'and break him. We come in from above, fast enough he has no time to react. His defences are focused outward, not upward. As soon as Yselda is close to him his magic will fail, and then we crash the orb down on his skull. All of us will die, but that is more than we could ever have hoped. If that is the price we *must* pay it. How fast can you go?'

The Orubor Rowan, with his careful braids and geometric tattoos, clicked his teeth and shrugged. 'Fast.'

Yselda stopped crying, and climbed to her feet. She was tall now, taller than Floré by a head. Her back was stooped, and she swayed in place, her ragged Stormguard commando tunic tight in place. Floré placed a hand to the girl's chest and her other to her cheek.

'Preserve the freedom of all people in the realm,' she said, and hated herself as she said it. Forcing the girl, giving her no choice. *I must.* Yselda smiled at her, her eyes still full of tears, but Floré could see in her the same relief that she felt inside. *It will all be over soon.*

'Suffer no tyrant,' they said together. 'Forge no chain. Lead in servitude.'

Slowly Yselda clambered to the chair next to one of the great wands and buckled herself in, and Rowan joined her.

'I'll lower the ramp as we go,' he said over his shoulder. 'It won't slow us down, but if you jump out before we land. Well. You might hit a nice pile of snow?'

Voltos gave something that was almost a laugh, but it caught in his throat.

'Farewell, Private Hollow,' he called, and Floré took his hand. Together they stood by the ramp as it lowered. Floré kept her gaze locked to Yselda's, trying to send her what strength she could. At the back of the ship she gripped the rim of the crystal window that bisected the orb, and Rowan slowly changed their orientation until he was facing straight down. The three robed Antian said nothing, but holding tight where they could they started to chant in low voices – Floré did not know what magic they were working, but they offered no objection to the plan, had said nothing at all.

'It's better this way,' Yselda said, and Floré's voice caught in her throat. *I must be strong for her.* 'Tell Cuss... No. He knows. Thank you, Commander.'

Floré began to sob. *She thanks me, for killing her.*

'Eyes sharp, Yselda,' she said, unable to articulate anything she felt, the sickening sadness, the horror at all Yselda was using. 'I'm sorry, daughter.'

'A fist of stone and magic,' Voltos said quietly, and Floré gripped him close. *Marta is with Cuss and Benazir. Marta is safe.* She looked at Yselda, slumped in her chair, staring out at the clouds below. The girl did not cry. She bit her lip and she stared down, gripping her buckles, resolute. Rowan said something in a tongue Floré didn't understand, and then she was thrown back against the wall with the acceleration as the orb of light flew down and down.

~

Yselda could not begin to describe her new senses, the horrible pain racking every inch of her. As they accelerated she had only a moment in cloud before they broke through to the storm below. In that moment she pictured her mother and her father and her brothers, Shand and Esme and Nat and Lorrie at the Goat and Whistle. She pictured Cuss and little Petron and Marta, Benazir, even Tomas.

They broke through clouds and the whole world was laid below them, a jumble of broken rock surrounded by scrambling people, with two figures at its top. In her heart Yselda reached for something, and she could see *more*. Time slowed for her. *Is this the skein?* She could see connection, disconnection, chance and possibility all laid out in light and sound and colour and other things she had no words for. She herself was a relic of this force, this chaos, this pattern. Nobody told her what to see or what she was seeing and so she sought in it and found pattern and connection but also disconnection and chance.

Faster. The orb around them was itself a horrible knot of complexity, and she could feel it pulling at the universe below as they flew down, and from herself there was an aura of pure energy and chance, *chaos*, disrupting every mote of pattern that came close to her. But not the orb – it was safe, insulated, walls of pattern surrounding pattern, buffers against the breaking waves. As they flew down she felt motes drift from the back of the orb – Floré and Voltos and the Antian witches, falling high in the sky so fast but so much slower than the orb. They left her sense, and she held her necklace tight.

Suffer no tyrant, Floré had told her, so many times. *I can do this one thing.* The orb covered the distance from cloud to ground in a heartbeat, and through the sight her new form afforded her, Yselda saw in slow motion Ashbringer clutching Tullen One-Eye closer. The man was an insane knot of connection and points, hurling flame and lightning out across the meadow, but then Ashbringer plunged her thumb into his eye and all his force and connection scattered and then Yselda was *there*, her chaos overlapping his pattern and she could see it breaking away, layers and shields and walls and power all slipping away from him in that heartbeat before they slammed into him, rock and steel and crystal travelling at impossible speed straight down. She could feel Rowan next to her, and Floré and Voltos and the Antian witches right at the edge of her senses, so high in the sky.

Impact.

Everything in the world exploded into pattern, and blackness, and then there was chaos and pattern, pattern and chaos, a dance of it, shapes moving out and away, some familiar and some strange to her, but all part of a dance that went on and on.

EPILOGUES:
THE BROKEN CHAIN

WHERE TWO FORESTS MEET

'We have harnessed the gods themselves, and the power they offer us. Where lesser men and beasts kneel at the feet of spirits, we hunt and harvest and fuel our magic. The pattern is power, and chaos may supersede the pattern – the truth is that there is no true pattern, and no succour. The world is full of opportunity, and with focus we can take the fragments we find and from them build our church. A church that worships those who have the intellect and audacity to step above the gods, and take their rightful place as rulers of this world.' – **Doctrine of the silent mind**, Ihm-Phogn of Cil-Marie

Brude hauled the pack higher onto her back and stared down at Pertcupar. When she was a little girl she had lived there with her mother and her brothers, six of them in a shack that was never strong enough to keep the wind out, the rain out, the endless storm. It had a peat-cut roof, and Brude and her eldest brother took turns each day to climb it and crunch any little rotvine growing its way up through the black sod. From atop the hill, she smiled. She had never seen it like this. *Home.*

Pertcupar was built in a low plain where two glens met, in the shadow of a mountain above. Brude had never seen the mountain before, but the sky was clear, a blue so pale as to almost be white. The sun shone high and strong above, and her heavy waxed cloak was rolled up under the ties of her pack. Brude flexed her arms and felt the heat of sun on her bare skin, so pale and stretched. Her bones still ached, her blood still had an acid taint that seemed to shiver whenever she focused on it, but with a blue sky above Pertcupar she could ignore it all.

The village was barely more than a hamlet – two roads of what had been stone ran off either side of an old black Ferron road that connected Urargent in the north-west to Nillen in the east. The stone was weathered and worn down by three hundred years of acid and rain, the hard geometry of architecture softened into something more organic, pitted and curved – what it had been before was tenuous, hinted at but never truly seen. The black road outside of the town had long grown over with strangling vine and bog and water, but stretches of it were still clear and in the town she could see it stark – the locals had been keeping the worst of the blight and rot pushed back. A tumbled stone building reinforced with peat and gnarled wood, and two dozen houses and crofts – that was Pertcupar, where she had spent her childhood. All around the town, paddies of dark water where eels swam, protected from wandering goblin or crocodile by thick briars of pepper-thorn that were tended with careful hands and jealously guarded metal.

'This is Pertcupar?' Amon asked, and she grinned at him. In the distance to the west and south the rotstorm was a wound on the horizon, but the air above them was clear, clear now all the way back to the Undal Stormwall. *Nillen, Urforren, Fetter-Dun, Talpid, Urargent – all free.*

'There used to be a forest, in each glen,' she said, 'back

before the rotstorm. Pine trees. You can find them buried in the peat, turned to stone.'

Amon dropped his pack to the bare rock – the hill they were on had been blown clear of dirt and peat and vine, and what remained was rock on rock intercut with seams of dark earth and rippling streams thick with roots. He undid his pack and spread out his waxed cloak on the stone, sitting and gesturing for her to join him. Brude swung her pack down and sat next to him, cross-legged. She was aware as ever of her overlong legs and the arch to her back, the way her skin felt so sensitive and so rough at once, as if every touch was a sparking flare up the jangle of her nerves. *Not today*, she thought. *I won't feel it, not today.*

They sat and stared at the little town and Brude tried to pick out her mother's house – Rol's house. Rol who had raised her children in the storm and kept them safe from it, for the most part. Rol who had sung them songs as the wind tore at the seams of their home, and who had baked them eels in pots of clay that she broke open, steaming and rich flesh inside to grow her children strong.

Amon passed her a skin of water. It tasted of peat, but the acid sting of the rotstorm hadn't polluted it. *So quickly the taint fades.* Brude drank gratefully, and together they watched as a crow flew low across the rolling moors below.

'Don't see that every day,' he said. Brude stared after the crow, a black hood and wings and a grey body gently curving as it flew. 'Used to be crows and all sorts in Ferron, they say. Little birds that would sing. I saw some, in the Northern Marches. Even in winter, birds singing and calling.'

'They'll come back,' Brude said, and threw a glance back at the rotstorm looming on the horizon.

'Still staying south?' Amon asked, and Brude kept her gaze on the haze of black and purple cloud but she smiled.

'Aye,' she said, 'south and west, out towards the open sea. Last scout flight had it almost at Cil-Marie, though we'd not fly too close. A lot of water opening up. Still south and west, a winter and a spring of south and west now. On this course it might miss Cil-Marie and head out to open water and... whatever is beyond there.'

They'd spent the last season tracking the rotstorm, mapping the lands revealed to the west, the ruins of old Ferron where the deep storm had made even rust-folk fearful to tread. The Iron Desert beyond Ferron to the west was suddenly more than a legend – Brude had seen the sands of it herself, endless black sands, seas of dunes from the frozen Storm Sea in the north down to where the rotstorm still held in the skies. The goblins and wyrms and rottrolls followed the storm, fleeing along with it. *What will happen if it truly passes over the sea? Will they try to follow it?* Brude shivered at the thought.

None had seen Anshuka's ghost since the bear was awakened, but the great wolf Lothal had been seen in the north and west, past Urargent – near to where the Iron Desert began in true. *He is fleeing the bear,* Brude thought, but Amon and others said perhaps he was headed home, wherever that may be. For the first time in three centuries the lands to the west were open. Brude did not know how to feel about it, any of it. There was so much opportunity. *But to have something is to have something that can be taken,* she thought, and her lips twitched.

'What do we do if it comes back?' Amon asked, and she could only shake her head.

'What we can, Amon. I'll fight no more wars, I hope. Look at the mountain!'

Brude pointed high above Pertcupar. The mountain was a jutting imposition of granite, a sheer cliff raising from a tumble of broken stone that loomed over the village, three softer sides rising to meet the cliff at its rough peak. Amon leaned close and followed her arm, up past the little village and the broken stone, up past clinging vine and pitted cliff. He laughed when he saw it. It was a waterfall, falling from near the peak of the hill and running down the sheer edge of the cliff face. Halfway down the cliff an outcropping sent the stream spiralling out over hundreds of feet of clear air as the rock undercut it and fell away, and the water turned to mist and dissipated out over the valley below.

Sunlight played through the mist, and colours danced. Brude let her arm drop and Amon put his hand in hers and leaned in to her shoulder.

'I spent fifteen winters here, and never saw that,' she said. She did not have to explain to Amon. He knew the oppression of the rotstorm, the cloud hanging a hundred feet over black earth, the constant rain and mist and fog and blight motes, the acid haze that danced through storm undaunted by wind, moving on arcane currents. 'I've never even seen the peak before.'

Amon took his other hand and cupped her chin, turned her gaze from the waterfall and the mountain beyond into his own.

'There is much to discover, Brude,' he said, softly, and then he smiled at her and kissed her, lingering a long moment.

Brude felt the shame and horror of herself buried beneath the rush of sensation. The monster she was, the horrors she had wrought. A life of violence. Children screaming in the caverns of the Blue Wolf Mountains, flame burning from her orb as she burned thatch and flesh, horses and cattle shrieking as her wands cut deep and she stole strength from the Undal every way she could.

'I don't deserve this,' she said, and Amon kissed her again and turned back to the mountain. When they had sifted the wreckage of stone and hell in Orubor's wood, when she had found what ruined remains of Tullen One-Eye there were to be found, she had felt relief, but not only relief. Fear, for herself and her people. Hatred, of herself and what she had done. All her strength had been arrayed against the deathless mage. *Perhaps that is what allowed the Stormguard and their demon to break his barrier above.*

Brude had seen the orb descend through storm and lightning, seen it fall faster than a stone, propelling downward. Behind it, figures falling – Antian, the Stormguard woman who she had taken from Ossen-Tyr. The orb slammed into Tullen and his Orubor, and Brude had watched an era end. Above, the falling Antian and Stormguard slowed as they fell, three robed Antian singing in chorus. She could see in the storm from where Tullen had held her, a hundred yards back, could see the Antian pulling at the skein to slow their fall. The Stormguard woman had survived, and afterward Brude understood. They had broken Tullen's pattern with their new crow-man, the girl Anshuka had changed. They had broken him as he focused on Brude and her demons, as he focused on whatever the broken Orubor Ashbringer had said.

I played my part in his ending, she thought, *but it does not wipe the blood from my hands.*

'There is work to be done,' Amon said, and he leaned his head back on her shoulder. He trusted his full weight against her, and she felt him relax. The crow was climbing up the mountain in slow spirals, wings flitting through the thin sheets of mist that cascaded slowly down the jagged cliffs. 'Mountains to be climbed, ruins to be delved. Monsters to be fought, Judges to be watched. Crops to sow. If you have a penance in your heart, it will match my own. But I'd face it together if you'd have me.'

Brude moved her arm around him and pulled him closer, and stared at the blue sky above. Her joints and sinews ached, her mind was sodden with the blood she had spilled, and her fingers twitched with the fear of what would happen. *If the storm changes its course. If the Undal break their word. If the Sun Masters of Cil-Marie come hunting orbs or Judges' bones.* She reacted to the fear the way she had for decades – she began to reach for the roiling storm inside her, the burning knot of pattern Anshuka's ghost had tied in her chest. It was there, the storm, there for her to hold, to keep her strong, *to do what she must.*

Amon raised his hand to hers and stroked it, and Brude let the storm fall away. She gazed up at the blue sky above, and held him close as a whisp of white cloud passed by far above, unhurried.

The Gauntlet and The Windbound Girl

> 'Bended wing and twisted neck
> To keep the wind behind you
> Aloft and higher sharpened eyes
> Your beak a blade for sinew
> Leave the rampart, find the sea
> Water, salt, and fortune
> No chain, no rope, no bond, no weight
> To keep the wind against you
> Leave the rampart, find the sea
> Water, salt, and fortune
> Leave the rampart, find the sea
> keep the wind behind you'

'Gull over Undal City',
Every Tree a Home, Janos Argarioch

'The current is intricate,' said the Unnamed Knight, his voice muffled through his unadorned helm of shining metal. 'Do not seek to impose upon it. Move with it, and by moving with it, influence it. The current is not one current – it is always divisible. There is wind above, and tide below. Do you understand?'

Marta frowned at the hulking Tullioch. Knight was muscled like a warrior, bigger than Rue even, and clad only in a loincloth of sharkskin and a belt of braided kelp. His scales were black and slick and he sat cross-legged with his tail curled below him, but she couldn't see his spear anywhere – normally it was always with him. She rubbed her nose and pulled at the sleeves of her tunic and tried not to tap her foot. *He hates it when I tap my foot.*

'How can I influence the current if you don't let me *feel* it,' she said, and that steel-clad face tilted ever so slightly to the left. They'd spent the morning talking about the difference between flame and heat, and a dozen half-burnt candles littered the coral floor between them. Marta reached a hand up to the back of her neck and felt her face flush at Knight's focus. *Stupid mask. Everyone knows he's just some Tullioch – who cares what clan?* Her stomach rumbled and with a glance out the window she saw the sun was climbing high – almost the end of morning lessons.

'You can feel it,' he said at last, and she blew out a breath and started tapping her foot. *Stupid Knight.* They were high in the Tullioch Shardspire, a few levels below the break where Tullen One-Eye had cut it centuries before. Marta jumped up to her feet and began pacing the room, and Knight didn't protest. *Too clever to ever lose his temper,* she thought with a twist of her mouth. *Not like me.*

Like the rest of the shardspire the room was wrought from coral, colonies of coral of a thousand types tended over a thousand years and encouraged through the true current – *the current they won't let me touch.* Marta sniffed and ran her hand over the wall and stared out one of the window slits, the wind snagging through it, making her eyes water. She had to step up on her toes to see out, to see the edges of the reef city below protruding from the water, the endless Wind Sea beyond. A gull dipped past the window and she watched it for a long moment, the way its wings curved to catch the wind. *Not flapping, not thinking – just flying.*

'When you have shown you can control yourself, your bonds will be broken,' Knight said, his voice rough and deep but calm as ever. Marta chewed her lip and ran back to the folded blanket that was her seat. 'The world has changed much since you were a babe, Marta. The Judges are unbound; the rotstorm moves further south each year; Caroban fights its wars across the straits. The bird and the whale travel far. Magic is not what it once was – but it is not *weaker*, Marta Artollen. It is simply different. Why have we bound you, human child? Why have you spent a decade at my feet?'

Marta settled herself into a cross-legged pose and kept as still as possible, watching her reflection in the sheen of Knight's helmet. Her ashen hair was down past her collar now, half that length again if she ever brushed the curls from it. Her face was distorted in the reflection – *stupid long nose made even longer.*

'Marta,' Knight said, and she could hear the faintest edge to his voice. 'Why are you here?'

Marta blinked and smiled up at him.

'Sorry, Knight,' she said, and he nodded. 'I'm here because I kept reaching for the current and changing it, but changing it takes energy. Looking too hard or diving too deep takes energy. Everything seems to take energy. It made me sick.'

'It almost killed you,' Knight said gently, and Marta looked down at her hands and rubbed her fingers. She remembered being sick – remembered a warm cottage and her pa, the cold stone of Protector's Keep and the Antian tunnels. *A cave surrounded in ice. Orbs of light.* Marta clenched her jaw and shook her head. *You don't remember that,* she told herself. *You were too little. You just know the story.* She didn't believe that, not really, but it felt better to pretend she didn't remember. Marta knew that if she could remember her pa, then she could remember the rest of it.

'And only a skein-wreck could help me,' she said eventually, and with a waved hand Knight relit the candle stubs. A dozen flickers of light, flame appearing where before there had been nothing but stillness and potential.

'A skein-wreck could help you,' he said. 'A diver of the true current can *teach* you to help yourself. To know your place in the world and all of its challenges, you must first know yourself. Would you like to try to feel, today?'

Marta nodded and breathed deep three times the way Knight had told her, long inhalations and exhalations. She let her mind look for the hook of the current below all things. It was always easy to find, but getting her thoughts to wrap around it and let it in was the trick. *Or let me in?* It was hard for her to even articulate. It was something between sinking into water, and drinking that water down, letting that water fill your eyes and ears and nose and throat... She focused and frowned and beyond the walls of the spire gulls called back and forth, long flat laughs to each other.

'Think about the difference between flame and heat,' Knight said, and Marta shivered and felt her mind catch. *There.*

Her mind caught the current and Marta let her eyes drift, let them take in the room. Over her sight was a layer of intricacy – light and colour, shape and movement and connection and potential. It wasn't just that – there was sound and heat and vibration, all sorts of things she couldn't put a name to. Colours that had no name, feelings that had no words. Knight had told her the Tullioch names for those sensations but she didn't need those words – *and I can't pronounce them anyway.*

'Think about heat and light,' Knight said, and waved a hand

at the candles. 'Think about observation and influence. How closely can you watch the flame before you influence it? Can you watch it without it influencing you? Can there be heat without light, or light without heat? Where does the flame begin and end?'

Knight kept talking, his slow deep voice asking endless questions. Marta kept her gaze loose and let the questions wash over her, turned her head around the room. The coral walls of the shardspire were living, a huge web of intricate connection – each mote of life so small that its connections were just at the limit of her sight. She could see wind currents outside, and below and above those, other strands of connection barely visible. Knight was something she couldn't look at too closely – she always struggled to describe him.

She looked down at the candles to start the exercise again but allowed herself a peek at him from the corner of her eye, the Unnamed Knight, her teacher – the skein-wreck of the Tullioch. The Tullioch claimed they always had a skein-wreck, but only ever one, and Knight would not answer Marta's questions about it.

Connection upon connection, from him and to him so much more than the rest of the world. He was denser than any other person she had looked at, more intricately patterned and more *confusing*, layer upon layer of pattern like armour, like the scales of a shark. At the same time, compared to anyone else she had seen, he was porous – great gouts and intricate ribbons of connection poured from him and to him in every direction in every colour and temperature and taste and vibration, and she felt herself getting lost looking for pattern, the pattern of Knight – *everything has a pattern. What is his pattern? Was my pa like him?*

'Focus,' Knight said, and Marta closed her eyes and opened them again facing the lit candles. *Heat and flame.*

Marta chose one candle, saw the flame flickering with her eyes, saw the heat dissipating with the skein, saw the patterns break down in the tallow, intricacies snapping and... *the energy inside. Is that it?*

Marta looked lower – she looked at the tallow breaking to make flame, and saw the pattern and sought it. Lower down the candle, halfway, she focused her mind and saw that pattern repeated all through, found one point and focused. *Can I break it?*

'Windbound, I call you,' Knight said, but Marta wasn't listening. *If this pattern breaks to make heat, does the heat make the flame?*

'I bound you myself. You can see deep in the current, can dive far, but the wind will keep you safe. Your mother wanted you safe until you were grown enough to look without changing – to observe without cost. This is impossible, you understand. There is always cost.'

There! Marta found the way the pattern broke, and without thinking she reached and twisted her hand and broke it. On the coral floor of the Unnamed Knight's rooms at the top of the Tullioch Shardspire, a candle burst into brilliant flame. Smoke and heat poured out and Marta watched it in the skein, the heat dancing and making new patterns – *flame*.

'Enough,' Knight said, and then the flame was gone, and Marta felt the skein fading around her until it was just them, just her eyes – her normal eyes, the light dancing through the window. Knight rubbed at the knuckles of one huge, clawed hand. Marta took in a great gulp of air. *When did I start holding my breath?* The candle lay in between them, a mess of charred tallow coating the floor. The wind tearing through the high windows caught the gout of smoke the candle had unleashed and within moments the air was clear and cold again, thick with salt.

'You should not be able to change things,' Knight said, his intonation flat, 'but the wind can only do so much. You begin to see the possibility – you see where energy can come from, and what it can do. Whenever you change the current, you are the candle. You must learn to keep yourself back. Do you understand?'

Marta grinned and flung herself up and across the room and hugged Knight tight, and the Tullioch slowly put an arm around her back. *I did it. I changed something.* She could feel no shiver of sickness, no fever, none of the pains she remembered so well from being little, just a vague sense of fatigue. *I changed something.*

'Thank you, Knight,' she said, and the Tullioch nodded his steel-clad head.

'Tomorrow, another lesson,' he said, and Marta scrabbled to pack away the stubs of candle and tapers and scraps of paper into her cloth bag. 'Do not look again, or try to change the current without me, Marta. Remember that you are windbound – you must learn to move with the current.'

Marta left the room smiling.

~

'Don't punch with your fist,' Cuss said, and with a firm hand adjusted her shoulders so the right dropped back an inch. Marta huffed a breath to blow her hair from her face, ashen curls tumbling right back over her eye. Cuss smiled down at her. He was huge – the biggest man she'd ever met, of the few humans at the shardspire. She'd seen a sailor from the straits who was taller, but Cuss was wide too. It was hot down in the reef city where their quarters were, far hotter than up in the shardspire. Marta rubbed the sweat on her face on the shoulder of her tunic. *Gross.* She could still taste charred fish in her teeth.

'Punch with your shoulder,' he said, moving to stand next to her and demonstrating with his own body. 'Your arm, your whole body.'

'Aye, Captain,' she said and swung again at the padded log they'd painted with the angry face. The reef city in the shadow of the shardspire was low and wide and their quarters were sunk below the water, walls of coral at the town edge holding back tide and wave, the intricate rooms and corridors of the city appearing like flat ocean from only a mile away. Above the courtyard there was only blue sky and gulls.

'Again,' Cuss said, and Marta hit again, and again, and again.

'You've got fish in your beard,' she said when finally he let her stop, and with a frown he went searching for it. His head was shaved back almost to stubble for summer, but he had the same thick brown beard as ever, a thousand different browns meshed into one mess of curls, every hair a shade darker than the chestnut of his skin. After a full thirty seconds he stopped looking for the fish that wasn't there and sighed and looked instead at her.

'That funny, Cadet?' he said, his face like thunder, and she snapped to attention.

'No, Captain sir, Cuss sir!' she said, and he snorted and threw a waterskin at her. Marta didn't manage to catch it with her fists all padded, and she spilled it half down her face when she finally managed to pick it up and take a drink.

'I'm sorry I burned the fish, Marta,' Cuss said, and she raised her fists and growled at him.

'No trial for fish-burners,' she said, and his smile faded. Standing in front of her he picked up his padded mitts and held out his palms to her, dropping to a crouch so his hands were at her head height. Marta jabbed and crossed and tried to use her whole body, and Cuss moved with her. They sparred for what felt like an age, until her breath was coming in gasps and her arms were like soaked driftwood lumps. Finally they stopped, and she put her hands on her knees. Jozenai the fat black cat was watching Marta from her customary perch on an old green cloak folded on a crate at the edge of the training courtyard. She was languidly cleaning fish from her paws with her tongue. *Lazy cat,* Marta thought. *She never has to fight.* Marta stuck her tongue out at Jozenai but the cat just blinked slowly at her, then rolled onto its back.

'Sprints!' Cuss yelled, and Marta began to run the courtyard width back and forth, skidding on the rough sand with every turn, lungs burning. Back and forth, back and forth, again, again, again. 'I know you can run faster! I know you'll have to run faster if you want to see the ship...'

Marta stopped running.

'A ship?' she said, and her voice was suddenly small. *A ship.* It had been spans, this time. *How many days?* She had been keeping count. Today would be forty days, forty days with just Cuss and Knight and Jozenai for company.

Cuss came to her and tugged the wraps at her wrists, retying the left one around her hand and cinching it tight.

'It'll be here in a few hours, Morae said.'

Marta looked at the door. *A ship. I need to wash. I need to find my book. I need—*

The blow caught her in the shoulder, a stinging hit from a rod of ash that had been soaking in a barrel at the edge of the courtyard. She hadn't even seen Cuss pick it up.

'Hey!'

Cuss was looking down at her, frowning, the wood rod in one hand. 'Why do we train to fight, Marta?' he said, and with a sudden burst of movement the rod of wood jabbed forward at her legs.

Marta leapt back. 'I need to get ready, Cuss,' she said, and he shook his head. He absently stroked the wooden pendant at his neck, simple wood with a charred mark on it, and he frowned.

'Hmm. No, that's not it.'

Around the courtyard he chased her with the sodden stick, swinging wildly to drive her forward. She started out laughing but after a few moments he still didn't stop – he sped up, stick jabbing at her feet and calves, her arms, her shoulders.

'Cuss!' she yelled at last, turning on him and stamping her foot. 'I need to get ready for the ship!'

'No,' he said, and the rod came down with a flick and cracked onto her knuckles. 'You need to tell me why I'm teaching you to fight.'

He swung again and Marta leaned into it and took the hit on her shoulder and punched him in the gut, and then rolled away and raised her fists. Cuss coughed and grinned at her.

'Simple question, and then we can get ready. Get it wrong, I'll be cooking all week – burning your fish.'

'So I can win!' she said, and tried to hit him again, but Cuss dropped back and shook his head. 'So nobody can hurt me!'

Cuss hit out again and the rod of wood smacked her hard on the arm, a sharp pain vibrating up her bones. She felt sick. She felt *angry*.

Marta leapt at him and swung her fists and he blocked her easily, once, twice, and then the third time he just stood there and let her hit him. She had to jump to reach his face but she did – she jumped and felt her fist hit his face and heard him laugh and then he had his hands up in surrender. He knelt and she hit him again, straight in the jaw. Cuss caught her swinging fists one at a time, and Marta vibrated with rage. *I need to get ready!* She had no words, could feel the heat rising in her cheeks, heat beyond any exercise. *Why does he make me so angry? Why is he being like this?* She breathed deep and Cuss locked eyes with her until she stopped struggling.

'I teach you to fight,' Cuss said, letting go of her fists and taking her hands in his and slowly peeling back her clenched fingers, 'so nobody can hurt you, yes. So you can win if you must. Yes. But firstly and above all else, so you can learn to control yourself. The world will make you angry. *I* will make you angry.'

He smiled at her and she felt the flush of shame blooming across her cheeks. Jozenai hopped down from her crate and sidled between them, twisting between their legs, black-furred face looking up, and opening her mouth expectantly, as if they were fighting over who would have the honour of giving her more fish.

'I'm sorry,' Marta said, not meeting his eye, and he cupped her chin gently and tilted her face up to his own.

'You can't control getting angry,' he said, 'but you can always choose what you do next. That is one reason we learn how to fight – if we must, we can fight. It is another option, but if we fight it will be because it is our choice. Do you understand why that's important?'

Marta nodded.

'Now,' he said, rubbing his jaw, 'show me that last punch again one more time, and we'll go get ready for the ship. It was a good punch!'

Marta stood back and bit her lip but he was smiling and so she showed him the punch slowly, the way her shoulder followed through, the turn in her waist, the way her off-hand stayed high. Cuss put a hand on her head.

'Punching me in the back of the head, *through* my face,' he said quietly. 'Go and get ready, and then let's head to the docks.'

They left Jozenai to nap in the sun and worked their way

through the alleys and arteries of the reef city, Marta racing ahead and waiting for Cuss at the edge of each district as he stolidly stomped along. Marta was barefoot like the Tullioch, her soles callused and strong, but Cuss was in ridiculous Undal boots. He'd pulled on his tabard and cinched his belt tight – a heavy axe hanging on a hook on one side of the belt and a pair of old steel gauntlets on the other. He stopped to chat with various folks *four times* on the way and Marta felt like she was going to explode. The little crabs that scurried the alleyways of the reef city scattered at the shadow of her hands as she waved them impatiently for him to *get a move on*.

'You're gonna boil in that,' she told him when he finally caught up at the end of the markets, but he just rolled his eyes. 'You're sure it's from home? The ship? Cuss? Is the ship from home?'

Cuss gestured at the thick wool of his tabard.

'No, Marta,' he said, voice thick with sarcasm, 'I just like dressing like this for every random ship.'

The trade dock was at the edge of the reef city to the north, sheltered from the winds gusting across open sea by the hulking mass of the broken shardspire behind – a hundred and fifty foot of coral blocking out a quarter of the sky. The fallen upper half of the shardspire had been slowly worked into the town walls centuries before, but the trade dock was the only place Marta had seen where the walls were above twenty feet – everywhere else, if a tide or wave surge came over even bigger than that they would let it come, and let it drain down into the rock below through whatever weird Tullioch magic they had.

It didn't make any sense to Marta – it felt like the whole city should be full of water. *I should ask Knight.* The dock had room for three dozen ships easily, but the Tulliochs' own ships were hidden at their own dock to the west of the city – Marta had been thrown out of there three times trying to see a Tullioch ship up close, instead of distant glances from a perch on the walls. The Tullioch ships were living things, coral and kelp, with sails that were grown and harvested whole, not stitched – the same material as the smooth seaweed they treated to make their cloaks and loincloths. Marta's trousers were the same hard-wearing material, but she wore the shirt of blue cotton the last ship from Undal had brought.

They waited two hours in the end, marching up and down the floating pontoons. Cuss was speaking to captains and sailors and old Trull the Tullioch harbourmaster. Marta did her own thing. She spoke to a sailor from a strait trader who gave her a copper coin in exchange for directions – the coin had a trident on one side and a man with a huge moustache stamped on the other, script she didn't understand. The sailor had her hair tied back with a twisted band of coloured leather across her head, so it was pulled tight across the front of her head and flared out wild behind. *Brilliant.*

She tied her own hair back in imitation after the sailor had gone, with a twist of cloth she ripped from her old handkerchief. She spent an hour walking the docks and looking at the ships, helping translate for one of the Tullioch dockers who was unhappy with the way a bunch of Isken were speaking to her crew, reading the ship names she could and looking at the intricate decorations of the sails, the garish dress of all the strange folks, the ornate figureheads and carvings that decorated the ships from the strait kingdoms.

She spent five minutes dipping her finger and the tip of her pocket knife in the water, trying to attract one of the little fish that lived beneath the docks, but they kept a wary distance and she could only watch them flit and dance. Hanging below the floating pontoons were drifting lines of kelp and strange translucent tubular plants that seemed to pulse open and closed with the ebb and flow of the water. Small crabs clung in and among them, and Marta lay on her stomach and stared at the little kingdoms beneath the water, watching the creatures scurrying. There were so many types of crabs – she had tried to learn them all, but whenever she thought she knew them there was another, or some variant of a type she had already learned that looked like something new.

She spent a long time there, until the distant crash of a falling crate broke her reverie. Finally she made her way to the open slot where the Undal ship was meant to dock, right at the end of the longest quay, and set herself up on a coil of rope and read her book.

'What is your book?' a Tullioch she didn't know asked, and so she spoke to him and learned his name, *Nuemar*, and his job, and all sorts. He was nice. The Tullioch were always surprised she could speak the shardkin tongue, clumsy as she was with it. She was still reading, rereading, thinking, when a shadow fell over her.

'Look,' Cuss said, and pointed out at the horizon where a ship was coming in – tall sides, two masts with sails full, the sea calm below her and the sky clear above. Marta clutched her book to her chest, the book her mother had given her – the book her father had written. They stood together and watched the ship draw closer and Marta could feel her heart fluttering.

Two people stood at the railing of the ship, both dressed in tabards of garish red with a bolt of lightning emblazoned across each chest. Squinting in the glare of the sun Marta could see the glint of Benazir's hook hand. Next to Benazir's slight figure, Marta's mother Floré wore a sword at her hip, a green cloak fluttering behind her in the wind. Marta waved with one hand and then both hands as the ship drew closer, and she yelled, a wordless whoop of joy and love and pure satisfaction.

Her mother had not wanted to leave, even for so short a time, but as the Undal ambassador to the shardspire she had to return twice a year to make her reports. Cuss had a hand on Marta's shoulder and he was yelling too and then Benazir was pointing to them and at last at the railing of the ship her mum was waving, her hands bare, smiling and ecstatic, ashen curls caught by the wind as the ship bore her home.

THE END OF BOOK THREE OF THE ROTSTORM

Acknowledgements

Thank you! If you have made it this far then you have my eternal gratitude. The Rotstorm has been an absolute dream come true, and it means the world to me that you've chosen to join me on this adventure. I hope you've found something in these pages that spoke to you. I've loved every second of crafting this world and diving into this story. Endless thanks to Holly who commissioned and edited all three books in The Rotstorm – your positivity and enthusiasm has been a consistent well to draw from, and the joy and seriousness with which you take the work in equal measure is lovely. I owe you a coffee, always. Thanks to Oliver for keeping a keen eye to windward.

Thanks to the Chainbreakers: Simone, Anna, Rich, Anthony, Erick, Abi, and Adam. Across this series you've given me invaluable insight and feedback, from when this was just a handful of scrappy pages and a pencil map, right through to the end. Thanks to Sophie for shepherding us to the finale, to Nic for giving The Rotstorm a place to live, and thanks to Clare, Jade, Polly, and all the Head Of Zeus team across departments who have been so supportive. Thanks to Fiona for her excellent narration. A deep thank you to Helena who copy-edited the series (and apologies for my inability to use an em dash properly). Thanks to the Head of Zeus art team and Patrick Knowles for the fantastic covers. Thanks to Eastercon, Bristolcon, Fantasycon, and CymeraFest who have kindly hosted me over the last few years to chat about The Rotstorm, and all the bloggers, podcasters, and fantasy fans who have written reviews and helped me try to spread the word! Thanks to Matt and the crew at The Broken Binding for being so supportive. Thanks to CDU for the caffeine.

Thank you to my mum and dad, and my brothers. I love you all. Thank you to Abi – without your unfailing belief and love there is no way I would have been able to do this. I am living my dreams every day. Thanks to the little dragon, inspiring me every day.

The Rotstorm trilogy is over... but it is a big world, hey? You've only seen this edge of the map, wanderer. I'll see you out there, perhaps, where the wild beasts roam – eyes sharp, blade sharper.

THE ROTSTORM TRILOGY

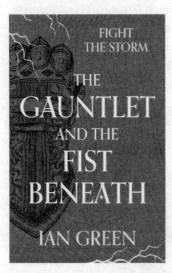

FIGHT
THE STORM

THE
GAUNTLET
AND THE
FIST
BENEATH

IAN GREEN

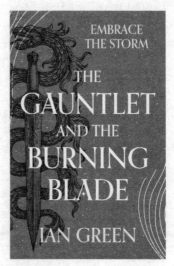

EMBRACE
THE STORM

THE
GAUNTLET
AND THE
BURNING
BLADE

IAN GREEN

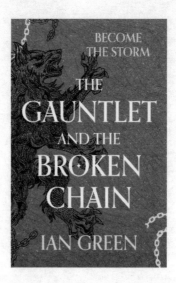

BECOME
THE STORM

THE
GAUNTLET
AND THE
BROKEN
CHAIN

IAN GREEN

FOR 312 YEARS THE ROTSTORM
HAS BLIGHTED THE RUINS OF THE
FERRON EMPIRE.

Born of an unholy war between gods themselves,
it scours the land with acid mists and deadly
lightning, spawning twisted monstrosities
from its nightmarish depths.

On the Stormwall, the men and women of the
Stormguard maintain their vigil – *eyes sharp, blades
sharper* – defending the Undal Protectorate from
the worst of the rotstorm's corruption.

But behind the storm front, something
is stirring, kindling the embers of an ancient
conflict and a plan to kill a god.

Will Stormguard steel be enough
to meet the coming tempest?

READ THEM ALL!